B.J. Daniels is a *New Yo...* bestselling author. She wrote ... as an award-winning newspa... thirty-seven published short s... with her husband, Parker, and three springer spaniels. When not writing, she quilts, boats and plays tennis. Contact her at bjdaniels.com, on Facebook or on Twitter @bjdanielsauthor

USA Today bestselling author **Barb Han** lives in North Texas with her very own hero-worthy husband, three beautiful children, a spunky golden retriever/standard poodle mix and too many books in her to-read pile. In her downtime, she plays video games and spends much of her time on or around a basketball court. She loves interacting with readers and is grateful for their support. You can reach her at barbhan.com

Also by B.J. Daniels

A Colt Brothers Investigation

Murder Gone Cold
Sticking to Her Guns
Set Up in the City
Her Brand of Justice

Cardwell Ranch: Montana Legacy

Steel Resolve
Iron Will
Ambush before Sunrise
Double Action Deputy

Also by Barb Han

The Cowboys of Cider Creek

Riding Shotgun
Trapped in Texas
Texas Scandal

A Ree and Quint Novel

Newlywed Assignment
Eyewitness Man and Wife
Mission Honeymoon

An O'Connor Family Mystery

Texas Law
Texas Baby Conspiracy
Texas Stalker
Texas Abduction

Discover more at millsandboon.co.uk

DEAD MAN'S HAND

VG

B.J. DANIELS

TROUBLE IN TEXAS

VG

BARB HAN

MILLS & BOON

First Published in Great Britain 2023
by Mills & Boon, an imprint of HarperCollins*Publishers* Ltd
1 London Bridge Street, London, SE1 9GF

www.harpercollins.co.uk

HarperCollins*Publishers*
Macken House, 39/40 Mayor Street Upper,
Dublin 1, D01 C9W8, Ireland

Dead Man's Hand © 2023 Barbara Heinlein
Trouble in Texas © 2023 Barb Han

ISBN: 978-0-263-30744-3

1023

This book is produced from independently certified FSC™ paper
to ensure responsible forest management.

For more information visit: www.harpercollins.co.uk/green

Printed and Bound in the UK using 100% Renewable Electricity at
CPI Group (UK) Ltd, Croydon, CR0 4YY

DEAD MAN'S HAND

B.J. DANIELS

This book is dedicated to my father, Harry Burton Johnson, who fed me lobster at fancy restaurants when things were going well—and free peanuts at a bar when they weren't. He taught me many of life's lessons and I'm sure that's why I'm a writer today. I had so much fun writing these characters because they were all close to my heart.

DEAD MAN'S HAND: A slang term used in poker for a two pair of black aces and black eights. The story goes that lawman and gambler 'Wild Bill' Hickok was shot while holding the dead man's hand, which is why it's considered an unlucky two pair in poker today.

Chapter One

DJ Diamond shoved back his Stetson before glancing from the cards in his hand to the three men and one woman sitting around the table. After hours of poker, he felt as if he knew all of them better than their mothers did.

Except for the woman. She had a better poker face than any of the men. Also, she played her cards close to the vest—or in her case, the red halter top she wore. The top had the initials *AL* monogramed on it. Not her initials. He'd bet she picked up the garment at a garage sale. Her blond hair was long, pulled back into a ponytail that made her look like jailbait. All of it was at odds with her sharp honey-brown eyes and her skill at the game. All part of her act to throw grown men off their game.

It was working. The men had trouble keeping their eyes off her as she leaned forward to ante up—forcing their gazes away from the huge pot of money in the center of the table.

DJ could feel the tension in the room around him, but he was as cool as a cucumber—as his uncle Charley used to say. He was aware of everything, though—including the exact amount of money in the pot as one of the men folded, but the other two stayed in, matching his bet, confident he was bluffing.

With luck, he'd be walking out with all the money—and the sexy young woman—before the night was over. And the night was almost over.

But right now, everyone was waiting on him.

He glanced down at his last five hundred dollars in chips for a moment, then picked them up and tossed them into the pile of money. "I'm going to have to sweeten the pot." Across the table, he saw the woman who called herself Tina shoot him a disbelieving look. He grinned and shrugged. "You want to see what I've got. It will cost you."

SADIE MONTCLAIR MUMBLED, "Arrogant fool," under her breath. She knew the Montana cowboy was planning on taking this pot and when he did all hell was going to break loose. She'd been reading the table since she sat down. The big doughy former football star next to her had a possible three queens. The guy in the expensive suit on the other side of her had to have had two pair, maybe even ace high. Luckily, the appliance salesman with the bad rug had folded. She'd marked him as the wild card of the group even before he'd started sweating profusely after losing so much money tonight.

She sighed as she looked at her jack-high straight with regret and tossed in her five Cs. Placing her cards facedown on the table, she leaned back, stretching, all eyes on her heaving chest.

"Let's see what you've got," the suit said, tossing his five hundred onto the pile of money and drawing the men's gazes again to the pot.

Sadie gave the arrogant fool across from her a shrug as she reached for the gun in her shoulder bag hanging off her chair. Her hand closed around the grip. She brought it out fast as the cowboy said, "Read 'em and weep," and fanned out his cards. An ace-high straight.

"You cheating bastard!" she yelled, kicking her chair back as she jumped to her feet. "Is it just him or were you all in on it?" she screamed as she waved the gun around.

The men were on their feet the moment they saw the gun in the hands of an angry woman, their chairs crashing to the floor behind them.

"You think you can cheat me, cowboy?" she yelled at him, wiping away his grin as she pulled the trigger.

The first report was deafening in the small dark room. Out of the corner of her eye, she saw the men scrambling for the door, the appliance salesman the slowest of the group. She fired twice more, putting three slugs into the arrogant fool cowboy's chest.

He fell backward, his chair crashing to the floor. She heard the others all rush out, the door slamming behind them before she stuffed the money into her shoulder bag, tossing the weapon in after it, and looked under the table. The Montana cowboy was lying sprawled on the floor, his Stetson beside him. "Arrogant fool."

Chapter Two

"I heard that," DJ Diamond said from the floor, and groaned. "Damn, Sadie. That hurt."

"That was pure arrogance to raise the bet again," she said. "You were just showing off. You can't keep pushing your luck—and mine."

He rose slowly, grimacing in pain as he tried to catch his breath. "Arrogant is shooting me three times. One wasn't good enough?"

"Three just felt right tonight," she said, cocking her hip as she watched him remove his shirt, then his body armor with the three slugs embedded in it.

"You must really hate me," he said, and grinned through his pain.

With his shirt off, it was hard not to admire the broad shoulders, the tapered waist or the vee of dark hair on the tanned chest that disappeared into his button-up jeans.

"What do you think?" he asked, raking a hand through his thick dark hair.

For a moment, she thought he was asking about the way he looked. She blinked, realizing he was asking about their take tonight. "Not bad."

He laughed. "Come on, we made a haul. Maybe I pushed it a little, but it worked out. Don't forget the cards."

She had forgotten them, which would have been a mistake. If one of the gamblers realized they'd been had, he might come back here and find the marked deck. She scooped up the cards and added them to her shoulder bag. "I'm hungry."

DJ SHOOK HIS head as the shirt and body armor went into the satchel he'd brought with him. He pulled a fresh shirt out and put it on. "You're always hungry."

"I'm so hungry I could eat steak and lobster."

"That might be a problem dressed the way you are," he said as he settled his Stetson on that head of thick dark hair, then stepped to her and reached for the end of one thin strap that kept her halter top up.

She caught his hand. "You didn't get *that* lucky tonight." It was an old joke between partners whose relationship was strictly business. But more and more, she felt an undercurrent between them, one she suspected went both ways. Yet she never knew with DJ.

He chuckled, giving her that Diamond grin that apparently worked on women everywhere. "I do know a good barbecue place and I know how you feel about ribs." He grimaced as he touched his own ribs.

"Don't you think we should get rid of the loot first?"

"Couldn't I at least count it before we hand it over?" He flashed his baby blues.

"You don't need to count it and neither do I. We both know the take. You're stalling."

"Can you blame me? We should get hazardous pay for this."

"We should get into a new line of work," she said, knowing that he never would. He was a born poker player with larceny in his blood. "One of these days… In the meantime, let's get out of here. That one player made me nervous."

"There's always one who makes you nervous," he said as he put an arm around her and steered her toward the alternate exit door.

"The one that's going to get us both killed one day," she said under her breath.

His cell phone rang. He removed his arm from Sadie's shoulder to step away and take the call. "What's wrong, Keira?" She was sobbing, begging him to help her. He stepped farther away, never mixing business with family. "You have to stop crying so I can understand you."

She let out a cry and suddenly the voice on the phone was male. "I'll tell you what's wrong, Diamond. Your sister owes me money. A lot of money. Otherwise, we're going to have to sell her parts to the highest bidder."

"ONE OF YOUR GIRLFRIENDS?" Sadie asked as he caught up to her at her SUV in a parking garage blocks away from where they'd held the poker game. She'd left him to his phone call. Now, though, she noticed that his face was pinched, blue eyes flinty; his usual charm had vanished. Her first thought was that one of his women had called him to say she was pregnant. Then again it could be some angry husband threatening to kick his adorable ass. "You all right?"

"It's just something I need to take care of," he said, his voice tight. "Back in Montana. I'll be gone for a few days."

She went on alert. "You need help?"

"No, but thanks. Don't worry, I'll be back."

"Keep in touch," she said, and opened her car door. She

saw him looking at her shoulder bag and shook her head. "You can't."

Nodding, he gave a shrug. "No, I can't. We had a deal. Don't worry, I'm sticking to it." He glanced around but she'd already made sure that the dark street was empty. As usual she wouldn't take the same route when she left, she would watch closely for a tail, she would take the usual precautions until tonight's take was locked up safe and secure.

Climbing behind the wheel, she closed the car door, but hesitated. She powered down the window. "DJ?" She'd noticed a tell she never saw at the poker table. He wasn't just nervous, he seemed...scared. "DJ, if—"

"I'm good. You take care."

"You, too," she said as she watched him walk, head down, toward his pickup parked even farther away. All her instincts told her he was in trouble. She reminded herself that he wasn't her responsibility. Theirs was a business partnership and nothing more. As long as they both stuck to the deal...

DJ SLID BEHIND the wheel of his pickup and rubbed a hand over his face. He'd tried to protect Keira from this life. He'd watched over her since the first time she'd shown up at the ranch—skinny, scraped up, hungry and scared. He suspected he'd probably arrived at the hardscrabble, run-down ranch in the same shape.

It wasn't much of a ranch, small by any standards. The only thing they raised was dust as criminals came and went. The place was straight out of an old Western movie set, a hideout where some came to recover from gunshot wounds. Others to cool their heels from the law. The ranch had been a dumping ground for lost souls. As the way of the ranch, no one asked questions. DJ and Keira had just been taken in like all the others, fed and clothed and conditioned to never know what to expect next.

Charley Diamond had been a small man with a hearty laugh and kind eyes. He was also a crook but with a code of the West. He helped those needing help—people like him down on their luck who always knew they had a place to recover. But he also took from the richer and pocketed the take.

When DJ had asked about his parents, Charley would rub the back of his neck and look up as if thinking. "Sorry, kid, I have no idea. You just arrived one day looking hungry and lost. Can't say who dropped you off. Doesn't matter. You're here now and I'm darned glad to have you. I could teach you a few things to help you survive for when you leave here."

DJ figured he'd been dropped off at the ranch just as Charley had said. He wondered, though, if his parents had promised to come back for him—and just hadn't. He also wondered if Charley knew more than he had told him. Not that worse things couldn't have happened to him—and to Keira. They both helped out around the ranch, earning their keep and becoming the only family either of them knew of—other than the man they called Uncle Charley.

When his uncle had fallen on hard times and lost the ranch, DJ was sixteen. Lucky for him, Charley had taught him the grift. Keira, who was six years younger, was too young for the road. She'd gone into foster care.

The next two years DJ spent staying one step ahead of the law and tough guys who wanted to kill him and his uncle. A born poker player, it didn't take DJ long though before he went out on his own way—eventually going legit since he found that he could make plenty of money without cheating.

He always kept in touch with Keira, made sure she had

what she needed, and once she finished high school, paid for her college education and her wedding. Uncle Charley had given her away, even though like DJ, he didn't care for her choice of a husband. Luca Cross lacked ambition, while Keira wanted it all.

DJ suspected that Keira might be the reason her husband had gotten involved with gamblers and loan sharks. Now they were using her to collect what was owed. The same way DJ had ended up where he was now—owing the wrong people for all the wrong reasons.

He started the truck. Tonight he'd made thousands of dollars. But it was money he couldn't touch. He tried to look at it as work—the same way Sadie did. Some nights, though, he'd enjoyed it more than he should have. He felt only a little guilty since the men who'd gotten fleeced tonight had all been handpicked by a man they either owed or had crossed. The boss was a man who always collected debts—one way or another. Even though Uncle Charley was dead, DJ, now twenty-nine, was still paying off his uncle's last debts. It was the way it worked in this world. Some inherited wealth, others inherited debt. A man paid that debt.

Shifting into gear, DJ headed to his apartment to pack for the first flight he could get to Bozeman, Montana. From there Keira would pick him up. He had no idea what he would find when he got there, but that was nothing new. He'd spent his childhood expecting the worst.

Chapter Three

On her fiancé's ranch outside of Lonesome, Montana, Ansley Brookshire felt as if she couldn't breathe. Time was running out. Her longed-for Christmas wedding was days away. She was about to marry the man of her dreams. Just the thought stole her breath and made her heart pound with both excitement and anxiety.

It was all perfect except for one thing. Recently, she'd found out not only that she'd been adopted—but also that she had a twin brother. Now that she knew, she couldn't imagine getting married without him at the wedding. She had this image of him giving her away. Her heart ached for the two of them to be united and brought into the family that she'd only recently discovered.

Unfortunately, she had no idea where he was, even who he was. Like her, he'd been sold or given away right after birth by a woman who'd told their biological mother that they both had died. Ansley's adoptive mother had only wanted a baby girl and swore that she never even knew there had been another baby.

No one knew what had happened to her twin brother, since the woman who'd sold the babies was now dead. Ansley's fear was that like her, her twin might not even know he'd been adopted. She just hoped he'd gone to a good family and had a better childhood than hers. While she'd lived on an estate, never been deprived of anything money could buy, she'd been lonely and wished desperately for a family. All her childhood, she'd seen more of her nannies and the household staff than her parents.

When Ansley had learned that she was adopted, she'd gone in search of her biological mother. It had been like taking a stick to a hornet's nest. But she'd found her birth mother and the happy ending she'd hoped for. She wanted the same for her brother. Unfortunately, all leads had gone cold.

Her only hope was that the PIs at Colt Brothers Investigation would find him before it was too late. One of those PIs was her fiancé, Buck Crawford, who'd been working tirelessly for weeks searching for her missing twin. All they had to go on was the tiny bracelet his birth mother said she'd had made for him with the initials DJ on it for Del Junior. They couldn't even be sure that he'd ever gotten the bracelet.

"Maybe we should postpone the wedding," Buck had said, but she hadn't had the heart to do that. They both wanted to be married soon. She told herself she was being too sentimental. A Christmas wedding was her dream and Buck was everything she'd ever wanted in a husband.

"No," she'd told him. "We're getting married. Anyway, I still have hope that we'll find DJ before the wedding."

Now the wedding was looming and still no leads on her twin.

"Ansley?" a female voice called. "Or should I call you DelRae?"

She hadn't heard a vehicle in the deep snow, but now she heard the front door close. Footfalls headed her way. She had to smile, wondering at twenty-nine years old if she would ever answer to the name her birth mother had given her. Or if she should even bother trying.

"In here," she called back to Bella Colt, a sister-in-law. Along with finding her birth mother, she'd also found her biological father's family—the Colt brothers of Colt Brothers Investigation and their wives. She now had four half brothers, Tommy, Davy, James and Willie, and their wives, Bella, Carla, Lori and Ellie. She'd instantly felt a part of the family.

On top of that, she'd also fallen in love with the brothers' best friend, Buck Crawford, a fellow PI at the agency.

Bella came into the living room where Ansley had been wrapping Christmas presents. "What in the world! Did you buy out all the stores in Missoula?"

She shook her head sheepishly. "I've never had a family to buy for before. My adoptive mother bought her own Christmas presents for me to wrap. My adoptive father had his secretary pick up something for each of us. He usually also had the secretary return anything Maribelle or I got for him, saying he didn't need anything. So shopping for all of you has been so much fun. Don't tell anyone, but I started shopping even before Thanksgiving. I couldn't wait."

"You really are too much." Bella hugged her awkwardly around the baby. James's wife Lori had given birth to two identical baby boys a few months ago.

Ansley motioned her friend into the kitchen. "Coffee?"

"I shouldn't." Bella lumbered in, both hands over her protruding stomach. "Water tastes so…watery," she groaned.

"Eggnog?"

"Don't tempt me," her friend said, and held her side for a moment. "They've been kicking like crazy. I suspect they've got my and Tommy's worst traits," she said with a laugh as she took a chair and the glass of eggnog. "It would be just like them to decide to be born in the middle of your wedding." All four Colt wives were her bridesmaids, with their husbands the groomsmen.

A silence fell between them as Ansley poured herself a cup of coffee and joined Bella at the table.

"Are you sure you don't want to wait?" Bella asked. "Even if Buck manages to find him, he'll be a complete stranger. Do you really want a stranger standing up with you at your wedding?"

Ansley laughed. "He won't be a stranger. I know him— that is, I feel like I do. He's my *twin*. He won't be a stranger."

Bella looked skeptical but let it go. "What if Buck doesn't find him before the wedding?"

"Then we go ahead anyway," she said, knowing how disappointed she would be.

"You could just postpone it," Bella suggested.

It wasn't like she hadn't thought about postponing the wedding. "Wait for how long, though? What if DJ's never found? Buck and I can't wait. We love each other. We want to get married." She sighed. "But at the same time, how can I start my life not knowing where my twin is, how he is or even if he's still alive? I've always felt as if there was a missing piece of me. Then I found you and the Colt brothers and Buck."

"And still something was missing," Bella said.

She nodded. "Once I found out that I had a twin who my mother called DJ for Del Junior, I knew I had to find him." She swallowed the lump in her throat. "Even if he can't be found by the wedding, we will find him. Buck won't stop looking for him."

"Neither will the Colt brothers. They were shocked to

find they had a half sister. Imagine their reaction to meeting a half brother. If he is anything like you, we are going to love him. We'll love him anyway," she said with a laugh and took a sip of her eggnog. "So, is it going to be Ansley or DelRae? Or are you going to answer to both?"

"I have no sentimental ties to the Ansley name or the Brookshire name. I love DelRae, I'm just not sure I'll ever remember to answer to it."

"I can understand that you might want to ditch your first name and last with both Maribelle and Harrison Brookshire headed for prison. But you also can't erase your past," Bella said. "You know my father almost went to prison at one point." She shook her head. "A long story for another time," she said, awkwardly getting to her feet. "I have some last-minute Christmas shopping to do, but I wanted to check on you."

She rose to show her out. She couldn't believe how close she'd gotten to her new family and in record time. She hoped the same would be true for her twin when he was found.

At the door, Bella turned to take her hand and squeeze it. "Don't give up hope. There's still time."

All she could do was nod and smile her thanks even as she felt sick with worry that time was running out. Worse, the news might not be good. Her twin might not have survived. Or he might want nothing to do with her and the rest of the family.

BUCK CRAWFORD DISCONNECTED and leaned back, feeling more positive than he had in weeks. "I think I might have found a lead," he said, leaving his office to walk out into the main reception area of Colt Brothers Investigation.

James looked up from his father's old desk expectantly.

The brothers had all done their best to find Ansley's twin brother before hitting a brick wall and being forced to move on to other clients. Buck was determined to continue looking for the missing twin right up until the wedding.

"It's an old friend of Judy Ramsey's who moved away after her house burned down." Buck remembered the vacant lot next to Judy's house. "Luella Lindley lived there and knew Judy during the time frame when Ansley and her brother were born. I'm hoping she's going to be able to help."

"For Ansley's sake, I hope so." He smiled. "Yours, too, since I know how badly you want to marry my sister. But what if you don't find him? Would you postpone the wedding?"

Buck shook his head. "I hope not, but Ansley has her heart set on her twin giving her away. Not that I blame her. I can't imagine what it's like to find out you have a twin brother you never knew existed. I'd want to find him, too."

"Let's hope she gets her happy ending. I just worry. Ansley lucked out. Even though the Brookshires weren't the family she'd hoped for, she had what most people would consider a good life. Then she got all of us." He grinned. "But it could have turned out a lot worse for her brother."

Admittedly, Buck worried about that as well. Ansley needed a happy ending and that meant finding her twin. Hopefully before the wedding. He didn't want to think about postponing the wedding. He wanted Ansley for his wife now. The waiting was killing him. He was anxious to start their lives together.

But until Del Jr. was found, dead or alive, he knew Ansley would be heartbroken. That was something Buck couldn't stand. He'd do anything to make her happy.

Buck couldn't help but think about all that Ansley had

gone through to find her birth mother. It had been dangerous. People had died, others had gone to prison. Both Buck and Ansley were lucky to be alive. He really hoped that wouldn't be the case finding her twin.

"Let's hope Luella Lindley has the answers we need," he told James. "I'm driving down to Casper, Wyoming, to talk to her in person. Don't mention this to Ansley. I don't want to get her hopes up."

Buck knew it was more than that. He didn't want to give her bad news with their wedding and first Christmas together just over a week away.

"CAN YOU TURN that off?" DJ asked after he and Keira were headed north away from the busiest airport in the state, Yellowstone International just outside of Bozeman, Montana. He wanted to put all this progress in the rearview mirror as they headed toward the mountains.

She reached over and turned off the radio and the Christmas music. DJ realized he'd lost track of not just weeks, but months. How could it already be this close to Christmas? It wasn't as if he celebrated the holiday. He had no warm and fuzzy family holiday memories. In fact, he was always glad once the season was over—not that it wasn't a good time financially for him and Sadie. The kind of people they dealt with were more reckless with their money this time of year, some out of Christmas cheer, most out of greed or desperation.

"Tell me what's going on," he said once they were on the open highway.

Keira's hands gripped the wheel seemingly tighter, her eyes galvanized on the road ahead as she chewed nervously at her lower lip. "I don't want you to get mad." Too late for that. "It was a mistake. He didn't know."

DJ swore. Of course Luca knew. No one gambled without knowing they might lose—and they might lose big if they didn't stop. "How much?"

"Seventy-five large originally," she said without looking at him. "I didn't know that he'd borrowed more to keep up with the interest payments."

He never lost his temper. It was bad for business. But right now...

"I wouldn't have called you, but..."

But there was no one else.

She concentrated on the road.

He chose his words carefully, determined not to take his frustration and anger out on her. "When you're involved with these kinds of people you don't go to another one and borrow more. That's a good way to end up in a ditch dead. Or in your case sold to the highest bidder. Who are these men your husband got involved with?"

"Do you remember Titus Grandville? He's an investment banker in the same building as his father's bank."

Is that what he was calling himself? "Crooks wear suits, too, baby sister," he said, and turned to stare out at the passing countryside while he tamped down his anger and tried to concentrate on the beauty. It had been so long since he'd been back here. He'd forgotten how breathtaking the snowcapped mountains were. The pines were so dark green against the cobalt blue of the big sky. He felt an old childhood ache for a place that he'd once thought of as paradise.

"Who's his muscle?" he finally asked.

She mugged a distasteful face. "Butch Lamar. He's the one you talked to on the phone. He's new in town. Hangs out on the Turner Ranch. He's friends with Rafe Westfall, the son of one of the men who used to live out at our old ranch." She shot him a look. "They're serious, DJ. The first time Luca couldn't pay, they beat him up real bad. This last time…"

"He still alive?" DJ asked, hoping so for selfish reasons.

"Barely. He's hiding out. That's why they grabbed me."

"Did you know?" he had to ask. Her silence said it all. He swore and turned on her. "You grew up with this. How could you let him?"

"*I didn't let him*. He thought he was—"

"Smarter, right?" DJ cursed under his breath. "And he thought he was going to surprise you, make you happy. How do I know this is the last time he's going to have to be bailed out?" He saw her jaw tighten.

"I'm divorcing him. I'm done. He's on his own after this."

He studied her, trying to decide if she was telling the truth or just saying what he wanted to hear. He made a living reading people, but his little sister was a mystery to him because he loved her so much. "Does he know that?"

"Yes. He says he was trying to make money to save our marriage."

"Bull," DJ snapped.

She swung her head in his direction. "Don't you think I know that?" She quickly turned back to her driving as the SUV swerved. "It's not the first time. We had to sell everything last time."

He found himself grinding his teeth and had to look out the side window again. In his line of work, temper was a real weakness and one he couldn't afford. But this wasn't business. This was personal.

Ahead, he saw the turnoff to Whitehall. "Take this exit.

We'll get a couple of rooms here and go into Butte in the morning." What he didn't say was that he wasn't ready to go back. Not yet. The city brought back too many memories.

"By the way, where is Luca hiding out?" He asked it casually, but Keira knew him too well.

"I don't want you to do anything to him."

He waited, counting off the seconds until she finally spoke as if she knew he'd find out even if she refused to tell him.

"Lonesome. It's a small town up by—"

"I know where it is," DJ said. "Why'd he choose it?"

She didn't answer right away. "He's staying at Uncle Charley's cabin up there."

Charley had a cabin? This was news. He thought that his uncle had lost everything back when he lost the ranch. And why outside of Lonesome, one of only a few small Montana towns that he noticed his uncle had avoided? When asked, Charley had been surprised that he'd noticed. "Some towns aren't worth the trouble." But he'd looked at him strangely, as if he wanted to say more but had changed his mind.

DJ had guessed that Charley had unfinished business in Lonesome. Those last few years of his uncle's life, he hadn't seen much of him. When he did see him, he worried that Charley was in more trouble than he could dig himself out of. As it turned out, that was true.

Charley always had his secrets. Now he knew that his uncle had a cabin that he'd somehow managed to keep— and Keira knew about it.

He glanced over at her, wondering what other secrets they'd both kept from him.

Chapter Four

Leaving Keira in Whitehall, DJ rented an SUV and drove to Butte alone. He found the investment banker's office on the top floor of the Grandville Building. He'd checked it out online last night as he prepared for this. A four-story brick edifice from the late eighteen hundreds that housed the Grandville Bank started by Titus's great-grandfather. The bank was still on the ground floor with two upper floors converted into condos and the top floor office space.

He found Titus Grandville in his corner office overlooking the historical section of downtown Butte. "Nice digs," DJ said as the banker motioned for him to take one of the leather club chairs. He declined and approached the man in the large office chair behind the massive desk.

Like all the Grandvilles, Titus was short and squat with a cowlick at the crown of his brown hair. While dressed like a respectable investment banker, he still looked like the thug he was.

"Let me understand the problem here," DJ said quietly, calmly. "You came after my sister to threaten her over debts run up by the deadbeat husband she is divorcing. Is that right?"

Titus narrowed dark eyes that were a little too close together. He dropped his hand below the desk. To buzz for security if needed? Or reach for a weapon? "I hope we can settle this like respectable gentlemen."

DJ laughed. "We'd have to be respectable gentlemen." He lowered his voice. "You need to leave Keira alone. What is it going to take?"

The banker smiled and leaned back in his large office chair, steepling his fingers on his round middle. Apparently, mentioning money made Titus less nervous. "Someone has to pay what's owed."

Grandville was enjoying this a little too much. He remembered him as a kid. To say there was bad blood between them was putting it mildly. Titus had always lorded it over him. Not that everyone in Butte hadn't known that Titus was a Grandville. Who knew what DJ was?

Just the sight of his smug face was enough to make him want to leap over the massive desk and take the man by the throat. But it wouldn't solve the problem. DJ had known the moment he heard Keira crying on the phone that he was going to have to come up here and pay them off. The very idea stuck in his craw because of his dislike for the Grandvilles.

"Settle for twenty-five."

Titus shook his head. "Seventy-five with interest on the loan adding up every day—"

"Fifty thousand and I don't throw you out that big window behind you," DJ said.

"Diamond, you have always been a loose cannon." Titus tsked. "All right. For old time's sake, seventy-five and no more interest as long as this is handled quickly. By the end of the week."

"And you never go near my sister again."

The banker nodded, but DJ didn't feel as if this was settled. "Do I need to say it? You never do business with Luca Cross again either."

"Why do you care about him?" Titus asked, sounding amused.

DJ didn't answer, afraid to voice his fear that Keira wouldn't leave the man because she still loved him. Love was a fickle, foolish sentiment, one he avoided when it came to women. Family was another story, though, maybe especially family you didn't share blood with.

"I'll get your money. But you do realize that I'm going to have to put together a poker game to make it happen. That all right with you?"

Titus rocked forward in his chair, taking the bait quicker than DJ had expected. "I could suggest a couple of players with deep pockets I'd like to see cleaned. Let me know when and where."

"You're welcome to come play as well," DJ said with a grin.

The banker laughed. "I'm smarter than that. And Diamond? I'll need that money by the end of the week."

As he turned to leave, the banker called after him, "So it's true. You're paying off your uncle's debts, too." Definite amusement in his voice.

DJ didn't trust himself to look back. If he saw that self-righteous look on Titus's face, he might just make good on his earlier threat.

As he left the building, he quit kidding himself that there was another way to solve this. He was going to have to pay, one way or another. He had the money in his savings account. Seventy-five grand wouldn't even make a dent. He could pay Titus off and walk away, but the very thought turned his stomach. He'd told Keira to stay put in Whitehall until this was settled. She'd be safe there—as long as she didn't do anything foolish like try to go to her husband.

DJ stopped for a moment as he tried to talk himself out of the plan that had come together the moment he'd walked into Grandville's office and seen Titus sitting behind his big desk. His good sense advised him to just pay the debt and forget it. Unfortunately, it wasn't just about the money. It hardly ever was.

He made the call to the one person he needed right now. "Sadie?" He hated the way his voice almost broke. It made him admit how much he wanted her help, as if a part of him worried that he couldn't do this without her, and that alone should have scared him. He'd come to depend on her. But even as he thought it, he knew it was a hell of a lot more than that. "I need you."

"I wondered how long it would take before you realized that," she joked.

"It's my sister. Her bad-choice soon-to-be hopefully ex-husband's fault. He's taken off and left her holding the bag."

"How heavy is this bag?"

"Seventy-five large."

"I can be on the next plane. Where am I headed?"

DJ closed his eyes for a moment, relief and something much stronger making his knees weak. "I'll pick you up at the airport outside of Bozeman. I'll be the cowboy in the hat," he said, needing to lighten the moment for fear he'd say something he couldn't take back. "I really appreciate this," he said, his voice rough with emotion. "Thank you."

"No problem, partner. I'm on my way."

SADIE DISCONNECTED, a lump in her throat. *DJ had a sister*? Why had she thought it was just him and the conman uncle who'd raised him? Not that DJ knew any more about her life than she did his. When they'd been thrown together, she'd just assumed that he was like her, from the same background, caught up in a world not to either of their making or liking. DJ had taken on his uncle's debt to the organization her godfather ran. The payments on that debt, which were almost paid, were what had kept them together.

She'd done her best to treat it like business, especially after her godfather had warned her against getting too close to DJ Diamond. But she'd gotten to know the man from sitting across a poker table from him all that time.

While she'd been shocked to learn that DJ had a little sister, she wasn't surprised that he would drop everything to bail her out. What worried her was that she'd never heard him sound like he had on the phone. Desperate? Anxious? Neither was good in this business, she thought as she quickly threw some clothing and money into a bag along with their decks of marked cards.

Two hours later, as she boarded a plane to Montana, she reminded herself that this might be the last time she saw DJ. Their "arrangement" was over. She'd told her godfather that she wanted out as soon as DJ's debt was paid. He'd been disappointed but not surprised.

"What will you do? You'll miss this," he'd said.

"I don't think so. I want a family." She didn't have to tell him that she also wanted to be as far away from criminal organizations as she could get.

"I understand," he'd said. "Your father was like that. Tell Diamond we're even. His uncle's debt is paid in full. My present to you since I can tell that you have a soft spot for him."

Sadie had only smiled. "Thank you."

"But you're not quitting because of him, right?"

"No, that partnership will be over," she said, hating how hard it would be to walk away from DJ Diamond. She'd grown more than fond of him. But she would walk away, she'd told herself.

"Good," her godfather said. "By the way, you're better at this than your father ever was, and he was pretty darned good." It had been her father who'd taught her that poker wasn't a game of chance. It was a game of skill, mental toughness and endurance.

"Never sit down at a table unless you know you can beat everyone there—one way or another," he'd said over and over. "You're going to lose sometimes, so never throw good money after bad. It all comes down to reading your opponents and knowing when to cash in and walk away."

Whatever DJ had going on in Montana, it was time to cash in and walk away. She would tell DJ when she got to Montana. She would also offer him the seventy-five grand so they wouldn't have to use the cards in her carry-on bag. He wouldn't take it, but she would offer. She feared that unlike her, he'd never be able to step away from the con. He enjoyed it too much. But eventually, his luck would run out. The thought made her sad. As her godfather had said, she had grown a soft spot for the cowboy.

BUCK CRAWFORD MADE the drive down to Casper, Wyoming, arriving in late afternoon. Luella Lindley lived in a small house in the older part of town. She was in her sixties, retired after being a telephone operator for years. She lived alone except for her three cats, George, Bob and Ingrid. She had a weakness for chocolate, her husband had been dead for almost twenty years, and she played bingo on Tuesday nights at the Senior Center.

He'd gotten all that information the first time he'd talked to her. Had she known Judy Ramsey? Yes. "We were like two peas in a pod," Luella had told him. "Sisters, that's what Judy called us, me being the older sister."

It took a good five minutes after ringing the doorbell for the woman to answer the door. She'd warned him that she used a walker and would be slow. Luella opened the door, leaning on her walker and smiling broadly. The smell of meat loaf wafted out, making his stomach growl.

"I hope you're hungry," she said, her blue eyes sparkling with excitement, giving him the feeling that she didn't get many visitors. "I made my famous meat loaf. Come on in. No need to stand out there on the front step." She turned and led the way into the house. "Have a seat." She went from the walker to a recliner. "Didn't expect a good-looking cowboy, although you did sound young on the phone. Are you really a private detective?"

"Yes, and you should have demanded proof of identification before you let me in," he said.

She laughed. "I saw you drive up. You didn't look that dangerous."

Buck knew he couldn't leave until he had meat loaf, so he let Luella talk about everything under the sun for a few minutes before he said, "What can you tell me about Judy Ramsey?"

"Sweet thing she was. Never had a lick of sense when it came to men, though," Luella said with a shake of her head. "Broke my heart every time she let some man hurt her."

"You knew her twenty-nine years ago. Did she tell you she was pregnant?"

The elderly woman nodded. "She was scared, but I could tell a part of her liked the idea of being a mother." She shook her head. "Turned out it was female problems. No baby. Never going to have one. By then, she'd realized she wasn't mother material."

"Did she tell you about meeting Maribelle Brookshire?"

"Read all about it in the paper. I have the Lonesome paper sent to me. The news is old by the time it arrives, but I don't care. It doesn't cost much and that is my hometown."

"So she told you about her deal with Maribelle to buy the baby if it was a girl?"

"No," she said after a moment. "I could tell something was going on, but no. She was devastated when she found out there was no baby. I didn't realize the main reason was because she'd already sold the baby to Maribelle Brookshire. I thought her behavior was due to a man, but then she began asking questions about babies… I had to wonder why since I knew she wasn't having any of her own."

"What kind of questions?"

"Like what they ate, how to burp them, how to even put on a diaper and what you needed to buy for a baby. I thought she'd gone crazy."

"If you've read the news, then you know that Maribelle and Harrison Brookshire are awaiting trial for Judy's death. I'm engaged to their daughter they bought from Judy, Ansley Brookshire."

"My goodness, isn't that wonderful. That poor child needs a happy ending. Those so-called parents of hers, they deserve the electric chair for what they did to her, not to mention poor Judy."

"Ansley had a twin brother. Do you have any idea what Judy might have done with him?"

Luella shook her head. "I can understand why she did what she did. I mean, that's how we became such good friends—her moving in next door to me. She couldn't have done that without the money she got from that woman. Not that I approve of her means."

"Is it possible she gave the baby boy to someone she knew in Lonesome? I would think that she would have taken him to someone she trusted, someone with knowledge as to how to care for an infant."

The woman nodded sagely. "You're thinking me."

"The birth mother wasn't in any shape to take care of the baby. Also she thought both babies had died. So Judy had to have taken the baby boy to a friend."

Luella seemed to squirm a little in her seat. "Is talking to you like talking to a lawyer, anything I say is just between us?"

Buck hesitated, but only for a moment. "I just want to find him. I don't want to get anyone in trouble, especially you."

"That didn't quite answer my question."

"She brought you the baby, didn't she?"

Chapter Five

DJ had never been happier to see anyone. He stared at Sadie as she came down the stairs at the Yellowstone International Airport—his second time there in days. He blinked realizing he'd never seen her in normal clothes. Today, she wore designer jeans, a pale blue cashmere sweater and furry snow boots. She had her sheepskin coat thrown over one shoulder, her leather shoulder bag on the other and the expensive carry-on in her hand.

She looked like a million bucks. Everything fit like a glove, and she fit in here in the Gallatin Valley where the wealthy came to find paradise. She could have passed for any one of them because, he realized with a start, she was one of them. Sometimes he forgot that she'd been raised in Palm Beach, rubbing elbows with the rich and powerful.

He knew he wasn't the only man staring at this breathtaking woman with her long blond hair resting around her shoulders. But when those honey-brown eyes found him, he felt like the only man in the world. She smiled, reminding him how amazing she was—and how unattainable.

His partner, Sadie Montclair, the smartest, funniest, sexiest woman he'd ever met, was off-limits in a big life-threatening way. Even if her godfather hadn't threatened him if he even thought about seducing her, DJ knew that she wouldn't look twice at someone like him. Not seriously, anyway.

"How was your flight?" he asked as he took her carry-on and led her outside into the cold, snowy December day to his rental SUV. "Thanks again for coming. You fly over so many mountains to get here. Sometimes the turbulence can get to you, but the view can be pretty spectacular."

"Are you really trying to make small talk, DJ Diamond?" she asked with a laugh as he climbed behind the wheel. She could tell he was nervous. He saw a flicker of concern in her gaze before she said, "Tell me about the people your sister owes this money to."

So like Sadie to get right to business. He tried to calm his nerves, having second thoughts about getting her involved in this. But while he kept thinking that he shouldn't have called her and she shouldn't have come, he was so glad that she was here. Maybe this was a mistake, but right now he couldn't help feeling relieved. Sadie balanced him; it's why they were such a good team.

He started the engine, stopped at the booth to turn in his parking ticket and drove out of the airport onto Interstate 90 headed west, mentally kicking himself for getting her involved in his family mess. "I shouldn't have called you."

"Of course you should have. If I hadn't wanted to come, I wouldn't have. I'm here for you. We're partners. It's just that you were acting like you'd picked up your girlfriend at the airport."

He nodded, swallowed and tried to relax. She was right. He wasn't himself around this version of Sadie. But he better pull it together. He cleared this throat and turned to business. "The men? Old money. Suits, ties, hired muscle.

Grandville is a cocky bastard. Would they kill Keira? Probably not. Would they mess her up? Yeah."

SADIE SAW THAT her words had hurt DJ. But she'd seen the way he looked at her as she'd come down the stairs at the terminal. It was going to be hard enough to walk away from this partnership as it was. She couldn't have him looking at her like that. Worse, she couldn't feel like she *was* his girlfriend he was picking up at the airport.

"Doesn't sound like anything we haven't dealt with before," she said as she took in the scenery as he drove, reminding herself that this was just another job.

She'd never been to Montana, but she could see the appeal. There was a winter wonderland outside her window. Everything was frosted with snow from the mountains to the pine trees, from houses to the fence posts they passed. Even the air seemed to sparkle with snow crystals. She couldn't help being enchanted as she saw a red barn with Christmas lights in the shape of a star on the side.

"I thought we'd make a big haul, pay off Grandville and get out," DJ was saying. "He's supplying at least one of the players, someone's pockets he wants us to pick. I'll find someone to front the game who can bring in a local hard hitter or two to the mix."

"Whatever you think is best," she said as she saw a snowman in one of the yards. "Montana really is like the photographs I've seen. It's beautiful."

He glanced over at her. "You should see it in the spring. That's my favorite time of year, when everything greens up after a long, dull, colorless winter."

"I'd like that," she said. "I was thinking on the way up here. I have seventy-five thousand that I could—"

"Not a chance," he said quickly.

"It's my money, nothing to do with my godfather, and I wouldn't—"

"No," he said, shaking his head. "Thanks, but no. If you don't want to do this, just say so. No harm, no foul."

"I told you. I'm here. I'll do it. I just thought…" She could see that she'd offended him. "Sorry."

He shook his head. "I can't take your money."

"I get it." Sadie considered him for a moment. DJ saved what money he made when gaming legally. He was a hell of a poker player. She was betting that he had a whole lot more than seventy-five grand lying around. So if he wanted to, he could pay off his sister's creditor. This wasn't so much about money, she suspected. This was about getting even. With this Grandville he mentioned?

"Want to tell me what you have planned?"

"Just a friendly game of poker." He grinned as he looked over at her. She knew that look. He loved this. "I'm keeping you under wraps. Butte's an old mining town. I've got you a room at a local historic hotel that's been completely renovated. It's fancy—just like you. Room service, a bar, order whatever you want, any clothes you need."

"Sounds like you've thought of everything. So I'm the mark," she said, and shook her head in amusement. "A new role, huh?"

"One that clearly you were born into," he said, his gaze taking her in again.

She tried not to read too much into the look. She knew DJ. He couldn't help the charm. The man had an appreciation for women. All women—she couldn't let herself forget that.

Sadie told herself that this was just going to be another poker game like so many others they'd played together. She knew the drill. The two of them had it down pat. But as she studied him while he drove, she had to ask, "You sure about this? Once things get personal—"

"Like your godfather says, otherwise it is only money."

"Don't kid yourself. He likes the money just as much as the retribution."

They drove in silence for a few minutes. "It will be our last time." DJ tapped on the steering wheel, seeming lost in thought. "I know we're close to paying my uncle's debt. However much he owes for interest, I'll pay it from my own money. I'm done." He glanced at her as if to see how she was taking the news.

She nodded. "Talk about like minds. I was going to tell you the same thing. My godfather says you're paid in full." He turned to give her a suspicious look. "I had nothing to do with it. He says it's time."

DJ turned back to his driving and chewed on that for a while. She was wondering if he would miss it. If he would miss her. "One last big score." When she said nothing, he asked, "You're really up for this?"

"We're a team. If this is our last time… I wouldn't want to miss it for anything."

His gaze locked with hers for a few earth-shaking moments. She felt heat rush to her cheeks and quickly turned away. Was this really their last game? Her heart ached at the thought of never seeing DJ again as she watched the snowy landscape blur past her side window. Probably for the best, she thought, because she seemed to be losing her resistance to his charm. She couldn't let down her guard now when it was almost over. She knew how DJ was with women. She didn't want to be one of them.

It surprised her, though, that he'd been ready to end their

relationship, even if it had been all business. Maybe like her, he'd decided it was time. Yet it made her uneasy, as if he was worried this was their last game for another reason. Just how dangerous was this going to be?

"You can still walk away," he said as if reading her mind.

He had to know her better than that. "Have I ever let you down?" she asked, still not looking at him.

"Never."

She heard something in his voice, an emotion she hadn't heard before. But by the time she dared look over at him, all his attention was back on the highway ahead.

BUCK HELD HIS BREATH. This was the first decent lead he'd had on finding the missing twin. He couldn't help but think of Ansley. He had to find the last missing piece of her. She'd risked her life to find her birth mother, who had been told that both babies died.

"Can I go to prison for this?" Luella asked, her voice cracking.

"You aren't going to prison," he said. "Unless you harmed the baby."

"Oh, good Lord, no," she said, sounding shocked. "I'd never hurt a precious baby. He was so sweet, so tiny, so precious. I didn't care where Judy had gotten him. I should have. I know that was wrong. I just wanted to help her. She was beside herself, afraid he wasn't going to make it. I assured her I could help."

He saw her hesitate and suspected he knew where she was headed. "You knew someone who could take care of the baby."

"I'm not saying who, but yes. We took him over there and my...friend who'd just given birth six months before was still breastfeeding. He took right to it like the little champ he was and perked right up."

Buck thought how easy it would be to find out if Luella had a daughter or daughter-in-law who'd given birth that year—but only if it came to that. "So you left the baby with her?"

"Only for a few days. I still didn't know where Judy had gotten the little darling. Had I been younger, I would have kept him. I wanted to, but there would have been talk. Lonesome is a small town." She shook her head. "It wasn't possible. But it was so hard to give him back."

"Back to Judy?"

She nodded. "She knew someone who wanted a baby." Luella began shaking her head even before he asked who. "I didn't want to know. I'd involved people I cared about already. I knew not to push it."

He tried to hide his disappointment. "You must have some idea. You were Judy's best friend. You knew some of the same people."

She looked away for a moment and he felt hope resurface.

As DJ TURNED off the interstate and headed toward uptown Butte, Sadie took in the city sprawled across the side of the mountain—except for the right side, where much of the mountain was missing. "They still mine here?" she asked in surprise.

"Butte is a hard-core mining town," DJ said. "It started as a mining camp back in the 1860s and quickly grew to become Montana's first industrial city." They passed large abandoned old brick buildings, the windows either missing or covered in dust. "It's fallen on hard times since then, but the Continental pit is still active as an open-pit copper and molybdenum mining operation. Mining still pays better than any other industry in the state."

"Which is why we're here," Sadie said. "Aren't miners… a bit rough to deal with if things go south, though?"

"We aren't taking the miners' money. We're after the people above them who make the big money."

She was relieved to hear that. With her godfather, he handpicked the players in the games she and DJ relieved of their cash. Even so, there were some who often made her nervous. She'd learned that you could never tell what a person might do—especially if you'd just spent hours taking his money.

DJ headed up the mountainside, passing more old brick buildings in what was obviously the historic district. She couldn't help being fascinated just thinking of the history here as he pulled down an alley behind a large old brick hotel. The sign on the top floor read Hotel Finlen.

Sadie shot him a look as he stopped at the hotel's service entrance off the alley, but he didn't seem to notice. "Butte has an amazing history—and so does this hotel. Charles Lindbergh, Harry S. Truman and even JFK visited the Finlen," he said with an enthusiasm that was catching. "I love this hotel and this town. Butte was once the largest city between Chicago and San Francisco. You'll like this place. The Finlen was architecturally inspired by the Hotel Astor in New York and was built to impress in 1924."

She couldn't help smiling at him. Clearly this old mining town meant a lot to him. "How do you know all this?" she asked, hoping he would talk about his childhood here.

"The Finlen was my uncle's favorite hotel. He often paid the bill so we could come back. That wasn't true of most other hotels we stayed in."

She laughed. "Do you always use the back door off the alley?"

"Used to a lot. But today?" He shrugged. "I know people here." Of course he did. He knew people all over Montana and the northwest after growing up with a conman uncle. Not that DJ had ever offered anything about himself or his past. Just as she hadn't. But her godfather had told her a few things about the man before he'd asked her to work with him.

"I want to keep our partnership quiet. I hate to ask you to walk around to the front of the building through the snow and slush, but we can't be connected," DJ said. "I need you to hang out here for a day or so. Like I said, buy expensive meals, shop, whatever. Throw money around. I'll contact you when I'm ready, but for this one you're a high roller."

"I think I'm going to enjoy being the mark," she said as he reached into the glove box and took out a thick envelope of money. She waved it away. "Thanks, but no. You don't get to be the only one to take the high road."

He looked as if he wanted to argue, before stuffing the envelope into his inside jacket pocket. "You'll get every penny back." He pointed up the street behind them. "It's easier to go that way. In this part of the older city, the streets and sidewalks are steep since they built the original city on the side of a mountain. I know how steep because I was the one who had to make the run for it so the employees chased me—and not my uncle."

His words hit her at heart level. She knew he'd had a rough childhood, but she hadn't known any details and now didn't know what to say. A cold silence seemed to surround the cab of the pickup for a moment. "It was a game for me," he said as if seeing her sympathy even though she tried hard to hide it. He grinned. "When we were flush, we ate lobster tail and steak from china plates on white linen tablecloths with real silver at the best places in town. True, when we were between scores, we ate whatever I could scrounge up—often from food trays left out in hotel hallways. But you'd be amazed what people leave. Like I said, as a kid it was a game. A scavenger hunt." He shrugged and she could tell that he wished he hadn't told her any of this. So why had he?

"Bet you could run fast." She smiled even though she felt more like crying as she thought about DJ as a boy outrunning hotel employees so his uncle didn't have to. "I can't wait to see this hotel that meant so much to you and your uncle." She met his gaze. "I like seeing this place through your eyes. Thanks for sharing. And don't worry about me. I'll do my part."

"I never doubt it. Thanks again, Sadie."

She hesitated, surprised how much she wanted to reassure him. He seemed so vulnerable here in this place that had been such an important part of his younger life.

But she was the one who'd kept their relationship strictly business. While she couldn't *not* have regrets, it was almost over. The thought made a lump rise in her throat as she climbed out, closed the door and headed back down the alley. As she walked she couldn't help comparing his life to her own. Hers had been a fairy-tale princess's existence compared to his. There was no way she couldn't help him get the money for his sister. But she still felt uneasy. She didn't know this place or these people. Nor did she and DJ have the protection of her godfather. They were on their own.

At the front of the hotel, she pushed open the door, lifted her chin and strode in as if she owned the place. It was time to go to work.

Chapter Six

Buck watched Luella turn away to rinse out a cup in the sink. Stalling. He held his tongue although it was killing him. He could tell that she knew something he desperately needed. He thought of Ansley, his love for her, their upcoming wedding. *Please.*

"I honestly don't know for certain," Luella said. "I swear."

"I believe you, Luella," Buck said. "But anything you can tell me will help. My fiancée is desperate to have her missing twin brother give her away at our wedding."

The woman sighed as she turned back to face him. "That is so sweet." She hesitated, but only a moment longer. "There was this young woman that Judy had befriended when she worked at that old folks' home down in Missoula. Her name was Sheila. I saw her a few times when she came up to visit." Luella shook her head, lips pursed in disapproval. "I didn't like the look of her, but Judy was a sucker for anyone less off than she was. Sheila had had a hard life apparently and looked up to Judy."

He could see where that would have pleased Judy, who'd had a tough life herself. "Are you telling me Judy gave this young woman the baby?"

"I fear she did," Luella said, her voice cracking. "Broke

my heart. That sweet innocent baby boy turned over to someone too immature, too irresponsible, too incapable of even taking care of herself let alone another life."

"How can I find Sheila?" he asked, hoping Luella had more than just the woman's first name to give him.

"I never knew her last name." His heart fell. "But I did hear from Judy that Sheila had gotten married. Said Sheila'd had a baby. Married some man named Grandville."

Buck knew the name. It was an old money Montana name. "You think the baby Sheila allegedly gave birth to was the baby boy Judy had given her?" Luella nodded. "You remember which Grandville she married?"

"Darrow Grandville," Luella said, not hiding her distaste for the man.

"I don't think I've ever heard of Darrow Grandville," Buck said, surprised.

"He was a cousin of the Grandvilles of Butte. Thought he was something, him and his fancy car, but I wasn't fooled." She shook her head. "I knew nothing good could come of it. Not a year later, Sheila was back—without the baby or the husband. Judy said Darrow had gotten into some kind of trouble and had to go underground, so to speak. I didn't ask about the baby. I didn't want to know."

"Underground?" he repeated.

Luella waved a hand through the air. "Some place outside of Butte, not really a ranch. The way Judy described it, the place was a hideout for outlaws. She always exaggerated, though. The ranch had a jewel in the name." She narrowed her eyes for a moment as if straining to come up with it. "Emerald Acres or something like that. I'm sorry. It's been too long."

"That will help," Buck said, hoping it was true.

"You think you can find him?" she asked, sounding as skeptical as he felt. "I mean for all we know, he didn't survive."

"I have to find him. Or at least find out what happened to him. If he's alive, his twin sister needs him at her wedding. As the groom, I'll turn over every rock looking for him."

As he left, he called the Colt Brothers Investigation office. "I need to find a ranch that existed near Butte almost thirty years ago. Might have been called Emerald Acres or something with a gemstone name."

"I'll put Tommy on it," James Colt assured him. "Anything else?"

"I'm also looking for a man named Darrow Grandville."

"Grandville? Like the Grandvilles of Butte?"

"A cousin apparently, a disreputable one possibly. He might have had my future bride's twin with him when he got into trouble and had to go to the ranch hideout."

"Great," James said. "I'd be careful with the Grandvilles."

Buck laughed. "Last I heard, they'd gone legit."

"Yeah. Crooks in high places are still crooks and even more dangerous. Also it's Butte. Tough town if you cross the wrong people."

"So I've heard."

"Let me guess," James said. "You're headed for Butte."

"Tell Tommy to call me if he finds anything on the ranch or Darrow. I might have to rattle some cages."

"I'll pay your bail," James said, and hung up.

DJ MENTALLY KICKED HIMSELF, wishing he hadn't told Sadie so much about his life with his uncle. He blamed it on being back in Butte. Memories assailed him the moment he started up the mountain to the old part of town. His uncle had loved

Butte. He'd made a lot of money here and had been almost killed doing it several times. His uncle always said that he wouldn't have survived if it wasn't for DJ.

The two of them hadn't just been on the run from hotel managers and the dozens of people his uncle conned. "If anyone asks you why you aren't in school, you need to have a lie ready," Charley had warned. "Otherwise, they'll take you away from me, put you in a foster home, force you to go to school. Believe me, that's the last thing you want to happen."

Charley had grown up being kicked from home to home before he'd taken off on his own at sixteen and learned the grift from old codgers he met on the street. He taught everything he knew about the con to DJ. Everything else, DJ had learned when he was young from reading and television. Most hotels had books lying around that people had left behind. If desperate, there was usually a Gideon Bible in a motel room.

Once he was older, DJ got his GED and applied for college. Four years later he had a business degree and a legit job that he held on to for almost seven years. Poker night was just a way to pick up some spare change. Then he heard that his uncle Charley needed his help. He quit the job that he later admitted he hated, but before he could reach his uncle, Charley was arrested and sent to prison. That's when he met Sadie's godfather and went to work paying off his uncle's debt and buying him protection while inside. Charley died in prison two years ago of a heart attack.

DJ seldom looked back. That was something else his uncle had taught him. "Spend time looking behind you and you'll trip over your own two feet," Charley used to say.

But being here brought so much of it back, the good, the bad and the downright ugly, he thought.

He tried to concentrate on setting up the poker game rather than going down a very bumpy memory lane. He'd picked up his phone to call Sadie a dozen times, needing to hear her voice, needing to know that he wasn't making a mistake, but he hadn't called.

He knew she was busy playing her part. She was a pro. Meanwhile, he'd been playing poker in penny-ante games around town, looking for a front for the game. He finally found Bob Martin, a small-time poker player with friends with deep enough pockets. It just couldn't be obvious that DJ was behind the game or that he needed players who had money to lose.

DJ told Bob that he knew of a woman with money to burn who liked to play poker but wasn't very good, and the game was set for Friday night. Bob said he even had the perfect place, a local poker spot in the back room of a Chinese restaurant in the older part of town. DJ called Titus with the time and place.

Then he called Sadie.

Buck was on the outskirts of Butte when he got the call. Up here, the snow was deeper, the day darker, as the sun would soon be disappearing behind the mountains that closed in the city.

"It was the Diamond Deluxe Ranch," Tommy Colt said. "It was owned by a man named Charley Diamond. Word is, it was an enclave for outlaws. Diamond lost it about fifteen years ago to back taxes."

"Charley Diamond? Why does that name sound familiar?" Buck asked. Tommy had no idea. "Think I'll see if Willie might recognize it. Anything on Darrow Grandville?"

"Dead. Killed in a bar fight twenty-four years ago."

Buck took the news like a blow. Ansley's twin would have been five years old. What had happened to him? "Tell me how to find the ranch."

"It's now part of a larger working ranch, so the place is probably not occupied." He gave him directions.

"Thanks." He disconnected and called Sheriff Willie Colt. "Charley Diamond," he said without preamble when Willie answered. "Ring a bell?"

"Charley Diamond? Nope, but if it's important I could ask around."

"If you wouldn't mind. He used to own a ranch up here outside of Butte. A place for outlaws to hide out apparently. Darrow Grandville might have been one of them. Grandville hooked up with a friend of Judy Ramsey's named Sheila. That's all I have on her. But she might have gotten Ansley's twin. Problem is, a year later, after hooking up with Grandville, she didn't have the kid anymore."

"I'll see what I can find out. Where are you?"

"On my way to visit the Grandvilles."

"Really bad idea from what I've heard about the family," Willie said, and disconnected.

Buck wasn't surprised that he had to push his way in to see Titus Grandville in his penthouse-floor office.

"I'm sorry, but if you don't have an appointment—"

He walked past the receptionist down the hallway. The views through the windows he passed were of historic Butte with its old mining rigs as well as decaying remnants of elaborate brickwork buildings from a time when it had been the largest city west of Chicago.

Titus Grandville was on his feet by the time Buck walked into his office. "I've already called security."

"I just need to ask you a couple of quick questions." He held out his hand as he approached the man. "Buck Crawford. I'm with Colt Brothers Investigation in Lonesome."

Titus raised a brow, but made no move to shake hands. "Private dick?"

Buck dropped his hand. "I prefer PI. I need to ask you about Darrow Grandville."

"I don't know anyone by that name. Had you called, I could have saved you the trip. Now if that's all."

"Darrow is your cousin. He was arrested in Butte about twenty-odd years ago and might have been staying out on the Diamond Deluxe."

"Before my time," Titus said.

"He might have had a woman with him. Sheila? And a little boy somewhere around one or two at the time."

Grandville was shaking his head. "I told you—"

"You don't remember, right. Well, I'm looking for the boy. He would be twenty-nine now."

"Why are you looking for him anyway?"

"Client confidentiality."

Titus smirked as he settled into his massive office chair. "He wanted for something?"

"A wedding. He needs to give the bride away."

Grandville laughed. "Quite the dangerous case you're on, PI."

"Maybe your father would remember," Buck said as he turned to leave. "I've got time. I'll drop by his place. Maybe his memory is better than yours. Shouldn't be hard to find him since your childhood home is on the historic register."

"Don't bother my father. He isn't well."

Buck was headed for the door.

Grandville was on his feet now. "I'm serious. Leave my father out of this. He doesn't know anyone named Darrow. Or Sheila or anything about a kid."

"I guess I'll see." He walked out with Grandville cursing after him.

SADIE HAD BEEN getting into her new role by spending money. She'd ordered room service and then gone shopping. She'd bought her godfather a Western bolo tie as a gift. She'd picked up a pair of red cowboy boots for herself along with some boot-cut jeans and a large leather purse with a horse carved into it. The purse was plenty big enough for everything she needed.

After she'd returned from an outing, the hotel clerk had called to say that she had a package down at the main desk. Inside it, she'd found a handgun like the one she usually used and ammunition. She'd cleaned and loaded it, telling herself that the next time she saw DJ would be no different than any other night she'd worked with him. Except she was playing a different role and her godfather wouldn't have set up the place and the players.

While it had been dangerous the other times, she'd felt as if things had been under control. She feared that wouldn't be the case this time as she loaded the gun and put it in her new shoulder bag. DJ was too personally involved this time, and that worried her.

After DJ's call, she now had the time and place. All she had to do was wait. She'd already planned what she would wear, who she would be. She and DJ had signals so they could communicate if needed. Usually, it wasn't needed because they both knew the other person so well.

Just the thought that this would be their last game together made her sad. She knew she was being silly. When her godfather had come to her about working with DJ, she'd thought he'd lost his mind.

"This guy is one hell of a poker player," he'd said. "With you as his wingman, the two of you can't lose."

She'd been skeptical at best, especially after she'd met him. DJ was too handsome, too cocky, too much a cowboy even without the Stetson. He seemed like a wild card—the kind of man who could get her killed.

But after one game, she'd been a believer. He was as good as her godfather had said. And under all that cocky cowboy arrogance there was something special.

Isn't that why DJ had gotten to her? Why she knew she'd risk her life for this cowboy without a moment's hesitation?

Was that what she was about to do?

Chapter Seven

Buck figured Titus Grandville would have called for security at his father's mansion. He decided to let security cool their heels for a few hours while he drove out to the old Diamond Deluxe Ranch first.

He drove south, down the mountain from historic Butte to a strip of newer businesses. Like a lot of towns in Montana, the old mining city had seen better days. Buck quickly found himself in the mountains.

Tommy had been right. There wasn't much left of the Diamond Deluxe Ranch and yet he could read the name branded into the weathered wood arch over the road in. A few outbuildings stood along the edge of the road. Through the pines he saw a dilapidated two-story farmhouse, the paint long peeled off, the porch rotted, little glass left in the windows. There was a chicken coop and what could have once been a bunkhouse.

Buck told himself there was nothing here to find, yet he knew he couldn't leave until he looked around. He had to climb up through a deep snowdrift that had blown in across the front porch. The front door was ajar, snow drifted across the weathered hardwood floor inside. He tested the floor. It creaked and groaned but didn't give way as he entered.

A stairway led up to the second floor. He could hear something moving around up there. Pack rats? He started up the stairs, more sounds of movement as small animals scrambled for cover. He found a few old mattresses, a pile of metal bed rails and a couple of broken-down dressers.

There was nothing here of DelRae's twin. For all Buck knew DJ had never even been here. The baby Sheila and Darrow Grandville had with them might not even be the missing twin. He coughed, aware of the dust and other scents in the air, none of them making him want to spend another minute here.

As he started for the top of the stairs, he saw something that made him stop. He recognized the painstakingly carved marks down one side of the door's wood frame. He still had those on the inside of his bedroom. It was a growth chart. Buck stepped closer and felt his heart bump in his chest. He crouched to read the crudely carved dates in the pine. A child had stood here to be measured. He leaned closer, running his finger over what appeared to be initials. DJ.

Buck broke into a grin. Ansley's missing twin had been here. His growth proved that he'd survived to live here at least until... He quickly did the math. His middle teens. That's when the dates on the marks stopped.

Frowning, he noticed that it wasn't just DJ's growth chart carved into this piece of old pine. He tried to make out the name. Keira? A younger child from the dates. He took several photos, anxious to call his bride-to-be. He hadn't found her twin, but at least he knew that DJ had survived to his teens in this place.

Buck did the math, comparing the last date on the chart to when Tommy had told him that Charley Diamond had lost the ranch. What had happened to these kids? DJ had been in his middle to late teens, but whoever Keira was, that child had been much younger. Where would they have gone? Social services?

He called Tommy, then he headed for Old Man Grandville's. He told himself that he'd call Ansley later with the news, hoping he would know more by then.

The Grandville home had been a mansion in its day. Built in the late 1800s during the city's opulent past on what was known as the richest hill on earth, it was the home of one of the city's high society. Three stories with gingerbread brickwork, ornate wood filigree and leaded glass windows, it had stood the test of time.

Buck parked on the steep street. No sign of security. He climbed out and walked through the wrought iron gate, up the sidewalk and onto the wide front porch. At the massive wood door, he rang the bell.

To his surprise, an elderly man in apparently fine health answered the door. He was dressed in slacks and sweater, loafers on his feet. He wasn't tall or handsome, but there was an air about him of arrogant dominance. He could see where the son, Titus, had gotten it from.

"Marcus Grandville," Buck said. "I'm Buck Crawford, a private investigator with—"

"I know who you are," the man said. "You're here about Darrow. Titus called and warned me you might be stopping by. I have a few minutes before I need to leave." He waved him into what had once been the parlor. Now it felt more like a den. "This shouldn't take long, but if you'd like to sit…"

He took one of the chairs facing the elderly Grandville.

"Darrow," Marcus said. "What about him?"

"He's your nephew?"

The older man gave a nod. "*Was* my nephew. Why are you asking about him after all these years?"

"He married a woman named Sheila about thirty years ago and they moved up this way. I'm trying to find Sheila."

"I have no idea where she is after all this time."

"But you met her."

"I suppose I must have."

Buck tried not to grit his teeth. "Did she have a child with her?"

Marcus frowned. He could tell that the man was about to say no when Marcus surprised him. "A boy with dark hair and pale blue eyes. One look at him and I knew he was no Grandville. Any fool could tell that. Any fool except my nephew."

"He thought the boy was his?"

"Darrow took after the other side of our family," Marcus said in answer.

"Sheila returned to Lonesome without the boy after they split," Buck said. "What did Darrow do with the boy?"

The man shrugged. "Had him with him the last time I saw my nephew. He was hanging around some ranch outside of town."

"The Diamond Deluxe?"

Marcus's eyes lit up for a moment. "Charley Diamond's place, that's right. Haven't thought about that place in years. Look, I have an appointment." He started to get to his feet, but Buck stopped him.

"I know the young man I'm looking for lived out at that ranch," he said. "I suspect your nephew left him out there. What I need to know is what happened to the boy after that."

The elderly man sighed. "Charley lost that place, you know." Buck nodded. "I think I might know who you're looking for. After Charley lost the ranch, he and a teenage boy were running cons around the state. You think DJ Diamond was the kid Darrow thought was his? Mind if I ask why you're interested in Diamond?"

"It's a long story, but he has family looking for him."

"Family?" Marcus huffed, looking skeptical, as he rose, interview over.

"One more question," Buck said as he rose as well. "Have you ever heard of someone named Keira?"

He saw the answer in the man's face an instant before Marcus caught himself. "I really have to go. Sorry I couldn't have been more help."

"On the contrary, you have been very helpful. I can show myself out."

"Titus," Marcus said the moment his oldest son answered the phone. "That PI from Lonesome was just here."

Titus swore. "Where were Rafe and Butch? They were supposed to make sure he didn't bother you."

"I sent them away," Marcus said with a curse. "I'm quite capable of taking care of myself and I was curious why he would be asking about Darrow and that woman, Sheila. Darrow's dead and who knows what happened to Sheila. Did the PI ask you about Keira?"

A worrisome silence, then, "No, why would he ask about her?"

"That's what I want to know. Didn't I hear that she owes us money?"

"I'd really like to know how you hear these things, Dad."

Marcus waved that off. "Why would the PI be asking about her?"

"I have no idea. Her husband, Luca, is the one who owes

the money, but we've been putting pressure on her. But we're going to get it settled by the end of the week. She got her buddy from the ranch to come help her out."

"What buddy from the ranch?" Marcus asked, afraid he already knew the answer.

"DJ Diamond."

Marcus swore. "That's who the PI was looking for. Why didn't you tell me that DJ Diamond was in town?"

"I had no idea you'd care. He paid me a visit, threatened to throw me out the window. But he'll pay off Keira's debt. Calls her his sister."

He didn't like this. As much as he loved his son, Titus often made poor decisions. Soon he would be in charge of their family fortune. The thought terrified him. "How much does Luca owe us?"

"Seventy-five. Diamond's a conman. Offered to settle for half the price. He's an arrogant fool like his uncle."

"DJ was Charley Diamond's protégé," Marcus said. "I wouldn't underestimate him if I were you. The last thing you want him to do is move in on our territory. Settle this and let me know when he leaves town."

"I can handle him. I have a plan."

"That's what worries me," Marcus said.

JAMES ANSWERED THE phone when Buck called the office. "I'm staying in Butte." Since going out to the Diamond Deluxe and talking to the Grandvilles, Buck was more convinced that DJ Diamond was the missing twin.

"Find something?" James asked.

"A few pieces of the puzzle seem to be coming together," he said. "It looks like the baby that Sheila and Darrow Grandville had was called DJ. That's assuming that Sheila did name the boy Del Junior or at least call him DJ." He told James about what he'd found out at the ranch inside the farmhouse owned by Charley Diamond, then about his visit to Titus Grandville.

"Titus Grandville." James said the name like a curse. "Anyone from this part of Montana has nothing good to say about that man."

"He pretended he'd never heard of Charley Diamond or the ranch," Buck said.

"These guys all know each other. Might not have traveled in the same circles but they're all connected."

"After Grandville lied to me, I went to see his old man."

"He's still alive?"

"Titus told me he wasn't well. Another lie from what I could tell. Marcus was more up-front, confirming what I'd already found out. Said he did remember the boy being with his nephew. Also said he remembered the Diamond Deluxe Ranch and DJ running cons with his uncle when he was a teen. I got the impression that Marcus doesn't know what Titus is up to, though, but I could be wrong. He definitely didn't want me talking to his father."

"Titus always was the worst of the bunch," James said. "And that was saying a lot."

"Marcus told me that after Charley Diamond lost the ranch, he and DJ traveled around Montana running cons." He didn't have to say that he was worried about the kind of man he was going to find.

"Buck, are you sure about this? Maybe finding him isn't the best idea."

"I can't stop now. I haven't told Ansley any of this. I'm thinking that I should wait until I find him."

"I think that's wise."

"I'm going to hang around and see what Titus is up to. I just have a feeling about him. I've rattled enough cages that I suspect he'll lead me to DJ if he knows where he is."

"Watch your back," James said. "You're in the Grandvilles' sandbox and we already know that they don't play nice."

SADIE TOLD HERSELF that she was ready. In the days since she'd arrived here, she hadn't seen DJ. She'd missed him. Knowing that this might be their last poker game together had her feeling melancholy. She'd known from the beginning that one day it would end. DJ would have paid off his uncle's debt. They would have no reason to see each other.

Her future felt hollow. She really hadn't realized how much she was going to miss that arrogant grin of his. Or the way she often found him looking at her. Every time, she saw that gleam in his eyes, it warmed her clear to her toes. She kept telling herself that she'd never fall for his charm. She didn't want to be one of his women. But now she could admit that the thought of never seeing him again made her ache with longing.

She was looking forward to tonight's game just to see him. Although she was nervous. She felt as if too much was riding on tonight. She'd taken an Uber part of the ride down the mountain and walked the rest of the way through the falling snow to get a feel for where she was. It appeared to be an even older part of the city, the area more industrial than residential or commercial. Even under a heavy blanket of the pristine new snow still falling, it looked as if this place hadn't seen better days in a very long time.

She didn't need to question why DJ might have agreed to this site. It was the kind of neighborhood where no one would hear a gunshot. But that was a double-edged sword when dealing with people you didn't know or trust.

As she stepped down the alley, she saw the door he'd described and the sign over it. It appeared to be the back entrance to a Chinese food restaurant—if still operational. She didn't see anyone else around, but knew she had the right place. DJ had been explicit in his directions.

The metal door was heavy as she pulled it open and looked down a long, dimly lit hallway. Time to get into character, she thought as she stepped in and let the door close loudly behind her. Swearing just loud enough to let the men know she was coming, she brushed snow from her coat and yelled, "Could you have found a darker place?"

The hall was long with several closed doors. She kept going, following the acrid scent of cheap cigars and the murmur of voices. At the end of the hall, she turned to the right toward another hallway. One of the doors was open a few yards farther. She could hear the men's voices more clearly along with the scrape of chair legs on a wood floor and the rattle of ice being dropped into a glass.

She stepped into the open doorway and, leaning against the jamb, she took in the men already starting to gather around the table.

"Why am I craving pot stickers?" she demanded, and laughed as they all turned toward her. As she entered the room, she removed her coat, sweeping in as if the place wasn't a dump. She'd worn designer jeans and a lightweight sweater that accentuated her curves but modestly. She wore a scarf loosely tied around her neck and diamond earrings that glittered every time she tucked a lock of her long blond hair back behind an ear. Her coat was a classic expensive wool. Nothing too flashy.

"Anyone save me a spot at the table?" she asked.

One of the men jumped up to pull out an empty chair for her. She wouldn't be sitting directly across from DJ, but she wouldn't be sitting next to him, either. "This should work," she said, and looked at each of the players as she sat down. "Good evening, gentlemen." She held her large leather bag in her lap.

"Buy-in is ten thousand dollars," said a florid-faced, heavyset man with the offending cigar in one hand and a drink in the other. He motioned to a makeshift bar set up over by a sad-looking couch. She saw a tray of mismatched glasses, a bucket of ice, several bottles of booze, a container with a dollar sign on the side, and a cooler on the floor with beer iced down. "Booze? Put your money in the kitty. I'm Bob. We're using cash, no chips. We're the Old West here. I'll need to see your money."

"I'm Whitney," she said as she met the man's gaze through the smoke, smiled and reached into her bag to pull out an envelope full of cash. She gave a tilt of her head. "Ten thousand. I'm betting you want to count it." She slid it over to him.

He thumbed through the hundreds, then passed it back with a lopsided grin.

Sadie took a thousand dollars from the envelope and laid it on the table in front of her. She wondered which players DJ had gotten into the game other than her and Bob. One of the men at this table was the real mark. Bob was the kind to have invited at least one of his buddies as well. The trick was figuring out who was who.

She'd never been more aware of DJ. Having him so close was like a separate pulse beating under her skin. She felt the heat of him and wanted more than anything to see that arrogant grin of his, to feel his eyes on her, to connect with the man who'd gambled his way into her thoughts and her heart.

Bob introduced everyone only by first name starting with the man to his right as he went around the table. Max, the large truck driver in the Kenworth jacket and T-shirt that read I Drop Big Loads. Her, then Lloyd in the canvas jacket and fishing shirt. Next to him was Keith, the youngest in a hoody, jeans and untied trainers. Then Frank, the oldest of the bunch with short gray hair and the air of an ex-military man or retired cop. He gave her a nod. She watched him line up his bills perfectly in front of him. And last but not least, DJ, sitting next to Bob.

Sadie tried to still the unease she felt as she looked around the table. It was an odd gathering. She noticed that only two of them were drinking, Bob and Lloyd, the fisherman. She had no idea who was the true mark. As she started to hook her purse over the back of the chair, it slipped and fell to the floor.

Lloyd started to reach down to pick it up.

"I have it," she said, and grabbed it before he could. He moved his chair over a little to make room.

"Sorry," he said, avoiding her gaze.

"Let's play some poker," Frank said impatiently. "I don't have all night."

"I agree with Frank. Let's play." Sadie bent down to retrieve her purse. As she did, she glanced under the table and saw Frank shift in his chair, his slacks riding up to expose the gun in his ankle holster—and froze.

Chapter Eight

Sadie tried to stay calm, but her heart was pounding as she straightened. She could feel DJ's gaze on her and wasn't surprised when he spoke.

"Excuse me," he said. "Does anyone else have a new deck of cards? No offense, Bob." He looked around the table, his gaze lingering on her for just a few seconds longer than the others.

She pulled her purse up on her lap, reached inside, but instead of pulling out a deck of the marked cards, she took out her lipstick and applied a fresh coat before putting it away. Out of the corner of her eye she saw Bob roll his eyes. Frank said something rude under his breath.

But it was DJ's reaction to her "abort" signal that she was most interested in. He stared at her for a moment before shaking his head ever so slightly. He wasn't going to walk away.

"We're going old-school tonight," Bob said, opening one of the packs of cards he'd brought. "Five-card stud, jacks or better to open, minimum bid ten bucks, no pot limit." Bob grinned. "That ain't too rich for your blood, is it, cowboy?" he said to DJ. He began shuffling with practiced expertise.

After a few more elaborate shuffles, he set down the deck and Trucker Max cut them.

Sadie could feel DJ's gaze on her and shook her head imperceptibly. She didn't have to look at him to feel his disapproval. She knew what was riding on this for him—and his sister. But she had also learned to follow her instincts. She'd felt uncomfortable the moment she'd walked into this room. After seeing that one of their opponents was armed—and possibly ex-military or a retired cop—there was no way she was going through with the original plan.

Unfortunately, DJ was ignoring her advice and now she had no idea what he was planning—except they wouldn't be using the marked deck of cards in her bag—and she hoped not the gun resting there, either.

So where did that leave them?

DJ HAD LIVED his life calculating the risk—and then playing the odds. But he'd never regretted it more than he did right now. He looked over at Sadie. He'd missed her. All the time he'd been putting things together, his thoughts had kept straying to her. He knew she was doing what he'd asked of her. That was Sadie. He could count on her. He just hoped she could count on him. She hadn't hesitated about coming to Montana to help him. He'd known she would fly up here to do whatever he needed done. He'd needed her, and of course she'd come.

What he couldn't understand was why. She didn't owe him anything. Half the time, he thought she didn't like him. It wasn't the first time he'd heard her call him an arrogant fool. He figured she'd be relieved now that they wouldn't be working together for her godfather. She was free.

He'd often wondered if there was a man in her life. He'd

been glad that she'd never mentioned one—let alone let him see her with anyone. DJ knew he'd never think any man was good enough for her. Not that she would ask his opinion.

Now he tried to read her face. The woman had the best poker face he'd ever seen. She gave nothing away. But he knew that she'd been worried. He'd seen her concern. She'd heard it in his voice. She'd known this was personal. They all knew that when it got personal, it got more dangerous. He wasn't just taking a chance with his own life; he was jeopardizing hers. He had no idea why she'd wanted to abort. He'd known her long enough that he knew she wouldn't have done that unless she'd seen something she thought he hadn't.

His gaze locked with hers, but only for a moment before she looked away. She thought he was making a mistake. He could tell that she was angry with him. It wouldn't be the first time. She'd called him an arrogant fool, an arrogant cowboy and probably worse. But tonight was the first time she'd refused to use the marked cards.

He trusted her instincts. She'd seen or felt something that had made her change her mind. She wanted him to walk away. Had she sensed that one of the players was a wild card? Or had she seen something that scared her? Not that it mattered. He couldn't quit now.

Sorry, Sadie, no can do. He wanted to tell her to trust him. But he feared her trust might be misplaced tonight. Charley had taught him the con, always warning him to step away from the table if he didn't think he could win. Poker was a game of skill, one DJ had perfected. But most everything else was a crapshoot. You read the situation as best you could, but ultimately, you had no control over what other people did—or didn't do. All you had were your gut instincts and years of learning to read people.

DJ hoped to hell that he knew what he was doing tonight. He'd gotten Sadie into this. He signaled for her to walk away after a few hands. Leave not feeling well. Make up a lie. Just leave.

But when he met her eyes, he saw not just anger but stubborn determination. Damn the woman, she would see this through. It was up to him now. Play out the hand he'd been dealt or throw in his cards and walk. He didn't have to look at Sadie. They both knew he wouldn't walk away.

SADIE CONCENTRATED ON the game and her opponents rather than DJ. She drew three cards on the first hand, picked up a couple of fours to go with the one she had, bet big and lost. The others noticed that she'd bet on a losing hand. She would play her part. But she would also be watching the table.

Frank had folded early in the betting, while Keith, slouching in his chair, was throwing good money after bad. Bob took the pot and passed the deal to trucker Max, and the game continued.

Sadie won and lost. So did DJ, although his pile of money kept growing. Keith, the kid, lost, got angry and stormed away from the table to crash on an old couch in the corner after Bob refused to spot him credit.

And then there were six of them and suddenly, the game turned serious. The pots got bigger, the smoke thicker, the smell of sweat stronger. Sadie felt the tension rise. She knew DJ felt it, too, but he looked calm, almost too calm.

Earlier, he had signaled for her to leave. *Cash out. Walk away.* She couldn't. She had tried to warn him. He hadn't listened. Her options were limited. Keep playing or quit and walk away from not only the game, but also DJ, and not look back. If she walked, that would be the end of them.

He would never trust her again—even with him being the one to tell her to leave. Their time together was ending as it was. She couldn't bear the thought that she'd let him down when he needed her most.

No, she thought, there was no way she was leaving him here alone. There was nothing more she could do but stay in the game and see this to the end. She thought about the gun in her purse and hoped she wouldn't have to use it. The load wasn't enough to do much harm to DJ if he had worn his vest under his shirt and jean jacket. But it would stop someone. Problem was that she didn't want to use it any more than she had the marked cards.

All she could hope was that her instincts were wrong, that Frank wasn't the wild card she feared he was, and that DJ's stubborn determination would carry them through as the cards moved around the table. Bob opened a new deck after a short break, and they continued.

Bob was losing and getting drunker. His dealing was sloppy. Sadie watched him. If she hadn't been able to smell the booze wafting off him, she might have been worried that it was all an act, and he was dealing off the bottom of the deck. He lost the next pot and handed off the cards to Max.

The trucker had been playing well. He and DJ had about the same amount of money in front of them. Lloyd the fisherman had played a conservative game, folding early, and yet staying in the game. The armed Frank was good at the game. Maybe too good. He gave nothing away, including his money.

Her turn was coming up again to deal. She'd lost just enough so that the others didn't take her seriously. As it got later, she found herself getting more nervous. The trucker began losing badly, hemorrhaging money. He wasn't smart enough to stop. She could see him getting more anxious.

Bob had begun to sweat as his pile of bills dwindled. He'd been making bad bets on even worse hands. He kept rubbing the back of his neck, shifting in his chair, getting up to make himself another drink he didn't need. He knew he was going down and this had been his show. The pressure was clearly getting to him.

"Come on, we don't have all night," Bob kept complaining. The trucker, too, was restless. Only Frank seemed unperturbed when the game slowed. All of it put her on alert.

DJ must have noticed that things were coming to a head. On the next hand, he raised the bet. The others either thought he was bluffing or just didn't want to fold in defeat, so they stayed in, no doubt convinced that they had the better hand.

They'd come to the end of the night, one way or another. Even Frank was in deep with this hand. Bob would be broke if he didn't win the pot, and Lloyd was down badly. The game was about over.

Sadie stayed in with three queens. "I'll call your bluff," she said, and met DJ's gaze with a look that said, "I hope you know what you're doing."

He grinned as she tossed her money onto the growing pile. He was going to have to show his hand.

BUCK HAD BEEN parked down the street from the Grandville building for hours and was beginning to wonder if he'd missed Titus, when the man came out the back door and headed for a large SUV parked across the alley. He seemed in a hurry as he slid behind the wheel.

From down the block, Buck was glad that his instincts had been right. Now he feared that he'd wasted his time.

Maybe Grandville would only go home for the night. But it didn't take long to realize that Titus wasn't headed home.

Instead, the man drove down the mountain to an older, more decrepit part of Butte. The streets became darker, the commercial buildings got more derelict looking before the banker pulled over, parked and after getting out, walked down the street to where he ducked into an alley.

Buck stopped down the block in front of an old gas station with a condemned sign out front. He checked his gun, put on his side holster and turned off his cell phone before tucking it into his coat pocket and getting out. It had been snowing off and on all day. Falling snow spun around him as he walked toward where he'd seen Grandville disappear. By the time he turned down the alley, huge lacy snowflakes were fluttering down, making it hard to see more than a few yards ahead.

His gut told him he was onto something even as his head said this might be a complete waste of his time. This night-time adventure might not lead him any closer to DJ Diamond because it might be nothing more than a booty call. Titus might have a woman he was secretly meeting. Not that this appeared to be a residential area.

At the top of the alley, he could see footprints in the snow. The new flakes hadn't covered them yet. They led to a back entrance of what appeared to be a Chinese food restaurant. The sign was faded. He wondered if the place was even still in business. He moved down the alley through the falling snow, his footfalls cushioned by the new snow.

At the door, Buck grabbed the handle and pulled, half expecting it to be locked. It wasn't. He stood to the side for a few moments listening before he peered in, then stepped through into the semidarkness, closing the door quietly behind him. He stood stone still for a moment to let his eyes adjust to the lack of light.

There appeared to be a solitary bulb at the far end of the hallway. He headed for it, following the murmur of voices.

SADIE HAD BEEN watching DJ closely. He hadn't cheated. But she could feel the tension in the room spark and sizzle. The pot was huge and DJ had already won a lot of money. Earlier he'd been playing with a stack of hundreds. A few minutes later, the stack had shrunk but not so noticeably that the others had seen him pocket the bills. He didn't want anyone to see how far ahead he was. He was playing smart, but she feared that wouldn't matter. Frank's being armed had her nerves frayed. Maybe he always came to games armed. Or not.

Sadie realized that she was holding her breath and told herself to breathe. She had to be ready if things went south. *When* things went south, she amended. The thing about carrying a gun was knowing when to pull it. The rule of thumb had always been: never pull a weapon unless you were going to use it—and quickly—before someone took it away and used it on you.

Her purse was hooked on the back of her chair, easily accessible—but not quickly. She had her gaze on DJ, but her true focus was on Frank, whom she was watching closely from the corner of her eye. If he reached down for the gun strapped on his ankle, she was going to have to pull hers. She would have only seconds to act.

For all she knew Frank wasn't a retired cop, but still an active-duty older cop. Even her godfather would have advised against shooting a cop—especially one with a loaded gun at a poker game. Ex-military or cop or just cop-looking older man with a gun, Frank was the wild card.

It had crossed her mind that Frank's true purpose here tonight might not be to play poker at all. She'd gotten the impression that DJ had enemies here in Butte. Her godfather had told her that teenage DJ had worked cons for years with his uncle until he went out on his own. She had no idea what kind of trouble DJ's sister was in, other than financially, or with whom. But if someone wanted to draw DJ out to even an old score, they now had him back in Montana on their home turf.

Sadie knew it was her fear making her think these things. But hadn't she, from the start, been worried that his concern for Keira had overridden his survival instincts?

She met his gaze across the table in those seconds as the last player threw his money into the pot and called to see DJ's hand. Her heart ached at the look in his eyes. He had known that this might be all about him. She held his incredibly blue eyes. *Tell me what you want me to do.* He gave a slight shake of his head. Nothing? He didn't want her to do *anything*? But it was what else she saw there that gutted her. *I'm sorry.*

No, she wanted to scream. DJ had to know her better than that. She wouldn't let Frank kill him in cold blood—not if she could prevent it. She could have heard a tear drop in the tense silence as DJ started to let his cards fall on the table.

Chapter Nine

Buck reached the end of the hallway and saw a short hall-way off to his right. One of the doors was partially open. The smell of cigar smoke wafted out. Quietly, he moved closer until he could look inside.

From what he could see through the haze of smoke, there was a poker game going on. He didn't see Titus, but he knew he was here somewhere. Even from the doorway, he could feel the tension in the room as thick as the cigar smoke.

There were five men and one woman at the table, another man on a couch in the corner. Past the woman he could see a pile of money in the middle of the table. High-stakes game, it appeared. He could smell the sweat and the booze. His anxiety rose. Where was Titus? Why had he driven down here tonight? The whole scene had Buck on edge. He'd seen gunplay break out over a game with a lot less at stake.

He heard the heavy man with the cigar say, "All right, DJ. Let's see what you've got." There was an edge to his voice.

Everyone seemed to be waiting on the cowboy who was about Buck's age. He had dark hair and even from here, Buck could see that he had pale blue eyes. DJ Diamond?

The room fell silent as if everyone in it was holding their

breath. DJ shoved back his cowboy hat and grinned as he let the cards drop faceup on the table.

EVEN BEFORE DJ'S cards hit the table, the room seemed to explode in a roar of voices and movement. Everyone was moving at once. Sadie had gotten only a glimpse of DJ's cards. He had a royal flush? No wonder everyone was yelling. She would have sworn that he hadn't cheated, but then again, DJ was a man of many talents.

She wanted to look at him, to see the truth in his eyes, but her gaze was on Frank. His chair scraped as he threw down his cards, one fluttering to the floor, and shoved back from the table.

Sadie reached into her purse, avoiding looking at DJ. If Frank came up with his gun, she'd be ready. Her hand dived into her purse, closing around the pistol's grip. She could feel movement all around her as players threw down their cards and rose, but her gaze stayed on Frank as he reached down. She gripped the gun tighter. She was about to bring it up when he straightened, coming up—not with a gun, but with the card he'd dropped.

As he threw the card on the table, his gaze locked with hers. But only for a second. Just long enough to tell her that she'd made a huge mistake. It wasn't Frank that she and DJ had to worry about.

DJ ALWAYS EXPECTED TROUBLE. So he wasn't surprised when cards went flying, chairs crashed to the floor, drinks spilled as all but a couple of players were on their feet and yelling.

The tension had been rising like the heat around the table. Too much money had changed hands and tempers were flaring. It was the name of these kinds of supposedly friendly card games.

But this one had gone south much quicker than he'd expected. Bob was on his feet and so was Max, the trucker, and Frank, the older man he figured Sadie had tagged as a retired cop. He'd figured both Bob and the trucker for poor sports if they lost too much. But it was the younger man in the fishing shirt who surprised him.

He watched in horror as Lloyd reached over and grabbed Sadie's wrist. She had her hand in her purse. Now he watched as Lloyd twisted her wrist, making her cry out and the gun drop from her fingers back into the large bag.

As he unarmed her, he rose to step behind her. Before DJ could move, Lloyd locked his arm around her neck, drew a gun and pulled her to her feet. DJ rose slowly, putting his hands into the air as the barrel of the gun was pointed at his chest. All he could think was that Sadie had tried to warn him and he'd ignored her. He thought he knew what he was doing. Arrogant fool.

"Everyone just stay where you are," Lloyd ordered as he motioned with the weapon in his hands. "This is between me and Diamond."

Max and Bob quickly stepped away from the table and the huge pile of money in the middle. "Easy," DJ said. "It's just a friendly game of poker."

"Like hell," Lloyd said as Keith left the couch with a bag in his hand. "Cash us out," Lloyd told him. Keith grinned as he began to scoop the money into the bag, taking not just the pot, but any money that had been in front of the players.

"What's the deal here?" Bob asked, sounding confused and scared. It seemed pretty clear to DJ what was happening. He'd been set up and was now being ripped off along with everyone else.

"I don't want any trouble," the trucker said, stepping even farther back. Bob and Frank had both frozen where they stood at the sight of the gun in Lloyd's hand. Bob looked jittery, as if he badly needed a drink. Frank on the other hand stood watching expressionless, seeming to be assessing the situation.

DJ expected someone in the room to do something stupid before this was over. But he figured Lloyd was expecting the same thing. The man still had Sadie in a headlock and his own gun pointed in the general direction of the three of them; Bob was to his right, Frank to his far left. The trucker had moved closer to the door.

Unfortunately, the table was between DJ and Lloyd, not to mention the gun or the man's arm cutting off Sadie's air.

"Got a message for you, Diamond, from Mr. Grandville," Lloyd said. "Pay up and get out of town. You're not welcome in Butte."

The tension in the room kicked up a few more notches. Frank swore and stepped farther back. "What the hell?" Bob said angrily. "DJ, you didn't tell me you were mixed up with the Grandvilles." He looked like he wanted to take a swing at him.

DJ felt the tension reaching a fevered pitch. Why didn't Lloyd and Keith just take the money and leave if that's what this was about? Because they'd come for more than the money. He had to get Sadie away from them. She wasn't part of this. Unless they knew differently. In that case, they were both as good as dead.

"Which Grandville in particular sent this message?" he asked, surprised how calm he sounded. "Titus or Marcus?"

"Does it matter?" Lloyd snapped.

"Actually, it does."

"They both want you gone, along with that PI from Lonesome who's looking for you," Lloyd said. "Seems you have family looking for you. You must owe them money, too."

DJ frowned. He had a PI from Lonesome looking for him? Something about family? That didn't sound right. Actually, none of this felt right. According to Keira, her husband, Luca, was staying just outside of Lonesome in the mountains at Charley's cabin.

He met Sadie's gaze, his full of apology. She was fighting to breathe but still looked angry and determined. He tried not to show how afraid he was for her. All his instincts told him that this wasn't going to end well, and he had only himself to blame. But he knew that he would die trying to save her.

SADIE WAS FILLED with a cold dread as she watched the scene unfold. Lloyd kept cutting off her air. She'd leaned into him, trying to relieve some of the pressure as she calculated what they could do to get out of this. It wasn't her nature to give up. There was always a way out of a mess, wasn't there?

She'd hoped that Lloyd and Keith would just take the money and leave. But she could see that it wasn't going to happen. This was personal.

DJ had realized it, too. She saw it in those blue eyes of his. She couldn't bear seeing his regret. He thought he was about to get them both killed. She wasn't ready to give up so easily. Also she knew that he'd risk his life to save her. She couldn't live with his blood on her hands.

For a moment she was overwhelmed with her feelings for the cowboy. He'd gotten her into this, and she should have been furious with him. But instead, all she felt was love, and that alone made her angry with herself, with him and with this jackass who had her in a headlock.

The Grandvilles had apparently set them up, that much was clear. Lloyd had known about her and DJ. He'd known she had a gun. He'd also known that they were here to make money to pay back Titus Grandville.

When he'd grabbed her, twisting the gun from her hand and dropping it back into her shoulder bag as he pulled her to her feet, she'd been taken off guard. She'd been so sure that Frank was the one they had to fear.

Now as she watched the others, feeling the pressure rising to the point where everything was going to blow, she knew she couldn't wait much longer to do something. These men weren't through with her and DJ. She didn't think they would kill everyone in the room. But they weren't going to let her and DJ walk away. She would have to act.

For a moment, she'd been distracted by Bob, who definitely looked as if he wanted to pick a fight with DJ. So she hadn't seen how Frank had maneuvered himself out of her line of vision—and Lloyd's—behind DJ. Keith had gone back to the old sofa and was busy counting the money.

She thought that no one had noticed Frank as he reached down and came up with the gun except her. If he fired, she feared Lloyd would shoot DJ. But before she could squeeze in her next breath, the door into the room was suddenly flung open.

"Everyone. Drop your weapons!" yelled a cowboy with a gun standing in the doorway. "Hands up! No one gets hurt!"

All she could think in that instant was *This is it. This is the game that will get me killed—and DJ, too.*

Chapter Ten

Sadie had no idea who the man was. But the distraction was enough that she saw what might be her only chance—and so did DJ. He launched himself across the table toward her and Lloyd as she drove her elbow into Lloyd's ribs and grabbed for his gun. But not quickly enough. As DJ crashed into them, the gun went off, the sound of the shot deafening in the confines of the room.

Had DJ been hit? Her heart dropped.

The force of his attack sent all three of them to the floor, Sadie still grappling for the gun. DJ climbed on top of Lloyd, pulling back his fist to hit the man in the face so hard it knocked his head back, banging it on the worn wood floor. For a moment, he appeared to pass out. She managed to get the gun away. As she pointed it at Lloyd's head, her hands trembling, she saw the blood. Just as she'd feared, DJ had been hit.

Lloyd blinked and tried to rise. "Don't tempt me," she said to Lloyd over the pandemonium that had broken out in the room.

"Everyone just settle down," the cowboy in the doorway yelled. "I'm Buck Crawford. I'm a private investigator looking for DJ Diamond. I'm here on behalf of his family. I'm not interested in whatever else is happening here."

A RESTLESS QUIET fell over the room. DJ pushed his forearm against Lloyd's throat as he took the gun from Sadie and pressed it into the man's side. He met Sadie's gaze. "Are you all right?"

She nodded, but he could tell that she was scared. He followed her widened gaze to his left arm, surprised to see that his shirt a few inches above his elbow was soaked with blood. His blood. He hadn't realized he'd been winged.

"We're going to get up," he said loud enough that the cowboy PI in the doorway could hear. He kept the gun against Lloyd's ribs as the three of them rose to their feet, Sadie next to him. She pulled off the scarf from around her neck and tied it around his wound as if she was nurse Nancy. DJ was both touched and amused. The woman never ceased to amaze him.

When he looked around the room, he saw that PI Crawford and Frank seemed to be in a standoff, both with weapons drawn and pointed at the other.

"I'm going to leave," Crawford was saying from the doorway. "But I need DJ Diamond to come with me. Then the rest of you can settle whatever this is all about."

"I want none of this," Max the trucker said, and headed for the door.

Keith, who'd been sitting on the sofa counting the money, looked to Lloyd as if asking what to do. DJ shook his head at the man and jabbed Lloyd hard in the ribs. The only way they were walking out of here was if neither Lloyd nor Keith put up a fight.

Crawford moved out of the doorway to let Max leave. Bob rushed out as well.

"I'm Diamond," DJ said to the PI, happy to have an escort out of here. "But I'm not coming without Sadie." He motioned to her. She quickly picked up her purse and coat to move toward the door. DJ just hoped they weren't jumping out of the frying pan into the fire by trusting the PI. But right now, it appeared he was their best bet.

Maneuvering Lloyd over to the sofa, he jabbed the man hard in the side with the barrel end of the gun and said, "Tell Keith to give me his gun."

"You won't kill me in front of witnesses," Lloyd challenged.

"Willing to bet your life on that?" DJ said. "You hurt my girlfriend. I'd just as soon shoot you as take my next breath." He dug the barrel into Lloyd's flesh, making him wince.

"Give him your gun."

Keith carefully took his weapon from between the sofa cushions where he'd apparently hid it when the PI had burst in armed.

"Now tell him to give me the money."

"You're a dead man, Diamond," Lloyd spat, but motioned for Keith to hand over the bag. The younger man did it with obvious reluctance. "You think you can get away with this? They'll be coming for you from every direction." Lloyd smiled. "Even those closest to you have already turned on you. Nothing can save you or your girlfriend."

DJ shoved Lloyd down on the couch. He held the gun on Keith and Lloyd as he reached into the bag of money, took a handful of bills and dropped them on the table before nodding to Frank. The older man slowly lowered his weapon as if to say, "Tonight never happened."

Then DJ backed over to Sadie and the PI. He took one last look at Lloyd and Keith. They weren't Grandville's real muscle. Just as Lloyd had said, Grandville would be sending the big guns after them before they got out of Butte. Meanwhile, these two thugs would be smart to get out of town before they had to face Grandville's wrath for what had gone down here tonight.

DJ grabbed the chair at the end of the table as the three of them walked out of the room. He closed the door, sticking the chair under the knob. It wouldn't keep the men from getting out, but it would slow them down.

Once outside in the alley, DJ breathed in the cold December night air. They'd dodged a bullet. Almost, he thought as he looked down at his arm and the blood-soaked scarf tied around it. With his uninjured arm, he pulled Sadie to him. She wrapped her arms around his waist, leaning into him, as they walked down the alley. He could feel her trembling. Or maybe it was him who was shaking inside. He was back in Butte and it was as if he'd never left.

"My truck is just up the street," the PI said. "I work for Colt Brothers Investigation out of Lonesome. We need to talk."

THROUGH THE FALLING SNOW, Buck saw that Titus Grandville's car was gone from where it had been parked earlier. He must have left when he thought his two men had everything under control. Or when the gunplay started. Buck hadn't heard him leave, but then again, he'd been busy.

He still couldn't believe they'd gotten out of that mess back there alive. Worse, he didn't know which side of the law Ansley's twin was on or what he'd just helped him do.

All he knew was that Titus Grandville was up to his neck in this—and so was DJ Diamond.

"I appreciate what you did back there," DJ said. "But right now, you don't want to be anywhere near the two of us. When those two back there report to their boss—"

"Titus Grandville." DJ shot him a surprised look. "I followed him to the game earlier. I'm pretty sure he already knows what went down tonight and that's why he's taken off. As far as being involved, I'm already more involved than you know. You owe me at least time to explain why I've been looking for you. My truck's down here. Let's get out of the snowstorm."

"You said you work for DJ's family?" Sadie asked once she climbed in the front of the crew cab and DJ got in the back out of the weather. Buck started the engine, letting it run as the heater warmed up the car. The temperature hovered around zero as the storm cocooned them below a thick blanket of fresh snow.

Buck turned in his seat so he could see both DJ and Sadie. He wondered about their relationship. "What I have to tell you might come as a shock. I'm not sure how much you know about your birth." He glanced at Sadie. "Or how much you want anyone else to know. I'm sorry, we haven't officially met." He held out his hand to her. "I'm—"

"Buck Crawford." She smiled. "I'm Sadie Montclair." She looked at DJ. "If he'd just as soon I not hear what it is you have to tell him—"

"No, she stays," DJ said as he looked from her to the PI. He'd kept so much of himself from the rest of the world, maybe especially Sadie because he hadn't wanted her to think the worst of him. But all that had changed tonight when he'd almost gotten her killed. He was still shaken at how close he'd come to losing her.

"Anything you have to say to me you can say in front of her," he said, his voice cracking as he shifted his gaze back to her and swallowed the lump that had risen in his throat. They had to make this quick. If the PI was right and Grandville already knew what had gone down here tonight, he would be sending more of his men for them.

"I'll give you the abbreviated version," the PI said, no doubt seeing how anxious he was. "About thirty years ago your mother was pregnant with twins, a girl and a boy. It was a rough delivery. She believed that you both had died. But you'd both been given away by a woman who thought she was doing the best thing for the two of you. I'm here on behalf of your twin sister, who is getting married at the end of this week. She didn't know about you until recently. Actually, she didn't know that the people who raised her weren't really her biological parents. Once she found out, she wouldn't stop until she found her birth mother. That's when she found out that she had a twin brother. I believe you are that missing twin."

DJ scoffed. Did he believe any of this? It sounded like a con. "That's quite a story."

"We won't know for sure until we get your DNA, but you look a lot like Ansley. The dark hair, the blue eyes… It's kind of incredible."

Incredible, DJ thought, feeling like he needed to ask what's the hitch. "So what's in it for you if I'm this missing twin?"

"I don't blame you for being suspicious. Other than finding my future bride's brother for her, I'm hoping you'll be at our wedding."

DJ felt his eyebrows shoot up as Crawford nodded.

"Ansley Brookshire is my fiancée."

"Brookshire?" That was a name he'd heard. It was right up there with Grandville—just not as old money. "Sorry if I'm having trouble believing this."

The PI pulled out his cell and flipped through the photos for a moment before handing the phone over to him. DJ stared down at the pretty woman with the dark hair and familiar blue eyes. His heart raced. Could this be true? "Other than I resemble her, what makes you think I'm the twin?"

"I've followed a trail from the birth mother to here," Crawford said. "I found your growth chart out at Charley Diamond's ranch. I'm pretty sure Darrow Grandville left you out there. It's a long story, but the sooner we get a DNA test the sooner we'll know for sure."

"If you're telling me that a Grandville was my father—"

"No," Buck said with a shake of his head. "If you're who I think you are, then your father is Del Ransom Colt, a former rodeo bull rider and the man who started Colt Investigations in Lonesome."

All DJ could think was that he couldn't trust this. Trust had always been an issue with him. Until he met Sadie. But hadn't he always wondered who he was, how he'd been left out at the ranch with Charley and if anyone had ever wanted him? He looked at Sadie as he handed her the phone with the picture of the young woman who could be his twin.

She glanced at the photo, her eyes widening in the same shock he'd felt. Maybe it *was* possible, but the timing couldn't have been worse.

A set of headlights bled through the falling snow that had accumulated on the windshield.

"All this is interesting, but we really need to get out of

here," DJ said. "Grandville's men are going to be looking for us." He waited until the vehicle coming toward them passed before he started to open his door. "I'm going to have to get back to you."

BUCK COULDN'T FIND Ansley's twin only to have him disappear again. "Look, I can see that you're in some kind of trouble," he said quickly. "Let me help you." He pulled out his business card with his cell phone number on it.

"Sorry, but you can't help," DJ said as he reluctantly took the business card and handed back Buck's phone. "A friend of mine is in danger. I have to get to her before they do."

"You might want to get some medical attention for that wound first," Buck said.

"I can see to it," Sadie said like a woman who'd done her share of patching up gunshot wounds. Buck had to wonder who this woman was and just how much trouble the two of them were in. But if Titus Grandville was involved, it was dangerous.

"I could help you more if you told me why Titus Grandville is after you—and your friend. If it's money, maybe I can—"

"It's more than money," DJ said. "But thanks for the offer. With me and Grandville it's apparently personal. My... friend's husband owes Titus money. He's pressuring her. I've got her hidden. After what went down tonight, I'm afraid of what they'll do to her if they find her, and I have no doubt that they are looking for her."

"DJ, if you go to her now, you'll lead them right to her," Buck said quickly. "I can keep all of you safe if you come back to Lonesome with me." He saw the answer and quickly added, "At least let me keep your friend safe until this is over. You can trust me."

DJ shook his head. He was clearly someone who'd been taking care of himself for so long that he was suspicious of help. But before he could decline the offer, the woman spoke.

"He's right. If you go to Keira now, you'll just be putting her in danger," she said, reaching back to take DJ's hand. "I trust him. He just saved us back there."

Keira. The name of the other child from the ranch. Buck could see that DJ was having a hard time trusting him. But there was something between these two, the woman he called Sadie and DJ himself. Apparently, DJ did trust her, because Buck saw him weaken.

DJ LOOKED AT SADIE, felt that lump form again in his throat as she nodded her encouragement. He'd almost gotten her killed tonight. He should have trusted her and aborted when she'd signaled for him to. But he hadn't. He'd been so sure he knew what he was doing. He'd trusted only a few people in his life. He realized that if there was one person he trusted with his life, it was Sadie. But did he dare risk Keira's life by trusting this PI?

He looked at Buck Crawford, reminding himself that Sadie was right—the man had just saved their lives back there. But it was Sadie's trust in the man that made him decide. "Her name's Keira Cross. She's in Whitehall at the Rice Motel. Tell her I sent you. She won't believe you, so you'll have to show her this."

He dug in his pocket and pulled out the tiny, tarnished gold bracelet with his initials on it. For a moment all he could do was rub his thumb over the *DJ* engraved in the gold. He'd had it from as far back as he could remember. It was why they'd called him DJ at the ranch.

He'd carried it for luck. He didn't even know who'd given it to him—just that it had been his talisman. He handed it to the PI. "Keira means a lot to me."

Crawford nodded as he took the bracelet and pocketed it. "I'll make sure she's safe." He handed his phone back to DJ. "Put your number in there. I'll call you when I have her." DJ took the phone again and keyed in his number, hoping he wasn't making a mistake. "The wedding is next Saturday."

DJ shook his head as he handed the phone back. "You aren't even sure I'm your future bride's missing twin."

"I'm not much of a gambler, but I'd put all my money on it. Next Saturday. It would mean everything to Ansley and me if you were there."

"Aren't you worried that I'm a wanted criminal who could be behind bars by then?" DJ asked, amazed by this PI.

"I'm a pretty good judge of character. Also, I know a good bail bondsman," Crawford told him. "I'll call you the minute I have Keira safe."

Chapter Eleven

"Can you ever forgive me?" DJ asked as he started the SUV's engine without looking at Sadie, and waited for the wipers to clear the windshield. He heard her buckle her seatbelt before she finally spoke.

"There's nothing to forgive," she said, her voice sounding hoarse.

His gaze swung to hers in disbelief. "I almost got you killed!"

"I'm fine." She wasn't. He could hear in her voice the scratchy sound of her bruised throat. It had to hurt since he could see the bruised area where Lloyd had held her too tightly. He gripped the wheel until his fingers turned white just thinking about Lloyd with his arm around her neck cutting off her air. "I should have listened to you and gotten out of there before—"

"I thought it was Frank. I saw his ankle holster and gun right after I sat down. He looked like former military or an ex-cop. I panicked."

DJ shook his head. "It doesn't matter. I was wrong. You went with your instincts, and they were right. I'm so sorry."

"You have nothing to be sorry for."

He shifted the SUV into Drive and started down the

street. "How can you even say that? If I had listened to you, we would have gotten out of there before Lloyd grabbed you."

"Would we have? I really doubt they were going to let us just walk out."

DJ didn't argue the point as he took a road out of Butte. It didn't matter which way he headed as long as it was out of town. "I thought I knew what I was doing. You were right. I was too personally involved. I believed that Grandville wanted his money bad enough that he'd let me win enough to pay him off. I underestimated him. I doubt now it was ever about the money."

Out of the corner of his eye, he saw Sadie nod. "Do the two of you have a history?"

"Back when we were kids," he said. "Just a couple of brief occurrences when our paths crossed. He was the rich kid. I was nobody. But I must have made an impression on him."

"You do have that ability," she agreed, and he saw her smile. "Do you think he might have used Keira to get you back in Montana?"

So like her to cut to the heart of it. For a moment, he couldn't answer. The thought hurt too bad. He refused to believe the kid he thought of as his little sister would betray him. "I'll ask her when I see her."

His words kind of hung in the air. Sadie didn't say anything. The only sound was the swish of the windshield wipers as he drove through the falling snow. He saw that he was headed for Helena. He knew he was waiting to hear from Crawford and simply driving to stay one step ahead of the men after them.

It didn't matter what town they reached as long as it had an airport, where he planned to put Sadie on a plane home.

It had been a mistake calling her and getting her up here. He'd selfishly wanted her with him, he could admit now. He hadn't really needed her. He'd been right about one thing, though…it had been their last game. He'd almost gotten her killed for nothing.

"You know that I have to finish this."

Sadie said nothing for a few moments. "What exactly is this?"

"I thought I was just coming back here to pay off Grandville and free Keira from the debt and her no-account husband. Now I'm not sure what this is. All I know is I never should have gotten you involved."

THE DRIVE TO Whitehall took longer than Buck had expected because of the storm. He didn't think he'd been followed, but he'd still taken precautions just in case. The one thing he couldn't let happen was leading Grandville's thugs straight to Keira Cross's motel room. He'd gotten DJ Diamond to trust him. Now Buck just had to prove that his trust had been warranted. It was the only way he was going to get the missing twin to his and Ansley's wedding.

He tried not to worry about DJ and Sadie or speculate on just how much trouble the two were in with the Grandvilles. DJ was the missing twin. Didn't the bracelet prove it? But how to keep him alive was the problem. There was nothing he could do about that—at least not at the moment. Once he had Keira and knew she was safe…

The snow was falling harder as he pulled up in front of the Rice Motel in Whitehall. It was still dark, the hour late. The crack of dawn wasn't that far away. For a moment he just sat in his pickup watching the snow, watching the parking lot, hoping she was inside number nine and that he would soon be calling DJ with the good news.

Still, he couldn't help being a little leery. This felt almost too easy. That and the one man's words back in Butte about DJ not being able to trust those closest to him. He didn't see anyone else in the parking lot and there were only a couple of cars in front of two of the other motel rooms. On the surface, everything looked fine.

Still, as he got out of the pickup, he felt the hair spike on the back of his neck. He moved quickly to the motel unit door and knocked. No answer. He knocked again, then he tried the knob, his anxiety growing. The knob turned in his hand and with just a little push, the door swung open.

"Keira?" he called again. "Keira?" It was pitch-black inside the room, but as his eyes began to focus, he could see that there was someone in the bed. She was either a sound sleeper or... He raised his voice. "Keira?" He took a step in, his heart in his throat for fear that Grandville's men had already gotten to her.

Buck heard movement off to his right side. He turned, but not quickly enough. He caught a glimpse of Titus Grandville an instant before he was struck with something hard and cold. He staggered and went down hard.

AFTER DRIVING NORTH toward Helena and the airport there, DJ tried Keira's cell. He couldn't risk the Butte airport. He'd already decided that he would get the PI to bring Keira to him. Somehow, he'd talk her into going to Florida with him. The Grandvilles might run Butte, their tentacles stretching even into the states around them, but they wouldn't come after them in Florida. If she wouldn't go, he'd know that she still loved Luca and had no intention of leaving him.

The call went straight to voicemail—just as it had earlier. Had trusting the PI been a mistake? Or had the Grandvilles been waiting for Crawford? If so, then they already had Keira. He tried Crawford. The call went to voicemail. Disconnecting, he felt worry bore deep into him. He told himself that he should have heard something by now.

"She could have stepped out to get something to eat," Sadie said, no doubt seeing his concern. She didn't sound any more convinced than he was.

He'd left a message for her to call, but his instincts told him she wasn't going to because she either couldn't or wouldn't. He'd been set up tonight at the poker game. Grandville had been two steps ahead of him the whole time. Keith and Lloyd had been low-rung thugs. Now Grandville would send his A-team after them, the men Keira had told him about, Butch Lamar and Rafe Westfall. Paying Grandville off was no longer an option. Maybe it never had been.

He'd had a bad feeling from the moment things had gone south at the poker game. Something was at play here, something that had him off-balance. He kept thinking about what Lloyd had hinted at, something about those closest to him turning on him. There was only one meaning he could get from that.

Keira.

If he couldn't trust her, Luca Cross was to blame, he told himself. Hadn't he worried that Keira was still in love with him, that she would go back to him, that he would get in trouble again? He told himself he shouldn't have ever let her marry the man, like he could have stopped her.

But even as he thought it, he knew he couldn't blame Luca. Keira had taken to life on the ranch even as a young girl, fascinated with the criminals who came and went. He'd caught her learning sleight of hand tricks by one of the cons when she was five. She'd been good at it. He'd seen the pride in her eyes.

"It's in her genes," Charley had always said with a laugh. "She was born to this life. As much as we don't want to be anything like our biological parents, we are part of that gene stew. Just need to make the best of the hand you've drawn. Remember that, DJ. Accept who you are."

He thought he had, even though he hadn't known his gene pool. But he had wanted to believe it didn't have to be Keira's future. He'd done his best to protect her, but he'd only been a boy himself back on the ranch. After that, he hadn't seen her much because he'd been trying to stay alive and not starve.

Thinking about his own biological stew, he wondered about this twin sister, if he really was her twin. Ansley Brookshire. She'd certainly landed in the lap of luxury, he thought uncharitably. By now she knew that if DJ was her twin, they weren't in the same league—not by a long shot. Maybe she would change her mind about meeting him— let alone having him stand up with her at her wedding. He wouldn't blame her if she did.

As Charley used to say, "It's all in the cards and how you play them." Isn't that what worried him? DJ thought. Was Keira in the game?

He refused to believe it. He called again and this time left a message. "Where are you?"

BUCK OPENED HIS eyes to darkness. For a moment, he didn't remember anything—especially where he was. On the floor in a motel room. It took him a moment to adjust to the light coming through the partially cracked blinds. As his memory returned, he rolled over so he could see the bed. Empty. He pushed himself up into a sitting position, his head a little clearer.

He was surprised to realize that his gun was still in his holster. How long had he been out? He checked for his phone. Still in his coat pocket. He hadn't been out that long even though it was now daylight outside—and still snowing, and Keira was gone. He couldn't be sure she'd even been the body he'd seen covered in the bed.

The only thing he knew for sure was that he had a bump on the side of his head the size of a walnut. Nor was there any doubt that Titus Grandville was behind this. He hoped he'd get the chance to return the favor.

As he felt steadier, he got to his feet. Turning on a light, he checked out the motel room. No sign of a struggle. No blood. He checked the bed. It had been slept in, but also no blood. Keira had either been taken—or had walked out on her own.

But whoever had hit him had been expecting company. Had they thought it would be DJ? They must have been disappointed.

He peeked out at the parking lot. His truck was still right outside, but the rest of the parking lot was now empty. The two vehicles he'd seen earlier were gone. Either they had been early-rising guests, or they'd been Grandville's men.

As he started to turn out the light and leave, he felt something in his other coat pocket. He carefully pulled it out. The unsealed envelope had *To DJ* written on the outside.

Buck frowned as he opened the flap and quickly read the contents. Pulling out his phone, he called DJ.

DJ HAD DRIVEN as far as Helena last night. They'd parked in a Walmart lot, sleeping in the back of the SUV. This morning, he and Sadie had eaten breakfast at a local truck stop. Now, not even a mile from the airport, he knew he had to make a decision. He hadn't heard from either Keira or the PI. Both could be dead, although he doubted Grandville would kill Keira—not until he got whatever it was he wanted out of DJ.

Crawford was another story. He'd trusted the man, still did because Sadie did. He just hoped he hadn't gotten the man killed. He was mentally kicking himself for involving other people in this when his phone rang.

With a wave of both concern and relief, he saw it was PI Buck Crawford. He picked up. "Was my sister there?" he asked.

"No."

He listened as the PI told him what had happened when he'd reached the motel room. The news didn't come as a surprise. He'd already figured that Grandville's men had found her. "Are you all right?"

"I'll live," Crawford said. "But apparently she left you a note."

He listened as Crawford read: *"'I saw them looking for me in town. I barely got away. I have no choice. I'm going to meet Luca up at Charley Diamond's cabin in the mountains north of Lonesome.*

Thank you for trying to help me, but I know things didn't go well up in Butte or you would have been back by now. Luca and I are going to head for Alaska. It's only a matter of time before Grandville comes looking for us if we stay here.'"

Keira, no, DJ thought. She was making a huge mistake.

He had to stop her, or she'd be running the rest of her life. "Any chance she left directions to the cabin?"

Silence, then Crawford said, "She did." What he didn't say, but DJ heard, were the words "almost as if she was hoping you'd go to the cabin to try to stop her." The PI continued reading. *"'I'd love to see you before we leave. In case you forgot where Charley's cabin is, here's the directions. If we miss each other, thank you again for everything.'"*

"DJ, you have to wonder why she'd leave you the directions to the cabin," Crawford said. "Are you sure you can trust her?"

He felt anger boil up inside him. "She's been like a little sister to me from the time she was just a toddler," he snapped. "Just give me the directions."

Again there was that slight hesitation before the PI read the directions.

"Thanks. Send me a bill," DJ said, hating that Crawford was thinking the same thing he was. If he went to Charley's old cabin outside of Lonesome, he could be walking into a trap—a trap set by someone he loved and thought he could trust with his life.

"You already know it isn't money I want," Crawford said. "Saturday at the only white church in Lonesome. Four o'clock."

He disconnected. He could feel Sadie's gaze on him and see the recrimination in her expression. The PI had done him a favor, gotten his head bashed in, and this was the way DJ repaid it. Of course she'd heard the entire conversation in the confines of the SUV. He could see that she agreed with the PI. Going up to the cabin was a mistake, maybe the last one he'd ever make.

But when she spoke, it was only to say, "So we're going up into the mountains to your uncle's cabin to meet her."

"Not *we*. Just me. I should never have gotten you involved in this. I'm putting you on the next plane to Florida."

"You know that isn't going to happen. I'm going with you because clearly you're determined to see her. You don't believe that she would turn on you and you could be right."

He held her gaze, but words stuck in his throat. He probably wasn't right; that's what hurt. Keira had betrayed him. He knew it and yet he refused to believe it until he heard it from her. And by then, it would be too late.

"I have to know," DJ said, fearing that the bond he and Keira had was never as strong as he'd thought. It was something he didn't want to think about right now. "I also have to try to save her if I can. Grandville will never let her go now."

SADIE FELT HER heart break for him. He and Keira weren't really brother and sister, but it didn't matter to DJ if they were blood or not. Some bonds were even stronger.

She could understand his loyalty and love for this girl he'd taken under his wing from an early age. Two children thrown together under strange if not terrifying circumstances. She thought of her own childhood. She'd been alone in an adult world that she knew wasn't normal. Her parents dead after their small private plane had crashed. If it hadn't been for her godfather, who knows what would have happened to her.

Ezra Montclair had taken her in, raised her, taught her the business as if she were the heir to his kingdom. She'd been all alone in that adult world. She would have loved to have another child to be there with her, let alone to watch her back. She'd learned to navigate through the many men who came to see her godfather. She'd learned to be invisible, to listen and learn, to not be a child.

"I envy the relationship you had with her," Sadie said at last. "I would have loved a big brother watching over me like you have Keira."

He said nothing, looking sick for fear he was wrong about her. Worse, that Keira had lied about the debt owed to the Grandvilles knowing he would come back to Montana to help her. If she'd deceived him, she had to know what Titus Grandville would do to DJ. She couldn't be that naive.

"I needed her as much as she needed me," he said. "She gave me a purpose."

Like paying off Uncle Charley's debt, she thought. Now that debt was paid. Keira in need had become his new purpose. But what after that? she wondered, realizing how driven DJ had been. First it had been just the fight to survive in the world he'd found himself in. Later, it was repaying even a dead Charley for giving him a home, an occupation, a way to survive once he was on his own.

She realized that she and DJ weren't all that different. Both Charley and her godfather had taught them well. They were survivors.

Chapter Twelve

DJ made his decision. "I need you to go back to Florida."
She started to speak, but he stopped her. "Sadie, I'm begging you. I'll take you to the airport so you can catch a flight
home. It has to be this way. *Please*."

She shook her head, raising a hand and cutting him off.
"I'm not letting you do this alone. You're wounded and you
need me. We're partners, remember?"

He shook his head. "That's over. Your godfather and I are
square. You and I are square, aren't we?" He held her gaze
and saw something so soft and vulnerable that he had to
look away. They were so much more than that, he thought
as his heart lifted, then fell. Hadn't he wanted desperately
to be with this woman—and not just as business partners.
Now that they had a chance to be together… "You know I
might be walking into a trap that could get me killed."

"Get us killed," she corrected. "But we stand a better
chance together, always have. We check out the cabin. If it
looks like a setup…" She drew his gaze back to her. "We
walk away. Together. One last game. If we realize we can't
win it, we throw in our cards and fold. There is no shame
in walking away when the odds are against you."

He knew what she was saying. It didn't have to end this

way. He had a choice. They had a choice. If he forced her on the plane… His heart ached at the thought that it would be over for them even if Keira hadn't betrayed him, even if he lived to tell about it. He couldn't imagine *never* seeing Sadie again. She would be walking away with a huge chunk of his heart he hadn't even realized he'd given her. But it would kill him if he got her hurt any more than he already had.

"I need to re-bandage that wound," she said as if the discussion was over. For her it was. "If you don't take me with you, I'll rent my own SUV," she said as if reading his mind. "I heard the directions to the cabin. I'm not leaving you, DJ. Not when you need me more than you ever have before. So don't even think about driving off and leaving me the first time I'm out of your sight."

He'd just been planning that exact thing. The thought made him sick inside that he would stoop to tricking her, since he'd always tried to be honest with her. She would go up to the cabin on her own. That kind of loyalty made the thought of Keira betraying him all the more painful. He saw her look around the SUV.

"Do you know what happened to the scarf I had tied on your wound?" she asked.

"I'm sorry. I must have lost it."

"It's not important." She met his gaze. "Keeping you alive is, though."

He couldn't take his eyes off her. The woman had always amazed him, but never as much as she did right now. Yet he couldn't help thinking that she'd picked the wrong horse to put her money on. "You seem to have some fool idea that you can save me from myself. What if you can't, Sadie? What if I've been a lost cause all along?"

She shook her head. "You have a twin sister who'll be standing at the altar soon waiting for her twin brother. You're going to show up and not let her down or die trying. She needs you and you just might need her and the family she's offering you. Now let me see your arm."

BUCK CALLED JAMES back at Colt Brothers Investigation the minute he got off the phone with DJ. He quickly told him everything that had happened.

"The man you believe to be Ansley's twin is headed up in the mountains to confront a woman he grew up with and is probably walking into a trap?" James asked. "What is wrong with him?"

"Apparently, DJ and this young woman, Keira, were raised together there on the ranch. He considers her his sister. He doesn't believe she would betray him."

"You told him he might have a twin sister, a real sister by blood?"

"I think he's worried it's a scam," Buck said. "You have to understand, he isn't very trusting and given the way he grew up, I get it. I'm on my way back to Lonesome. I have a scarf I found in my pickup with his blood on it. I'm hoping Willie can get us a DNA sample from it to confirm that DJ Diamond is Ansley's lost brother. He looks way too much like her not to be. Stubborn to a fault like her, too. Also I followed a trail from Lonesome and the woman who sold the babies to DJ Diamond. It's too much of a coincidence for him not to be the missing twin. The real kicker, though, is that he had the gold bracelet his birth mother had made for him with the initials DJ on it. I get the feeling it's his talisman, his good-luck charm. He's the real deal."

"Where are you headed now?" James asked as if he already suspected Buck's next move.

"As soon as I get back to Lonesome, I'm going to hook up to my snowmobile trailer and head up into the mountains. Keira Diamond Cross left directions to the cabin where she said she'd be waiting. DJ will be coming from the west side of the mountains. I plan to beat him to the cabin. I can't let him walk into a trap."

"Even without the blizzard, the freezing temps and killers possibly waiting at this cabin?"

"I can't let Ansley down." It was more than that. He liked DJ Diamond. He didn't want to see anything happen to him or to the woman with him.

"Getting yourself killed would be much worse than not having her brother at her wedding," James said. "There would be no wedding without you. That's why I'm going with you."

"Me, too," Tommy said, making Buck realize that he'd been on speaker.

"You have a pregnant wife," both Buck and James said at the same time.

"She's not due for a month," Tommy protested. "Stop by my place with the trailer. We'll throw on a couple more snowmobiles. Safety in numbers, you know."

Buck chuckled. "I'm on my way. But one more thing. DJ has a woman with him, Sadie Montclair. See what you can find out about her."

SADIE CHECKED DJ'S WOUND, cleaned and bandaged his upper arm against his protests that it was just a flesh wound. It had been a clean shot, tearing through skin and flesh and fortunately missing the bone. It had to be painful, but he didn't show it. So like DJ, she thought. The man was the strongest, most determined man she'd ever known. He was also the kindest and surprisingly, the gentlest. His heart was so big, which she knew was why he was in so much emotional pain over Keira. The one thing he wasn't was a lost cause, no matter what he thought. She hoped she could prove that to him before it was too late.

The weather report they heard on the radio was dire. It was still blizzarding across the state. Residents were advised not to travel except in cases of an emergency. Sadie listened to the steady clack of the windshield wipers. They were doing their best but seeming to struggle to keep up. Because of the falling snow and the wind whipping it, visibility was only a matter of yards.

DJ seemed oblivious to the blizzard and the snow-covered road. She watched him drive, his strong hands on the wheel, his expression calm, maybe too calm, his amazing blue eyes intent on what road he could see ahead.

"Florida didn't seem to diminish your winter driving skills," she said, hating that the whirling snow outside the cab was making her nervous. She was born and raised in Florida. She hadn't even seen snow until she was in her teens. She'd never been in a storm like this one. How could something so beautiful be so treacherous?

"Driving in the snow is like falling off a bike," he said.

"I believe the expression is like riding a bike," she corrected, playing along.

He grinned over at her for a second. "We'll be fine. You trust me, don't you?"

She knew he meant more than with his driving in this storm. "I trust you with my life."

He shook his head almost ruefully. "That's what worries me."

A Christmas song came on the radio. He reached over and turned it off.

"What do you have against Christmas?" she asked, feeling a need to fill the silence, but also wanting to know more about this man. All the hours she'd spent with him and yet she knew little of his early life at Charley Diamond's ranch.

"Nothing against Christmas. Just never was something we celebrated at the ranch. Charley said it was a scam." DJ laughed. "He said a lot of things were a scam. He should know."

She laughed. "See, we have even more in common. My godfather didn't celebrate holidays either. Said they were businessmen's trick to play on people's emotions so they felt guilty if they didn't spend more money than they had. I never cared about the present part of Christmas."

For a moment, she watched snow flying around them in a dizzying blur. "But I did love the lights and the decorations. I always felt that there was something special about the season beyond all the commercialism. We were far from a religious family, but there was something spiritual that I felt at Christmas." She fell silent before adding with a laugh, "I always wanted a real Christmas tree. Did you have a Christmas tree at the ranch?"

"No."

Sadie felt him turn toward her for a second before going back to his driving.

After a few minutes, she realized she wasn't getting any more out of him. They drove through the whiteout with only the clack of the wipers and the hum of the heater. She kept losing sight of the road ahead. She felt as if they were driving into a wall of white with no idea of what was on the other side. The snow had a claustrophobic quality, no longer as beautiful as she'd first thought. It now felt dangerous.

The weather report on the radio continued to get worse. Many of the highways were closed due to a lack of visibility. The snow kept getting deeper on the highway. She realized that she couldn't remember the last time she'd seen a car go by, let alone a snowplow.

Through a break in the whirling snow, she saw a sign. DJ slowed and turned onto a narrower road. This one led up higher into the mountains. The snow quickly got deeper. The SUV broke through the drifts that the wind had sculpted, sending a shower of white flakes up over the windshield.

Sadie was relieved that DJ seemed to know how to maneuver in the deep snow filling the narrow road. That wasn't what had her worried, though. It was why he was driving in a blizzard when roads were closing, drivers were told to stay home, plows couldn't keep up. This part of the state was closing down and yet DJ kept going as if racing toward his destiny.

She'd seen determination in him many times before, but not like this. She could only hope that Keira had been telling the truth. She and her husband might already be on their way to Alaska. What would DJ do if he missed them? Would that be enough proof that Keira hadn't betrayed him?

The road wound up the mountain. The wind was reduced with the thick pines on each side of the road so the snow wasn't as drifted. They kept climbing. Sadie remembered being in awe of the winter wonderland DJ had brought her to. Now it had a lethal quality that unnerved her. It was bad enough that they were probably driving into a trap—

and that's if they survived the blizzard and the drive up this mountain.

You trust me, don't you? DJ had asked.

I trust you with my life.

"It should be right up here," DJ said as they topped a small hill and he turned up an even more narrow road. He started up it. They hadn't gone far when she heard a spinning sound as the tires fought to find traction—and failed.

The SUV came to a stop. DJ tried to get it going again, but the whine of the tires told her that they weren't going any farther. DJ backed up and made a run at the hill. The same thing happened: tires spun, no traction. Only this time, the pickup slid off the road, and the driver's side dropped into what appeared to be a narrow ditch—not that she could tell with the snow so deep.

"Stay here." He jumped out, leaving the engine running, the heater cranked. He was out of the SUV, cold rushing in as he exited, then he disappeared into the storm. Sadie hugged herself and waited, not sure where he had gone. To see how stuck they were? But when he didn't return, she began to worry. What if something happened and he didn't come back? The thought raced past, kicking up her pulse and making her stomach churn. She was completely out of her element. How long could she survive out here? She quickly shoved the thought away. DJ would come back. If he could.

She checked to see how much gas they had. Less than half a tank. She reached over and turned the key. The engine stopped and so did the heater. An eerie, deafening quiet filled the vehicle. She felt the cold surround the SUV and begin making its way in. Moments ago, it had been almost too warm. She shivered, realizing she wouldn't survive long if DJ didn't make it back.

The air inside the truck was getting colder by the second. How long had she been sitting here? How long had DJ been gone?

She tried to see outside. The wind would occasionally part the falling snow enough that she could see pine trees. Had they reached the cabin where he was to meet Keira? Surely he wouldn't have gone in to face Keira alone knowing he could be walking into a trap! She should have jumped out and gone with him, but he hadn't given her a chance.

But even as she thought it, she knew that was exactly what he would do to protect her. She buttoned up her coat and reached for her scarf before she remembered that she'd used it to put over DJ's wound and he'd lost it somewhere. She must not have tied it tight enough.

She dressed as warmly as she could manage; still, she hesitated. Should she go after him? She wasn't even sure which way he'd gone or if this was the road to the cabin. Leaving the pickup seemed like a bad idea since the alternative was to go out into the snow and cold. Snow had accumulated on the windshield. Soon she wouldn't be able to see out.

She reached for the door handle and stopped. Through a break in the falling snow, she caught movement. She held her breath, unsure what was up here in these woods. Animal? Or human?

Her heart bumped hard against her ribs as DJ appeared out of the storm. Relief made her weak for a moment as he opened the door and climbed in.

For a startled moment, she didn't recognize him with his

hair and coat covered with snow. Flakes clung to his long dark lashes. "Are we— Is this—"

He must have seen her relief and her fear. "Sorry, I didn't mean to leave you alone for so long. Charley's cabin is on up the road about halfway up the mountain."

"Keira?"

He shook his head. "But someone's been here. There is food and firewood. I found a branding iron with the Diamond Deluxe, a diamond shape with a D inside. I hurried up and built a fire so it would be warmer for you once we climb up the mountainside. It's a pretty good hike up."

"No problem," she said without hesitation. Anywhere was better after sitting here thinking the worst might have happened.

"We'll be warm and dry. I saw older tracks in the snow. I might have already missed her. Otherwise..."

Otherwise, she could be coming once the storm passed, he didn't say, but she knew what he meant. He pulled the SUV key and met her gaze. "Don't worry. I've got everything covered."

She'd heard these words before, so they didn't give her much assurance. The thing about DJ Diamond, though, was when things went south, he always came up with a backup plan. Whether he'd thought of it before things went bad or not was debatable. But he'd always managed to save them. She just hoped he hadn't met his match this time as she climbed out into the Montana blizzard.

BUCK HEARD THE relief in Ainsley's voice the moment she answered the phone. "Are you all right? I've been so worried about you."

"I'm fine. I'm sorry I haven't called sooner." There was

no way he was getting into everything that had happened since he'd last seen her. Eventually, Ansley would know most of it.

"Did you find him?" Her voice cracked. He could hear the hope and felt his heart break for her. He'd wanted so badly to have good news for her.

"I think I've found him, but we won't know for sure until we get the DNA results."

"That's wonderful news," she cried. She sounded so relieved. She really did have her heart set on him giving her away at the wedding. He wished he could have talked her into putting off the ceremony until spring, but she'd wanted a Christmas wedding and he would give her anything.

He told her what he'd learned and about going out to the Diamond Deluxe Ranch and what he'd found out there.

"His name is DJ Diamond?" she said. "It has to be him if he had the gold bracelet our mother had made for him. And he grew up on a ranch, that's great."

He didn't know how to tell her. It was one reason he hadn't called until now. He'd put it off, telling himself he wanted to be sure that DJ Diamond was indeed her twin. But the truth was he didn't know how to tell her about the life her twin might have lived.

"It wasn't that kind of ranch," he told her now. They were about to start their lives together. He didn't want there to be any lies between them. She needed to know the truth, as hard as it was going to be to tell her—let alone for her to hear. He told her about everything that he'd learned. For a moment there was only silence on the line. "Ainsley, are you there?"

"You're saying he's a criminal?"

"No. Maybe. I'm not sure. He was raised by an uncle who

was a conman who apparently taught him everything he knows. From what I can tell he makes his living gambling."

"What aren't you telling me, Buck?"

He sighed. "Right now DJ's on the run after a poker game went badly. He has a friend who's in trouble and he's determined to save her. James, Tommy and I are going after him, but we aren't the only ones anxious to catch up to him and this friend of his he grew up with. There are some powerful men also after him. I don't want to upset you, but I think we should postpone the wedding."

Chapter Thirteen

On the climb up the mountainside to the cabin, DJ mentally kicked himself. Sadie should be winging her way to the sunny shores of Florida right now—not trudging through thigh-high snow with him. He should have been more insistent. As if that would have changed her mind. He imagined himself physically putting her on a plane home. That was just as ridiculous as thinking he could make her do anything she didn't want to do.

But bringing her up here… A gust of wind whirled fresh snow around him. He caught a glimpse of the cabin above them almost hidden in the tall pines.

"A little longer and we'll be there," he said to her as he stopped to let them both catch their breath. They were used to Florida and sea level. He looked at her, trying to gauge how she was doing—and not just from the climb. He'd gotten her into this, something he deeply regretted. It was bad enough that he'd been possibly tricked into coming back here—let alone that he'd dragged Sadie into it. He couldn't bear the thought that Keira had purposely drawn him back to Montana on a lie so that Grandville could get retribution for some old grudge.

Pushing the nagging thought away, he said, "You doing okay?"

"I'm good," she said, and flashed him a smile. It wasn't one of her brilliant, knock-a-man-for-a-loop smiles. This one was part worry, part sympathy. He wanted to tell her that he'd be fine no matter what he found out, but he couldn't lie to her because she would see right through it. If Keira had turned on him... He hated to think of the pain it would cause. That's if she didn't get him killed.

"It's not far now," he said.

"Lead the way, partner."

A few minutes later, they waded through the drifted snow up onto the porch. As he opened the front door of the cabin, he gave a slight bow and waved her inside. He had no idea how long they would be here. At least until the storm passed. Where was Keira? Had she gotten caught in the storm? And what about the Grandvilles? Were they on their way as well?

Keira had chosen the perfect isolated place in the mountains for her husband to hide out. It was also a perfect place to get rid of someone. Bodies often didn't turn up for years in these woods. He tried not to think about what might happen if Keira showed up. If she was telling the truth, she and Luca might already be headed for Alaska. He realized he might never see her again if that was the case.

Or she and Luca might be planning a visit to the cabin— just waiting for him to arrive. Keira knew him. She would know that he would come to the cabin. Wasn't that why she'd left the note?

His head hurt thinking about it. He could no more see the future than flap his arms and fly. Yet his gut told him he couldn't trust her. Maybe he never could.

He looked over at Sadie, fighting the feeling that they were sitting ducks and hunting season was about to open.

SADIE STEPPED INTO the cabin and glanced around as DJ closed the door behind them. She'd caught the scent of smoke the last half dozen yards up the mountain and now welcomed just being out of the storm.

A fire crackled in an old rock fireplace against the right wall, but from what she could tell, it wasn't putting out all that much heat yet. She beat the snow off her boots before she stepped toward the heat and took in the rest of the cabin.

It was compact and open. The living area consisted of the fireplace, two upholstered chairs and a kindling box sitting open. Inside it, she could see twigs and pine cones, old newspapers and matches. Turning behind her, she saw what served as the kitchen. It consisted of a sink with a bucket under it. A propane stove and an old icebox-type refrigerator. Pots and pans hung over a small cabinet that she assumed held utensils and possibly flatware.

DJ was right. It appeared someone had been here recently. She saw a package of store-bought cookies open on the top of the cabinet. "No electricity, right?" she asked as she peeled off her gloves to hold her hands up to the fire. Her fingers ached from the cold. So did her cheeks.

"No electric, no cell service, no internet," DJ said, "but there is a root cellar–type enclosure in the back against the mountainside with canned food that isn't frozen. There is also a stove with a propane tank and a pile of dry wood under a shed roof on the side of the cabin. We won't starve and we won't freeze."

She couldn't help but smile at him as she took in the rest of the cabin. She suspected DJ often looked for a silver lining in even the darkest of clouds. There was a back door with some storage along the wall. To the right of that was a double bed taking up the corner of the room near the fireplace.

As she began to warm up, she took off her coat and dropped it into one of the chairs. She saw that they had tracked in snow, but she wasn't ready to take off her boots. Her toes were just starting to warm up.

DJ threw some more wood on the fire. She could feel the heat go to her face. Her fingers and toes began to tingle, then sting. Her cheeks ached, but she began to relax. They were safe for the moment and as he'd said, they wouldn't starve or freeze. That was enough for now.

"Not bad, huh," DJ said, and grinned.

Partners to the end, she thought. "Not bad."

He turned toward the cupboard over the stove. "Let's see what there is to eat. I don't know about you, but I'm hungry after that hike."

TITUS GRANDVILLE STARED out at the snowstorm in disgust before spinning his office chair back around to face the two men standing there with their hats in their hands.

"Let me see if I've got this straight," Titus said, trying to keep his voice down. "You lost Diamond, you lost the money and now..." His voice began to rise. "You say you can't go find him and the money and finish this because it's snowing too much?"

Rafe Westfall looked at him wide-eyed. "It's a *blizzard*. Some of the roads are closed. How are we supposed to—"

"We'll find him," Butch Lamar said. "We know Diamond's headed up into the mountains. Keira left him a note with directions to Charley's old cabin. She swears that Diamond will show. If she isn't worried, why should we be?"

Titus swore. "Because you're standing in my office, dripping melted snow all over my floor instead of being up in the mountains waiting for him."

"We're going to need snowmobiles," Butch said. "There's no way anyone is driving very far in the mountains right now. We'll find him. We're taking Lloyd with us. But what do you want us to do about the woman with him?" The banker gave him an impatient look. "We'll take care of all of it," Butch said quickly. "Don't we always?"

Titus could have argued further, but it would have been a waste of time. "Diamond thinks he can come into my town and make a fool out of me? I don't want him or his girlfriend coming out of those mountains. Is that understood? By spring there should be not enough left of his body to know how he died, right?"

Rafe nodded. "The animals will see to that."

"Make sure you dump the remains where some horn hunter doesn't stumble across them this spring."

"You got it," Butch said. "We'll let you know when it's done."

Titus shooed them out of his office and told his secretary to get maintenance to come up and clean up the mess the two had made. Then he sat back and looked out at the whirling snow again.

His father wasn't going to like this. Then again, Marcus didn't like the way he ran much about the business. It was time for Marcus to step down, but the old fool was healthy and stubborn and still thought he was running things.

"This kid was Charley Diamond's protégé. His legacy. Hell, practically his flesh-and-blood heir," Marcus Grandville had said on the call this morning. "So he outsmarted you last night and walked away with the poker money. Cut your losses. I'm warning you. We don't want him coming back to Butte. From what I've heard, he's in a position where he could do great harm to our business."

Titus still didn't believe that. Diamond was a cheap con-man. But even if he did believe it, things had progressed such that it was too late. He had Keira Cross right where he wanted her and thus he had DJ. He couldn't tell his father that the reason he wanted DJ dead had little to do with the money lost last night or even the embarrassment of DJ getting the better of him. No, this went way back to when he was a kid. Humiliation was something that had stuck with him all these years—and DJ Diamond had witnessed it.

Now it was just a matter of finishing this. Then he would run the business as he saw fit. But he wondered if it would be possible as long as his father was alive.

"ARE YOU SURE I can't help?" Sadie asked as she heard DJ banging pots and pans in the tiny kitchen behind her. He'd told her to just take a seat in front of the fire, warm up and relax. He was going to cook.

"You cook?" she'd questioned.

"I can cook," he'd assured her. "But this will be more a case of opening canned goods.

"I've got everything under control," he called back now.

She stared into the flames, wondering how true that was. If what Lloyd had told him was true, Keira had set DJ up. Meeting her up here in the mountains seemed like a death wish. Was DJ really that sure he could trust this girl he'd called his little sister?

She thought about PI Buck Crawford. She didn't doubt

that it was true, DJ had a twin sister. She knew there was more to the story. Hadn't the PI said that DJ and his twin's mother had thought both babies had died? That they'd later been given away? Sadie just hoped there was some good news to be had with his biological family. She wasn't sure how much more bad DJ could take—especially if Keira betrayed him.

"I hope you're hungry," he said from behind her, startling her out of her thoughts. She caught a whiff of something that smelled wonderful and felt her stomach rumble. "It's my own concoction. I hope you like it."

He handed her a bowl and spoon. "It's a can of spaghetti mixed with a can of chili. I added a few spices I found." He sounded so eager as he waited for her to take a bite.

She breathed in the rather unusual mixed scents, filled her spoon and took a bite. Surprisingly the canned spaghetti and the chili actually went together. "This is delicious."

"Don't sound so shocked," he joked.

She took another bite. "Seriously, it's really good."

He laughed, shaking his head before returning to the kitchen to load his own bowl. He joined her in front of the fire in the opposite chair. "You really like it?"

"I love it. I hadn't realized how hungry I was until I tasted it."

She could see that he was pleased as he began to eat his. They ate in a companionable silence. The only sound the occasional crackle of the fire. Outside, the snow continued to fall as if it were never going to stop. She could see flakes fly by the window, whirling through the pines outside. Sometimes she heard the soft moan of the wind. Outside there was only white. With a start she realized something. They were snowed in here. Trapped.

The thought startled her until she reminded herself that if they couldn't leave, then no one could get to them. The rental SUV was down the mountain, blocking the road. She couldn't help but wonder. Where was Keira?

As she finished her dinner, DJ offered her more, but she shook her head, pleasantly full. He took her spoon and bowl and went to finish off what he'd made. She found herself lulled by the crackling fire, the warmth, the fullness in her stomach.

It felt so pleasantly domestic that she could almost forget why they were here in this cabin and what they would be facing when the storm stopped. As she glanced over at DJ, she wanted to pretend that they had stumbled onto a magical cabin and they could stay here forever, safe from a dangerous outside world. In here, no one could hurt them.

Childish wishing, she thought. There were no magical cabins, no place safe from the dangerous outside world because of the life they both had lived—and were still living. Was she kidding herself that she could stop doing this? Just get off, like climbing from a merry-go-round? Could DJ?

Otherwise, *they* were that dangerous world.

MARCUS GRANDVILLE KEPT going over his morning conversation with his son. The fool had authorized a poker game with DJ Diamond and two of Titus's men. The PI Marcus had met got involved. DJ walked away with the money after besting Titus's men.

"What kind of foolishness was this?" Marcus had demanded. "I told you to settle and get him out of town. What about that didn't you understand, Titus?"

"I couldn't just let this bastard come into town, set up a poker game, take us to the cleaners and walk away. One of your associates, Frank Burns, was in the game. DJ was thumbing his nose at us."

"So what?"

"You're beginning to get soft in your old age if you'd let a Diamond come into our town and do whatever he damned well pleases."

"Oh, and you handled it so much better? DJ Diamond did exactly what he planned and now he's left town after rubbing your face in it. Isn't that why you're so upset? You thought you could outsmart him and you failed."

"He hasn't gotten away," Titus said. "I have him right where I want him. I have Keira Cross, the woman he calls his little sister. I have her and therefore, I have Diamond."

"What are you talking about?"

"I'm using her to get DJ. I know exactly where he's headed and when he gets there, I'm going to make sure that he never comes back to Butte again."

Marcus shook his head, thinking now that he should have tried to talk his son out of this plan. Titus had always been a hothead. He didn't understand business, legit business; he never would. He wanted to be the tough guy, the schoolyard bully. He didn't even know how to pick his fights.

Now he'd sent Rafe, Butch and Lloyd into the mountains. Marcus knew what that meant. Titus wouldn't be happy until Diamond was dead. He swore under his breath as more of the conversation got under his skin.

"You used to let Charley run all over you. I'm not going to let DJ Diamond run roughshod over me."

Marcus shook his head. Titus could never understand the respect he and Charley Diamond had for each other. "I let him run his small-time cons in my town. Because I knew that he could never hurt me unless I did something stupid and tried to keep him from making a living here. You never learned how to make deals because you always have to win. You think I've gone soft? I'm washing my hands of this whole mess. You're on your own just like you've always wanted. If you're looking for my blessing, you're not getting it. You're making a huge mistake. Probably your last."

Now he regretted his words. He feared for his son. Worse for what this might do to the Grandville name—and their business. Titus was a fool, and he was about to prove it to the world.

DJ FINISHED EATING the rest of what he'd made, then cleaned up the dishes in the water he'd heated on the stove. He couldn't help smiling. He could see Charley in this cabin. It was comfortable and yet simple, like Charley himself. Why his uncle had never told him about the place still surprised him. Especially since Keira knew about it.

He pushed the thought away as he finished the dishes, dried them and put them away. Returning to the fire, he found Sadie sound asleep. He stared down at her, feeling a wave of affection for her that threatened to drop him to his knees. When had he fallen in love with her?

He felt blindsided. All that time when he'd been flirting and joking with her knowing she only saw him as an arrogant fool, she'd somehow sneaked into his heart and made a home there. She was right. He was a fool.

Leaning down, he kissed her forehead, then carefully, he picked her up and carried her the few feet to the double bed. He took off her boots and covered her with several of the extra quilts on a rack by the bed. She stirred a little but went right back to sleep. It had been a long, exhausting day, after a long, uncomfortable night in the back of the SUV.

For a moment, he watched her sleep. She looked so peaceful, as if she didn't have a care in the world. He realized that he didn't know if she had a man in her life. He knew she lived in a penthouse condo next to the ocean, that she drove a nice car that she'd bought with money she'd earned herself, that she had Sunday dinner with her godfather each week and that she didn't like the mustache DJ had grown shortly after they'd first met. He'd shaved it off before the next time he saw her. But that's about all he knew about her.

Turning away, he went back to the fire. He was exhausted but knew he wouldn't be able to sleep. His heart ached for so many reasons. Now he felt as if he'd come to a crossroads in his life. He could keep looking back at the paths he'd taken or he could look to the future—a far different future than he had ever imagined.

Was it possible that he had a twin sister? Ansley Brookshire. A blood relative. And he had a mother who'd believed that both he and Ansley had died at birth. And family, half siblings.

For so long he'd wondered who he was and why no one had wanted him, thankful that Charley had taken him in when he had no one else. If true that Ansley was his twin, it brought up a lot of questions. Like what had happened to separate them? Where was their mother? Why hadn't someone come looking for him sooner?

He realized he wasn't all that sure he wanted to know the answers. Maybe it would be better not to know the truth.

He glanced over at Sadie sleeping on the bed. Partners. More than partners. Did she feel the same way about him that he felt about her?

His beating heart assured him she had to. Why else was she here risking her life to help him?

He thought about Keira and questioned why he had to know the truth. Why he had to face her. He would be facing his past. If she'd betrayed him, then nothing had been as he'd thought.

Once the storm stopped, he would know the truth. If Keira had betrayed him, she might not even come to the cabin. Instead the Grandvilles' thugs, Butch Lamar and Rafe Westfall, would. He told himself that right now they would have the same problem he did, so he didn't expect them until the storm blew through. According to the weatherman the last they'd heard on the radio, the storm wasn't supposed to let up until the day after tomorrow.

So they had time, he told himself. He had time to decide what to do.

He'd always had a different idea about what made up family. Not blood. Not love. Not even loyalty. Family had been Charley and Keira. At best, he'd hoped they would have his back. Now, he feared both would have sold him out to save their own skins. And that could be exactly what Keira had done.

Either way, he couldn't worry about it now, he thought as he rose and stepped out on the porch. He listened as the snow blew past. Absolute silence. No sound of a vehicle. Nothing but the whisper of wind blowing the falling snow. He could feel the temperature dropping as he went around the side of the cabin to get more firewood. It would be a long night.

He was just glad he'd found this cabin. He didn't think they would have survived in the pickup even with the engine running and the heater going. They would have run out of gas, run out of hope, fairly soon. He told himself he could relax a little as he went back inside. Sadie was safe.

Now all he had to do was keep her that way.

Chapter Fourteen

Buck had been sure he could beat DJ and Sadie up to the cabin. He and the Colts had the shorter drive if they were anywhere around Butte, but DJ had also gotten a head start. But as they had just started up in the mountains a tire blew on the snowmobile trailer. They had to take the machines off to fix it. They'd lost any chance they had at getting to the cabin before DJ, and now it was getting dark.

The conditions had been worse than even he and Tommy and James had thought they would be—especially in the dark, but no one suggested turning back. It became apparent quickly that once they reached the mountains, they wouldn't make it all the way to Charley's cabin.

"Don't Francis and Bob Reiner have a cabin up here?" James had asked.

Buck tried to calculate where they were. "Not far ahead." His pickup was bucking snowdrifts. It wouldn't be that long before they couldn't go any farther by truck. They'd have to take the snowmobiles, but not in this storm in the dark. In his headlights, he could barely make out the narrow road through the pines.

"Watch for the sign," he said. "We can spend the night

there and try again in the morning. DJ is going to be having the same problem on the other side."

They'd gone a few miles when Tommy said, "There's the sign."

Buck turned and drove up the road toward the cabin, but he didn't get far before the truck high-centered on a huge drift. The wind whipped snow around them as he shut off the engine.

"That's as far as we're going," he said, afraid this had been a mistake. He hadn't been surprised when James and Tommy had insisted on coming along. Sheriff Willie Colt was standing by, offering a helicopter when the storm stopped, if needed. So far no crime had been committed. Buck was hoping to end this without gunplay, but that would depend on what they found up here on this mountain.

They grabbed their gear and started up through the whirling snow, breaking through drifts, until they reached the front door of the cabin. The Reiners never locked the front door, saying they'd rather not have anyone break in. They didn't keep guns or liquor, and nothing worth carting out of the mountains to pawn. They'd never had a break-in or anything stolen.

James opened the door as Buck grabbed a load of firewood from the overhang on the porch. Within minutes they had a fire going in the woodstove.

"I can tell you're having second thoughts," James said after they'd eaten one of the sandwiches Lori had sent.

"I should have come alone," Buck said.

"Wasn't going to happen, so get over it. If you feel really bad, you can take one of the kid bunk beds. I'm going for the double bed in the only adult-sized bedroom," James said with a grin. "Looks like Tommy has already taken the couch." Tommy was sprawled out trying to get a bar on his phone.

"You can take the truck back in the morning," Buck told him.

"I'm not worried about Bella," Tommy denied. "Baby's not due for a month and you know Bella, she wouldn't want me worrying. Just wanted to check in, that's all." Buck and James exchanged a look.

"Just in case you are worried in the morning, take the truck. Charley's cabin isn't that far by snowmobile. I am wondering if Keira Diamond Cross didn't get us all up here on a fool's errand while she's on her way to Alaska."

"That could be the best scenario," James said.

"Maybe for her. That still leaves DJ to deal with the Grandvilles if I'm right and this woman he calls his little sister set him up."

"I guess we'll find out tomorrow," James said, and yawned. "Try to get some sleep. Tomorrow could be a busy, eventful day."

SADIE WOKE TO the smell of something frying. She opened her eyes to see DJ at the small stove. It felt too early to wake up and yet there was DJ with a pancake turner in his hand humming softly as he cooked whatever was sizzling in that huge cast-iron skillet.

Next to the bed, she could see that there was fresh wood on the fire. How long had he been up? Or had he ever come to bed? She tried to remember going to bed and couldn't.

Had DJ put her under the covers last night? She threw back the heavy quilts covering her, not surprised to see that she was fully clothed. DJ wouldn't have taken advantage of her exhaustion. No, he had a code of honor that he followed. The thought touched her, warming her heart.

If he wanted to bed her, he'd seduce her. The thought made her swallow as she saw her boots were positioned next to each other beside the bed and slipped them on.

"Is that breakfast I smell?" she said, walking the few yards into the kitchen. It was still storming outside. She couldn't see anything but snow through the windows, as if the cabin had been wrapped in cotton.

"Hey, sleeping beauty. I wondered if you planned to sleep all day." He was grinning, those blue eyes of his bright in the white light coming through the windows. Looking at him, it was as if he didn't have a care in the world except what to cook next. She could see that he felt at home here as basic as the place was. That, too, made her smile.

"What is that?" she asked, taking in what was frying in the skillet.

"Are you telling me that you've never had Spam?"

"I've never heard of it," she said skeptically.

"Well, then you are in for a treat."

He was giving her the hard sell, which was making her even more skeptical. *"You made flour tortillas?"* This man continued to amaze her.

His grin broadened. "I found flour in an airtight canister and canned shortening and salt. Voilà! Flour tortillas and Spam and canned salsa. This morning, we feast. Shall I make you a Diamond burrito?"

She nodded, laughing as she did. "I'm guessing this isn't your first time eating canned meat."

His grin faded a little as he shook his head. "We could sit at the kitchen table," he suggested, nodding toward a folding table and chairs that he'd set up near the front door.

She hadn't noticed. But she did notice that it looked like fresh blood on his shirtsleeve. "Right after breakfast, I need to re-bandage your arm." He started to argue but she talked over him. "I'm sure I can find something to use here in the cabin."

"There's a first aid kit in the top drawer over there," he said, nodding in the direction of the cabinets along the wall to the back door. She marveled at how he'd made himself at home. It made her wonder about the man he called Uncle Charley. Apparently they had a lot in common.

BUCK AWOKE IN the middle of the night to snow. He'd hoped that the storm would have stopped. It hadn't. He heard Tommy and James moving somewhere in the cabin. He tried his cell phone. No service. According to his calculations, they still had a way to go before they reached Charley Diamond's cabin. He had no idea if DJ and Sadie had made it there. Or what they had found if they had. His stomach churned at the thought that he might be too late.

James had been subdued last night. Tommy seemed restless. Was he worried about Bella? Bringing them along had been a mistake, Buck told himself, then was reminded how much trouble he would have had changing that tire last night in the storm if he'd been alone.

"You two okay?" he asked as they began to put on their warm clothes to leave.

"Let's do this," James said, and looked at his brother. Tommy nodded.

"It's only a half mile up the road before the turn to the cabin. I doubt we'll get that far before we have to unload the snowmobiles and go the rest of the way on them. With luck, DJ and Sadie are still okay."

Both looked solemn as he glanced outside. All he could see was white. Out of the corner of his eye, he saw James check his weapon. Tommy did the same. Buck had already made sure his was loaded, even though he didn't want any gunplay.

But he'd heard stories about the Grandvilles and the men who worked for the family. DJ had already been shot. Guns were a part of this world—and the one Buck now considered his new career as a PI. Most private investigators, though, didn't even carry guns. Few had ever been forced to use them.

Unfortunately, Buck feared today would not be one of those days.

That's when he heard the buzz of snowmobiles. More than one. All headed their way.

DJ HANDED SADIE a plate with her burrito on it. "I gave you extra salsa. I know how you love your hot peppers." His grin was back and she tried to relax, telling herself that they wouldn't be up here in the mountains all that long. Once they reached civilization again, she'd insist he have his wound checked out. She worried it would get infected. Better to worry about a flesh wound than what might happen before they got off this mountain.

If she had to, she'd call her godfather. He'd know someone who knew someone who knew someone who would check out the gunshot wound and not report it. Not that she wanted her godfather to know where she was and why. He wouldn't like it, that much she knew.

"Keep it professional," he'd warned her. "DJ Diamond will make a great partner for what I have him doing, but beyond that..." He shook his head. "He's not boyfriend material, so don't get too attached."

At that time, she hadn't met DJ yet and had rolled her eyes. "You don't have to worry. I won't touch him with a ten-foot pole."

Her godfather, who had already met DJ, had said, "Keep it that way. I've been told he has an irresistible charm that's like catnip for women. I hear you're falling for his routine, and I'll put someone else with him."

She'd been fine with that at the time. Now she knew that no one could have done the job she and DJ had for her godfather. Her godfather knew it, too. He'd just assumed now that DJ had paid off his uncle Charley's debt that his goddaughter wouldn't be seeing the young Diamond again. She'd let her godfather believe that because she'd thought it was probably true. Once she told DJ that his bill was paid in full, he'd be gone.

Sadie hadn't admitted to herself, let alone DJ or her godfather, that it was the last thing she wanted. She had more than a soft spot for the cowboy.

"Well?" DJ asked. When she didn't immediately respond, he glanced at her plate and the half-eaten burrito on it. She hadn't even realized that she'd taken a bite. Half of it was already gone.

"Delicious. Sorry, I was just enjoying it. Do you need me to tell you that you're a great cook?"

He was eyeing her as if he'd seen that her mind had been miles away. "Great, huh?"

"Great," she said and ducked her head to take another bite. "I'm a Spam fan now."

"Good to hear, since we might be eating a lot of it, depending on when this storm lets up. But I hope you know that I can see through any lie that comes out of that mouth of yours," he said quietly, his gaze on her mouth.

She swallowed the bite of burrito, her cheeks heating under the directness of his look.

Sadie heard it about the same time as DJ did. He set down his plate and was on his feet in an instant. By the time he reached the front window, she was beside him. "Someone's coming, aren't they?"

"Stay here." He pulled on his coat, one of the weapons in his hand as he went out the front door, closing it behind him, before he stepped off the porch and disappeared into the falling snow.

DJ DIDN'T GO FAR before he stopped to listen. He could hear the whine of the snowmobiles somewhere on the mountain. It didn't sound close, but it was hard to tell.

Who was it? Keira? Or someone else foolish enough to try to get to their cabin in this storm? Someone like Butch Lamar and Rafe Westfall? Not Titus. He didn't do his own dirty work.

It had sounded as if the machines were busting through snowdrifts. He waited for the buzz to get louder, signifying that they were headed this way. But that didn't happen. The sound died off. They weren't headed here. At least not yet, he thought as he went to the woodpile.

But now he was on alert. It had felt as if they were alone on the mountain. Just the two of them. And he'd liked it. Liked it a lot more than he'd wanted to admit. Now he feared they didn't have that much more time together.

Sadie looked up expectantly when he came through the door. She'd taken their plates to the sink and was washing them. But next to her on the counter was her gun, fully loaded, he knew.

"Whoever it was didn't come this way." He was relieved. He wanted this time before seeing Keira. He realized that he also wanted this time with Sadie.

"You think they were looking for us?" she asked.

"Didn't sound like it. Our tracks would have been covered and they wouldn't have been able to see the SUV up here hidden in the pines and snow. As long as it's snowing, I doubt they'd be able to see the smoke from our fire." Unless they stopped, got out and smelled it.

He saw her visibly relax as he took off his boots and coat and hung them up, his gun tucked in the back of his jeans. The other gun he'd taken from Rafe and Butch was on the mantel behind a large wooden vase. Both were loaded if needed. He hoped it wouldn't come to that, but then again he couldn't imagine any other way out of this. If the Grandvilles' thugs showed up, then Keira had to be in on the setup—even if she didn't show herself.

"Thanks for breakfast," Sadie said, drying her hands on a paper towel. "Where did you say I could find that first aid kit?"

"First, I brought you something."

She frowned quizzically. "At the local convenience store you stopped at on your way back in the cabin?"

"Something like that. It's right outside the door on the porch."

Sadie was still giving him a questioning look as she stepped to the door, opened and saw a small evergreen tree leaning against the side of the cabin.

"I thought it was small enough that we could find something to decorate it with around the cabin."

She turned to stare at him. "A real Christmas tree."

He shrugged. "You said you never had one. I found an axe near the woodpile and since it is the season…"

Tears welled in her eyes, and he felt his heart ache. It had been impulsive and such a small thing to him, but so much more to her. "DJ."

He heard so much in those two letters. He cleared his throat. "I'll make a stand for it."

"Thank you."

He could only shrug again, half afraid of what he'd say— let alone do—seeing the emotion in her eyes.

HE'D CUT HER a Christmas tree. Sadie feared she would cry if she tried to speak so she could only nod as she closed the door. His thoughtfulness was almost her undoing. She went back to the fire, warmed her hands and steadied herself before she asked, "Where did you say that first aid kit was?"

She was surprised to find that her hands were trembling as she opened the box with the red cross on it. DJ had taken off his shirt. She'd seen him without one enough times, but seeing him half-naked in the close confines of the small cabin made it much more intimate.

Sadie tried to concentrate as she took off the old make-shift bandage. She could feel DJ watching her closely. She cleaned and gently put antiseptic on the wound before she re-bandaged it. Closing the first aid kit, she started to stand to return it to the cabinet when DJ laid a hand on her arm.

She froze as his touch sent a bolt of electricity charging through her at the speed of lightning before it settled in her center. She tried to breathe but it made her chest hurt.

"Sadie." He'd never said her name like that. Low, husky,

loaded with a jolt of emotion that she recognized even though she'd never felt it with such intensity.

She slowly raised her gaze to his. What she saw in those unusually pale blue eyes made her heart kick-start. She let out the breath. She hadn't realized that she'd still been holding the first aid kit as DJ took it from her and set it aside.

Her mouth went dry as he locked eyes with her. She tried to swallow as he rose and gently pulled her closer. She wanted to drag her gaze from his. She wanted to pull away, but all the reasons this was a bad idea evaded her. She wanted this, and from the look in his eyes, he wanted it just as desperately.

Drawing her closer, he bent to tenderly kiss her. Her lips parted of their own accord and she heard a soft moan escape him. He dragged her to him, the look in his eyes telegraphing the message *Stop. Me. At. Any. Time.*

But stopping him was the last thing she wanted. He pulled her against him, her soft to his hard, and then they were kissing like lovers. His hands slid down her back to her behind. He cupped her, pulling her against him. She heard his moan.

He drew back to look at her. She could see he was begging her to stop him. He didn't want to hurt her. He didn't want her to just be another of the women he'd bedded and walked away from.

"If you stop now, I will never forgive you," she said, her voice breaking.

He shook his head. "You have no idea how long I have wanted this. Wanted you."

"So what's stopping you?"

He chuckled. "Your godfather will kill me. But he'll have to wait in line." He swept her up into his arms and carried her over to the bed. The moment he set her down, she pulled him down with her. The kiss was all heat. Their tongues met, teased, then took. They tore at each other's clothes in reckless abandonment.

There was no turning back as he bent over her breasts, sucking, nipping, teasing with his tongue. Outside the wind howled at the eaves, the snow fell as if never going to stop, and inside DJ made love to her as if there might not be a tomorrow. Later, after they were curled together trying to catch their breaths, he whispered next to her, "You intrigued me from the first time I laid eyes on you. Then I got to know you."

She chuckled as she turned to him. "I could take that a number of ways."

"You were pretty and smart and sexy as all get-out. Sitting across from you all those nights, I wanted you, but I also wanted more than anything I'd ever had with another woman." His gaze met hers and held. "When you got off that plane the other day... I knew. I love you, Sadie Montclair."

"You don't have to say that."

"I've never said it to another woman—even at gunpoint. I wasn't sure how much longer I could work with you and not...step over a line that would end it."

She'd never seen him this serious. "DJ," she whispered as she moved to kiss him.

He looked uncomfortable, as if he'd opened his heart, laid it out in front of her and now felt too vulnerable. "If I'd just known that all it would take was a misshapen little evergreen tree to get you into bed..." he joked.

Sadie knew this man so well. "I didn't sleep with you because you brought me a Christmas tree. I've wanted this for a very long time too." She smiled and said, "I fell in love with you as hard as I tried not to. I love you, DJ. Do I need to tell you that's the first time I've said those words to a man?"

He shook his head. "So it wasn't my imagination? This has been building for some time?" She nodded.

"I never thought..." He didn't have to finish. She knew what he was saying. He never thought the two of them would ever be together like this. "I did think about you and me, though. But I saw us in a fancy hotel with silken sheets and room service. Nor did I ever think it could be so amazing, not even in my wildest dreams." He traced a finger along her cheek to her lips.

She smiled. Her gaze locked with his. "The room service here is quite good and I don't need expensive sheets with a high thread count. Just being here with you like this..." She touched the washboard of his stomach. "I feel I'm never going to get enough of you."

He laughed as he grabbed her and rolled her over so she was flat on the bed and he leaned above her. "Let me see what I can do about that." He bent down to kiss her gently on the lips before he trailed kisses down her neck. She closed her eyes, remembering that his favorite song was something about a slow hand.

Chapter Fifteen

When DJ woke beside Sadie, he was afraid that earlier had been nothing more than a dream. In the corner was the small Christmas tree they'd taken a break from lovemaking to decorate together with the silly things they'd found in the cabin. It made him smile it was so ugly and yet so beautiful all at the same time. Then they'd gone back to bed to make love and had fallen asleep.

He glanced over at Sadie and wanted to pinch himself. He'd never thought he'd even get to kiss her. The woman had captivated him for so long, but it had been strictly hands-off, all business. He ran his gaze down the length of her naked body, memorizing it the way he had earlier with his fingertips, with his tongue, with his lips—as if he could ever forget.

Remembering made his heart beat faster. He'd never experienced this kind of pleasure and pain, and knew it was why he'd never put his heart in jeopardy before. The emotions he was experiencing were the most joyous he'd ever known—and the most terrifying. Yet his pulse drummed with more than desire as he realized he couldn't bear to ever walk away from this woman. He felt as if he would die with the longing. As if he wouldn't be able to breathe—and wouldn't care if he did.

He'd never felt anything like this, and it scared him more than having killers after them. This woman had stolen not just his heart, but his body and soul. He'd always felt protective of her, but now—

Her brown eyes opened, her gaze on his face as if she'd felt him looking at her. He smiled, not in the least embarrassed to be caught. "I'll never get tired of looking at you."

He saw the heat in her eyes as she reached for him, but just as quickly, she froze. Her gaze shot over his shoulder to the front of the house. He felt himself tense and quickly estimated how long it would take him to get to the weapon behind the vase on the mantel.

"It stopped snowing," she said in a whisper filled with regret.

He felt it, too. Being here like this, he'd forgotten the outside world for a while. Now it came rushing back in. With the storm stopped, someone could get to them. He felt both dread and regret. "We'd better get up."

She nodded but didn't let go of his forearm. Looking into her eyes, he knew she was afraid this might be their last time together. He bent toward her for a kiss, and she cupped the back of his head, drawing him closer.

He wanted this so badly, and not just for today but always. He knew he would do whatever it took to make sure that happened as he lost himself in her. One way or another, they would be together. Partners to the end, he thought.

BY THE TIME they were out of bed and dressed, the sun had come out. The sunshine lit up the freshly fallen snow. It glittered like diamonds, so bright that it was blinding.

Even the pine needles under the cover of snow caught the rays and glistened.

"It's so beautiful," Sadie said from the window. "Like a field of diamonds." She turned as DJ came in through the back door, reminding herself how dangerous it could be.

"I found a shovel in the shed behind the cabin," DJ said. "I'm going to dig out the SUV and then we're getting out of here."

She stared at him in surprise. "What about Keira?"

He shook his head. "Hopefully she's on her way to Alaska."

"Are you sure about this?" She couldn't bear the thought that he'd have regrets. That their lovemaking had been the cause of him wanting to leave.

DJ's look was heartbreaking. "I don't need to look her in the eye to know the answer. I just didn't want to believe it." He shrugged. "At some point, you have to quit trying to save a person."

She wasn't sure he was still talking about Keira. She quickly stepped to him and put a finger to his lips. She shook her head slowly until his gaze met hers and held. She kissed him, wanting desperately to be in his arms, to assure him that she wasn't ever going to give up on him. But even as she had those thoughts, she realized how much she needed this man.

She'd always been independent, determinedly so. While her godfather had raised her and made sure she had anything she wanted, she'd been on her own since she was eighteen. She could take care of herself, something she prided herself on. She'd never needed a man to take care of her.

Nor had she ever wanted one badly enough to even consider giving up her independence, let alone admitting that need. Until DJ Diamond. Neither of them had relationships that had lasted. The two of them as partners had been the longest for both of them.

Her need for DJ filled her with panic that she might lose him. They'd finally admitted how they felt about each other. She'd kept it bottled up for so long. It was unbearable even letting him go down to get the SUV unstuck. That need was an excruciating ache, so physically painful that she wanted to beg him not to leave for fear of what would happen.

But as she met his eyes, she saw that they couldn't stay up here on this mountain forever. Eventually they would have to leave and go back to the real world. If their love for each other couldn't withstand that, then there was no future for them.

She stepped back, feeling bereft. Love hurts. The words from a song now resonated in her heart, in the pounding of her blood.

"That vehicle we heard before," she asked. "Keira?"

He shrugged. "Could have been Grandville's men. Could have been anyone."

She knew it could also be PI Buck Crawford—with more of the PIs from Colt Brothers Investigation. Crawford was determined to get DJ to his twin's wedding. She could only hope that was the case and that DJ made it. He had family waiting for him.

BUCK WOKE TO the sound of the snowmobiles. He sat up, banged his head on the upper bunk and swore. What time was it?

Climbing out of the bed, he hurriedly pulled on his boots since he'd slept in his clothes in the cold cabin.

Before he got his second boot on, James opened the door. "You hear that?"

He nodded. "Sounds like more than one."

"Sounds like they're headed our way."

"Willie?"

James shook his head. "The sheriff's department doesn't move that quickly, especially in a snowstorm. You think it's DJ?"

"I doubt he had access to a trailer and snowmobiles. Grandville's men."

"That's what I'm afraid of," Tommy said from the doorway. "They must have seen your truck and the snowmobile trailer outside the cabin. Sounds like there are three of them coming up the mountain. What do you want to do?"

"They aren't looking for us, right?" James asked.

"Guess we'll have to find out." Buck pulled on his second boot and rose.

By the time they reached the cabin's front door, all three snowmobiles and their drivers were sitting outside. Buck opened the door and stepped out, James and Tommy following.

"Where's DJ Diamond?"

"Who wants to know?" Buck asked over the rumble of the three snowmobile engines.

"Butch, it's that PI I told you about." Buck recognized the man's voice who'd spoken. Lloyd from the poker party. He seemed nervous, his hand on the weapon at his side.

But it was Butch Lamar he kept his eye on. He'd met other men like Butch. Grandville's lead thug was a big man, with a face that had met too many other men's fists and an unfriendly attitude. They were always looking for a fight. They liked beating people up. They constantly were looking for someone to knock that chip off their shoulder. Butch Lamar was one of them.

Buck assumed the third man was Rafe Westfall. Both Butch and Rafe had AKs hanging across their chests and pistols at their hips over their winter clothing.

"We have business with Diamond," Butch said.

He knew what kind of business. "So do we. Also we have the sheriff on his way just in case your business includes hurting Diamond or the woman with him," Buck said.

Butch wagged his head as if amused. "I don't think you know who you're dealing with."

"Trust me, I do," Buck said.

"And where's this law? I don't see any law. Rafe, do you see any law?" He turned back to Buck. "From the looks of it, we have the upper hand here. He touched the AK-47 strapped to his chest. This is a dangerous place to be for you boys. Anything can happen up here this time of year. A man could get himself killed really easy."

Butch's words hung in the air. An open challenge.

James saw Lloyd go for his pistol before Buck did. He drew his weapon from behind him and fired at the same time Lloyd did. Buck was drawing his gun as well when Butch gunned his snowmobile, the others following suit as they sped off, Lloyd hunched over his machine in pain, the snow where he'd been sitting on his machine dotted red with blood.

Buck turned quickly to James, who was holding his side. He looked at Tommy who hadn't had a chance to go for his gun. He was thankful since it could have been worse if they had pulled their weapons. "Get inside. Let's see how bad you're hit."

"Not bad," James said as he was helped inside the cabin to a chair.

"I'll be the judge of that," Buck said. "Tommy, disconnect the snowmobile trailer from the truck."

"Aren't we going after them?"

"No, you're taking James down the mountain so Willie can get a helicopter to take him to the hospital."

As soon as Tommy went outside, Buck looked to see how badly James had been hit. There was a lot of blood. He did what he could to stop the bleeding and prepare the wound for traveling. "Keep this on the wound," he said of the gauze and bandage he'd found in the bathroom cabinet.

"I know what you're thinking," James said. "But you can't go after those three alone."

"You need to get to the hospital," Buck said. "Tommy needs to take you. Once you're where you can use your phone, get Willie to send up deputies and Feds. Don't worry about me. I'll be fine," Buck said.

James shook his head as Tommy came back in. "The truck's ready. How's James?"

"He needs to get to the hospital. You're taking him," Buck said, expecting more argument. But one look at how pale James had gone and Tommy nodded. "He's lost a lot of blood. I did what I could. Get him off this mountain."

James grabbed Buck's arm. "I'm planning to stand up with you at your wedding, man. Don't let me down."

Buck smiled. "I'll be there. Now go. They might decide to circle back. I want them to think we all left. Tommy, drive the truck down following their tracks to their vehicle. They would have busted through the drifts. It should make the going easier."

"You do realize that we are going to have to disable their vehicle, right?" James said.

"You need medical attention. Tommy, don't listen to him. Just get him to the hospital. Tell the sheriff hello."

"Willie will be coming like gangbusters," Tommy said. "Just keep yourself safe until he and the troops arrive."

ANSLEY HAD BEEN waiting anxiously by the phone. She'd wrapped the rest of the Christmas presents she'd purchased and put them around the tree. She'd cleaned the kitchen, made a batch of cookies and was just about to ice them when her phone finally rang.

Hurriedly, she scooped up her cell. "Buck?"

"Sorry, it's me," Bella said. "I'm in labor."

It was the last thing she'd expected to hear.

"Don't panic," her friend said quickly. "I called my doctor. He said not to come in until my contractions were more consistent and much closer together. I've called Lori. She just put the twins down for a nap. She assured me that I might not be having this baby for hours—or maybe not even today. She called Ellie while I called Carla. Ellie's in Seattle at her law firm. Carla didn't pick up."

"I'll be right there," Ansley said, knowing that Bella had to be wishing she'd reached someone with at least pregnancy experience. She checked to make sure that the stove was off. The cookies could wait. "I'm leaving now."

Bella laughed. "I know I'm being silly, but this is all new and I'm nervous."

"I am a great hand-holder," Ansley assured her. "Have you been able to reach Tommy?"

"No, that's the other thing. I haven't heard a word since

they went up into the mountains yesterday. I know he doesn't want to miss this. He better not miss this." Her voice broke.

"I'm sure he'll be back before you even have to go to the hospital," she said, not sure of that at all. She knew nothing about giving birth or babies. But after she and Buck were married, she couldn't wait to learn. "Sit tight. I'll be there before you know it."

The moment she disconnected, she tried Buck's number. It went straight to voice mail. "Hey, it's me. Bella's in labor. Hope you're all right. Come back. Bella needs us all. I need you. I should never have sent you on this ridiculous mission." She hung up close to tears. Maribelle was right. She was a spoiled rich girl. Even as she thought it, she knew that wanting to have her twin at her wedding wasn't outrageous. It was her deepest desire. Unless, of course, her twin was a possible, even probable, criminal on the run and this ended up getting the people she loved killed.

DJ TOOK THE shovel down the mountain to the snowbound SUV and began digging. He needed the physical exertion. He went to work, shoveling as his mind raced. He kept thinking about Keira. Had he really been ready to jeopardize everything just to know whether or not she had betrayed him?

His thoughts rushed back to Sadie and the time they'd spent in the cabin. He didn't want to leave here for fear the bubble would pop. He'd told her that he loved her, but he wasn't sure that was enough. She'd said she loved him, too. But what would happen when they got back to the real world? If they got back?

He stopped to listen, hearing snowmobiles but far off in the distance; he glanced back up the mountain. He knew

Sadie had taken the SUV keys the moment he couldn't find them. She didn't trust him and with good reason. He would do anything to protect her, even leave her behind if it came to that. But right now, he wasn't sure that Keira wouldn't show up. The cabin was no longer safe since the storm had passed. Keira might not be the only one coming for them.

Going back to his shoveling, he thought about Ansley Brookshire, his alleged twin sister, who was going to all this trouble so he'd be at her wedding. She really could be his twin, he thought with a chuckle. She was determined enough and they did look like they could be fraternal twins.

But how would she feel when she met him? She was a Brookshire. The name meant money. He was willing to bet that her childhood had been nothing like his own. She probably didn't realize who she might be inviting not only to her wedding but also into her life.

He tried to imagine being part of this family Crawford had told him about. He would have been a complete fool not to realize that this was the fork in the road, the crossroads he'd felt coming. His deal with Sadie and her godfather had come to an end, but that didn't mean that he and Sadie couldn't have a future. A twin sister was offering him a family. And then there was Keira, who was either going to Alaska to live with her no-account husband or setting him up for a fall.

DJ stopped shoveling. With luck, he should be able to drive the SUV out now. He leaned on the shovel as he tried to catch his breath. He'd made a decision about his future. He and Sadie were leaving.

Glancing back up the mountain, he smiled to himself. It was a no-brainer. Let go of the past, let Keira go to Alaska, leave the poker game money for the Grandvilles and walk away. One call to Marcus Grandville once they got off this mountain could end this.

He took a deep breath of the cold mountain air. It was almost Christmas. He thought of their Christmas tree back in the cabin. He was ready to experience the magic of the holiday through Sadie's eyes.

At the whine of a single snowmobile high on the mountain, he dropped the shovel. Whoever it was, they were headed this way and fast. Sadie. He had to get to her. He took off through the deep snow as he raced up the mountain, knowing that he would never reach the cabin before the snowmobile did.

Chapter Sixteen

Sadie had felt a chill as she stood on the porch and looked down the mountainside to where she had seen DJ shoveling. The breeze dislodged the fresh snow from the pines, sending it streaming through the sunlight, making the flakes gleam like glitter. The mountainside was so quiet it was eerie. DJ had said that they were leaving. He wasn't going to wait for Keira. He wasn't going to leave her, either. She had the keys to the SUV in her pocket, so she knew he'd be back. But if she hadn't taken the keys, would he have left?

If so it would have been to find his sister. He still wanted the truth, she knew that. No matter what he said, he had to know if Keira had betrayed him, set him up to die. Sadie shuddered at the thought. How could anyone want to hurt DJ? Once you looked into his heart and saw what was there, it seemed impossible.

She thought of their lovemaking. He'd been so gentle with her, as if he was afraid she would break. Yet she'd sensed the urgency in him. He'd wanted her for a long time. The man had amazing control, she thought with a wry smile. All the time they'd worked together, he'd joked, but he'd never let it go past that.

Sadie wouldn't have known how he felt if she hadn't

seen it in his eyes. She'd thought she'd caught glimpses of it over their time together, but she'd never trusted it until now. DJ had said he loved her, something he'd never told another woman, and she believed him. Their lovemaking had been more than sex. There was a connection between them that felt so strong. The thought of losing it, losing DJ, made her stomach roil. They needed to get out of here, she thought urgently.

She hugged herself, shaken by that sudden almost warning. A part of her never wanted to leave this cabin, never wanted to go back into that world where things were complicated. Here, life was simple. But she knew they couldn't stay for so many reasons; Keira and Grandville's men were only part of it. DJ would never be happy with a life like this.

That was the problem, she thought, as she watched the breeze send the new snow into the cold morning air. She wasn't sure what it would take to make DJ happy. She wasn't sure he even knew himself. Could she make him happy once they left here?

Sadie just knew that it was important for him to make it back for his twin sister's wedding. She had no doubt after looking at Ansley's photo that it was true. He was the missing twin. He was born into a family that would love him. They'd gone to a lot of trouble to find him. It appeared to be the kind of family neither of them had ever had.

She silently urged DJ to hurry and get the SUV unstuck. The woods seemed too quiet. She felt a chill as she thought of Keira. Where was she? Had this been a trap? Sadie couldn't imagine what was in the woman's heart to do such a thing to DJ. She'd been glad to hear DJ say he wasn't staying around to wait for her. If not for the storm, she feared they would already know Keira's true intentions.

After everything that had happened between her and DJ since she met him, she would risk her life for his. She might have to let him go once they got off this mountain, but she couldn't live without knowing he was alive somewhere. She wanted to be able to think about him and imagine him in his Stetson sitting at a poker table. He'd be grinning, holding the winning cards in his hand because he was the best player at that table, and nothing was going to keep him from proving it.

Sadie heard the sound of a snowmobile. At first it was distant, but it was coming this way and fast. Her heart lurched. She looked down the mountain and didn't see DJ. He must have heard it, too.

She hurriedly stepped back inside the cabin and started for the mantel and the gun there when she heard the snowmobile engine stop. The silence was deafening. Until the back door of the cabin flew open, and she reached for the gun.

ANSLEY FOUND BELLA pacing the floor, her hand on her swollen abdomen, looking close to tears. "It's going to be fine," she assured her the moment she walked into the large ranch lodge. "I called Buck and left a message. I know they will turn back the moment they get it."

Bella didn't look any more convinced than Ansley. Who knew when they would get the message? Or if they would, since there was spotty cell service at best in the mountains and with this storm…

"Did you hear the avalanche report on the radio this morning?" Bella asked, sounding scared. "They're warning people to stay out of the mountains. The new snow on the old is too unstable. They said it is like a powder keg about to go off."

"Let's sit down," Ansley said. She'd heard the report. Like Bella, she was worried, but she couldn't show it. Bella was already upset enough. It couldn't be good for the baby. "I'm sure the men know what they're doing."

She didn't know the mountains around here, but she'd skied at both Bridger Bowl and Big Sky. There, though, the ski patrol cleared the cornices before letting skiers on the slopes. Cornices formed high in the mountains could be kicked off by anything– even a sound.

"I hope you're right," Bella said. "All this fresh snow, it just makes me so nervous."

Ansley felt the same way. Every year backcountry skiers and snowmobilers were caught in avalanches, many of them not surviving. Once the snow began to shift… The mountains would be extremely dangerous right now and Tommy, James and Buck had all gone up there.

"How far apart are your contractions?" She led Bella over to the living room couch, anxious to change the subject.

"They're sporadic," she said with a sigh. "But this girl is kicking like crazy. She is ready to come out of there."

"Why don't you put your feet up?" Ansley suggested. "Relax as much as you can. Your Christmas tree is beautiful. Tell me you didn't climb up on a ladder to decorate it yourself."

Bella rolled her eyes, seeing what she was trying to do. Still, Bella explained that Tommy had insisted she hire a crew to decorate the house. "He didn't want me overdoing it. Now I'm afraid maybe I did anyway and that's why the baby is coming early." She was clearly fighting tears.

"You don't know that," Ansley said, getting her some

tissues. "We aren't even sure the baby is coming today." They sat in silence for a few minutes. "I feel like this is all my fault. If I hadn't been so determined to have my twin at my wedding..."

"Don't be silly," her friend said, sniffling as she wiped her eyes. "It's your determination that got you to us. None of this is your fault. We all just want your wedding to be perfect. Buck won't let you down, trust me. Anyway, this is what our men do. We wouldn't love them so much if they weren't the way they are."

Ansley nodded, knowing it was true. Buck was as driven as the Colt brothers in righting wrongs, helping people, finding out the truth. She loved that about him. All of them had helped her find her family and now they were doing their best to help the man Buck was convinced was her twin.

"So who do you think this woman is with DJ?" Bella asked.

"Sadie Montclair? I'm not even sure Buck knows. But he says there's something between them."

"Romantically?" Bella's eyes lit, making Ansley laugh.

"You are such a sucker for a happy ending," she teased. "I heard Davy is manning the office. I'll call him and see if he knows anything about her."

As she gave Davy what few details she knew about Sadie Montclair, Bella had another contraction. Ansley had been timing them, knowing that she might have to take her to the hospital soon. "Davy's going to call back."

They talked about baby names, baby clothes—"Have you seen the little overalls they make for girls?" Bella had cried. "I couldn't resist. I got the denim ones and the Western shirts that match."

"For a newborn?" Ansley asked in surprise.

"No, that would be silly. I got the twelve-month size and while I was at it, picked up the twenty-four month size as well." Bella laughed. "Tommy is actually worried that I might go overboard on baby clothes. Can you imagine?"

Ansley's phone rang. She quickly picked it up, hoping it was Buck. "Davy," she said trying not to sound disappointed since she was the one who'd asked him for the favor.

"If she is the Sadie Montclair of Palm Beach, Florida," Davy said, "then she has quite the mob connection. I found a socialite photo online that tagged her as the goddaughter of Ezra Montclair, Palm Beach business mogul. He's her godfather, all right."

Bella was waving her hand. "Well? Who is she?"

"Any word from the others?" Ansley had to ask before she hung up.

"Nope. Not yet. Don't worry. They know those mountains. They'll be fine."

"Thanks." She disconnected, even more worried. Davy was worried, too, but who wouldn't be given the weather?

"What?" Bella demanded after breathing through another contraction.

"I think we should get you to the hospital," Ansley said, rising. "Your contractions are more consistent and are now ten minutes apart."

Her friend looked surprised that she'd been timing them. "What about Sadie?" she asked as she lumbered to her feet.

Ansley helped her. "Seems Sadie's godfather might be the head of the mob in Palm Beach, Florida."

"Get out of here," Bella cried.

"Which is exactly what we are doing," she said, steering her toward the door. "Should we call your doctor to let him know we're coming in?"

Bella shook her head. "He's on call. He knows." Her face crumpled. "What if Tommy doesn't make it?"

"I'm sure he'll show up at the hospital as soon as he's out of the mountains," she said, and realized Bella meant what if Tommy doesn't make it out of the mountains. "Do you have a bag packed for the hospital?"

"It's by the door. Tommy insisted."

"I'll grab it." As Ansley picked it up and turned, she saw Bella standing by the door looking back at the house as if she might never see it again.

"Let's go see if this baby is coming today or not," Ansley said too brightly as Bella turned to look at her, tears in her eyes as her water broke.

SADIE TURNED, not sure who she would find standing in the doorway as her hand closed around the grip of the gun. She blinked, startled by the tiny, slim blonde who stared back. But she was more startled by the gun in the angelic-looking woman's hand. She took a wild guess. "Keira."

"Who are you?" the blond woman demanded.

Sadie was debating whether or not she could pull the gun from behind the vase, let alone shoot this woman who DJ considered his little sister. She eased her hand off the grip and pretended to hold on to the mantel for support. "I'm Sadie."

"Sadie, of course. You're that mobster's daughter DJ's been working with down in Florida."

That pretty much summed it up, she thought. Although her father and her godfather considered themselves businessmen who played the odds and used the system to their benefit.

"Where's DJ?" Keira asked, taking in the small cabin and seeing for herself that he wasn't there.

"The last time I saw him, he was headed for the outhouse out back. Actually, I thought you were him returning. He must have heard you coming and took off."

The blonde stepped deeper into the cabin, letting the back door close as she moved away from it. "He wouldn't leave you behind," Keira said, smirking. "I know how he feels about you." Sadie stayed by the fire, turning her back on Keira to warm her hands, and considered her chances if she went for the gun. "Get over here so I can see you."

The gun was in reach, but she could feel the blonde's sights on her back. It was clear that this wasn't the first time Keira had held a gun. There was no reason to believe that she wouldn't use it, Sadie thought as she turned to look at the woman. Sadie had talked herself out of tough spots before, but her instincts told her that trying to reason with this woman would be a waste of breath. There was something in Keira's eyes, something dark, something soulless. She'd seen the look before in some of the men she and DJ had played poker with. It was a terrifying pit to look into, seeing raw greed and hate, knowing there was violence there.

"Sit down," Keira ordered. "In that chair there." She pointed with the gun as she moved closer. "We'll just sit here and wait, although I don't believe he went to the outhouse."

Sadie shrugged as she took the chair as Keira had instructed while her would-be killer stood next to the fireplace wall so she could see both the back as well as the front door. DJ would have heard the snowmobile. He wouldn't just come walking in unaware of what might be waiting for him.

But he would come back to the cabin. He would know it was Keira. He had thought he could leave without facing her. But now that she was here… He wouldn't be able to help himself. He'd want to hear it from her.

Sadie just hoped that this woman didn't kill DJ as he came in the door. Her instincts told her that Keira wouldn't. She would want him to realize what she'd done, for whatever reason. She would want to make him suffer first.

Counting on that, Sadie considered what she could do to stop Keira. Unfortunately, it would be hard to disarm the woman from this chair in front of the fire. Sadie felt tense, waiting for the sound of DJ's boots outside on one of the wooden porch boards. He would be armed, but she really doubted he would fire a weapon before he would ask questions. Keira would know that. Maybe that's what she was counting on.

Sadie caught sight of the Christmas tree DJ had cut for her and they'd had so much fun decorating. They'd laughed so hard as they tried to outdo each other, finding the wildest things to put on that puny tree's limbs. Yet when they'd finished, it looked wonderful to Sadie.

"This is the best real Christmas tree I've ever had," she told DJ.

He'd hugged her and said, "And I thought my childhood was bad."

A sob rose in her throat. She pushed it back down. Now more than ever she needed that poker face that DJ said she was famous for. She couldn't let Keira see what she was feeling. It would make her and DJ more vulnerable.

"He probably went looking for you," Sadie said, wishing it were true. He could have taken off on foot. Or he could still be down digging out the SUV. Now she wished she'd let him take the keys so he could have left in search of his sister. But she doubted he would have. Things had changed between them. She knew DJ was somewhere outside this cabin. He would soon be opening one of the doors and walking into a trap—just as Sadie had feared and Keira had no doubt planned.

BY THE TIME DJ neared the cabin, he could no longer hear the snowmobile's engine. Heart lodged in his throat, he slowed as climbed up to the back door. Sounds in the mountains were often amplified and hard to pinpoint exactly where they were coming from. But there had been no doubt about this earlier sound, he thought as he caught sight of a snowmobile sitting in the pines above the cabin.

He stayed to the trees, keeping the cabin in sight as he approached. He told himself that Sadie was all right. It wasn't like he'd heard anything coming from the cabin. Anything like a scream. Or a gunshot. Yet he knew she was no longer safe, as if his heart now beat in time with hers.

As he reached the side of the cabin, he saw the footprints from the snowmobile sitting in the nearby pines to the back door. He looked around for other tracks. Only one person had gotten off the machine and entered the cabin. Could be PI Crawford.

All his instincts told him it wasn't. Just as he knew it wasn't one of the Grandville men either. The tracks in the snow were too small.

It was Keira.

DJ stood for only a moment considering his best play. He knew the odds. They weren't to his liking. Sadie was in there. He told himself that she was still safe. He would have heard a gunshot. He would have heard a scream. All he heard even now was silence.

Even if Sadie hadn't been inside with Keira, there was no walking away from this. There hadn't been since getting the call drawing him back to Montana. Keira was either here to tell him goodbye before she left for Alaska or she'd come here to earn whatever Grandville had paid her.

He thought about her as a little girl. She'd been so skinny, so pale. He remembered her eyes that first day. He'd had trouble meeting them, afraid of what horrors she'd already been through. Like him, she had no one. Whoever had dropped her off wouldn't be coming back for her and he thought she'd known it.

He'd thought he could protect her, erase whatever had happened to her before Charley's ranch. He'd been a fool. Sometimes you can't save a person. That was a lesson Sadie had never learned.

Tucking the gun into the back of his jeans, he walked to the back of the cabin, hesitated only a moment and opened the door.

Chapter Seventeen

DJ stepped into the cabin. His gaze went to Sadie first. She was sitting in the chair in front of the fire. She gave him a look that said she was all right. He shifted his gaze to Keira, the woman he'd called his little sister since the day she'd arrived at the Diamond Deluxe Ranch.

She stood over Sadie, holding a gun on her. He remembered her wanting to learn to shoot when she was about nine. She'd been so determined that he'd taught her. She'd been a natural, knocking off the cans he'd put on the fence one after another. He remembered the joy in her expression now and felt sick.

When he spoke, his voice was much calmer than he felt. "Keira, want to tell me what's going on?"

"Seems pretty obvious, doesn't it?" she said.

"Sorry, you're going to have to spell it out for me. Talk slowly, you know I never was as quick at catching onto things as you were. Bet you excelled at college."

She shook her head, anger flaring in her eyes. He feared he'd taken it one step too far. "Right, you worked, you paid for my college. Subtle reminder, big brother. You think that made up for what you did?"

"I'm sorry, what exactly was it that I did, Keira, that you

would betray me?" he demanded. "Why would you do this to me? I've always been there for you."

"Not always," she snapped. "You let Charley put me in foster care. You and Charley just left me."

"Keira, I was a kid myself. You were a child much younger than me. There was no way you could have gone with us. That life was no picnic. I was terrified most of the time because people were chasing us, some trying to kill us. There were days when we had nothing to eat, no place to stay but out in the woods."

She shook her head stubbornly. "You abandoned me."

"That's not true. Once I went out on my own, I started sending you money. When it came time for you to go to college—"

"I didn't go to college, DJ. All I ever wanted was what you got—to live the con. I would have been better at it than even you. Look how I conned you."

He stared at her, still disbelieving. "This was Luca's idea, wasn't it?"

"See, that's why you fell for it. You wanted to believe an idea like this could only have come from a man. Keira couldn't have come up with this on her own." She huffed. "It was all my idea, DJ, and it worked." She looked so satisfied that he felt even sicker inside. He'd thought he'd protected her from this life, but he'd been wrong. She'd done this to show him but also to get even for him leaving her all those years ago.

"What did you do with the college money?" he asked.

She smiled. "Taught myself a few tricks of the trade. You wouldn't know, living down there in Florida working for the mob."

"I've been paying off Charley's debt. It's not the glamorous life you think it is." He hated that she'd grown into a hardened woman already, so hard that she'd sold him out to Grandville. "How much do you get for delivering me to them?"

Her smile was all greed and misplaced glory. "Two hundred grand. Like you, Grandville wanted to treat me like a child, or worse, a woman who doesn't know what she's doing. But he sees me differently now."

DJ was sure that Titus did see her differently now. "You can't trust him. He'll turn on you like the venomous snake he is, Keira." But even as he said the words, he could see that she didn't believe him. She'd thought that she'd won Titus Grandville's respect and there was no telling her different.

She tilted her head, listening, but not to him. He heard it too. The whine of snowmobiles in the distance. Grandville was coming with his thugs to get retribution, as if he and his ilk needed a reason. Charley was at the heart of this. Years ago, he remembered his uncle embarrassing Titus on the street in Butte with a card trick. At the time, DJ had looked into the young Grandville's furious red face and worried Titus would go to his father and make things harder for them. He seriously doubted that Titus had ever forgotten the humiliation—or the young threadbare-dressed boy who'd witnessed it. Titus had felt small in front of DJ, a kid he'd ridiculed and felt superior to.

Suddenly DJ felt tired and defeated. He was sick of old grudges and feuds. He'd come up here to save Keira. Worse, he'd gotten Sadie involved. For that, he would never forgive himself. Not that he would have long to regret his mistakes. Titus planned to kill him, but what Keira didn't realize was that the banker wouldn't leave any witnesses.

DJ looked at Sadie. He saw that familiar glint in her eye.

She knew the score, but clearly she wasn't ready to give up yet. How had he ever gotten involved with such an optimist?

SADIE HAD TAKEN in the situation. She knew DJ had a weapon on him, but she doubted, even after everything he'd heard, that he was capable of shooting Keira. But Sadie now didn't have that problem. She saw the woman as a product of her own greed, using her childhood as her excuse, blaming everyone but herself for the way her life had turned out so far.

The problem was how to play this and not get DJ or herself killed. She couldn't do anything from this chair, though. She had to take a gamble, something she was apparently born to do.

As she began to clap, Sadie got to her feet to face Keira. "Thank you for this wonderful reminder of how lucky I am not to have a sibling. What a heartrending moment to have witnessed. To think I used to want a little sister."

Just as she'd hoped, her act caught Keira off guard.

"I told you to sit down there and not move," the woman cried, swinging the gun in Sadie's direction.

Holding up her hands, she'd stepped back toward the fireplace and the gun now within reach behind the vase. She'd also distracted Keira, who was having trouble keeping her gun on both of them.

DJ had moved toward the kitchen, putting the two of them on each side of Keira.

"You move again and I'll shoot you," Keira cried. "That goes for you, too, DJ."

"Other than to get me killed, what is it you want?" he asked, sounding bored.

She took a few steps back, bumping into the bed as she

tried to keep them both within sight. "For starters, I want the money you took from the poker game in Butte and any other money you might have on you."

"It's yours," he said. "But I'm going to have to move to get it."

Keira raised the gun so it was pointed at Sadie's head. "Try anything and I kill her."

The sound of the snowmobiles made all three of them freeze for a moment. The sound grew louder, closer. Time was running out. Sadie looked at DJ. *Tell me what you're thinking. Give me a sign.* Otherwise, Sadie was going to do whatever she had to.

THE MOMENT TOMMY and James left in the truck, Buck climbed on one of the snowmobiles, drove it off the trailer and went after Grandville's thugs. He hadn't gone far when he saw the blood on the fresh snow and remembered that James had wounded one of them. A little farther, following the tracks the three had left, he saw a snowmobile sitting without a rider, idling. As he drew closer he saw the body lying next to it on the far side. He cautiously approached. Within a few feet, he saw that it was Lloyd, and he was dead. He appeared to have been shot not once, but twice, the last time between the eyes.

Buck looked to the dark pines ahead, feeling sick to his stomach as he thought about the kind of men he was dealing with. He knew where Rafe and Butch were headed. Charley Diamond's cabin. Were DJ and Sadie there? What about Keira Cross? He gunned his engine; the snow machine roared past the abandoned one as he followed the tracks that he knew would lead him into more trouble than he'd know what to do with.

Ahead, he could see the snowmobile tracks where they had crossed the mountain above the tree line. He'd been following three, now two. But now he saw another track. It, too, had gone in the same direction. His heart sank, as he knew it must belong to the other person on this mountain DJ and Sadie had to fear. Keira.

He just hoped that Tommy and James got word to Willie and the rest of the law in time. He could use all the help he could get since he had a bad feeling Keira had already found DJ and Sadie.

THE BUZZ OF the approaching snowmobiles got louder. DJ could see that Sadie was planning something. He wasn't sure it would make any difference if he was right about who was coming. If it was Grandville's men, they were toast. Keira would be the least of their problems. "You hear those snowmobiles approaching?" he asked his sister, and saw her self-satisfied expression. She thought like he did that they were Grandville's men. "They're going to take the money away from you and kill you. You'll never see the two hundred grand. You'll never see Alaska."

She laughed. "I was never going to Alaska."

"Luca will be so disappointed," he said, wondering if Luca wasn't on one of the snowmobiles headed this way.

"I dumped Luca. He's history. He was just dragging me down. I should have known he'd never get me the start-up money I needed. I realized I'd have to do it myself."

"So you went to Titus. I actually thought he was the one who'd suggested you betray me. But it had been your idea. Good to know. Let me get you that money," he said as he moved toward the bed.

"You can't shame me, DJ," she said angrily. "This life is about doing what needs to be done no matter who it hurts."

He chuckled. "It doesn't seem to be hurting you, Keira. In fact, as smug as you're acting, I get the feeling you're enjoying this."

"So what if I am?" she demanded, waving the gun in his direction as he started across the room.

It was just what Sadie had been hoping for.

SADIE MOVED QUICKLY, deciding at the last moment not to go for the gun behind the vase. She'd already figured out that Keira was cold enough that she might shoot DJ just out of meanness rather than drop her gun. So instead, Sadie went for the woman with the gun.

Even as she launched herself at Keira, she figured the woman would be expecting it. That's why she stayed low, hitting her in the knees, taking her down with a thud that seemed to rattle the entire cabin. Keira managed to get off one shot. Sadie heard it whiz by over her head as she landed on top of the skinny and yet feisty woman. She was already going for the gun when DJ put his boot down on Keira's wrist before she could fire again.

Almost casually, he leaned down and took the weapon from her. Keira kicked at Sadie, grabbing for her hair like a street fighter. Sadie punched her in the face, Keira's head flopping back and smacking the floor. She went still but didn't pass out.

Not that Sadie trusted her. "Please get me something to tie her up with," she said to DJ.

"Let me," he said, handing her the gun as he reached for a dish towel and began to rip it into strips. By the time he'd tied Keira's hands she was kicking and screaming, then pleading with him to let her go. "I'll split the money with you," she cried in desperation.

He shook his head, looking at her with pity. "I don't need the money. I have plenty. I could have paid Titus off without making a dent in my savings."

She stared at him. "Then why didn't you?"

"Because he knew I would try to make the money in a poker game. He would have his ear to the ground making sure that at least one of his men was in the game—and that it would end badly. I wanted to beat him at his own game. Now I wish I'd paid him off and walked away. I won't make that mistake again."

"DJ, let me leave with the money," she pleaded. "I need a new start and you're probably right about Titus double-crossing me."

"Sorry, little sis. It's too late," he said as he dragged her over to a chair and shoved her into it. He appeared to be listening as he tied her to the chair.

Sadie heard it, too. Silence. No sound of the snowmobiles. They both looked toward the back door.

Keira began to laugh. "What did you do to make Titus Grandville hate you so much?"

"ANYONE HUNGRY BESIDES ME?" DJ asked as he stepped into the kitchen and began to bang around in the pots and pans.

Sadie stared at him and so did Keira. He'd heard the snowmobiles stop on the mountain behind the cabin. Whoever it was had probably already surrounded the cabin. Any moment they would come busting in.

"Sadie, would you mind helping me?" he asked without looking at her.

She moved to stand next to him. "DJ?"

He handed her the opened container of canned meat and a sharp knife, the size that might fit in the top of a boot. "Why don't you cut the ham into slices," he said, still without looking at her. She saw that he had the larger of the two cast-iron skillets on the stove, the grease he'd put in it getting hot.

She glanced behind her at Keira, who was trying to get to her feet as the back door slammed open with a crash. The man in the doorway was big and rough-looking. He was carrying an AK.

"Now isn't this a cute little domestic scene," he said.

"Help me, Butch, they were going to kill me," Keira cried. "Cut me loose," she yelled louder when he didn't move. "I have the money. Hey, I'm talking to you."

Butch started over to the chair and Sadie saw another man standing just outside. He also carried an AK.

"Could you move any slower?" Keira demanded of the thug.

Out of the corner of her eye, Sadie watched Butch walk over to the woman. "Where's the money?"

"I'll get it for you as soon as you untie me," she snapped.

He pulled a knife and began cutting the strips of dish towel from her ankles and wrists.

"Hey, watch it with the knife, you big dumb—"

He raised the butt of the rifle and brought it down hard on her head. The sound reverberated through the small cabin. Sadie's gaze shot to DJ. His eyes were closed; he was gripping the edge of the counter.

"Your sister's taking a nap," Butch said from behind them. "Now where's the money?"

DJ's fingers loosened on the counter. His blue eyes flashed open. "Don't you want breakfast first?" he asked without turning around. His voice sounded strained as he took the ham she'd sliced from her and dumped it into the hot skillet, where it quickly began to sizzle and brown. The skillet was smoking hot. "Toast? What do you think?" he asked Sadie.

Her mouth felt dry. She didn't know what to say, let alone think. DJ was making her nervous. These two thugs were armed with weapons that could saw them in half and he was cooking breakfast?

She heard Butch come up behind them. "I'm sure you're one hell of a chef, but I didn't come here for breakfast, and you know it. Where's the money?" Butch swung the gun toward the front of the cabin and pulled the trigger on the AK, turning the front door into kindling. "Unless you want some of this, you'd better get me my money."

BUCK STOPPED IN the shelter of the trees and shut down his sled. He couldn't hear the two on the snowmobiles in front of him. He figured he must be close to Charley Diamond's cabin because the machines hadn't been silent for long. He could see the trail the two had left to a spot high on the side of the mountain.

As he followed its path, he saw a huge cornice that the blizzard had sculpted high on the peak above the cabin. The cornice hung over this side. He felt a chill.

He'd been caught in a small avalanche as a teenager on a backcountry ski trip. He'd been terrified and fascinated by the power of snow when it started moving. New snow was 90 percent air, yet one foot of it covering an acre weighed more than 250,000 pounds.

In an instant, that cornice could break off and slide. Thousands of tons of snow could come roaring down that mountain at the speed of a locomotive and with the same impact.

He could see the old avalanche chute where trees and rocks had been wiped out next to Charley Diamond's cabin. It wouldn't be the first time a cornice high on the peak had avalanched down. But this time, the cabin might not be so lucky.

The sound of gunfire inside the cabin made him jump as he swung off the snowmachine, lunging through the deep snow. While the snowmobiles had busted a trail, there was still a good two feet of snow below their tracks he had to break through as the gunshots echoed across the mountainside.

Reaching the cabin, he saw three snowmobiles parked outside. Two belonged to Grandville's muscle; the other must belong to Keira since he didn't think DJ and Sadie had brought any.

He moved toward the back door where the machines were parked, weapon drawn, knowing he would be outgunned. Just as he reached the door, all hell broke loose inside.

Chapter Eighteen

The contractions were coming only a few minutes apart when Tommy walked into the hospital room. Ansley felt her heart float up at the sight of him. He went straight to the bed to take his wife's hand. "Heard our girl is coming early," Tommy said, and smiled at Bella, who, in the middle of a contraction, growled at him.

"Buck?" Ansley asked hopefully.

"He's still up on the mountain," Tommy said, his smile fading. "I had to bring James down."

She felt a start. "What happened to James? Is he all right?"

"He's going to live, the doc said." He turned back to his wife. "Lori was on her way up here to check on Bella when I brought James in. She's in the waiting room while he's in surgery. The bullet went straight through. Doc said that was good."

Bella was oblivious to their conversation as she panted through yet another contraction.

"I'll just be down the hall," Ansley told her friend, and hurried out. James had been shot? Buck was still up on the mountain? She found Lori in the waiting room on the surgical floor.

"What happened?" she cried as she rushed to her.

"James was shot."

"But he's going to be all right?"

"He lost a lot of blood." She sounded close to tears. Ansley was close to them herself. "Willie's headed up there with a helicopter, deputies and EMTs. The Feds aren't far behind, he said."

She nodded but couldn't speak. "I never should have asked them to find my twin," Ansley said.

Lori took her hand. "None of this is your fault. This is what they do."

"You sound like Bella."

"Welcome to being a wife of a private investigator."

"I want to be a wife of a private investigator," Ansley wailed as Lori pulled her into her arms.

"I've known Buck Crawford my whole life," Lori said. "He'll be standing next to you on Saturday. He might be bruised and battered, but he'll be there. Sorry, not funny." She drew back to look at Ansley. "Buck will be there and if there is any way on this earth, your twin brother will be with him."

Ansley desperately needed to believe that finding her missing twin wouldn't cost her everything.

"How's James?"

She looked up to see Davy Colt coming through the door.

"He's in surgery," Lori said.

Davy glanced at his half sister. "Just got the preliminary DNA report from the blood Buck found on that scarf left in his pickup," he said. "DJ Diamond is definitely your twin."

Ansley began to cry. Buck had done just what he'd said he would do—find her missing twin even if it killed him. She couldn't lose them both.

"SETTLE DOWN," DJ said to Butch as the sound of gunfire died off. "I'll get your money." He knew the money was only an excuse. "Let me take this off the fire." He picked up the pot holder next to the stove, grabbed the handle of the largest skillet and swung around fast.

The sizzling canned ham hit Butch first so he was already screaming when the blistering-hot cast-iron skillet slammed into his face, not once but twice as the AK was wrenched from his hand. The first strike stunned him, the next knocked him to his knees. DJ was about to hit him again when he saw Rafe raising his AK and heard Sadie scream a warning.

Everything seemed to happen too fast after that. DJ saw the winter-clad figure come up behind Rafe. Crawford. The butt end of the PI's handgun came down on the thug's head hard. Rafe dropped, but as he did he pulled the trigger on the AK. Bullets sprayed across the cabin.

When DJ saw what was happening, he grabbed Sadie and threw her down, landing on top of her. As he threw her to the floor, he saw Keira's body jump with each shot before the bullets arced toward him and Sadie on the floor. He'd felt Sadie take one of the bullets even as he tried to shelter her from them. It was as if the bullet punctured his heart. For a moment he couldn't move, couldn't breathe. Beneath him, Sadie wasn't moving, either. His worst fears had come true. He'd gotten Sadie killed.

In the silence that followed, the earth seemed to move. He heard a whump sound, then Crawford yelling. He rolled off Sadie, praying he was wrong, that she was fine. But one look at her and he knew she wasn't. More yelling. He wasn't even sure it wasn't him yelling as he scooped an unconscious Sadie up into his arms.

"We have to get out of here." Crawford was shaking his shoulder. "We have to get out of here. Now!"

He could hear a roar, thinking it was in his ears, but it appeared to be outside as if a runaway train was headed for the cabin.

"This way," Crawford said, dragging him through the demolished front door, off the porch and into the pines away from the cabin. "Keeping going. Don't stop."

He could hear what sounded like trees being snapped off as the roar grew closer. Looking back he could see nothing but a cloud of white. He kept going until Crawford yelled for him to stop. DJ fell to his knees, still holding Sadie in his arms, and the PI rushed to him. Buck took off his coat and spread it on the snow. "Put her down here."

DJ didn't want to let her go.

"Let me check her wound," the PI said.

He slowly released her, laying her on the coat in the snow. He could see that she was still breathing but losing blood from a wound in her side. He stripped off his coat and put it over her, then removed his bloody shirt to press it against her side. He didn't feel the cold. He didn't feel anything as the cloud of snow around him began to dissipate.

"Stay here. I'll get a snowmobile. Help is coming. We just need to get to a spot where a chopper can land," Crawford said.

DJ looked back toward the cabin. It was gone. All he could see was a few boards and one wall sticking up out of the snow farther down the mountain. Charley's cabin was gone and everything in it. Keira. He closed his eyes and pulled Sadie closer as he heard the PI coming with the snowmobile.

Chapter Nineteen

Dressed in his Western suit, Buck rode the elevator up to the recovery floor. He found DJ next to Sadie's hospital bed. He was sitting in a chair, his elbows on his knees, his head in his hands. The anguish he saw there was nothing like what he saw in the man's eyes when DJ lifted his head.

"How is she doing?"

DJ swallowed, nodding, dark circles under his eyes. "The doctor said she should recover—once she's conscious. If she regains consciousness."

"I'm sorry. I know you don't want to leave her, even for a minute," Buck said. "But your twin sister needs you."

DJ shook his head. "She's better off without me. Can't you see that I'm trouble? The people closest to me get hurt. Ansley doesn't need that."

"She needs you, flaws and all. You have no idea how much trouble she's gone through trying to find out the truth about her birth parents," Buck said. "She is no shrinking violet. She's strong. She can handle just about anything, even you." He smiled to soften his words.

"What if my past comes back and I put her life in jeopardy?"

"You'll have family." Buck reached into his pocket, took out the gold bracelet and handed it to DJ. "You'll want this back. Your birth mother had it made for you. She called you Del Junior before you were born, and Ansley DelRae. She wanted you to know your father. You have more than just your twin, though she is definitely a force to reckon with. You're a Colt. You have four half brothers. One's a sheriff, the others are PIs. You also have your birth mother, who is just as anxious to meet you as Ansley is. She didn't know the truth until Ansley came to town looking for her. But you'll hear all about it from your mother, from your twin, from the rest of the family. DJ, you'd be a fool to pass up a chance to be part of this family. You won't be alone. We have you covered."

DJ put his head in his hands for a moment. "I don't want to disappoint her. I've already disappointed two people I swore to protect and got one of them killed."

He could have argued that Keira got herself killed, but he knew that wouldn't help right now. "Believe me, I know what you're feeling. I don't want to let Ansley down, today especially. I promised her I would find you and if at all possible get you to our wedding."

DJ raised his head, took in Buck's suit, and then looked down at his bloodstained clothing. "Do I look like I'm dressed for a wedding?"

"You will. Like I said, we have you covered. The wedding will be short and once it's over, you can come right back here. Your family is waiting."

"Family, huh." Buck could tell that he was thinking about Keira. "Charley always said you can't overcome your genes," DJ said. "I never knew what that meant until now. Now that my DNA makes me officially a Colt, I guess I don't have much choice."

"You always have a choice," Buck said. "But you'd be a fool to pass up accepting the rest of the Colts as family.

Hell, I've been trying to get them to adopt me for years. DJ, I promise I'll have you back here as fast as possible. I brought you some clothes."

"I don't have a present."

"You are the best wedding present either of us will get today. Trust me, once she sees you…"

DJ rose and went to Sadie's side. He leaned down to kiss her forehead, then turned to Buck. "I need to meet my twin before the wedding," he said. "I know you ran the DNA test, and it proves I'm her brother, but I need to know here." He tapped his chest just over his heart.

Buck nodded, hearing the determination in his soon-to-be brother-in-law's voice. "You got it. She can't wait to meet you, either."

ANSLEY STARED INTO the mirror. Today was her wedding day. Brushing her dark hair back, she promised herself she wouldn't cry even as her eyes filled with tears.

"You are going to ruin your makeup," her mother said, and handed her a tissue. "Buck will show. Nothing on this earth can keep him from marrying you today."

She took the tissue, dabbed at her eyes and nodded. "I know it's bad luck to see each other on your wedding day but—"

"Buck called you. He told you he made it out of the mountains. He's going to be here."

"Have you heard how James is doing?" Ansley asked.

"He came through surgery fine. The doctor said he was lucky. The bullet missed vital organs. It was just the loss of blood they were worried about, but you know Lonesome. Once word was out that blood was needed, people turned out to help. Bella and the baby are doing great. It's all good news."

She shook her head. When she'd talked to Davy, he'd told her that Willie and deputies from the sheriff's department had gone up to help search for bodies. Buck could have been one of them. She still worried that he'd been injured and didn't want to tell her. "I shouldn't have put so much pressure on Buck to find my brother. What was I thinking? Me and my perfect Christmas wedding. Without Buck—"

"Oh, honey." Her mother took her in her arms. "Buck will be here and if I know him, he'll have your twin brother with him. That man will move heaven and earth to give you the wedding you've always wanted." She drew back to look at her daughter. "You just have to believe."

Ansley nodded. She did believe in Buck, trusted him with the rest of her life. But she was set to get married in less than an hour and there had been no word from Buck since that one phone call. She couldn't help being terrified that something horrible had happened up there, that she would die alone because Buck Crawford was the only man for her.

Her cell phone rang. She grabbed it up. "Buck?"

"Hey, honey."

"Are you all right?" she cried.

"I'm fine. I'll tell you all about it when I see you. Actually, after the wedding, if that's okay. I know I'm calling it close." Tears of relief began streaming down her face. "There's someone here who wants to meet you before the wedding. He's right outside."

She heard the tap at the door and quickly wiped at her tears, her mother handing her another tissue. The door opened and standing there was her twin brother. She would have known him anywhere. Their gazes met and locked. As tears filled his eyes, she began to cry in earnest as she ran into his arms.

Chapter Twenty

DJ was beside Sadie's bed when she opened her eyes. She blinked, her eyes focusing on his face for a moment before she said, "Tell me you made it to the wedding."

He laughed; it felt good. Sadie was awake. She was going to make it. He couldn't remember ever feeling this overjoyed. "You just made my day and I've already had the most amazing day."

She smiled. "Tell me." She sounded weak, but back from wherever she'd been. He never wanted to come that close to losing her ever again.

So he told her about wanting to see Ansley before the wedding. "It was…incredible," he said, his voice cracking. "I was afraid. I didn't know what to expect. I had no idea what she was like and yet when I saw her…" He shook his head. Sadie reached for his hand, squeezing it, tears glistening in her eyes.

"She told me that she always felt as if a part of her was missing," he said after a moment. "I understood at once. How can a person yearn for something they didn't even know existed? I realized at the cabin that I'd tried to fill that need with Keira. The problem was, she never saw me as family. She never felt the immediate closeness I felt when I saw my twin. It was like a bolt of lightning."

"And the wedding?"

He chuckled. "Of course you'd want to know about that. It was perfect. All of the Colts were there except for James, who's still recovering. I'll fill you in later. But Lori had him on her phone so he got to be there via the internet. I met all my half brothers."

"And your mother?"

He nodded. "It was strange. She's nice. Buck was right. I like all of them. They made me feel like...family."

She smiled. "I figured as much."

"It's a complicated story about my mother and father. He was Del Ransom Colt, one hell of a bronc rider and one hell of a private eye, according to the family. I was named for him. Del Ransom Jr., thus the DJ. Apparently, I come from a long line of rodeo cowboys." Sadie laughed, then winced in pain. "You need to rest."

"So do you. I'm so glad you made the wedding."

"Me, too." She squeezed his hand and closed her eyes. He stayed there watching her breathe, thinking about everything. He didn't move until the sheriff popped his head in and motioned that he was needed out in the hall.

He kissed Sadie on the forehead and went out to talk to his half brother Willie Colt. They'd met on the mountain in passing.

"How is she?"

"She's conscious," DJ said. "The doctor said she should have a complete recovery."

"Good," Willie said. "I'm going to need to ask both of

you some questions about what happened up on that mountain. If now isn't a good time for you…"

"No, I'd just as soon get it over with."

AFTER DJ LEFT her hospital room, Sadie found herself in tears. She hardly ever cried. But seeing DJ, seeing the change in him since meeting his twin and the rest of the family, filled her heart with joy. It would take him a while to get used to it. He'd already lost so much. It would be hard for him to accept this gift of family, but in time, he would and he'd be better for it.

Sadie thought of the pain she'd seen in his eyes on the helicopter ride to the hospital. He'd held her hand, begging her to stay awake. "I can't lose you," he said again and again, his voice rough with emotion, his blue eyes swimming in tears. "I can't lose you."

She remembered little after that until she opened her eyes and saw DJ beside her bed wearing a Western suit and bolo tie. He looked so handsome in the suit, so different from the Montana cowboy she'd known. Wiping her tears, she closed her eyes, surprised how exhausted she felt.

When she woke again, her room was filled with women all about her age. They introduced themselves as Carla, Davy's wife; Ellie, Willie's wife; Lori, James's wife; and Bella, Tommy's wife. The Colt women had brought her gifts, wanting to meet her. Ansley was with them.

"Shouldn't you be on your honeymoon?" Sadie had asked.

"Buck and I aren't going anywhere until all of you are out of the hospital," the pretty dark-haired woman told her. "It's my fault since I desperately wanted my twin at the wedding. I could have gotten you all killed."

Sadie shook her head. "Your search for DJ actually saved our lives. We wouldn't be here now if it wasn't for your husband."

Bella had just given birth to a little girl with dark hair and Colt blue eyes. "She's precious," Sadie said after looking at the photo, since the infant was still down the hall in the nursery after coming a month early.

The women were fun, laughing and bringing cheer to the hospital room. They were all so excited about DJ being found, commenting on how much he looked like Ansley.

"We brought you a few things you might like," Lori Colt told her.

Bella had produced a dusty-rose-colored nightgown. "DJ said dusty rose was your color. I promise it's more comfortable than a hospital gown."

They also brought her flowers, candy, lip balm, lotion, a scented candle. They promised that their next visit they'd bring ice cream and small fried pies from Lori's former sandwich shop.

True to their word, they showed up the next day with the treats and lots of laughter and stories, often about the Colt brothers and growing up around Lonesome.

Sadie couldn't imagine, not after growing up in Palm Beach. Here the mountains came right down to the small western town. Pine trees grew everywhere. She wondered what it was like when it wasn't covered in a thick blanket of snow. She thought about what DJ had said about his favorite season, spring in Montana. She had never lived in a place that had seasons.

"How is DJ doing?" she'd asked. She didn't need to explain herself. They knew at once what she was asking since they knew that he had practically been camped out at the hospital.

"It's like he's always been part of the family," Carla, Davy's wife, said. "I think at first he was nervous, but once he met his brothers, I think he realized how much they all have in common."

"If you're asking if he plans to stay," Bella said, always the one to get to the heart of things, Sadie had realized, "he knows he's welcome. The brothers told him that there's a section of the ranch that is his for a house, if he wants it. They also told him that the ranch is as much his as theirs. I heard them talking about raising more cattle."

"It's the way Del would have wanted it, all of his off-spring together," Lori said.

"I'm sure DJ is overwhelmed by all of your generosity. I certainly am," Sadie said, wondering why DJ hadn't mentioned any of this to her. Because he was going to turn it down? Or because he was going to take their offer? Probably because it was all overwhelming and he hadn't made up his mind yet.

"Bet you're ready for a nice juicy burger," Carla said. "We'll bring you one tomorrow."

"When are you blowing this joint?" Bella inquired. "We want you and DJ to come out to the ranch for dinner. I'm also throwing a New Year's Eve bash if you feel up to it by then."

"We've worn her out enough for one day," Lori said. "She doesn't have to make any big decisions right now."

"Except about the burger," Ellie said. "You want that loaded?"

She laughed and nodded. "Fries?"

"Of course fries," Bella cried. "What do you think we are?"

They'd all left laughing and Sadie found herself looking forward to their next visit even as she realized the visits would soon be ending. The doctor said she was healing nicely and would be able to leave soon—long before New Year's Eve.

TITUS GRANDVILLE HATED his father butting into his business. Worse was when his old man showed up unannounced at his office. He'd had no word on what had transpired up in the mountains. Butch had promised to call the moment it was done. He hadn't called. The storm had stopped. The plows were running, the roads opening up.

Nerves on end already, looking up and seeing Marcus walk in only angered him. "What are you doing here?"

His father didn't answer, merely came in, pulled out a chair and sat down across the desk from him.

"Hello?" Titus snapped. "I really don't need this right now. I'm busy. I have work to do. What are you doing here?"

"This used to be my office," his father said. "You probably don't remember when you and your brother Jimmy used to play on the floor in here. You always took Jimmy's toys."

"Why are we talking about my dead brother?" Titus demanded. He knew his father still blamed him for the car crash that had killed Jimmy. He'd felt enough guilt over it; he didn't need the old man to rub it in, especially today.

"I always wondered why you didn't cry at the funeral."

Titus was on his feet. "Would love to wade through the past with you, Dad, but not today. You need to leave."

"Things didn't go like you planned them, did they?"

He felt the hair rise on the back of his neck. "Why would you say that?"

"Because I saw the cops as I came up the back way."

It was the smugness on his father's face. All of his life, his father had tried to tell him what to do. "You never trusted my instincts," Titus snapped. "Not even once. You never said, 'Good job, son.'"

"You never gave me reason to," Marcus said as two uniformed officers filled his office doorway.

"Titus Grandville?" one of the officers said as he stepped in. "We need you to come with us."

"What's this about?" Titus asked innocently as he saw his father get to his feet.

"We're arresting you for the murder of Keira Cross and attempted murder of DJ Diamond and Sadie Montclair as well as the deaths of Lloyd Tanner, Butch Lamar and Rafe Westfall and the shooting of PI James Colt."

"Is that all?" Marcus Grandville said with a laugh as he moved out of the cops' way.

"You realize that you can't prove any of this, right?" Titus said.

Titus looked around for a way out, his gaze going to his father who was standing back, smiling as if to say, "Told you so." It was something he'd heard all his life. He'd killed the good son, his father's favorite, and Marcus had never let him forget it.

"Enjoying this, old man?" Titus said as one of the cops began reading him his rights and the other cuffed him. Soon he would be doing the perp walk through the Grandville building out to a squad car. "You've been waiting for this day, haven't you?"

His father nodded, then grimaced, his hand going to his chest as he fell back against the wall and slumped to the floor. One of the cops hurried to him and quickly called

911 to report that the elderly man appeared to be having a heart attack.

"Go ahead and take him down to headquarters," the cop said to the other cop as he began to do CPR on Marcus.

Titus stared at his father, wondering why the cop was bothering. "You're wasting your time. He has a bad heart. It's rotten to the core. There's no saving him."

The cop jerked on his arm, dragging him to the door.

"I want to call my lawyer," Titus said. "I'm going to sue you and the police department for false arrest. You have no proof that I've done anything." On the way out of his office he saw two men in suits coming toward him. The one in the lead flashed his credentials. FBI. He waved a warrant.

"When it rains, it pours," Titus said, and smirked at agents demanding to see all records and confiscating all computers and phones.

Before they reached the street, EMTs raced past them on the way up to the top floor. Titus looked out at dirty snow in the street and told himself he'd be out of jail before the EMTs reached the top floor. He was a Grandville, the last of them, finally. All of this was his. He was finally taking his rightful place. These people had no idea who they were dealing with.

WHEN SADIE WOKE later that evening, the nurse told her that she had another visitor. She was glad to see Buck Crawford enter her room. "I heard you were getting better. I had to see for myself."

She smiled at him, sitting up a little. She knew little of what had happened up on the mountain. DJ had glossed over it when she'd questioned him on one of his many visits. Clearly, he hadn't wanted to relive it—not that she could blame him. "Tell me what happened after I was shot. It's all such a blur." She listened as he told her about the avalanche.

"Keira?" Buck shook his head. "She took one of the bullets. She was gone before the cornice broke and fell. We barely got you out before the avalanche hit the cabin. Her body will be recovered and when it does, DJ said he plans to have her buried next to Charley Diamond on the mountainside cemetery back in Butte."

"And the Grandvilles?" she asked.

"Titus was arrested earlier today in Butte. One of the men from the poker game, Keith Danson? He's turning state's evidence against Titus. He might never get out of prison. The FBI has been investigating him for some time apparently. They raided his office earlier. I suspect whatever they find added to murder and attempted murder..." He shrugged. "I'd say the reign of the Grandvilles is over, since his father died of a heart attack during Titus's arrest."

Sadie shook her head. It all sounded too familiar. "How is DJ?" she finally had to ask.

"He won't have any trouble with the law," Buck said. "Both Butch Lamar's body and Rafe Westfall's bodies have been retrieved from the avalanche. I'm sure their connection to Titus Grandville will be of interest to the Feds, but DJ is in the clear."

"So it's over," Sadie said, thinking of DJ.

"It doesn't have to be," Buck said as if reading her thoughts.

She smiled, wishing it were true. She was DJ's past. These people and this town, they were his future. He'd come by the hospital constantly to see how she was doing. Each time, she asked about his new family and each time, he would smile and tell her. She saw that he was indeed over-whelmed by their acceptance and even more so by their love.

When the doctor told her that she was being released in a few days, she knew it would be best if she didn't see DJ again once she left. He had to learn a lifetime about him-self, about his mother and his father, about the family he had only recently found. But he was fortunate that he had people to tell him the stories, to fill in the gaps in his life, to share memories of his father. He also had his mother, who was now part of the Colt family circle. She, too, had missed out on so much, but at least she'd gotten to watch the Colt brothers grow up.

Sadie had no idea what DJ's future held—just that he needed to sort it all out. She wanted him to have this time. They both needed it. She could admit it now. She loved DJ Diamond and always would. Which was why she couldn't say goodbye. It would hurt too bad. She also knew that he would try to get her to stay and she might if he asked. She couldn't imagine ever loving anyone as much as she did him. Her heart couldn't take a long goodbye.

On the day she was to be released, the nurse came in to tell her that she couldn't leave until a wheelchair was brought up for her. "Then please hurry," Sadie had said. "I have a plane to catch." The nurse gave her a disapproving look but turned and left.

Sadie pulled out her phone and called her godfather be-fore she could change her mind. It was a call she'd been put-ting off and was grateful when he didn't answer. She left a voice mail. "Headed home. Will see you soon."

Chapter Twenty-One

DJ told himself that he was ready to look toward the future as he hurried up to Sadie's floor at the hospital. Yesterday, he'd put Keira to rest in the cemetery next to Charley. He still couldn't help feeling as if he'd failed her even though he knew Charley would have told him that it all came down to genes.

He'd been rediscovering his own genes. He was a Colt from his dark hair to his blue eyes. The more he was around his twin and his half brothers, the more he saw himself in them. They'd taken a different path in life, but they weren't that different. The Colt brothers risked their lives at their jobs—just as they'd risked them in the rodeo. It seemed something in their blood craved adventure. They were all gamblers at heart.

Pushing open Sadie's hospital room door, he couldn't contain his excitement. He couldn't wait to tell Sadie what he had planned. He'd never bought flowers for a woman before, and he felt uncomfortable holding the large bouquet. There was so much he had to say to her, words that had been stacking up, ready to burst out of him since he'd admitted how he felt about her.

Just the thought terrified him. He'd told Sadie that he

loved her at the cabin, something he'd never said to another woman because he'd never felt love like that before her. Over the time they'd worked together they'd become more than colleagues. They'd become friends. It was no wonder that he'd fallen for her.

But she'd never taken him seriously. She thought he chased more women than he did. He'd let her believe it, a mistake, he realized some time into their relationship. From the beginning, she'd made it perfectly clear that it was hands-off. If he needed a reminder there was her godfather, who'd also warned him with the threat of violence not to fall in love with Sadie. Their arrangement had been strictly business.

Until Montana. Until they were snowed in at the cabin high in the mountains just before Christmas. Until they'd let their true feelings out.

Now, though, they had to decide about their future. He knew what he wanted, but he wasn't sure Sadie would. He knew that wouldn't be a deal breaker for him. He loved her. He'd go and do whatever she wanted. It would be hard though to leave Montana, to leave the family he'd found, especially to leave his twin. He and Ansley had bonded instantly.

As he stepped into Sadie's room, he stopped cold when he saw the stripped bed and the woman from housekeeping readying the room for the next patient. For just an instant he thought the worst.

"She…she…tell me she didn't…"

The woman looked up. "Leave? She checked out this morning."

That wasn't possible. "But she wasn't supposed to check out until this afternoon."

"She checked out early."

She'd just checked out without letting him know? "Where did she go?"

The woman shrugged. "You might ask downstairs."

He looked down at the bouquet of flowers. "That's you, Diamond, a dollar short and a day late," he whispered to himself as he turned around and left the room. Uncle Charley used to say that when he messed up. He'd really messed up this time.

Downstairs he inquired as to where Sadie Montclair had gone and found out that she had been trying to catch a flight to Florida. Without saying goodbye? Maybe something urgent had happened to her godfather. Otherwise… Otherwise, she'd gone home, back to Florida, back to the life she was born into. Their partnership over, she felt there was nothing keeping her in Montana?

He thought about their time together in the cabin. His chest felt hollowed out, his heart crushed. She'd said she loved him. Clearly, she'd changed her mind. Otherwise, why would she just leave without even saying goodbye?

It wasn't like he'd asked her to stay, he reminded himself. But how could he? He not only had little to offer her, but also he'd put her life in danger and might again if she stayed with him. Wasn't it better to let her walk away? It wasn't like he was a prize. Why would she want to marry him?

"What are you doing?"

He recognized the voice calling to him. As he came out of the hospital, he turned to see Buck Crawford on his way in. "Shouldn't you be on your honeymoon?" he asked Buck.

"Ansley postponed it until we knew that James and Sadie were going to be okay. Wasn't Sadie being released this afternoon?"

"Apparently she left early. She's gone."

"I take it you missed her. So go after her," Buck said.

DJ hesitated, feeling lost. "She apparently already made her decision about me."

Buck sighed. "I'm going to give you some unsolicited advice, brother-in-law. When you find the woman who makes you doubt everything about yourself and at the same time makes you believe you're superhuman, you hang on to her."

He shook his head. "I'm not sure she feels the same way."

"One way to find out," Buck said. "Press your luck. Love is a gamble, but when you win…" He broke into a huge grin.

As he started to go inside, DJ said, "Did Ansley send you?"

His brother-in-law just laughed. "She said it's a twin thing."

SADIE HAD PLANNED to take a taxi home, so she was surprised when her godfather picked her up at the airport.

"Is everything all right?" she had to ask as she climbed into the back of the town car beside him.

"That's what I want to know," he said. "When I heard you were flying home, I was worried."

"I'm fine. The doctor said I will have a scar but other than that…"

He took her hand. "I'm sorry."

She turned slowly to look at her godfather, frowning in confusion.

"I shouldn't have brought DJ Diamond into your life."

Sadie shook her head. "I was the one who followed him to Montana."

"When I met him, I knew he was trouble. I just thought

the two of you would be a good match. I had no idea that you would fall for him."

"I never said I—"

"You don't have to. I know you, Sadie. What I want to know now is what are you going to do about it?" She stared at him. "Don't tell me that you're going to let him get away with breaking your heart."

"It wasn't like that. I was the one who left. It's better this way."

"For whom? You look like someone kicked your dog. You've never backed down from a challenge. Why are you running now?"

Sadie shook her head, thinking about the small cozy cabin, making love in front of the fire with the snow falling outside. It had been magical—but it hadn't been real life. It was a fantasy few days in a snowstorm. To read any more into it was beyond foolish.

"Please don't insult my intelligence by trying to tell me that you aren't still in love with him."

"Even if I was, I can't believe you'd want me to marry him," she said, shocked by this conversation. "You're the one who warned me not to fall in love with him."

Her godfather shook his head. "But you did anyway and now you come back here looking like you let him steal your heart and you're afraid to go get it back. No goddaughter of mine would give up so easily."

"I'm your only goddaughter." She frowned. "Aren't I?"

He smiled, something he seldom did. "You are indeed. Does he love you?"

How did she answer that? She thought of him beside her hospital bed. She thought of the way he'd looked in her eyes, the way he'd held her, kissed her, made love to her.

But how did she know that she was any different from the other women DJ had seduced?

As if reading her mind, her godfather said, "Don't be a fool. That cowboy has been smitten with you from the start. But if you don't believe it, go back there and ask him. He'd be a fool if he wasn't and DJ Diamond is a lot of things, but he's not a fool."

"You make it sound so simple."

"Love?" He chortled a laugh. "It's the most complicated and confusing, excruciatingly painful and exasperating emotion there is. But it's what makes life worthwhile. Stop being a coward and find out how that man feels about you. How can it be any worse than the way you're feeling right now?"

"Want to tell me about the woman who broke *your* heart?" she asked.

"No, I don't," he snapped. "And Sadie? Take the private jet, if you want. And if he says he doesn't love you, shoot him. I have people who will take care of the body."

"I wish you were joking," she said, but had to smile. "Thank you."

DJ COULDN'T BELIEVE it when he got the text from Sadie.

I'm sorry I left the way I did. I love you. If you can forgive me, I'll be flying into Yellowstone International Airport tomorrow afternoon at 4. I'll be the one wearing the red cowboy boots.

He read the text twice. He'd really thought that he'd never hear from her again. He'd been telling himself that he had to let her go. A part of him believed that she loved him, but maybe love couldn't conquer all—no matter what his twin said. His heart had been breaking since finding her gone. Now he was almost afraid to trust she'd be back again.

Except this was Sadie. This was the woman he loved. He'd had to let her go even though he'd been planning to go after her. He read the message again—just in case he'd misread it.

He smiled and tried to still his pounding heart before he responded with his own. I'll be wearing my hat.

Then he headed for the airline ticket counter to cancel his flight to Florida that was leaving in an hour. Sadie loved him. His smile was so big it hurt his face. Sadie loved him. Love had brought her back. Just as love had him wearing his lucky boots as he planned to fly to Florida and try to get her back.

Okay, maybe Ansley was right. Maybe love could bring two very different people together. Just as it had brought him to this family of his. He pulled out his phone. He couldn't wait to tell his twin.

"Didn't I tell you that nothing can stop true love?" Ansley cried. "You two were meant for each other. It is high time you told her what's in your heart. But first here's what we need to do."

SADIE WORE HER red cowboy boots. The first time she met DJ, he'd been wearing a pair of worn cowboy boots. She'd commented on them, suggesting he buy a new pair.

He'd laughed. "Sorry, sweetie, but these are my lucky boots."

"Call me sweetie again and not even your lucky boots can save you."

She could laugh about it now. Especially since she was

wearing her boots because she needed all the luck she could get as she got off the plane.

"He needs time with you and the rest of his family," she'd told Ansley when she'd called.

"He needs you. He loves you and you love him. That makes you family. You need to come back. He's hurting."

"So am I."

"Do you love him?"

"I do." Her voice had cracked. "I just don't know where we go next."

Ansley had laughed. "You think there's a road map? It's a leap of faith. None of us can see the future. We just have to believe that something amazing is ahead and enjoy each day. DJ told me you were an optimist."

"He did, did he?"

"All he talks about is you," Ansley said. "He wants to make a life with you. He has a plan."

She'd laughed. She was familiar with his plans. "A plan?"

"He'll tell you all about it when he sees you. He isn't going to let you go. My brother is no fool, even though sometimes he acts like one." They'd laughed. "Tell me you'll give him a chance. You know he loves you."

She did know, she thought as she looked around for DJ in the crowd at the Yellowstone International Airport. She spotted him standing against a nearby wall, his Stetson cocked on his dark hair, those blue eyes taking her in as if she was a cold drink of water in the desert. He pushed off the wall and headed toward her as she descended the stairs.

The way she'd left without saying goodbye and having been gone for a couple of days, she thought they'd be awkward with each other. That they no longer had anything to say. That they would realize not even love could sustain this relationship.

She watched him approach, her pulse hammering.

"Sadie." That one word filled her heart like helium. DJ looped his arm around her waist and picked her up before she reached the bottom step. He swung her around, taking her in his arms as he put her down. For a moment, he just looked at her, then he kissed her passionately.

She heard cheers and clapping, but they were a distant sound. Her heart was beating too loudly in her ears as DJ drew back.

"I love you, Sadie Montclair. Marry me." He dropped to one knee. "Love your boots, by the way," he whispered, then said, "Be my wife, be my partner, be mine."

She smiled. She knew this man. This wasn't such a leap of faith. Yet she couldn't speak as she looked into his eyes. All she could do was nod and fall into his arms as he rose. There were more cheers and clapping than before as some of the crowd joined in along with the entire Colt and Crawford clan.

All she could think was that from now on these would be her lucky boots as she was swept up in this large, gregarious, loving family.

Did it matter what the future held? Not as long as she and DJ faced it together. She was putting her money on the two of them. It wasn't a safe bet, but she was ready to play the odds.

Chapter Twenty-Two

It was their first Christmas holiday together. Also their first with DJ's family. Sadie had never seen anything like it and she could tell that DJ was just as overcome by it all. The Colts had a variety of holiday traditions—including all getting together at Bella and Tommy's because they had the largest space. There was a mountain of food and holiday treats, games and prizes, and more presents than she'd ever seen.

Because of everything that had happened, even the holiday had been put off until they could all be together.

"Ansley," Buck cried as he finished bringing in all the presents his new bride had purchased.

"I might have gone a little overboard," she admitted. "But it's our first Christmas, the first with my family, the first with my twin."

Buck smiled and raised his hands in surrender. "Given all that, I'm surprised you exhibited such self-control."

Sadie and DJ had gone shopping even though everyone told them it wasn't necessary. "The two of you are our presents," Ansley had said, and the others had agreed.

"It's just because you don't know us very well," DJ had joked. "By next year, you'll feel entirely different."

Still, they'd shopped together. It had been fun. Even DJ had enjoyed it. Sadie could tell that he'd never had anyone to buy for, other than Keira, and they'd never celebrated holidays together.

They went to Bozeman, hitting all the shops, and then had lunch in a quaint place along Main Street.

This large, exuberant family was something so new for them both that they grew quiet after they ate. Sadie thought that it was all just starting to sink in. When DJ spoke, she knew he'd been thinking the same thing.

"Can we do this?" he asked, meeting her gaze.

She didn't have to ask what he meant. The two of them, she felt, were solid together because they knew each other given everything they'd been through. "We can do anything we set our minds to."

"Are you sure we aren't too broken?" DJ asked.

Sadie chuckled. "Isn't everyone in one way or another?"

He shook his head. "What worries me is that I really like them. I don't want to let them down. Especially Ansley."

"You won't." She reached across the table to take his hand. "We have the rest of our lives yet to live. Our pasts are…unique, but they have also made us stronger. We're survivors. We can do this."

He smiled then, squeezing her hand, and she let go. "I've never asked you what you wanted out of life."

"To be like everyone else." She said it quickly and shrugged. "Promise you won't laugh?" He nodded solemnly and crossed his chest above his heart with his finger. "I want a family. I want what the Colt women have."

"To be married to private eyes?"

She shook her head. "They have a sense of community I've never had. They're all excited about their kids growing up together. Bella is convinced the kids will rule the school. I have no doubt hers will." She laughed. "I want Montana." She saw his surprised expression.

"I never thought you'd leave Florida."

"I want to see spring here," she said, glancing toward the restaurant window. Christmas decorations hung from the streetlights. Snow was piled up along the edge of the street. Everyone outside was bundled up against the cold. "I want to see the grass turn green, to feel the sun bring back life. I want to grow a garden and catch a fish out of the river." Her voice broke. "I want an ordinary house with a swing set in my backyard and a couple of kids out there playing on it."

He laughed. "You want a lot," he joked. "Just a couple of kids?"

"I'd discuss more," she said with a grin.

DJ turned serious. "You haven't mentioned this husband of yours."

She smiled. "I want him to be anything he wants. Lover, father, best friend. You want to raise cattle to go with that Stetson of yours, I'm all for it."

His eyes seemed to light up. "My brothers want to make the Colt Ranch a true ranch. There's plenty of land and they've offered me a section for our house. I have money to buy whatever we'll need."

"You know I have my own money, so we can pretty much do anything we want." She met his gaze, her heart in her throat. Was it possible? Could they do this? "Wouldn't you miss the grift?"

"Sounds like raising cattle might be enough of a gamble."

"I'm serious. You love what you do."

"I used to, but I've lost my taste for it. I'm like you. I look around Lonesome and I feel the need to put down roots. I want a swing set in my backyard. I want a couple of blond towheads out there who look just like you but are trying to see how much higher they can swing. You do realize that if you and I had kids they'd get some of my genes."

She smiled. "Would that be so bad? I happen to love your jeans. Especially the way they fit you."

He locked eyes with her. "We could do this, you and me. We could make a good life here in Montana. You'd have to learn to ride a horse."

"You know how to ride? You never told me that."

"I was raised on a ranch."

"Charley had a horse?"

"A couple of wild ones that Keira and I used to try to ride." At the mention of Keira a shadow crossed his face for a moment. "Our kids will have horses. Apparently rodeoing is in my blood."

"So I've heard. Let's cross that bridge when we get to it," she said. "But I'd love to have a horse of my own. Bella rides all the time. I know she'd teach me."

He nodded. "I can see us here."

"Me, too." She felt her smile widen. "I love you, DJ. I have for a very long time. You do realize that my godfather will want to give me away."

"Yes, your godfather. You sure he's good with this, you and me?"

She nodded. "He gave me his blessing." She didn't mention what else he'd said as DJ leaned across the table to steal a quick kiss.

They both grinned. They'd found not only their way to each other, but to a family and a place to make a home and a life neither of them had ever expected.

They could do this. Together. Partners forever.

JUST BEFORE MIDNIGHT on New Year's Eve, Sheriff Willie Colt stood, raising his glass as he looked around the table. As the oldest of the Colt brothers and prodded by his wife Ellie, it was up to him to speak before they rang in the new year. Bella and Tommy had thrown quite the party as usual. The whole family was here, and it had grown considerably since last year.

"It's been quite the year, wouldn't you say?" Everyone laughed.

"What a couple years this has been," Willie said as he looked around the huge table. "When James got hurt on his last bronc ride and came home, we all expected him to do what we usually did, heal up and go back. But instead he started digging into Dad's last case, the one he'd never solved before his death. We couldn't have known where that was going to lead."

There were murmurs around the table. "James gave up rodeoing to reopen Dad's private investigative business. It was the beginning of Colt Brothers Investigation. Tommy was lured back and then Davy. I was determined not to join this ragtag bunch," he said, and laughed.

"Instead, I joined the sheriff's department as a deputy to find out what had really happened to Dad that night when he was killed on the railroad tracks. I ended up finding something that I loved more than rodeo, law enforcement, and that led me to Seattle, and we all know how that ended."

More laughter around the table.

"We got Ellie," Bella said, and the other women all joined in with cheers. "Turned out to be a great deal."

"It wasn't like we ever expected you to fall in love, let alone get married," James said.

"We figured you would be Lonesome's old cranky bachelor," Tommy said.

"He's still cranky," someone said.

Willie waited until the laughter died down. "The four of us are now married, some of us fathers. There's been a few surprises along the way." He looked in the direction of Ansley and DJ and smiled. "Happy surprises," he added. He watched Ansley hug her brother and Sadie, tears in her eyes.

"We hadn't wanted to believe Dad's pickup being hit by the train was an accident. We now know it was. Also, we learned a lot about our mother, who was a mystery to us all." He glanced down the table at Beth. "I know Dad loved our mother, Mary Jo, but I also know that she made his life very hard. He found true love the second time with Beth, Ansley and DJ's mother. Sometimes we don't get the happy endings we want, but in the end we're so thankful for family. I wish Dad were here to see this. I like to think he'd be proud. I know I am at what you've all accomplished."

He cleared his voice. "Now we're about to start another year and I for one can't wait to see what this amazing family has in store for it." A cheer went up. He looked over at his wife. Ellie was glowing.

"Are you kidding me?" Bella cried. "Ellie?"

Her sister-in-law smiled and nodded. "There is a little Willie in the works." That brought on more cheering along with groans from some of the brothers and remarks like, "Never thought you had it in you, bro."

"It's almost time," someone called out, and everyone looked to the clock on the wall. They rose from the table as the countdown began. "Ten, nine, eight, seven..." The joy in the room rose as their voices joined to ring in the new year.

"Six, five, four, three, two... Happy New Year!"

Willie took Ellie in his arms and kissed her. All around him he watched his brothers and their wives and girlfriends kiss and hug. Noisemakers came out and confetti filled the air along with balloons. Bella never did anything halfway, he thought. This year she had a lot of help from the family since she had a new baby girl.

Willie laughed, hoping his father was watching all of this. This was the family he'd started. Willie hoped he'd be proud.

Epilogue

Ansley felt as if her feet weren't touching the ground as she looked out past the American flag flapping in the backyard breeze to her husband standing with the Colt men by the barbecue grill. Her husband. She would never get tired of staying that.

"You have been smiling way too much for a woman about to turn thirty," Bella said as she put her daughter down in the playpen in the shade. Daisy immediately began cooing and waving her arms at the bird mobile hanging over her head. Her twin boy cousins were in another playpen, also in the shade. Both were sacked out. Their older sister, Jamie, was playing in the kiddie pool not far from where the men were grilling lunch.

"Isn't it wonderful to have so much family?" Ansley said, knowing that Bella had also been an only child. So had Lori and Carla and Ellie. Probably why all of them wanted numerous children. "Just think, Daisy will grow up with all these cousins. Won't that be fun?" Carla and Ellie were both pregnant. When Ansley had gone looking for her birth mother she could never have imagined finding this much family.

"Don't try to change the subject." Bella looked down

to where Tommy was standing. As if feeling her gaze on him, he looked up and smiled. She smiled back and glanced down at their daughter. Ansley knew Bella had to be thinking about how close she'd almost come to losing him the day their baby was born.

"What's going on with you?" Bella said. "I can tell you're holding out on me."

Ansley smiled as she saw her twin standing with the other men. Just the sight of DJ brought her such joy. She'd been so afraid that they would never find him and when Buck had, she'd been so afraid that she would lose them both. When he'd walked in before her wedding...

Tears filled her eyes at the memory. She made a swipe at them, embarrassed at how emotional she'd been lately. "I'm happy, that's all," she said. "I love my life and you're a part of that."

Bella made a rude sound. "Okay, fine. Just keep it to yourself, but I have to tell you, you should never play poker. Your face gives everything away."

She laughed as she scanned Bella's backyard. Soon she would have a backyard of her own. Her brothers and Buck's father and brother had been helping with the new houses being built on the Colt Ranch for her and Buck—and for DJ and Sadie. She couldn't wait until theirs was finished.

Past the men at the barbecue grill, Lori and Ellie were uncovering the salads and desserts on the table under the umbrella. Sadie was busy putting serving spoons in everything. Ansley could tell they were laughing and was amazed how Sadie had become one of them so quickly. Having all of these women come into her life was a joy she'd never anticipated when she'd come looking for her birth mother.

Speaking of her birth mother, where was she? Running

late probably, because she was working even on a holiday. Being the mayor of Lonesome was a full-time job, one Beth took seriously—just as she did motherhood. She was going to make a wonderful grandmother. Ansley started to go help with the other women when Bella stopped her.

"Ansley!" Bella demanded. "No one is this excited for her thirtieth birthday, not even you."

She couldn't help but smile. Her happiness just seemed to overflow these days. "It's my birthday! Mine and DJ's. It also just happens to be the Fourth of July." They were also celebrating Davy's birthday as well since his was only a few days ago.

Bella was giving her a side-eye when suddenly her eyes widened. "Oh, you are not." She was laughing and smiling. "Does Buck know yet?"

"No, and don't you dare tell him. I want to surprise him tonight during the fireworks show."

Her friend's eyes filled with tears. "I am so happy for you. So happy for all of us. I never imagined that our children would be raised together on this ranch. We're all going to get sick of each other," she joked.

She pulled her into a hug. "I'm so glad you came into our lives and brought DJ and Sadie. You know they'll be getting married soon. I love weddings. Can you imagine what it is going to be like when all of our kids go to school?" Bella asked as she looked down at her daughter, who'd fallen asleep. "The Colt kids will rule the school. Along with the Crawfords and Diamonds, of course. The teachers won't know what hit them."

Ansley saw Buck look up at her. Their gazes met and she realized that he knew. He gave her a wide grin. So much for waiting until the fireworks. They'd already had their fireworks and now they were going to have a baby.

DJ PULLED SADIE ASIDE. "It's not too late. You can change your mind about marrying me." He waved a hand, taking in all the family gathered today. "I suspect it will always be like this."

"I certainly hope so," she said, stepping into his arms. "Happy birthday." She kissed him and let him lead her into the cool of the pines and out of sight of the others.

He held her at arm's length as he studied her. "I wouldn't be here if it wasn't for you. I almost lost you because of it."

She shook her head. "We *are* here now. Together. There is no looking back anymore. You changed my life...don't you realize that?"

DJ smiled. "How did I ever get so lucky?"

"I guess you played to your strengths."

"Whatever the reason, thank you for being my partner. I'm sure you had your doubts when your godfather suggested we work together."

Sadie laughed. "It was when I met you that I really had my doubts. What was I supposed to do with this arrogant Montana cowboy?"

"Save him from himself," DJ said, and pulled her closer for another kiss.

"Do you think we could sneak away during the fireworks show?" he asked.

"You're incorrigible," she said with a laugh.

"I just can't seem to get enough of you." He kissed her and drew back. "Okay, we should go back to the barbecue. Everyone will be talking about us."

"Everyone is already talking about us. They wonder what a man like you is doing with a woman like me."

He drew her close again so that their bodies were molded together. "I hope you told them."

Laughing she pulled away. "I love your family."

"*Our* family. They are pretty fantastic, aren't they? Ansley is nothing short of amazing. Do you know that she started her own jewelry business without the help of her rich family? Talk about determination."

Sadie nodded, smiling. "She's a lot like her twin. She just wouldn't give up hope that Buck would find you and bring you to the wedding."

"Thanks to you I made it. I wish you could have been there."

"All that matters is that you made it and just in time."

"You know me, I like to call things close to the wire," DJ said.

"Yes, I do know that about you."

He met her gaze. "I'll be early to our wedding. Are you sure you want to be the wife of a rancher? Us living on the Colt Ranch. Me, raising cattle."

"After all those years of being all hat and no cattle?" she joked. "I suspect you were born to ranching. You love a gamble."

He grinned. "You know me so well."

"Don't I, though," she said as he put his arm around her waist and led her back toward the barbecue and their new family.

"Your godfather still coming to our wedding this spring?" he asked, sounding a little worried.

"He's going to give me away. He said he wouldn't miss it for anything. He wants to ride a horse while he's in Montana and eat steak, he said."

"So he isn't coming just to make sure I'm good enough for his goddaughter?"

She smiled over at her fiancé. "Oh, he's definitely doing that. But I wouldn't worry too much if I were you. He's the one who brought us together, so he only has himself to blame for the way it turned out."

DJ pulled her closer. "Thanks, I feel so much better." He grinned. "Have I told you how much I love you and that I can't wait to marry you?"

"I believe you have mentioned it." She matched his grin.

"You did save me, you know," he said quietly. "The odds were against you and me, and yet you bet on me."

She cupped his handsome face in her hands. "I'd bet on you any day, DJ Diamond. I love you and I always will."

They heard their family calling to them. The barbecued ribs were ready.

"Hungry?" DJ asked.

"Starved," she said. He put his arm around her, and they headed back toward the Fourth of July picnic birthday party. "Ansley asked me what your favorite cake was. When I wouldn't tell her, she said, 'Fine. Lori will make my favorite then.' Wanna guess what it is?"

"Chocolate?" DJ asked with a grin.

"Chocolate."

"Did she mention that we are twins?" he joked as they joined the party. "You are aware that twins run in my family, right?"

"How else can we keep up with all these Colts otherwise?" Sadie said, and laughed. She couldn't wait to have babies with this cowboy. "In fact, I was thinking. After the party... I mean, it is your *birthday*."

* * * * *

TROUBLE IN TEXAS

BARB HAN

All my love to Brandon, Jacob and Tori, who are the great loves of my life. To Samantha for the bright shining light that you are.

To Babe, my hero, for being my best friend, greatest love and my place to call home. I love you with everything that I am. Always and forever.

To Shaq and Kobi, the best writing buddies ever.

Chapter One

Even the slightest movement caused Reese Hayes's muscles to scream as she tried to rally herself awake and sit up. The sound of muffled voices penetrated the darkness. Did she know one of them? A sense of familiarity was followed by bone-penetrating terror. She had a headache so fierce she feared her brain might splinter.

Questions were hammering against the backs of her eyes. What happened? Where was she? Who was there?

The feeling of icy fingers wrapping around her brain made it next to impossible to think. A fog thicker than a San Francisco morning felt like a weighted blanket, pinning her to a hard, cold concrete floor. Groggy, Reese couldn't recall the events that had gotten her here...wherever *here* was.

Trying to move at all was as productive as spitting on a lawn and expecting the grass to stay green over a long summer with no sprinkler. The tight grip of claustrophobia seized the air in her lungs. Understanding the gravity of the situation, Reese mentally pushed aside her panic. She needed to focus—not on the fact that she was in a blacked-out room lying on a hard surface, unable to move without head-piercing pain, but she needed to mentally lock on to something she could control and hold onto for dear life.

Reese concentrated on her breathing. She listened to the voices, trying to make out whom they belonged to or, at the very least, get some information as to why she was there. Any hint of where she was would be welcomed, because she had no clue. She felt like an out-of-focus camera lens trying to zoom in on a target while multiple things were going on. The only thing she remembered was that she'd been outdoors and there'd been some kind of red building in the background, which made no sense under her current conditions. A staticky sound, like when Granny fell asleep without turning off the TV years ago, caused her muscles to tense.

Breathe. The idea was so much easier than the execution. She winced as she tried to feel around and gain her bearings. The voices became more distant until they almost faded completely. She listened for other sounds—a vehicle engine, the sound of water, anything. The wind whipped outside and when she really concentrated, she could hear rain droplets tapping against a windowpane. Good to know there could be an escape route nearby. She tried her best to ignore the nausea that was causing bile to burn the back of her throat. There was nothing she could do about that now.

For a split second, she prayed this wasn't happening, that this was a nightmare. But the pain confirmed that it was very much real.

Survival instincts kicked in. Adrenaline pumped through her veins. She attempted to roll onto her back.

Not much happened. The reason suddenly dawned on her. Her hands were tied behind her. Now that the shroud was lifting, she could feel her body better. Her eyes were adjusting to the darkness, too. And her senses were sharpening.

She tried to kick and immediately noted that her ankles

were bound together. Was there something around that she could use to free her hands?

Squirming, she went headfirst into a wall. So much for ignoring her headache. Undeterred, she tried to feel around but there was nothing except for air behind her.

She heard the whisper of a male voice. He was close.

Reese strained to listen. She couldn't make out his words. There was nothing familiar about him. Was he the mastermind behind her kidnapping or just a willing accomplice?

What was the motive?

She had no real money to speak of other than a small amount that she'd saved up after working for the past ten years. She didn't own the kind of business that would warrant an abduction for extortion or revenge purposes. She didn't work in law enforcement. Her job in the Dallas fashion industry, which she'd started straight out of high school, wouldn't cause anyone to tie her up and leave her in an abandoned building.

Were there others here besides her? She was afraid to speak. Wouldn't she have heard something by now if there were others in here? There would have been breathing, or the sound of someone trying to move. Right?

The idea of being alone sent a cold chill racing up her back. She'd been a target. At twenty-eight years old, would she be too old for human trafficking? Since this couldn't be work-related and she had no idea what she'd been doing when the abduction had taken place, her thoughts snapped to things she'd read about. No one would take her for ransom. Hold on a minute, she might not personally have enough money to garner attention, but her family did. She was a Hayes and her grandfather, who'd been the patriarch of the family for as long as she could remember, had recently passed away.

Reese had been asked to come home to Cider Creek to discuss the ranch. Had she recently inherited boatloads of money? That would certainly draw attention.

Wouldn't she be the first to know? Or was someone hedging a bet? While her mother was still alive, Reese highly doubted she was about to inherit the ranch. Sometime down the line, she would most likely be given a piece of the family legacy along with her siblings. She had no idea how well the place was doing. She'd left right after high school, just like her brothers and sister. Since their grandfather ran a tight ship and had built the business from scratch, she assumed all was well.

At this point, she guessed this could have to do with a possible inheritance she had yet to learn about, or it came down to being a random occurrence. One might keep her alive. The other could make her dispensable if she created too much of a problem.

At least she was beginning to get some of her wits back. This was good. She could come up with a plan to get herself out of here and to safety. She had no idea where her purse might be, so that was an issue. She always carried two cell phones with her. One for A-list work clients and another for people like suppliers when she was helping put together an event. Those were B-level calls. Her A-list cell phone included VIPs in the industry, fashion magazine editors, top-level models who were hard to book, etcetera.

Most of the time, she had a cell glued to her palm. Where had hers gone? Because her A-list cell kept an almost constant buzz going. Even with an assistant, Reese had to handle the most important clients herself. She did well for herself but she was by no means a millionaire.

Why was it that she could remember what she did for a living, her family and the fact she had two cell phones, but couldn't for the life of her remember what she'd been doing to end up in a place like this? Trauma?

Reese might have been from the small town of Cider Creek originally, but she'd been living and working in downtown Dallas long enough to take necessary precautions. Safety measures that included locking doors and arming the alarm in her apartment every night. She knew better than to walk alone in an empty parking lot day or night, and had read enough warnings to remember that most abductions happened during the day. She was aware of her surroundings whenever she went out.

The sounds of some kind of commotion broke into her thoughts. A chair scraped across the concrete against the backdrop of mumbled curses and hurried footsteps.

A shot rang out before an engine roared and then tires spit gravel. Suddenly, one set of heavy footsteps filled the space. It was decision time. Reese could yell for help or stay quiet.

"Hello?" The familiar male voice and blast from the past sent momentary shock reverberating through her.

Darren Pierce?

"HELP ME. PLEASE."

Three words were all it took for time to warp and Darren Pierce to be transported back to the last day of high school. What the hell was Reese Hayes doing here? Even after all these years, he would recognize that voice. The desperation cut straight through his question—and his heart—as he made a beeline toward her.

The jerks who'd been squatting on his property had run off fast. But how had she gotten here?

Before his brain had time to come up with a response, he opened the door to a shed inside the old equipment building that he probably should have torn down years ago. The shutters had been closed and too little light came in from the building. The electricity had been knocked out in the last storm. He flipped on the flashlight app as Reese said his name. He flashed the light against the back wall and saw her. The second his gaze caught hers, all those old feelings surged, along with a threat to derail common sense. She'd walked out on *their* future, not just her family and the town. But, right now, she was in danger and he couldn't hold the past against her. Besides, if life had turned out differently, he never would have had the twins. Those girls were everything to him.

Darren closed the distance between them in two strides. He took a knee and ran the light the length of her body.

"Where does it hurt?" he asked.

"The back of my head feels like someone tried to drive a nail in it," she said in the voice that used to bathe him in warmth and light a dozen fires inside his chest. Now? He shoved aside those thoughts as he took stock of the situation. Her hands were behind her back. Her ankles were bound. The kind of anger that he might have acted on as a teenager if someone set him off pushed to the surface.

Darren immediately began ripping the electrical tape to free her hands. He moved to her feet next and freed them in a matter of seconds. Even in this light, she was still beautiful. Reese had a thick mane of dark-roast hair and espresso-colored eyes to match. Olive skin didn't hide the flush to her cheeks when she smiled or got nervous. He remembered the way her face flushed a second before their first kiss in the biology lab, when they'd been forced to stay after to help clean up. The teacher disappeared down the hallway and a moment had happened between them that had replayed in his thoughts far too often over the years.

As far as kisses had gone, theirs might have been innocent. Not much more than her cherry lips pressed against his own. But the effect had been a lasting imprint and the kiss he'd compared all others to. Then again, his first would always hold a special place in his heart. He'd written it off as to be expected, rather than go down the route of being irreplaceable.

The minute she could sit up, she wrapped her arms around his neck and held tight. "Thank you."

"No need for thanks," he reassured her. She didn't need to feel indebted to him. He did, however, have a growing list of questions. Her body was trembling—from fear, he expected, causing more anger to surface. Right now, he needed to get her out of there. "Can you walk?"

"I think so," she said as he lifted her to standing. Her knees almost immediately buckled. He steadied her, looping his arm around her. "Guess that's not as easy as I thought it was going to be."

"My horse isn't far," he said. He needed to get her out of this building, since he had no idea if those jerks were coming back or if they would bring friends. He'd spooked them away. His initial thought had been poachers. He ran into them from time to time on his small property. Growing up on a cattle ranch, he knew what to look for.

There'd been something different about this group, though.

"I might not be able to make it on my own," she said,

flexing and releasing her fingers a few times, as if she was trying to bring back the blood.

"I already called the law to investigate, but I can't risk sticking around. We need to go. I can carry you," he said. "I'll give you my weapon in case they come back. You keep watch and buy us some time if anyone surprises us." Normally, he would be fine with sticking around for a fight, but the crown of her head was caked with blood. He wouldn't have moved her at all if there was a way around it.

She nodded.

He handed over his Colt .45, then scooped her up in his arms, ignoring the electrical currents that vibrated in his body. He chalked up the feeling to muscle memory as he bolted toward the door.

"Do you know what day it is?" he asked as he exited the old equipment building. He'd moved the shed inside to keep it out of the elements while he figured out what to do with both.

"Monday," she said with a whole lot of uncertainty in her voice. "Is that right?"

"Yes," he confirmed. At least she had the day of the week right. She knew his name, too, so that was another good sign she might not have a concussion. "What about the month?"

"December," she said, sounding a little more confident this time.

"Right again," he said. There was a good chance she would be okay. He would still call in the doctor. "Do you know the people who ran off?"

"No," she said hesitantly.

"Any idea what that was about?" he asked as he approached the tree line, where he'd left Blaze, his mare.

"I have no clue," she said as she watched their backs while

he sprinted through the woods toward his horse. Working on a horse ranch kept him fit. Plus, there were the extra workouts, which had to be temporarily suspended while he had the twins. He needed to be in shape to chase after those little angels.

"We'll figure it out," he said, glancing at her and seeing the physical pain that her trying to answer seemed to create. Her face twisted. Even in pain, she was more beautiful than he remembered.

But he also recalled how she'd stomped on his heart and never looked back, so he intended to keep his guard up.

Chapter Two

Wrapped in arms like bands of steel, Reese surveyed the trees for fear one of the jerks who'd abducted her—and abduction was all she could think about at this point—would come back. No doubt, the bastards would be prepared for Darren this time.

Gratitude sprang to her eyes in the form of tears as he zigzagged through the trees and toward safety.

"This is Blaze," he said as they approached a beautiful ginger mare. Tied to a tree trunk, she stood tall and threw her head high in the air, as though nodding, when they reached her. "She's a good girl."

"She's stunning," Reese said as he hoisted her onto the saddle.

He mumbled a thank-you as she kept watch, looking for any movement other than branches being nudged around by the wind while he took up the reins. The rain had stopped, and lucky for them had not saturated the ground, which would make getting away on horseback faster.

Ignoring the thunder in between her temples, she sucked in a breath when Darren's arms closed around her from behind. Awareness skittered across her skin as he held tight to her, his chest against her back as he squeezed his thighs around Blaze, telling her to go.

She couldn't count how many times they'd ridden his horse Peanut, or how much teasing he'd endured for the name. It didn't matter that Darren had named the paint horse when he was ten. Peanut was stuck with the name, and so was Darren.

One hand wrapped around the saddle horn and the other holding the weapon, Reese kept her eyes on the trees. Since it was December, there were no leaves to hide behind in this area. The clouds shielded their eyes from the sun, but other than it obviously being daytime, she had no clue what time it was.

Had this been about robbery?

Her missing purse indicated that was a possibility, but did robbers kidnap people and stick around after getting their bounty? Maybe her purse was somewhere back in the old building. They'd gotten out of there so fast, she didn't think to search the place. Wouldn't a robber have knocked her on the head, stolen her handbag and hurried away? Instead, she was taken to a specific place, where several men had stuck around. There'd been no female voices, as best as she could recall. And then, somehow, Darren Pierce had arrived.

To spare herself the agony that thinking was causing, she pushed aside her thoughts. Besides, Blaze's canter was enough to scramble her brain.

Seeing him again reminded her of everything she'd had to give up to get out of Cider Creek. At eighteen, she hadn't realized how long the nights were about to become, or how lonely living by herself might be. Darren's uncle had offered her a chance to leave her life behind. Young and naive, she'd jumped at the opportunity to get away from her grandfather.

He'd helped her with the transition and the two had become involved romantically, much to her later regret.

Darren stopped in front of a small, tidy barn big enough for a pair of horses, and then helped her down. Standing there, for a split second it was almost like she had gone back in time, and was in his family's barn, looking into those serious eyes. His irises were the most incredible shade of brown, surrounded by clear white rivers, framed by thick, almost black eyelashes. His curly hair was always in need of a haircut, his face was almost too hard, and there had been just enough scruff on his face to give her goose bumps when his skin had come in contact with hers as he feathered kisses on the nape of her neck.

Reese shoved away that unproductive memory. It had her wanting to grab a handful of shirt and tug until his lips met hers. She missed the way he looked at her when they used to stand this close. It was gone now, which was a good reminder they were no longer a couple. She'd shut that down when she took off, too young to realize the tug at her heart when she thought about him would last a decade.

Coincidence might have brought them together again, but the reunion was temporary at best. She needed to assess the damage and then figure out how to get home to Dallas. Cider Creek, actually, she corrected herself.

"How are your legs now?" Darren asked.

"I think I can manage with a little help," she said.

Darren nodded, then removed Blaze's tack and ushered her into a stall where there was hay and water waiting. When he turned around to wrap an arm around her, his face twisted, as if touching her brought on physical pain. Since this didn't seem like the right time to apologize for leaving town and then dating his uncle, she kept her lips closed. She knew Darren. He would never forget what happened or forgive her despite her reasons.

The house was log-cabin style but modern. Everything seemed new, from the pine beams to the granite countertops. The living room and kitchen were open-concept and the place had Darren's warm and comfortable feel to the decor.

Two steps in and she took note of two walkers, the kind for babies to run around in. There was a pair of pink swings off to one side around the granite island.

Was Darren married with kids?

"I'm sorry to intrude," Reese said to him. "I'll arrange transportation. I'm sure your family needs you."

"The twins are with their grandma and law enforcement will have questions for you," he said to her. She immediately screwed up her face, because his mother had passed away when they were teenagers from a rare and aggressive cancer.

"Your in-laws," she said as he helped her to the brown leather couch. There was a flat-screen TV on top of the fireplace mantel.

"Something like that," he mumbled so low she could barely hear. He didn't look like he wanted to explain, so she left the subject alone. Instead, she glanced at his ring finger and was surprised when there was no band or tan line.

Shelving those details under the heading "no longer her business," she eased onto the soft leather.

"What can I get you? Water? A pillow? A blanket?" he asked, then checked his phone. "The law just arrived to the site."

"Do you mind asking them to look for my purse?" she asked. "I take it everywhere with me. And my phones. I'm lost without them." The work messages might be stacking up despite her competent assistant stepping up to cover.

"Is there someone you can call? Someone who can handle work for a few hours?" he asked, holding out his cell.

"I have someone, who I hope will be fine. But, seriously, who remembers anyone's number anymore?" she asked, a little embarrassed that she couldn't remember the number to her right-hand person.

"We can do an online search later," he suggested.

"Right," she said, blinking a couple of times, as though the movement could help with her nausea. Those systems weren't even connected. "You asked if I needed anything. Water would be nice." Her mouth was as dry as the year she licked a hundred stamps for Christmas cards. She'd feared her tongue might stick to the roof of her mouth for the rest of her life.

He went to the kitchen and brought her back a glass of water. In a flash, she saw the same hungry look in his eyes from years ago.

Or maybe it wasn't there at all. It was possible she saw what she wanted instead of what was there.

DARREN CHIDED HIMSELF for letting his gaze linger a few seconds longer on Reese's delicate features. There was something decidedly fragile about her right now that brought out his protective instincts. All he could say in his defense was that he must be a glutton for punishment.

"I'll call the doctor," he said as he walked back to the kitchen. Distance was good. It helped him stay focused. He made the call to Dr. Stacie and got her voice mail. Darren had barely hit the end button on his cell when it rang. It was the good doctor herself.

"Everything okay with the babies?" Stacie Larson asked,

sounding panicked. To be fair, his call had come out of the blue.

"The girls are fine," he quickly reassured her. "I have a friend who was hit in the head before possibly being robbed. Think you can swing by? It's after hours and the nearest hospital is—"

"Far," Stacie said. "I know."

"Do you mind doing me this favor?" he asked, figuring it would be easier not to move Reese again now that he had her on the couch. Plus, Stacie moved four miles away from him to help with the twins.

"Your house?" Stacie said after a heavy silence. He had no idea what the sudden attitude shift was about. Or did he? She was aunt to his twins and overprotective.

"Yes," he confirmed. "It's important to me or you know that I wouldn't ask."

Stacie let out a sharp breath.

"I'll leave now," she agreed before ending the call without warning.

He turned to Reese, who'd made herself comfortable on the couch, and said, "Help is on the way."

"Are you sure bringing a doctor here is a good idea?" she asked.

"The law will want to stop by and question you after checking out the equipment building," he explained as he retrieved a glass of water for himself.

"Can they do that at the hospital?" she asked.

"I guess so," he said. "Why? Are you uncomfortable here?"

"This is your family home," she said. "I feel like I'm intruding."

"You're not," he said, realizing he might not be rolling

out the red carpet, but he didn't want to throw her out, either. He wasn't built that way. If someone needed a hand up, he couldn't turn his back. Call it the cowboy way, but it was ingrained in him. "I want you to stay."

"Won't your wife have an issue with me being here?" she asked. The question was fair given their history, he supposed.

"If you're talking about heightened teenage hormones making us feel in love, that happened a long time ago," he clarified. "We're grown adults now, I have children and no residual feelings toward you." The lie about his feelings tasted sour on his tongue now that he heard the words out loud. For a split second, he'd convinced himself that he actually believed it. Correcting it now didn't seem like the right play. He fell back on defense, realizing he couldn't leave it like that. "Which means that I'd like to help and no one will question me about it."

Half a dozen emotions played out across her features before she settled on the one that he never could quite read. All those years ago, he'd known she was holding something back. All this time later, she didn't seem any closer to letting him in on the secret.

"I appreciate your kindness, Darren," she said. Hearing his name roll off her tongue wasn't helping with those old unresolved feelings that were trying to surface. Reese had sent him a text to let him know she was leaving town and taking a job with his uncle. She'd said the two of them should take a break and figure out who they were without each other. The next news he heard was the two started dating. Talk about gutting an eighteen-year-old. He would have warned her about the man, but it would have come off as jealousy and his hurt pride wouldn't allow him to contact her once she blew him off. He'd licked those wounds for a solid year.

Darren told himself forgetting the hell he went through because of her would be a bad idea. Keeping the recollection near the surface would help him stay focused.

Besides, the twins would be back tomorrow and his normal life of diapers and everything pink would resume.

"It's settled then, right?" he asked. "You're staying for a while?"

"Yes," she said. "But the minute anything changes, you let me know."

Why did she always have her running shoes tucked next to the door? Or maybe a better question was, what had made her that way?

"Deal," he said, figuring this wasn't the time for questions even she most likely didn't have answers to. He bent down and picked up Iris and Ivy's favorite blanket. The feel of the silk lining in his hands connected him to the girls, and to the life he'd made long after his fool heart had been broken into pieces that never seemed to fit back together quite right again. There were too many jagged edges now that could cut through his chest if he breathed the wrong way.

"How well do you know the doctor?" she asked, sitting up. Her face twisted in pain with the move and her hand came up to her forehead, like she could somehow dull the ache by touching it.

"My daughters are her nieces," he replied. "But I have other questions right now."

She nodded as a look of dread washed over her. He'd seen the look before whenever he talked about the possibility of life after high school in Cider Creek.

"I've been trying to remember what happened and have been drawing a blank," she admitted.

"Do you know why you were near my property?" he asked.

"Nope," she sighed in a way that detailed her frustration. "I assumed they brought me here. Whoever *they* are."

"Any recent fights with anyone?" he asked. "Does anyone wish you harm?"

She caught his gaze and held it.

"If you're asking if I have enemies who would knock me out, abduct me and then hold me in a random building, then I couldn't say," she stated. "I hope I don't know anyone who is capable of this kind of cruelty."

He lowered his head when he said, "Sorry to hear about your grandfather."

"Don't be on my account," she countered. "You, of all people, should know Duncan Hayes and I weren't close."

"Still," he continued, "it's a loss."

Reese shrugged as she said, "I guess so."

When did she get so cold? Then again, their history suggested she'd been heartless since the end of high school. Did anyone really ever change?

Chapter Three

Duncan Hayes was the reason Reese and her siblings couldn't get out of Cider Creek fast enough. The only hitch back then had been the thought of leaving Darren. At eighteen, she thought she was being smart about her life, putting her future before her heart. She'd looked up the statistics on successful marriages of high-school sweethearts. They weren't good. Plus, she didn't think she would be good at marriage, anyway.

Besides, sticking around Cider Creek was never an option for her. Darren had family to think about and their ranch needed him to stay on to survive.

"Why would someone bring me here?" she asked, suddenly wondering if this incident could somehow be tied back to him.

He shrugged.

"I haven't seen or heard from you in years," he pointed out. The slight edge to his tone suggested he didn't care for the tables being turned.

"I'm trying to look at this from every angle," she elaborated. "Please don't think I'm attacking you in any way."

Darren sat there for a long, thoughtful moment. He al-

ways got quiet when conflicting thoughts battled for control. "We're good."

No. They weren't. The two of them were anything but
on good terms. Darren was being kind enough to help her
despite their rocky past, and she appreciated him for his
generosity. They'd left on bad terms all those years ago and
the set to his jaw, along with those piercing eyes when he
looked at her, told her where they stood. He was tolerating
her because he lived by a code that said he helped anyone
in need. Ranchers were always there for each other. Too bad
her grandfather hadn't been there for his family in the way
he had been for the community. Watching everyone admire
the man who'd made everyone's lives miserable had been a
tough pill to swallow. Folks in town revered Duncan, and
the rest of the family had put up a believable front that they
were a strong unit. Only those precious few who got close
to her or one of her siblings learned the truth. Duncan was
a piece of work. The first word that came to mind was *con-
trolling*. The second would have gotten her mouth washed
out with soap when she was little.

Anger burned through her chest. Why couldn't she block
out her grandfather instead of the last few hours?

Darren's cell buzzed at around the same time the front
door swung open. A look of hesitation crossed his features
before he went for his phone. A blonde woman walked in
the door as he studied the screen. He glanced up, then nodded and hitched his free thumb toward Reese.

"I'm Dr. Larson," she said, making a straight line toward
Reese. The doctor could best be described as pretty. She was
also tiny, but there was nothing delicate about her manner-
isms. Shoulders square and stiff, starched shirt tucked into
neatly pressed navy slacks, everything about her said she

was put-together and serious. Her hair was slicked back in a ponytail that fell past her shoulders. Powder-blue eyes and pink lipstick softened her look a couple of notches, making her seem more approachable.

"Reese Hayes," she said as she took the outstretched hand. "It's nice to meet you."

The good doctor glossed right over Reese's comment. Those blue eyes looked Reese up and down as if she was sizing her up for a coffin.

"Thank you for coming on such short notice," Darren said.

The quick nod and chilly reception gave Reese the impression these two were more than just friends.

"Tell me what happened and where it hurts," Dr. Larson said, setting her bag down on the floor as she perched on the edge of the solid oak coffee table. She kept one hand on the handle. A stethoscope hung around her neck. Black ballet flats peeked out of the bottom of her pant legs.

Reese explained what little she knew. She pointed out where it hurt the most.

"It looked like she took a blow to the back of her head, based on the blood in her hair," Darren said from across the room. When the doctor didn't respond, he looked up from his phone and said, "Stacie."

Reese couldn't help but wonder just how close Darren and Stacie were, even though it wasn't any of her business. Tell that to her brain, because it wanted to know the exact nature of their relationship. It didn't help when Darren joined them in the living room, choosing to sit next to Stacie so close that their thighs touched. While he didn't seem to think twice about it, a flash of emotion crossed behind Stacie's eyes.

There was a familiar air between the two of them, too. She didn't get the girlfriend-and-boyfriend vibe. Although, it would serve Reese right if he flaunted a beautiful, successful woman under her nose to remind her of what she'd lost when she'd left town—him.

"I noticed the blood," Stacie said dismissively as she flashed a small light she'd retrieved from her bag in Reese's eyes. The exam and questions that followed seemed routine, like she could perform it in her sleep.

When everything was put away, Stacie closed the bag. She leaned forward, elbows on her knees, and clasped her hands together. "I cleaned up the wound on your head. There's a pump knot with a little cut that should heal fine on its own without sutures. My biggest concern right now is your lapse in memory. It's not uncommon in the case of trauma to block out the events leading up to the incident. Unfortunately, there's no quick fix or guarantees. In some cases, the memories come back. In others, they're gone for good. The brain goes to great lengths to protect us from memories that might cause us additional pain."

"What about her headache?" Darren chimed in. "How long will that last?"

"I was getting to that," Stacie said. "You can take OTC medication as directed to alleviate your headaches. If they get worse, give me a call. I can write a prescription for something stronger even though I'd prefer not to for the next couple of days."

Reese wasn't much on taking pills. "I'll be fine with ibuprofen."

Stacie nodded. "Avoid alcohol and driving for a few days until you're feeling better again."

The alcohol was no problem, but the driving meant she

couldn't get back to Dallas or her job any time soon unless she asked Darren for another favor or made a major request from her assistant who needed to be in the office.

"Okay," Reese agreed. She needed to come up with a plan to get home, preferably in the next couple of hours. She was still holding on to the hope her purse and cell phones would be found by the law. She could ask Darren as soon as Stacie left. Her keys were inside her handbag as well. She was at a loss without it.

Reese cracked a small smile. Here she was thinking about car keys when she didn't know where her vehicle was. It could be totaled or in a ditch somewhere at this point. Or both. Those details were still blank.

She might be putting too much stock in one option, but maybe the law could tell her where her vehicle was and in what condition.

"Other than that, rest," Stacie said with an emphasis on the last word. Her gaze narrowed the next time she opened her mouth to speak. "For the record…" Her lips clamped shut almost as fast as they'd opened. Had she thought better of speaking her mind? "Suffice it to say I'll be nearby if anything comes up."

Darren immediately stood up, bringing Stacie up with a hand on her elbow. "I'll walk you outside."

Reese would like to be a fly buzzing around for that conversation.

"There's no need," Stacie said as she bent down to pick up her bag. She gave Reese another up-and-down stare with ice in her eyes. "I know where the door is. I can show myself out."

Rather than tell the good doctor that she had nothing to worry about, Reese took the high road and thanked the woman. Stacie must feel threatened by Reese's presence. She wanted to say, "Believe me, honey, you have nothing to worry about." Darren would never move beyond the past and Reese had no right to ask him to despite her heartstrings being tugged by his presence.

Darren's stubborn streak was a mile long and he would never forgive her.

DARREN WALKED BEHIND Stacie as she cut across the lawn toward her vehicle. Part of him felt the need to protect Reese from Stacie, and the other part—the one that had been burned—said Reese was a grown woman capable of handling her own affairs.

"Hey, what just happened?"

Stacie whirled around on him, index finger up and pointed like she was about to poke him in the chest. At least she wasn't ready to smack him with her medical bag. "What?"

"Come one. Don't play games," he countered. "Not even a Texas summer could melt the ice back there."

Stacie blew out a sharp breath that he was certain would freeze rain. "Is it wrong that I'm overprotective of my nieces?"

"It is when there's no reason to be," he said.

"Who is she then?" Stacie asked, moving her pointer finger toward the door.

"Someone I went to high school with a long time ago who ended up on my property, tied up in my equipment room," he replied.

She sucked in a deep breath. "Why? Who would do that to her?"

"Those are good questions but all I know for certain is that she was being held against her will," he confided.

"Oh," Stacie said.

"And now the law is out there looking for clues about who did that to her and why because she can't remember," he continued.

"I was off base, but that doesn't mean I wouldn't do it all over again if it meant protecting those babies," Stacie conceded. The bull-in-the-china-shop routine was starting to fade as some of the tension in her face muscles eased. "It's only been a year and—"

"What?" he interrupted. "You think I've somehow forgotten her?"

"Well, no, but—"

"I haven't," he said. "And I won't. But it has been a solid year and I will get back on the dating horse at some point."

"With *her*?" Stacie blurted out. A look of embarrassment flashed across her features.

"Does it matter?" he asked. "Someone will come along at some point. I'll be ready to kick-start that part of my life again."

Stacie stood quiet for a few moments. He could see this was hard on her. Him moving on was another reminder that her baby sister was gone. He didn't want to get into the details of just how complicated his relationship with his wife had become before the pregnancy, or the fact that he wasn't a hundred-percent certain the twins were biologically his. The guitar-player ex-boyfriend from Hazel's past might share their DNA.

"I guess not," Stacie admitted after another long pause. "You have a right to live your life. I do realize that."

"If I start falling down on my duties as a father, I hope

you'll call me out," he said, knowing full well he would never do that to his girls. The statement was meant to placate their aunt.

"You can count on that," she said with a half smile. It was better than nothing.

"Good," he said. "Thanks again for coming out on such short notice."

"Call me if her condition worsens," Stacie said. "Every patient is different, but the vitals are strong on this one. My guess is that she'll be fine in a couple of days."

"That's good news," he said, then they said their goodbyes.

"You need to be careful with this one," Stacie warned as she got inside her sedan.

Rather than debate those words, or explain himself, he turned toward the house. "Drive safe."

Darren cut across the lawn as his cell buzzed again. He checked the screen about the same time he reached the door. After a quick scan of the message, he opened the door and stepped into the living room. "The sheriff is on his way."

"Any chance he found my personal belongings?" Reese asked as she immediately sat up.

"He didn't say one way or the other," Darren admitted. "Are you hungry?"

Reese crossed her arms over her chest. "That ibuprofen sounds good if you have any." Her body language tensed. The reason most likely had to do with Stacie.

"I do," he said. "Can you eat something first? It's not good to take on an empty stomach."

The way she scraped her teeth across her bottom lip told him she had questions but wasn't sure she should ask them. "I could probably eat a piece of toast if you have bread."

"What about a sandwich?" he asked as he moved toward the kitchen.

"Turkey?" she asked.

"Always," he said before stopping himself. Every day after school, she'd had a turkey sandwich at his house. He made sure it was stocked since it had been her favorite, a habit that stuck to this day.

"I could try," she said, taking one of the throw pillows, then hugging it against her chest.

He fixed the sandwich and then brought it into the living room. Sitting next to her on the couch wouldn't be the smartest idea, so he took the leather chair instead.

"Something has been niggling at the back of my mind and I can't for the life of me figure out what it is," she said, picking up the sandwich. She took a bite and made a face.

"What just happened?" he asked.

"Nothing," she said, recovering almost as fast. "This is great."

"That's not what your face said a second ago," he argued. "Come on. I'm a big boy. Tell me what's wrong with the sandwich."

She shot him a look he recognized as an apology, then said, "Mayonnaise."

"You used to like it slathered on both sides," he insisted.

"I'm a mustard girl now," she said, then took another bite. "But don't even worry about it. I'm used to it now."

He moved to the kitchen, then brought over a paper towel and handed it over. "Do you want to wipe the mayo off?"

With effort, she chewed the bite then swallowed. "Yes, please."

After wiping off most of the spread, she polished off the

sandwich in no time. He handed over ibuprofen and a re-filled glass of water.

"Camree Lynn," she said with an ah-ha look on her face.

"What does she have to do with you being here?" he asked. Her best friend had disappeared off the face of the earth in tenth grade and never resurfaced.

Chapter Four

The name had popped into Reese's mind out of nowhere. "I don't have any other details. Just her name but this feels important."

"Is it possible you found out information that led you here?" Darren asked.

She shrugged. "Anything is possible, I guess." Without her cell or purse, she only had her memory to rely on, and it wasn't very dependable at the moment.

"We have a name," he said.

That didn't mean much without additional context. *Useless* didn't begin to describe how she felt. Her head ached. The sandwich had eased some of her nausea. "It's awful to have a blank where there should be something, especially when that something might have been the reason for this." She held up her wrists to show the deep groves and red slashes.

"At least you're going to be fine," he said. "The rest can be figured out."

Reese took in a deep breath, then exhaled.

"Plus, the sheriff might find your belongings and the law will be all over figuring out who did this to you," he said.

"I don't think I've ever been more scared in my life waking up to find that I'd been bound," she admitted before flashing her eyes at Darren. "Don't feel sorry for me."

He shot her a confused look.

"I'm not telling you any of this so you'll have sympathy," she clarified. Walking away in the manner in which she had, with a text instead of a person-to-person conversation, had been a jerk move.

"Not a problem on my side," he said so fast it almost made her head spin.

"Good." She was glad to clear it up. Looking around, she had so many questions about his life here. Would he answer any of them? Tell her that his life was none of her business? If he did, she wouldn't exactly blame him. Since trying to remember what happened and how she'd ended up here only gave her more of a headache, she decided it couldn't hurt to ask a few questions about his personal life. "How old are your babies?"

"Eighteen months," he responded, folding his hands together and staring at the carpet. It was the move he'd always done when he was uncertain about something. Why do it now?

"You don't know for sure?" she asked.

"What?" He looked up at her and one of his eyebrows shot up. "I know how old the girls are. Eighteen months, like I said."

"You did the thing you used to do…" she began and then stopped. "Never mind. That was a long time ago. I don't know what I'm talking about anymore." People changed after a decade, especially when they'd only known each other as kids. Well, in high school, anyway. Darren had a number of habits that were probably different now that he was an adult, and a father. *A father.* No matter how many times she repeated the word in her head, it would still seem strange. If the twins—girls, based on the explosion of pink in the room—were a year and a half old, that meant they were born when he was twenty-six years old. Gestation took almost a year, so he would have been twenty-five when they'd been conceived. Since he wasn't wearing a wedding band, she assumed either he'd never been married, or he was divorced.

Darren would have done what he would have believed to be the "right" thing and proposed after a pregnancy announcement. Ten years might have passed, but she'd bet her savings account that Darren maintained his sense of honor. Call it cowboy code or whatever, but it was the reason he still held the door open for a woman, unless she asked him not to. It was the reason he was helping her now. And it was the reason he wouldn't ask her to leave unless he knew she would be okay.

Helping her because he still had feelings after all this time wasn't even a serious consideration.

When she looked over at him, he was studying her.

"I asked if you wanted more water," he said.

Her glass was empty. "Yes, please. If you don't mind."

"It'll hopefully help with the headache," he said, then stood and picked up the glass from the coffee table.

Darren moved into the kitchen. As he walked, she forced her gaze away from his strong, muscled back. He'd grown into his tall frame from the last time she'd seen him.

"Do you still work on the ranch?" she asked, needing to talk to work off some of her nerves at being back.

"The one my parents owned is mine now," he said as he refilled the glass. "Been that way since not long after you took off." The way he said those last few words sent daggers to the center of her chest. Without her cell, purse or keys, she was stranded here until the sheriff arrived. Making small talk didn't seem like the right plan. She should have known he wouldn't want to have anything to do with her outside of making sure she was safe. Conversation was probably asking too much.

Darren walked over and set the glass down on the table. His cell buzzed, indicating a text was coming through. He checked the screen. "The sheriff has been diverted on a call. He says it might be a while before he can get here."

"How far are we from Hayes Cattle?" she asked.

His face twisted. "Hour and a half, give or take. Why?"

"I've taken up enough of your time and generosity," she said, figuring he would want a break from all this so he could pick up his babies. "It might be for the best if I call to see if one of the hands can swing by and pick me up now that I think about it. If any of my things are found, we can always come back."

Going home reminded her of something she needed to do…but *what*?

"To be honest, you were found on my property and that makes this case my business," he countered after a thoughtful pause. "Unless you have a good reason, I'd appreciate you staying put. My children live in this home with me, and I need to know exactly what happened and how this case goes."

Reese caught his gaze and looked him dead in the eye. "You're sure that's what you want? Me in your house?"

The question caught him off guard based on the face he made. "You're here. I'm not asking you to leave."

"What if the sheriff takes a long time?" she continued. "Being in the same room with me after all these years can't possibly be high on your list of ways you'd like to spend a day."

"I didn't expect you to show up, but here you are and there are other rooms if I'm bothered," he said. "Time has passed and we've both moved on. This isn't high school anymore, Reese. We're grown adults who have pushed beyond a childish breakup." The manner in which he said those words made her feel otherwise. There was a tension in his jaw that only occurred when his coach had yelled at him during practice, or his father had dressed him down for being late to finish chores even when he had homework and tests to study for.

"If you're sure my being here doesn't bother you," she said, figuring he'd made good points about this being his home and where he was bringing up his children. He deserved to hear firsthand what the sheriff had to say. Plus, he'd been nothing but helpful so far, even if he had to force himself to be cordial.

"I'd tell you if I was," he said.

Would he, though? A small piece of her thought he might be as curious about her as she was about him. Then again, it had been a long day and she could be misreading his actions.

DARREN WAS DOING his best. Finding Reese on his property after all these years was one thing. Who would bring her here and why? As morbid as this sounded, even to him, why would someone hold her here instead of immediately killing her? More than one person had to be involved unless she'd come up on poachers who couldn't afford to let her go, but didn't have it in them to kill her. They might have been trying to figure out what to do with her, which may have included doing things *to* her. Anger made his blood run hot at the thought she could have been raped. There'd been more than one person present in the old equipment shed—a building that was going to be torn down the minute he received clearance from the sheriff. More of that anger boiled when he thought about his daughters being the ones inside there when they were older.

The building was dangerous. It had to go. He'd tear it down with his bare hands if it meant no one would ever be bound inside those walls again.

Darren issued a sharp sigh as he caught Reese suppressing a yawn.

"The sheriff won't be here for a while," he said. "You're welcome to change out of those clothes into something more comfortable and grab a nap." He gave her a sympathetic look. "It doesn't sound as though you remember any of your clothing being removed at any point during your abduction." He used the last word for lack of a better term.

"A shower sounds like heaven," she said, shaking her head. "I would like very much to wash this dirt off me."

"I'm sure I have something around here that you could change into," he said, forcing an image of her naked and in the shower out of his thoughts. "Even if it's just a T-shirt and a long robe."

"Okay," she said.

It occurred to him that her clothing might be considered evidence. "I have a paper grocery-store bag to put your things in. The sheriff might need them for evidence."

"Right," she said on a heavy sigh. "That's a good point actually." She crossed her arms over her chest and rubbed them like she was suddenly cold. "I can't imagine what kind of monsters would do something like this to another human being. I'm not sure what happened, but…" Her voice trailed off.

"You might have gotten in the way of poachers," he said, trying to find a way to offer some reassurance. "You weren't physically assaulted, which is a good sign." Hearing those words come out of his own mouth made a knot tighten in his gut. The fact any woman had to worry about being attacked once she left her home tipped his blood to boiling. Having daughters made him even more aware of the dangers women faced, and the feeling he wouldn't always be there to protect them sickened him to no end.

What happened to Reese today was a harsh reminder of what could happen to any woman. A random occurrence would mean the danger was gone. Poachers would move on and move out.

"You might have had something to do with it," she said, dropping her gaze to the carpet. "I have so many questions about what happened and why." She rubbed her arms again. "It might have been unintended, but you saved me from…whatever it was those men planned to do with me. Thank you."

"You're welcome," he said. "I'm just relieved you're okay." *Okay* was a relative term. She was shaken up, which was understandable.

She nodded.

"How about that grocery bag and shower," she finally said, pushing up to standing. As she took a step, her leg gave. In one quick motion, Darren was by her side, catching her, keeping her from falling on her backside. "I'm fine." She righted herself quickly, pushing him away as she regained her balance. "It's all good. I probably sat too long. That's all. I'm better now."

He took a step back. "Okay." The other possibility was that she'd lost her balance from the head injury. Stacie had given the green light, told them that Reese was medically sound. She also said to call if he had any concerns.

Reese wiped her hands down her shirt and took a couple of steps. "See. All good here."

It didn't erase his concerns, but seeing her walk without falling was a good start. "I'm right here if you need an arm to hold on to."

"I got this," she said in a tone that reminded him of her independent streak. Reese had always been the silent observer. She was so quiet in a room, it had been easy to overlook her for most of their lives. Except that he'd noticed her in middle school before she grew into her looks...and she'd been beautiful. Still was, which bothered him more than he wanted to admit.

He stood there, waiting for the inevitable question.

"Which way to the bathroom?" she asked.

"Down this hallway," he said, pointing toward the guest area. "I'll grab a few things and meet you in the hallway outside the door. There are unused toothbrushes underneath the sink."

She nodded and left the room. After gathering a few supplies, he stood outside the bathroom door and knocked.

The door opened enough for him to slide the items into her hands.

"Take your time in there," he said. "If I hear from the sheriff, I'll let you know."

After receiving confirmation, he headed back into the living room and grabbed his phone. A quick check of local news didn't reveal anything about the abduction.

He made a quick call to check on his daughters, and found

out they were doing fine. As he held his phone, he looked at the wallpaper on his phone. The picture of his wife holding their newborn twins wasn't something he believed he'd ever replace. The girls were older now and their looks had changed so much. It might be time to update the photo.

A noise sounded from the hallway. Darren jumped to his feet and made a beeline for the bathroom door. He accidently stepped on Ivy's favorite rattle and almost face-planted. His reflexes were solid. A quick hand up to grab hold of the fireplace mantel saved him. The girls' belongings were strewn around the living room, but he liked seeing reminders of them everywhere, especially on nights they slept over at Stacie's, or at their grandparents'. Being poked in bare feet wasn't as heartwarming as he hopped around, cursing, but at least this time, he had his shoes on. Thank the stars.

"Everything good in there?" he asked, standing at the door.

"I'm all right, but your shower curtain might not survive," Reese said with a moan of what sounded like embarrassment.

"Mind if I open the door?" he asked.

"Give me a sec," she said. The naked image of her wasn't one he needed burned in his thoughts.

Another noise sounded in the living room, sending an ominous feeling rippling through him. "Hold on. I'll be right back."

Chapter Five

Reese didn't like Darren's tone. She'd heard it before when there'd been trouble brewing. After what she'd been through today, it sent her pulse through the roof. Had the person who'd abducted her—and abduction was the only logical explanation, since there was no way she'd go with a stranger willingly—figured out where she was?

The thought had her racing to get dressed. Since her clothes were in a paper bag in the hallway, she shrugged into the oversized T-shirt and then the bathrobe. She kicked the shower curtain to one side to clear a path to the door, then reached for the door handle.

The door opened before she got to it.

She gasped, bringing her hand up to cover her mouth.

Darren took one look at her face and held his hands up, palms out, in the surrender position. "It's fine. A bird took a nosedive into the glass patio doors. They're reflective, so birds sometimes make the mistake of thinking they can fly right through."

"I thought maybe the guys found me here and were coming for me," she admitted. A glance at the mirror as she walked past revealed a ghost-white reflection. She took in a couple of deep breaths to calm her nerves.

"Believe me," he said, "I was under the same impression."

"It's dangerous for me to be here," she pointed out. "You have a family, Darren. If anything happened to you or your girls because of me, I would—"

"You didn't bring this fight to my doorstep," he interrupted. "Someone else did and it's not your fault. Until we know who is behind this, I highly doubt we'll figure out why it happened. Unless by some miracle, you get your memory back."

This didn't seem like a good time to say he was, in fact, the last person she'd wanted to bump into in or near Cider Creek despite the growing part of her that was happy to see him. Even the tiny worry lines creasing his forehead made him look better than he had years ago. She doubted it worked like that for anyone else. Darren was different. Special.

"That may very well be true," she said, thinking he had a good point. "I could make sure that I'm seen somewhere else. Draw these jerks away from you and your girls instead of toward."

"Careful, Hayes," he said, then turned toward the living room. Out of the side of his mouth, he added, "I might actually think you've started caring about someone besides yourself."

Those words stung more than she wanted them to. Was there truth to them? She couldn't argue that she'd been in self-preservation mode at eighteen years old.

Living at Hayes Cattle had become hell thanks to her grandfather. Reese had watched her mother hang on to a life that didn't exist anymore. Why she'd stuck around the cattle ranch after her husband's death was something Reese might never understand.

The real reason her mother was calling everyone home was still a head-scratcher. Even more than that, all four of her brothers were making plans to upend their lives to move home or be around more. It was insanity and they'd lost their minds if they believed she would leave the city to return to a place that never quite felt like home to her in the first place. Then again, work jeans and overalls were the standard-issue clothing for the ranch. No high heels needed.

Camree Lynn had made all the difference. Reese's best friend had made living on the ranch survivable. The two had been inseparable by freshman year. Reese couldn't count the number of nights they'd stayed up, dreaming of shaking the dust of their little town off their feet and moving to a big city like Dallas, where people ate more sushi than steak. Fort Worth was where all the cowboys lived. Dallas had businesspeople and fashion designers. It had restaurants and bars.

Camree Lynn had been Reese's saving grace.

An involuntary shiver rocked her body thinking about the past, about her friend and her unsolved disappearance. There was always something niggling at the back of Reese's mind that she could never quite reach. It was almost as though she'd blocked out part of her memory. Trauma, she decided. She'd shut down back then, but pretended to be fine after overhearing Duncan trying to convince her mother to send her to a "home for disturbed children," as he'd put it. Reese learned a valuable lesson in whom she could trust. Her mother put up an argument, but Duncan usually got what he wanted in the end. But not that time.

Immersing herself in her job—a job she loved despite the long hours and hard work—was so much better than thinking about Cider Creek. Reese realized she remembered her mother calling everyone home.

"You coming?" Darren's voice startled her out of her reverie. There was a cold quality to it that she probably deserved, but didn't like. Since she couldn't remember why she'd shown up in the first place, how she got here or who was after her, trying to leave didn't make a whole lot of sense. Selfishly, she wanted to stay, if only to be in the presence of someone who actually cared if she lived or died. Of course, her family did. Putting them in danger didn't seem like the best of ideas. When it came to no-win situations, this one took the cake and ate it, too.

"My mom wants us all home." She tightened the belt on her robe and then followed the voice into the kitchen area, stepping over baby paraphernalia along the way.

"Is that why you're here?" he asked.

"Has to be part of the reason but something tells me there's more," she said.

He nodded.

"What's it like?" she asked as he leaned a slender hip against the granite countertop.

He shot her a confused look.

"Being a father?" she asked.

"Scary," he said almost instantly. The quick response was honest. It had been his blink reaction to the question. "Great. The best thing to ever have happened to me. Tiring. Roll every intense emotion you've ever had into a ball, and there you go."

She smiled. His face lit up even when he talked about the tiring part.

"What about you?" he asked. "You change your mind about ever wanting kids?"

"Me?" She twisted up her face. "No. I couldn't do that to a child."

"What? You'd be a good mother," he said.

"Because I had such an amazing example?" she countered.

"Your mom is a sweetheart," he said without hesitation. He would know better than her now, considering she hadn't set foot in Cider Creek in ten years. Of course, she texted with her mother and made time for the occasional phone call. She sent flowers on Mother's Day and Christmas.

"She's a pushover. She let my grandfather walk all over her while she lived in the shadow of a marriage that didn't exist," she said, almost wishing she could take the words back. They sounded harsher when she spoke them out loud.

Darren stood there for a long moment, looking deep in thought. "Doing what's right for others even if it hurts you isn't being weak."

She shook her head. "I wasn't saying she was…" Actually, she was doing just that whether she wanted to acknowledge it or not.

"Speaking of family," Darren said through clenched teeth, "how's my uncle?"

Reese didn't mean to suck in a breath even though she did. "I wouldn't know. I haven't worked for him in five years."

"You mean the two of you aren't dating anymore?"

Taking in a slow breath did little to stem the pain from what felt like daggers straight to her heart. The relationship with his uncle hadn't been something she'd planned. Looking back, the man knew what he was doing, though. He'd seduced her in a matter of months, made her believe she was special and then laughed when she'd confronted him about the others he'd been seducing, too. He'd casually said there'd been no mention of commitment. True enough, the words had never been spoken, only assumed. At least, on her part. And he'd never explicitly said he was seeing other people, not even in so many words. All those late nights at the office, when he'd sent her home alone with work, hadn't registered as him cheating. Then again, he'd made a good point. He couldn't cheat on a relationship that didn't exist in the first place. "No. We aren't."

Rather than stand there and continue this conversation, she moved to the patio doors. Tears welled in her eyes as she realized just how much she'd hurt Darren by leaving and how foolish she'd been to believe a much older, more experienced man when he said words she never would believe from someone her own age. Just like she'd always suspected, true love equaled devastation and misery. To find proof, all she had to do was take a look in Darren's eyes.

DARREN FIXED A pot of coffee. Since he'd already checked on the babies, there wasn't much else he could do there. Being busy had become a way of life since the pregnancy, forget once the twins were born. Six months was too young to lose their mother and he'd had no idea how he was going to bring up the babies on his own. Then, Stacie had shown up, ready and willing to pitch in. His in-laws came next and he started to think he might actually pull this whole thing off and bring up healthy young women.

Seeing Reese again reminded him of what could happen if he messed up the job.

Kids needed parents. Preferably both, even if they lived under separate roofs, which was where he and his wife had been headed before the twins had been conceived.

Darren shook off the memories. Thinking about the past was about as productive as trying to milk a bee. Besides, walking down memory lane made him relive all the hurt he'd experienced when Reese had walked out. How foolish had he been at eighteen to believe he'd found the love of his life?

Right now, his heart only had room for two girls—Ivy and Iris.

Reese didn't turn to look at him. "She likes you," she finally said after staring out the doors for a few minutes.

"We're family," he said, reaching for a mug.

"No," she said without hesitation. "She *likes* you."

"Stacie?" he asked. "She's just concerned about the twins, trying to make sure I'm doing a good enough job now that her sister is gone."

"I'm sorry," Reese said quietly. "It must be hard to lose the love of your life and the person you decided to build a family with."

Darren didn't know how to respond, considering he had lost the love of his life once. She should have been the mother of his children, but wasn't. The smart thing to do would be to keep a safe distance between him and Reese, in case any of those old feelings decided to rear their ugly heads and come back to bite him in the backside.

"It's never easy to lose someone," he said, deciding not to go into more detail than that. First loves had a way of gutting a person, making it hard to go all-in with the next one no matter how great they might be. What he'd felt for Hazel was good. He'd loved her as much as he could love anyone after having his heart stomped on. None of which was Hazel's fault. She'd loved him in her own way, too.

"I can't imagine," she said, but an emotion crossed her

features that said she had some idea. Was it his uncle that she missed?

Darren couldn't let himself go there without anger boiling. Since getting mad wouldn't change the past, he shifted focus. Besides, anger never fixed anything. In fact, it usually led to someone popping off at the mouth and making the situation a whole lot worse.

"I'll check on the sheriff," he said, figuring the abduction was a whole lot safer subject. He retrieved his cell phone and checked the screen. He'd missed two calls from Stacie. "I need to make a call."

Reese nodded.

"Coffee is ready if you'd like a cup," he said. "Mugs are on the counter."

Receiving two calls from Stacie back-to-back set his nerves on edge. He walked over to the front window and returned the call.

"Is everything all right with the girls?" he immediately asked, concerned Stacie had information his former in-laws didn't want to deliver. He'd checked on them a little while ago but little kids were unpredictable and he'd learned the hard way were a danger to themselves half the time.

"Yes," Stacie said. "Sorry. Didn't mean to worry you. I just didn't like the way we left things earlier and wanted to make sure everything was okay between us."

Darren let out a sigh of relief.

"We're good," he said, trying to will his racing pulse to calm the hell down.

"Are you sure?" she asked. There was a quality to her voice that was different. Jealous? Was Reese right about Stacie wishing there could be more between them? He'd met her first, before Hazel. They'd gone out once but nothing happened because they'd gone to the restaurant where her sister worked as a waitress. As it turned out, Stacie was the practical sister. She studied and not much else. They'd run out of things to say to each other before the appetizers arrived. Hazel was the untamed sister. She was like a tornado who blew threw his life, turning everything upside down. Conversation with her had been easy. Sex had been fiery, but he found out later that there wasn't as much love between them as there was friendship. It was what he missed about her most despite her betrayal.

Hazel had asked her sister for his number, she'd given it, so he'd assumed she'd been just as bored on their date as he'd been. "I'd tell you if we weren't."

"How is she?" Stacie asked, not mentioning Reese by name. He'd pinned the situation right. He'd heard jealousy in her tone. Since he was going to start dating at some point, he needed to find a nice way to tell her that anything besides friendship was out of the question. At least it was on his side.

"Better," he said.

"Does she remember anything else?" Stacie asked. He figured she wanted Reese out of his home as fast as possible. The quicker she remembered, the faster she would leave.

"Nope," he admitted. Reese's words came crashing into him. Did Stacie want to step into her dead sister's shoes?

Chapter Six

Reese couldn't help but listen to the phone call between Darren and Stacie. It had to be the doctor, based on his answers.

The woman, no doubt, wanted Reese as far away from Darren as possible. Did she not realize how much disdain Darren had for Reese? After grabbing a fresh cup of coffee, Reese headed into the living room. She noticed a small picture on the fireplace mantel of a woman holding the twins. They couldn't have been more than a few days old. The woman was beautiful. The resemblance to her sister was clear, even though the two looked like opposites. Stacie was put-together. Everything about her was neat, from her blown-out hair to her neatly trimmed nails. The woman in the picture had big bright eyes and wild hair. She was smiling but there was a sadness in her eyes. Reese couldn't help but wonder what had happened to her.

Her heart went out to the babies, who would grow up without their mother. Based on all the baby supplies, Darren was a good provider. Based on her own experience, unconditional love and acceptance was all she'd needed growing up.

At the ranch, reminders of her father had been everywhere even though no one talked about him. Had it been too painful for her mother? Seeing Darren as a single father, and how hard that must be, was opening her eyes to what her mother might have gone through.

Kids weren't something Reese had ever wanted. She wasn't one of those girls who sat around watching future brides say yes to a dress. She'd never flipped through bridal magazines, not even if that was the only option while sitting in a waiting room. And she'd never been one to fantasize about what her own wedding might look like someday. But she sure as hell didn't expect someone to cheat.

As a kid, she wondered if there was something wrong with her. Camree Lynn had teased Reese about her lack of interest in marriage and family a few times. Her friend used to say that Reese would change her mind when she found the right person. As much as she'd been infatuated with Matias Ossian, Darren's uncle, love had never been part of the equation. But there was an even bigger problem. Reese had no interest in finding the kind of love she assumed her mother had with Reese's father. The kind that had doomed her mother to a lifetime of pain and heartache. For what? A few good years?

No thanks.

"I have to go, but I'll call you if anything changes," Darren said as Reese tuned back into his conversation with Stacie. Reese couldn't help but wonder if Darren had loved his wife in the all-consuming way people described. There'd been a distance in his eyes earlier that made her want to ask questions. The answers were none of her business, so she kept her mouth shut.

Darren studied his screen. "Sheriff is on his way."

"Oh, good," she said. "It'll be nice to wrap this up so I can get out of your hair."

Those words seemed the equivalent of a slap in the face

to Darren. He opened his mouth to speak and then clamped it shut.

"I was just thinking it would be nice for all of this mess to be cleared up so you can get back to your family," she said. "The longer those jerks are out there, the more time you'll miss out on with your twins."

Again, he started to speak and then stopped himself.

"I'm actually not trying to offend you," she said by way of defense.

"Didn't think you were," he responded. "If I wanted to, I could send you somewhere else and get on with my life after giving my statement to the sheriff."

Well, this was going nowhere fast. Being without her phones made her jumpy. She couldn't fathom how many messages would be waiting when she finally checked in.

The sound of gravel crunching underneath tires drew their attention toward the front window. Reese walked over and peeked through the blinds.

"He's here," she said.

Darren joined her. "You're about to meet Sheriff Red Courtright."

"Sounds like a good ol' Southern boy," she said, wishing she was back in Dallas, where she would be giving a statement to the police.

Red Courtright looked the part. He was tall and slim, and in head-to-toe khaki-colored clothing. He was wearing a cowboy hat that was nearly blown off and carried away in the wind. His belt buckle was huge and he had on boots. Exactly the picture someone would get in their mind when they pictured a small-town sheriff.

Darren opened the door as the sheriff's boots hit the porch. "Come on in, Sheriff."

Red Courtright nodded as his gaze shifted from Darren to her and back. He tipped his hat and said, "Ma'am."

Once inside, the trio exchanged handshakes. Reese introduced herself as she studied the middle-aged man who had remnants of red in his now-light hair. His front teeth were donkey-sized, and up close she could see a dotting of freckles on overly tanned skin.

"I'm afraid I have bad news," he said.

Darren motioned toward the kitchen table that had three chairs and two highchairs tucked around it. "What did you find out?"

"Your equipment building burned," the sheriff informed.

Darren smacked the table with his flat palm. "What the hell?"

"It burned to the ground before the law or volunteer fire-fighters could save anything," the sheriff continued.

"I thought they were already there collecting evidence," Reese said.

The sheriff shook his head. "My mistake."

"I'm guessing that means any evidence or DNA went up in flames, as well," Reese stated. It was brilliant when she really thought about it. There would be no trace left behind of the person or persons who'd abducted her, leaving the trail cold unless her vehicle or a witnessed showed up.

"Afraid so," the sheriff said.

"And the call that you mentioned?" Darren asked. "Was it possible that was made to draw you away from the scene of the crime?"

"It's looking that way," the sheriff said, shaking his head. "We can't trace the call back to a name." His fisted hand smacked the table. "Which means we'll put even more resources on this thing to find out who did this to you." His gaze shifted to Reese. "Mark my words, the perp will be behind bars soon."

"I appreciate it, Sheriff," she said. This area most likely didn't see the kind of crimes common in a big city like Dallas. Another reason to get home as soon as possible. Dallas PD would be more equipped to handle criminals in her opinion. She would point that out but figured it wouldn't make her popular with the sheriff. Since she needed him to be on her side, she decided not to comment on his inefficiency. "Was anything recovered in the area? Like my cell phones or handbag?"

He shook his head.

"We have Reese's clothing," Darren offered. He retrieved the paper bag and handed it over to the sheriff.

It didn't mean the other items were lost forever, considering she had no idea when she'd last had them on her person.

"We'll run these through forensics to see if we pick up any fibers," the sheriff said, then put up a hand like he was stopping traffic. "Before you get any ideas, I send these off to be analyzed and it'll take time for anything to come back. The real world isn't anything like what you see on those TV shows, where someone makes a call or pulls a favor. Investigations take time and I plan to be thorough."

"What about my car?" she continued, picking up the thread after nodding.

"There hasn't been an abandoned vehicle found," he admitted. "I'll need the make and model so we know exactly what we're looking for."

"I drive a teal Lexus," she said. "It's the smallest sport utility." From the corner of her eye, she saw Darren stiffen. She wanted to point out that she hadn't used a dime of family money for the purchase and it was already three years old by the time she bought it. Her body tensed as a reaction to him.

Reese reminded herself to breathe.

"NX 200t?" the sheriff asked.

"Yes, sir," she responded with a little more vigor than was probably necessary.

He paused long enough to shoot off a text. Then, he held up his phone. "Word is spreading as we speak. If your vehicle is in the area, we'll find it."

If she had her cell, she could put in a call to her landlord and find out if it was parked in her spot by some strange circumstance. No one in her building seemed eager to get to know one another, so it wasn't like she had any friends or could call one of her neighbors to check for her.

The thought stopped her in her tracks. How long had she been a resident? Four years now? And she didn't know anyone she could call? The thought made city living sound far less appealing when she thought about it like that. Then again, with the last name Hayes in a town like Cider Creek, small communities could be suffocating.

DARREN LEANED ACROSS the table and folded his hands. Not only had a crime occurred on his property, but he'd also been hit with a fire. It was too late to put up surveillance equipment. He was cursing himself for not thinking of it sooner. No one in their right mind would return to the scene of a crime when deputies and the sheriff were sure to be there.

Then again, this bastard had drawn law enforcement away. Poachers came here for white-tailed deer, desert bighorn sheep and the like. The illegal hunters were smart and they would think to cover their tracks. If they worked this area enough, they would know what kind of law enforcement they were working with as well. Were they too easy of an answer, though?

They could have scared Reese away without going through the motions of tying up her hands and feet. As a counterpoint, they wouldn't appreciate having a witness running around who could describe them or offer information on their whereabouts. She might have popped off at the mouth, or one of them might have recognized her as a Hayes and decided to try to cash in. He was just running through random ideas here, hoping something sounded right. A few things didn't add up. Like why would she have been on his property in the first place. She wouldn't be there for the fun of it.

"Has any member of the Hayes family been in contact with your office?" he asked the sheriff.

Sheriff Courtright's eyebrows shot up. It didn't take but a few seconds for him to figure out the implication Darren was making.

"As in reporting a ransom demand?" the sheriff asked.

"Yes," he said. "What if the persons who abducted Reese intended to ask the family for money?"

The Hayes last name seemed to finally register. His eyes widened and he got a look of recognition on his face.

"You're of *the* Hayes family of Hayes Cattle," the sheriff said to Reese. "You should have mentioned that before. I'd like to offer my sincerest condolences about your grandfather. Duncan Hayes was a good man."

"Yes." Reese looked like she forced a small smile. "Thank you." It also appeared as if it was taking everything inside her not to make a comment about the kind of man her grandfather really was. It must be eating her up inside to be told the man was such a good person when she knew the opposite was true at home.

"No, no one from the family has made a call to my office," he said.

Darren had had an insider's view to the family dynamic. Reese was the baby of the family. Everyone left before she came of age. Did she feel abandoned by her siblings? She must have on some level.

He hoped the twins stayed close throughout life. Their grandparents were older. They had Stacie if anything happened to him. But mostly, they had each other. They'd held hands the second they were placed next to each other. The image had melted his heart. Nothing else mattered—the second he laid eyes on those tiny angels, his heart had gone all in.

"With Mr. Hayes's death, I'm surprised it's taken this long for the vultures to come out if that was the original plan," the sheriff stated. It looked like he'd made up his mind about what happened already. "My office will do everything in its power to bring these men to justice before it happens again. If I were you, I'd be careful from now on until these perps are under lock and key. If they tried once, there's nothing stopping them from trying again."

"Are you certain that's what we're dealing with here?" Reese asked. She tilted her head to one side, like she used to do when she disagreed with someone but didn't want to call them out on it.

"It's a theory that makes sense," he responded.

She gave a slight nod, which told Darren she realized the sheriff had made up his mind at this point, and his idea was far-fetched. Arguing wouldn't do any good. In fact, he went so far as to tuck his cell inside his front pocket.

"I've got a lot of work to do on my end," he said. "Thank you for your statement. Is there a way I can reach you in case I have follow-up questions?"

"I don't have my cell," Reese admitted, looking a little more than flabbergasted that the sheriff was ready to walk out the front door.

"You can reach her through me for now," Darren said, figuring the two of them were going to be joined at the hip over the next few hours, anyway. Possibly more. The thought should have repulsed him, or at the very least make him hot under the collar. With her here, he had a better chance of finding out what really happened so he could ensure it never happened again.

"Well, all right," the sheriff said before nodding toward Reese. Was he incompetent? Red Courtright didn't come across as the brightest bulb in the bunch. "If you'll excuse me. I have work to do."

Reese nodded and thanked the sheriff for his time. Her words came out almost robotic, but the sheriff didn't appear to catch on. His grin was almost ear-to-ear before his face turned serious and he offered more sympathy for her loss.

Darren walked the sheriff outside, and then returned to the table.

"It's quick and convenient," Reese said, then added, "I'll give him that much."

"Shouldn't be too difficult to prove him wrong," Darren said.

"What am I supposed to do in the meantime?" she asked, her tone more defiant than defeated, even though he detected both. He'd always loved her quiet confidence.

"Stick around here," he said, wondering if it was a good idea. There was no other choice if they wanted to get to the bottom of this thing. Trusting the sheriff seemed like the quickest way for Reese to end up abducted again. This time, the bastards would be more prepared.

Were they watching his house right now?

Chapter Seven

Reese blew out a breath that depleted all the air she had in her lungs. She gave herself a moment of self-pity, but she'd learned a long time ago not to wallow there.

Taking in a deep breath, she decided to regroup.

"I can tell we're not working with a whole lot upstairs when it comes to the sheriff," she finally said to Darren, pulling the straps of her robe tighter. Granted, she might have on a long T-shirt underneath, but she had no plans to give any sort of peepshow.

"Believe me, I noticed, too," he said. "There's a decent deputy we can call who I've worked with before when tracking poachers."

"Except now that the high-profile name of Hayes is involved, I imagine the sheriff will want to run the show," she countered. Red Courtright might not have the highest IQ, and that was just a guess on her part, but he had to be savvy to have been elected to this job. Savvy or connected to someone prominent in the community. Hell, it could have been her grandfather who'd helped the man get elected for all she knew.

"That's a fair point," Darren conceded. "Reaching out

might put my deputy in a bad position, so I'll table the thought for now."

"Sounds like the best course of action," she said, realizing she'd go stir-crazy if she sat here much longer and did nothing. Her friend's name kept coming full circle in Reese's thoughts. "I keep thinking about Camree Lynn."

She looked over at Darren, who sat a little straighter at the mention of her.

"Do you want to talk about her?" he asked. No one liked to say her name too loudly after she'd gone missing. The sheriff back then decided she was a runaway based on her journals, where she said she couldn't wait to get far away from Cider Creek.

"We can," Reese said, wondering if there could be a connection. "To your point, she disappeared a long time ago."

"You were her best friend," he pointed out, not that he needed to. It had been common knowledge.

"Which is why I know she didn't run away," she said. "She would have contacted me back then to let me know a plan so I could go with her. If anyone was going to run away, it would have been me."

"The sheriff at the time collected evidence from your text messages, your laptop and, if memory serves, your journal," he said.

Having someone dig into her personal thoughts was the worst kind of awful for a teenager. Since Duncan Hayes had been an "upstanding" citizen, the sheriff had returned her personal items to him. He'd made no secret of reading every page, and all the frustration she'd vented about him came to light. She'd been mortified. But it served him right on some level since he was the one who'd forced her to turn over the items in the first place in the name of cooperation.

"That's right," she said. "It gave my grandfather an eyeful."

"Your mother intervened," he pointed out.

"As best as she could," Reese stated. "There was only so much anyone could do when it came to Duncan Hayes. Every time someone speaks his name with reverence, I want to roll my eyes." It was probably a jerk move to hate him now that he was dead, but she had a long history of not liking the man, and he'd given her every reason to.

"He was bigger than the room," Darren agreed. "Used to scare the living daylights out of me, threatening to take me out back behind the barn and whip me if I ever laid a hand on you."

"It almost sounds noble when you put it like that," she said, "but he was only ever worried about me or my sister Liz coming home knocked up. His concern had everything to do with keeping up appearances. He didn't care if I ruined my life one way or the other as long as he came out smelling like a rose."

"That's probably true," he admitted. "It's probably parenting that's making me soft now, but I'd like to believe he cared about you and that had something to do with his reasoning."

"Did you know Rory has a daughter?" Reese asked.

"Your brother? When?" Darren asked.

"Liv is almost thirteen years old," Reese said. She heard the hint of pride in her own voice even though she'd never met Liv face-to-face.

"How did that happen?" he asked before putting a hand up to stop her from answering and, therefore, stating the obvious. "I *know* how it happened. How is it that no one knew?"

"Duncan Hayes ran Rory off the second he found out

him and his old girlfriend got pregnant," she informed him. More proof that her grandfather had only cared about his own image. "My brother hid his child from the family all these years after Duncan practically forced him out of town at eighteen and Rory was too embarrassed to tell anyone until recently."

"There goes my hope your grandfather couldn't be all bad," he said.

"Believe me when I say that I wish it wasn't true," she said. "But those are the facts and we never spoke about it to anyone."

"What happened to Rory and his daughter?" he asked.

"My brother started a successful construction company and brought his daughter up on his own after his girlfriend decided being a young mother was too hard," she said. The news had come across in a group text and, rather than come home, Reese had called her brother to get the details. Rory had practically begged her to come back to visit so she could meet Liv. Was that the real reason she was in Cider Creek? "Liv sounds like a real sweetheart. A firecracker, but a sweetie nonetheless."

"Sounds like I need to call him for parenting advice," Darren said.

"You seem like you're doing all right so far," she said, hearing the hint of pride in her own voice.

Darren didn't look so confident in his abilities. "I've been able to get the hang of changing diapers and wiping more behinds than I ever wanted to see and, believe me, I'm exhausted. More than during any calving season I've ever experienced. I've rocked each one of the girls through their colicky phase and stressed over their first colds and fevers.

The thing is, I feel like this might actually be the easy part. Like, it only gets harder from here."

"You're probably just remembering all the trouble you used to get into as a teenager," she said with a small smile. "You weren't a bad boy, but you liked to play pranks and generally give teachers a run for their money."

"That's exactly what I'm talking about," he said with wide eyes, like she'd just caught on to something. "There's probably going to be some karmic retribution for all my past sins."

She swatted a hand at him. "You did things but it's not like you were a criminal. You were actually a good kid."

"I doubt Coach Waterston would agree with that statement," he countered.

Darren had tucked one of those fake blood capsules people use at Halloween into the man's favorite ball cap. The baseball coach had a habit of hitting himself with the flat of his palm on top of his head before he ripped into someone, and that someone was usually Darren.

"To be fair, you got kicked off the team for that one," she said. "You paid your dues by not being allowed to try out for the baseball team ever again."

"If that was the only prank I ever played, I wouldn't be worried," he said.

"I guess you were a handful back then," she said. "But you calmed down a lot when we were together."

"You finally gave me a reason to stay out of detention," he said. "You were never there."

"Because I never spoke to anyone, except you," she pointed out. "I kept my head down and did my work. I did everything I could to deflect attention rather than draw it to me."

"You were always quiet, but it got worse after Camree Lynn disappeared," he remembered.

"That's what happens when your best friend goes missing and no one believes you when you say she wouldn't run away," she said.

"I get the part about reading her journal and finding out how badly she wanted to leave Cider Creek, but surely that wasn't all they had to go on," he said.

"No," she said. "There was more. She had been fighting a lot with her parents, who were getting divorced. The whole situation shook Camree Lynn up pretty badly. She threatened to run away a couple of times, but I know for a fact she was only making those threats to get attention. She told me so herself because she decided her parents might try to work things out if they believed the divorce was affecting her badly."

"Sounds like Camree Lynn to think something like that," he mused.

"Her parents were too far gone to bring their marriage back," Reese said. "They sat her down and told her as much and I'm pretty certain she was talking to guys she shouldn't have been in chat rooms even though no evidence was found."

"A troubled teen who was known to threaten to run away could have made for an easy mark for a creep," he said.

"My thoughts exactly," she agreed. "But the sheriff didn't think so. Neither did her parents. They got it inside their heads their daughter was making a play for their attention and would come home within twenty-four hours."

"I remember the case," he said. "Camree Lynn never came back to school. A body was never found."

"Because they didn't look for one," she quipped. "It's

hard to find someone when you don't even bother to search for them."

"Even teachers believed she ran away, from what I remember," he said. "They were overheard talking about her in the teacher's lounge."

"What if she didn't?"

MUCH MORE OF this talk and Darren would go pick up his twins and never let them leave his sight again. Like he said before, as hard as this stage was, he feared this was going to be the easy part of bringing up children.

"You mentioned her before," he said to Reese.

"She was on my mind," she admitted.

"There could be other explanations than you thinking you'd found her trail," he said.

"How did you even know that I was thinking that?" she asked.

He shrugged, not really wanting to recall all those little details about her that he'd been trying to shut out of his thoughts for a decade. "But it makes sense that you would be returning home at some point because of your grandfather's death. Have you been back since he passed?"

She shook her head and then twisted her fingers together. "There hasn't been a reason to."

"Family," he said. Although, she'd made it clear that family wasn't exactly a priority for her.

"We've been spread out until recently," she said. "My sister Liz is probably the last person who would come home."

"Do you talk to them on a regular basis?" he asked.

"No," she admitted. "Pretty much all I do in Dallas is work."

"Sounds about right," he said.

"What's that supposed to mean?"

"Believe it or not, I wasn't trying to offend you," he insisted. "I was all about work until the girls came along."

Reese released a slow breath and then locked gazes with him. He wasn't ready for the gut punch that came with meeting her eye-to-eye.

"You look different," she said. "Good."

"I'm the same person, Reese."

"No," she argued. "You seem a lot more settled now."

"Kids have a way to doing that to a person," he snapped, figuring he could be insulted out there, but didn't have to put up with it in his own home.

"I didn't mean it in a bad way," she replied. "It's good, actually. I mean, when we were young, you had a restless quality. Like you were always searching for something to fill... I don't know—a void. Now, you have a confident air."

"Funny, bringing up the girls makes me feel like I have no idea what I'm doing in life or otherwise," he said.

"I guess you just seem comfortable with not knowing everything," she said. "Like, you know you'll figure it out along the way."

"What choice do I have?" His girls were the reason. And Reese was right, he would move heaven and earth to make sure he found answers to every question that pertained to them.

"Not everyone is as good a father as you are, Darren."

"You haven't even seen me with my daughters yet," he said. "How can you make a statement like that?" Why should he care so much that Reese Hayes seemed awestruck with any aspect of his life?

She shook her head. "I don't have to. It's in your eyes. It's in your determination when you talk about them. It's easy to see how much you love them and how devoted you are to them."

He hoped it was enough because there was no rule book when it came to parenting. One would think twins would have the same needs, but Ivy had an independent streak a mile long, whereas Iris was content to be with her sister all the time. He was going have his work cut out for him later in trying to make sure Iris understood Ivy's independence wasn't a rejection. When Ivy was tired at the end of a long day, her sister's presence comforted her the most.

"I appreciate your kindness," he said to Reese. But it was a little too early to pat himself on the back in the parenting department. "It means a lot. But this whole game is a crapshoot and it feels like any misstep could damage these things that I love more than life itself."

The jury was out on whether or not he would be a good dad after going the distance with his girls. He couldn't imagine the horror Camree Lynn's parents must have endured at losing their daughter at such a young age. It was against the natural order for a child to die before the parents.

Speaking of disappearances, he had an idea.

Chapter Eight

"Since it's likely you were coming home at the time of the abduction, for lack of a better word, maybe you were making a pit stop first. Something about Camree Lynn's disappearance."

Darren had a point.

"What do you suggest we do?" she asked.

"Look for another disappearance. Something recent and something nearby," he continued. He held up a finger, then disappeared into what she assumed was the master bedroom.

Reese refilled her coffee mug and moved to the kitchen table as Darren returned with a laptop tucked underneath his arm.

"I do most of my paperwork while in bed after the girls go to sleep," he explained, but it was unnecessary. How he handled his business was up to him. She remembered from growing up on a cattle ranch how much paperwork was involved. Folks had several misconceptions about cattle ranching and the first one was that ranchers spent all their time herding cattle. There was far more tagging, tracking and recording than anyone realized. Another was that ranchers were all wealthy. Ranching was hard work and most barely kept their heads above water.

Duncan Hayes might have been a son of a bitch, but he'd been a keen businessman. His cold heart was good for something.

"I like the idea of looking for a connection," she said.

"We'd be searching for a serial abductor," he explained.

"Would so much time elapse in between, though?" she asked. "How could that be the same person if they just now struck again?"

"We might be looking for someone who moves around a lot for their job or travels. They might have fixated on Camree Lynn for one reason or another, but taking someone so close to home would draw a lot of unwanted attention," he said. "The person would wait a long time before striking here again."

"If at all." Reese took in a deep breath. "Sounds logical." All those old feelings of helplessness surfaced as she thought about her former best friend's disappearance. It was funny how kids always blamed themselves for things they have no control over. "I thought if I'd asked her to sleep over that weekend, she might still be alive because she would have been with me instead."

"If someone targeted her, they would have waited for another opportunity. It wouldn't have made a hill-of-beans difference," he quickly countered. His reassurance meant more to her than he could ever know.

Darren opened his laptop and hit the power button. He entered a search for "missing teen + Cider Creek" and then sat back. "There are a few hits for missing teens but Cider Creek is crossed out."

"What if we try 'missing teen plus Texas'?" she asked.

The results narrowed by a slim margin.

"We can scan the headlines to see if we recognize any of the towns nearby," he said.

"Here's one that isn't far," Darren said. Robb City was forty-five minutes east. "The missing person is a high-school sophomore. Tandra St. Claire is her name."

"Any details about the case?" she asked, scooting closer to him so she could read the print on the screen.

"She's been gone almost two weeks now," he said.

"What about the family?" she asked. "Did they make a statement?"

"The father swears his little girl was taken and that she didn't run away," he said. "Mother blames the father for cheating on her and asking for a divorce."

"Trouble at home," Reese said quietly. It sounded a little too familiar.

"They might speak to us if we can find their address," he said.

"I happen to know Camree Lynn's mom still lives at the same place," Reese said. "We could go talk to her. A lot of time has passed, and she might have done her own search-ing for her daughter. She could have information that could help us tie the cases together."

"Let's go," he said, checking the time as he bit back a yawn. It was eight o'clock.

Reese glanced down at her clothing, or lack thereof. "I can't go out like this."

"I probably have something in the laundry room for you to borrow," he said.

She shot him a look that said she didn't want to wear an-other woman's clothes, especially if it was someone he was dating, had dated or had been married to.

"Stacie left a jogging suit here once," he explained. "You two look to be about the same size."

She wanted to ask why Stacie was leaving clothing at his

home but suspected it was a sure sign someone was staking a claim. As if the way the doctor had treated Reese earlier wasn't enough to convey the message. Since her only other option was a T-shirt and bathrobe, she agreed. Liking the idea wasn't a requirement. Going outside half-naked was probably still frowned on.

Facing Camree Lynn's mother wasn't something she was looking forward to. Virginia must have been devastated. After losing her only daughter, Virginia didn't show up to school anymore. To be honest, the whole time period was fuzzy for Reese. When Stacie mentioned the part about the brain blocking out trauma for survival purposes, it had resonated. Reese was sure she'd done that exact thing to avoid thinking of her best friend's disappearance.

As much as Darren seemed overprotective of his daughters now, she'd read kids were at far greater risk of being abducted by a stranger at around age fifteen, like Camree Lynn. It was an early stage of independence, a phase of rebelling against parents and testing boundaries. Camree Lynn had fallen into the right age category, but Reese doubted that her friend would do something foolish like meet in person with someone she didn't know from the internet. Besides, the law would have checked her computer and social media sites. At least, Reese hoped that would be the case. The past sheriff had been a little too quick to classify Camree Lynn as a runaway. Was there something in her journal that Reese didn't know about? As close as they'd been, it wasn't impossible to think her friend had kept some secrets to herself.

Teenage years were hard enough with hormones and all the insecurities that came with transitioning from a fully dependent kid to an independent adult. There wasn't enough money in the world to make Reese want to go back to those days. The only bright spot in high school after Camree Lynn's disappearance had been Darren, and she'd broken his heart. He was right about one thing. The toughest years for his girls were ahead. Stacie seemed plenty eager to step into the role of mother.

There must be a story behind the way she looked at him. One that ran deeper than her loving the girls and wanting to pitch in to help because she missed her sister. Those two things might be true, but Reese had picked up on more.

Darren returned with the offering, folded up in outstretched arms. Reese took the warm-ups. Now, she was going to get to wear the woman's clothing. That wouldn't go over too well if they ran into Stacie. Reese hoped it wouldn't happen. She had a feeling Stacie believed Reese was homing in on what she'd designated as her turf.

Reese had a few choice words for Stacie should the woman confront her. Besides, she'd known Darren first.

Clearly, she was going down a rabbit hole. "I'll be right back."

Five minutes later, she was changed and ready to go. The jogging suit fit well enough. A little tight in the chest area, but she could make it work. Besides, beggars couldn't be choosers, as the saying went.

Could she get information from Virginia Bowles? Or would her former best friend's mother slam the door in Reese's face?

DARREN DIDN'T HAVE shoes that would fit Reese and she couldn't go out barefoot. So when she came out of the bathroom wearing her shoes, he was relieved.

"I cleaned them," she said, motioning toward her ballet flats. "Kept them because I didn't figure they would be much use as evidence, and I needed something to use to walk." She issued a sharp breath and her face twisted up like she was in pain. "Ballet flats and sweatpants—high fashion at its best."

Darren couldn't help but chuckle. He'd read on the society page about her career. Small-town Girl Breaks into Dallas Fashion Scene.

"Let's roll," he said, leading the way to his vehicle.

It was a quarter after nine by the time they made it to the home of Virginia Bowles. Lights were still on.

"Do you know if Mrs. Bowles ever remarried?" Reese asked Darren as they sat in his idling vehicle in front of her house in the cul-de-sac with half-acre lots.

"I heard she did," he said. "Couldn't say how it worked out, though."

"Guess we'll find out," Reese said. "I just wasn't sure if I should still call her Mrs. Bowles."

On the ride over, Reese had closed her eyes and leaned her head against the headrest. The quiet didn't bother him. It was a rare moment in a house, or car ride, for that matter, when there was peace. Being around Reese reminded him of feelings that had been dormant too long. Delving into the past also reminded him how dangerous secrets were. He'd held on to his for a long time. Could he use Reese as a sounding board? Test the waters by telling her the one he'd been holding in?

The quiet gave him time to think rather than just blow and go 24/7. Thankfully, he worked outside fixing fences and caring for his family's ranch, which was small in comparison to Hayes Cattle. At this point, it was a legacy to his girls should they want it, and taking over kept him close to the land he loved, unlike Reese who couldn't get out of town fast enough.

Was she happy?

Had her life in Dallas worked out the way she'd hoped? Or maybe it was as simple as needing to get far away from Cider Creek and…him.

He'd nursed a bruised ego over that one for longer than he cared to admit.

"I'm sure she'll recognize you," he said. "Let her lead the way on the conversation and we should be fine."

"Okay," Reese agreed, rubbing her temples as though staving off a severe headache. The ibuprofen was back at the house. He regretted not grabbing the bottle. They could stop on the way home if they could find an open store. Cider Creek and the surrounding area practically rolled up the streets by eight o'clock at night. To eat out later, he would have to go to Austin.

"Are you?" he asked. "Okay?"

"My head feels like it's splitting in two," she said. "Other than that, I'm peachy."

Her attempt to lighten the mood made him crack a smile. Not because the joke was good. In fact, it was corny. It was the way she made eyes at him, like they suddenly went back in time and she made that same goofy expression she used to whenever she tried to make him laugh.

They had laughed, which was something he didn't do a whole lot of anymore, not even with his girls. At least, not like this. The ranch barely made ends meet and he was determined to keep everything running without hiring anyone. If he sold his place, it would cut down on expenses but there was something unsettling about taking over the home his parents had built their life in despite buying fold-up cribs for the place. Too painful?

"What is it?" Reese asked. He glanced over and realized she was studying him.

"Family stuff," he said, dismissing the conversation with his tone.

"I'm here if you want to talk," she said. "Which, I mean, you probably don't want to after all the bad blood between us. It's okay. I mean, I understand why you wouldn't want to talk to me, of all people, about your family."

She always repeated words when she was nervous and was having a hard time spitting out what she wanted to stay.

"I'll keep that in mind," he said, unable to throw her a bone. Her time in town was temporary and his life was too busy for casual friendships with people who lived far away. Besides, why should he trust her again? "Ready?"

Darren cut off the engine to his SUV.

"As much as I'll ever be," she said after a pause.

He got out of the vehicle and then rounded the front. It might have been a long time since he'd had a female over the age of two inside his SUV, but he hadn't forgotten the manners ingrained in him. He opened the passenger door and held out a hand to help her down. She took the offering and the electricity he'd been doing his best to avoid crackled in the air between them, vibrating up his arm, his elbow and into his chest.

Darren sighed. She was still as beautiful, if not more. From the dark-roast hair to eyes so beautiful they looked right through him, Reese Hayes made heads turn, including his. This close, it was hard to breathe. It was almost like his ribs were locked in a vise.

Since staring into her eyes was a mistake, he turned toward the ranch-style brick home. Reese took the hint and led the way. There was no gate or fence in the front yard. None visible on the side, either.

They were able to walk right up to the front door and knock. A little yippee-sounding bark, if it could be called that, fired off from the other side. It only took a few seconds for the porch light to flip on.

Reese positioned herself in front of the peephole. Mrs. Bowles, or whatever her last name was now, would hopefully recognize Reese and open the door. Folks might be friendly but they were known to have a shotgun around, too, so Darren made sure he kept his hands where someone on the other side of the door could see them.

"Mrs. Bowles?" Reese asked. "It's me. Reese Hayes."

Darren didn't want to get too caught up in the fact Reese wasn't married. One thing was certain—he wanted to throw a punch if he ever saw his uncle again. Matias never showed his face again after luring Reese away from town with a paid summer internship in Dallas. The man was considerably older than Reese, seventeen years to be exact. And though, technically she'd been an adult—she'd turned eighteen on April twentieth—a thirty-five-year-old had a helluva lot more experience under his belt.

Even so, it had been a little too easy for her to cast Darren aside. Some of those wounds must still be tender if he was thinking about it while standing on the porch of the mother of a friend who'd been missing for thirteen years.

Chapter Nine

The door opened a crack and someone picked up the barking beast. A sliver of Camree Lynn's mother's face could be seen. From the looks of her, the last thirteen years had been hard.

"Reese?" Virginia Bowles, or whatever her last name was now, sounded like she was in shock.

"Yes, ma'am," Reese responded. "It's me. And I know it's been a long time but—"

The door swung open and in the next second Reese was being brought into a hug. "I didn't think I'd ever see you again. Heard you'd moved to Dallas and dusted this town off your boots years ago." Virginia took a step back. "Let me look at you." Tears welled in the older woman's eyes. This might have been what Camree Lynn would have looked like if she'd lived into her midfifties. Platinum-blond hair, brown eyes and a heart-shaped face. Mrs. Bowles's skin had that worn-in, leathery look. Too much time in the sun during Texas summers could easily add years to a face. She had sunspots and a mole just above her lip, just like the one Camree Lynn had.

Reese fought back the sudden urge to cry. "May we come in?"

Mrs. Bowles stood there, stunned. She shook her head like she was shaking off a brain fog. "Of course."

The door swung open, and it seemed Mrs. Bowles noticed Darren for the first time. "You're the Pierce boy."

"Darren. Yes, ma'am," he said, his voice smooth as silk. He had a deep timbre now that had a way of sliding over Reese and through her. He seemed able to touch a place deep inside her that no one had discovered.

"Come in," the older woman said, holding her arm out. She was dressed in work clothes despite the late hour. "I'm catching up on emails. Don't mind the mess."

She walked them into the eat-in kitchen, which had a laptop and a stack of books. "I'm going back to school, so ignore these and have a seat anywhere you like."

Mrs. Bowles's home had always been spick-and-span, with a place for everything. Only a couple of necessities were allowed to be on the kitchen counters. This place wouldn't exactly qualify for an episode of *Hoarders*, but it would if they had a tidy edition.

"What are you studying?" Reese asked as she took a spot at the table.

"Accounting," she said without hesitation before turning in front of a cabinet. "Can I get either of you something to drink?"

"Water, if it's not too much trouble," Reese said.

Darren nodded. "Same for me."

"Two waters coming right up," she said, smiling. After filling two glasses with ice and water from the fridge, she brought them over and set them down on the table. "It sure is good to see you."

The look in her eyes said it was also painful. No doubt being around Reese brought back a lot of memories of Camree Lynn. She had worried that showing up here would bring back painful memories for the woman.

"What makes you want to study accounting?" Reese asked, unable to find the right words to ask what she really wanted to know, without some type of lead-in.

"Ever since Evan left…" She flashed her eyes at them. "He was my second husband."

Reese nodded.

Camree's mother sighed sharply. "Well, ever since he took off with his bookkeeper, I've had all kinds of time on my hands. Figured I'd find out what was so great about a numbers person."

"I'm sorry to hear it, Mrs.—"

"Virginia," she interrupted. "Please. Call me Virginia."

It would take some getting used to, but Reese figured she could manage. "Will do, Virginia."

The older woman smiled as she took a seat across the table from Reese and Darren. "What can I help you with? I know you didn't come all the way down here from Dallas to find out what I'm studying these days."

"Thank you for seeing us without any advanced warning," Reese began, taking advantage of the opening while hoping the words would flow. "It's about Camree Lynn."

Virginia heaved a sigh, and it looked like her body deflated. "I thought maybe that's the reason you were here." She lifted her gaze and inhaled a breath. "I read about the girl in the news. Tandra. My phone rings every time a reporter digs around in a case that might look anything like my girl."

Reese didn't know one way or the other if the story brought her back near Cider Creek to investigate. Although, it would make sense as the reason she'd gotten herself in danger if she'd been poking around in the wrong place. She cursed trauma for stealing her recent memories.

"Yes," she said, unsure if it was true or not. To be fair, they had just read about Tandra.

"Do you see similarities?" Virginia continued.

"I'm not sure," Reese admitted. "But I'd like to learn more about what happened with Camree Lynn." She put up her hand to stop Virginia from saying anything just yet. "And I know it was a long time ago."

"Dear child," Virginia said. "Where do I even begin? I miss my daughter every day. I wonder if she's alive. I think about what she might have become. Would she have gone to Dallas with you to work, in art and fashion like the two of you always planned? Would she be as successful as you?"

"I'm not—"

"Don't be modest, sweetheart," Virginia protested. "I've followed your career." Her chest puffed out a little. "I've been proud of you."

Tears welled in Reese's eyes. "It means a lot to hear you say that, Virginia."

"You deserve it, dear," Virginia continued. "And I can't help but think the two of you would have stayed lifelong friends."

"That was the plan," Reese stated.

Virginia dropped her gaze. "The divorce was hard on my daughter."

"Yes," Reese agreed. There was no use lying at this point.

"I didn't know what to think at first," Virginia said. "When Camree Lynn first…disappeared. We'd been fighting. The family was a mess." She looked up and searched Reese's eyes. "We never should have dragged her into our marital problems."

"I doubt you could have hidden anything from her," Reese said.

Virginia nodded. "That very well might be true. Still, I believed the law when they said she'd run away."

"And now?"

"No one stays mad this many years, do they," Virginia stated it like it was biblical truth. "She would have come home a few months later, after she'd had a chance to cool off. I tried to tell the sheriff the same thing, but he brushed me off. With the divorce, well, it was a little too easy to say she ran off to Houston or Dallas in an election year. Otherwise, he would have allowed a killer to stalk a young person in his county, right under his nose."

"Doesn't bode well on election day, does it," Darren said. The disdain in his voice reminded her that he'd been friends with Camree Lynn, too.

DARREN CLENCHED HIS back teeth. Being lazy on a job was one thing. A law-enforcement officer being lazy on the job was enough to make him see red. If the sheriff had treated Camree Lynn's case correctly, would she be sitting here at this table with them? Would her mother's smile reach her eyes? Because it sure as hell didn't now, and he couldn't blame Virginia one bit. The thought of losing one of his girls...

His grip around his glass was tight enough to break it, so he forced himself to cool off and set down the glass.

"No. It doesn't," Virginia said about his election-day comment. She placed her palms on the table. "Not a day goes by that I don't think about my Camree Lynn. I called police in Houston, Dallas, Austin. They weren't any help."

Darren could only imagine the pain. He prayed like hell

that he would never have to experience something as awful as losing a child.

"Funny thing is, you lose everything with your child," Virginia continued. "Oh, at first everyone is wonderful. They see you at the grocery store and can't wait to give you a hug and tell you what your child meant to them. After a while, it calms down and then you become this visual reminder of how awful it is to lose your baby. Folks see you in the soup aisle and skip it." She waved her hands in the air. "I'm sure they don't mean to come across as coldhearted. It's like they can't face you any longer because you remind them of what *they* could lose."

"I'm so sorry," Reese said with the kind of emotion that said she meant it.

"You were just a child yourself," Virginia said. "I imagine you were doing the best you could just to survive every day."

"For the record, I never believed she ran away," Reese stated.

Virginia rocked her head. "I know. Looking back, I should have listened." She studied a spot on the table in front of her. "What's the saying? Something about 'out of the mouths of babes.'"

Reese nodded. Darren had heard the saying, too.

"You're right, though," Reese said. "None of the other adults listened to me, either. Not the sheriff or my grandfather."

Virginia reached across the table for Reese's hands. "He was so hard on you."

"Yes," Reese said. "My mother tried to stick up for me but she was too... I don't know what the right word is."

"Political?" Virginia said.

"A pushover," Reese corrected. "At least in my view."

"Your mother was in a difficult position with your grandfather with the way he held the ranch over her head," Virginia stated, like it was common knowledge.

"What do you mean?" Reese asked.

"He used the ranch to keep her under his thumb," Virginia said. "Don't count your mother out, though. She was as strong as they come but she'd never worked a day in her life outside of the family business. Duncan used it against her, too. The bastard."

Reese's surprise was written all over her face. "Hold on a minute. Are you telling me that my mother would have happily left the ranch if my grandfather hadn't threatened her with the purse strings?"

"That's right," Virginia confirmed. "He must have realized she would leave after her husband..." Virginia locked gazes with Reese for a few seconds. "Logan died. Your mother had six hungry mouths to feed. Seven if you count your grandmother, who was from a generation of women who didn't have the option of making their own living. She had medical bills, too. Your grandfather on your father's side threatened to cut your mother off if she didn't bring you all up on the ranch."

Reese sucked in a breath. "I'm starting to understand my mother a little better."

"Marla was a strong woman," Virginia said. "I've always admired her for doing what was right for her family even when it put her in a bad position. She knew how to be delicate, whereas I was always more headstrong in life."

"The two of you were friends?" Reese asked, surprised.

"As much as we could be considering our lives were so different," Virginia said. "Our daughters, however, were best friends and we both approved. I'm afraid I was so

caught up in my own misery with my first husband that I ne-
glected Camree Lynn. And then she was gone. For months,
I believed she hated me. That she couldn't wait to leave
home to get away from the fights. I can't count the number
of times she threatened to run off." Virginia covered her
mouth with her hand, like the words were almost too horrible to speak out loud. A few tears rolled down her cheeks.
"I'm sorry." She shook her head. "You would think it would
get easier. It's just, I never really talk about her anymore.
Her father and I lost contact after the divorce. Without her,
there wasn't much left for us to talk about. And then my
second husband didn't know her, so I just stopped."

"I have twin baby girls," Darren stated. "Every day, I
make mistakes with them. I worry if my tone of voice is
too harsh or if they're sleeping all right. I check their cribs
several times a night to make sure they're still breathing."

Virginia smiled through tears that ran freely down her
face. "How old?"

"Eighteen months," he responded.

"How precious," Virginia said. "Do you have pictures?"

He fished his cell phone out of his pocket and thumbed
through the pass code before tapping the photo icon. A smile
crept across his mouth as the first photo filled the screen.
"Here they are in all their glory." He turned the screen so
Virginia could see.

"They're beautiful," she said as her gaze immediately
shifted to study him and Reese. "I can't tell which one of
you they favor the most."

"Oh, they're not mine," Reese said. "I'm not...haven't
been... We haven't seen each other in years."

Virginia balked. "I wondered how you would have

pulled off a secret wedding and a life working in two different cities."

"That would be impossible," Reese said with a little too much enthusiasm. He tried not to be offended that she seemed so ready to ship him off with someone else. Anyone else. He resisted the urge to say the logistics might be tricky but not impossible. Not for two people who were in love. With technology, long distance was no longer an issue. Except he could admit that he needed someone in the same area now that the twins were in his life.

Virginia looked like she was biting her tongue. Yes, they'd been a couple in high school, but she must not be aware of the fact Reese had easily chucked their relationship for a job then dated his uncle, no less.

"We went our separate ways after high school," he said, figuring it summed up the past in the most respectful way to both of them. "We had different goals." He also didn't see the need to point out her goal had been to date the first man who came along with a job offer. That was probably being harsh and he was most likely speaking from his ego—an ego that had taken more than its fair share of hits years ago.

Hazel might not have lit the same fires inside him as Reese, but he'd loved his wife in his own way. A voice in the back of his head reminded him that she'd betrayed him, too. Maybe that was just his curse with the opposite sex. They were bound to deceive him at some point.

"Did the law ever return any of Camree's personal belongings?" Reese asked after clearing her throat. The change in subject was a welcomed reprieve.

Virginia handed his phone back to him. "Yes. As a matter of fact, they did. Said nothing was relevant to a runaway case."

"What about her journal?" Reese continued.

"Still under her mattress," Virginia said. "I put it there because I knew she'd be so angry if she knew we'd read it."

Reese shifted in her seat. "Mind if I take a look?"

Chapter Ten

Virginia studied Reese as though the woman was trying to make up her mind as to just how bad of an idea it might be to disturb Camree Lynn's things again.

"Please," Reese added for good measure.

"What would be the point?" Virginia asked. "Unless you think you can bring her back by rooting through her things." Virginia blew out a breath. "I always felt guilty for letting the sheriff read her personal thoughts. Then again, I thought she'd come back once she cooled off."

Reese feared Camree Lynn was gone forever. A body had never been found. There was no closure for anyone who missed her. For a split second, she saw an image of Virginia sitting at this table, staring at that front door, expecting her daughter to come busting through in a fit of rage about her journal becoming public property. It made her sad all over again. The kind of sadness that had her cry in her pillow every night and refuse to go to school or speak to anyone other than the law or Darren. Sheriff Webb had been the sheriff back then. He'd had asked a few questions about Camree Lynn's mental state but even then, Reese believed the man had made up his mind. Looking back, talking to her had been ticking a box on a form rather than digging for information in an investigation. To Sheriff Webb, it had been an open-and-shut case.

"I'd like to explore any similarities, like we said before," Reese said honestly.

"It won't bring her back," Virginia protested.

"No. I'm sorry, but it won't. It might bring closure and justice, though," Reese pointed out.

"Camree Lynn isn't here to tell me what she wants one way or the other." Virginia threw her hands up in the air. "So I guess it won't do any harm now."

"We can see the journal then?" Reese asked, just to be certain they were on the same page. Getting a close-up look at how hard parenting was made her soften toward her own mother. Seeing Darren second-guess himself as a dad brought home how difficult the job must be. Hearing about the ultimatum her mother had faced burned her up even more about her no-good grandfather. What had the man done for the family besides build a successful cattle ranch? Reese had walked away from the family money at eighteen and had no plans to ask for a red cent. The money wasn't hers. She hadn't worked for it and had no business taking it as far as she was concerned.

Virginia stood up and placed her palms on the table as she leaned toward them. "Yes. You can see the journal. I've read over it a dozen times and couldn't find any clues. But you knew her better than anyone else." She shrugged. "Maybe you'll find something the rest of us missed. By the time we realized she wasn't coming back, the trail was cold."

"I'll do my best," Reese promised.

Virginia excused herself and went down the hallway. Darren had been quiet during the journal discussion. He sat back with his arms folded. Had Reese said something to offend him? His jaw muscle ticked like he was clenching his back teeth. It could be the heaviness of the situation, the fact that his daughters lived in a small town where a crime this heinous could occur or he was angry with her. She'd seen the look before. Usually, it meant the latter.

"Everything okay?" she asked, figuring it was better to speak up now than hold her tongue.

"Sure," he responded with a tone that said the opposite was true.

Reese wasn't ready to let it go. "Did I say something wrong?"

Before he could respond, Virginia came back into the room, holding Camree Lynn's journal high in the air. *The Starry Night* had been Camree Lynn's favorite painting. She'd been obsessed with it, so her journal was wrapped in a cover with a picture of the famous oil painting. "Here it is."

"Do you mind if we take it with us?" Reese asked.

Virginia emphatically shook her head. "In a strange way, I feel like she might come home expecting it to be tucked underneath her mattress. If it goes…"

Overwrought with emotion, the older woman struggled to get the words out. Reese could only imagine how difficult it must be for Virginia to sit across the table from her presumably dead daughter's former best friend.

She handed over the journal. "Take pictures of anything you want, but the journal must stay here."

"Okay," Reese said, taking the offering as Virginia reclaimed her seat across the table from them. Reese couldn't help but reach out for Virginia's hand to comfort her. She had no idea if the gesture made a difference, but when Virginia looked at her with gratitude in her eyes, Reese was humbled.

There'd been the occasional interaction with Virginia in a grocery-store parking lot years ago. Or a wave at the post office. But this was different. They were speaking to each other as adults who were on the same page about what had happened to Virginia's daughter and Reese's best friend.

Reese was also seeing parenting in a new light, and the job was even harder than she'd imagined it would be. Had she been too hard on her own mother? Judged her too harshly when Reese didn't have all the facts? The hard answer was yes. But she wished her mother had mentioned the ultimatum or explained the reasons she stuck around when Duncan Hayes had been a class-A jerk.

She liked her grandfather even less now and she didn't think that was even possible.

Refocusing on the journal, she flipped page after page until she reached the end. There were mostly scribbles, random thoughts, and sketches. She'd forgotten how much Camree Lynn liked to draw.

"She was good, wasn't she?" Virginia asked as Reese used her index finger to trace the outline of a teddy-bear drawing on the last page.

"Very," Reese agreed.

"She was going to start taking art classes in Austin on Saturdays," Virginia said.

"I didn't know that," Reese replied.

"Because I hadn't told her yet," Virginia said wistfully. "Her father and I decided to find classes for her as a way of apologizing for all the arguing we did with her around." She flashed her eyes at Reese and then Darren. "If you do nothing else as a parent, hold your temper. Count to ten. Walk out of the room. And I don't just mean with your children. Do it with your spouse as well."

"Thank you for the advice," he said with genuine appreciation in his tone. "My wife died a year ago."

Reese's heart nearly cracked in half at hearing him talk about the mother of his children to Virginia.

"I'm on this road by myself," he said. "It's nice to get a female perspective, and from someone who has a lot of experience."

Virginia clutched the center of her chest. "Dear boy. I remember you being a handful in your youth." She looked at him with such appreciation. "Look how you've grown into an amazing person. Your girls are lucky to have you. And don't you think for a second you're not going to be enough."

Darren nodded. "Thank you."

Virginia sucked in a breath. "I just remembered something. The sheriff never took me seriously because I believed my daughter ran away for a long time, but then I remembered two people had interactions with her that, looking back, made me think twice."

"Who were they?" Reese asked, leaning into her elbows that were already on the edge of the table.

"Phillip Rhodes and…" She snapped her fingers but Reese's body tensed at the mention of that name.

DARREN WITNESSED A change in Reese. It was almost as though her muscles coiled. He made a mental note to ask her about it in the SUV on the way back because her lips pressed together like they were locked.

"And the Archer boy," Virginia continued. "What was his first name?"

"They have three boys in that family. All close in age," Darren said as Reese seemed to have suddenly gone mute. "Andrew, Alexander or Aiden?"

"Aiden," Virginia confirmed. "Aiden Archer."

"What made you suspicious of these two?" Darren asked.

"Phillip Rhodes was a summer camp counselor at the Camp Needles," Virginia said. "He seemed to take an extra interest in Camree Lynn when he was here, but he always got nervous if he saw me."

Darren didn't put a lot of stock into the comment. "That could be any teenager around a girl's mom, especially one he likes."

Virginia nodded. "That's true, but I would see him stand close to her with his back turned to me. Later, I found out he wasn't a teenager even though he looked like one. He was twenty-four at the time of her disappearance."

"Did the law list him as someone she might have run off with?" Darren asked.

"I'm not sure if you remember but the camp closed the next year, so he never came back. The sheriff dismissed my concern. Said there was no evidence linking Rhodes to Camree Lynn because no crime had been committed."

"She was fifteen at the time she went missing," Darren said.

Virginia's lips thinned. "The sheriff said fifteen was the most common age for runaways. He said she'd be back once she realized how hard life was. Said she'd most likely return home on her own accord by month's end."

Darren took in a deep breath to calm his rising anger. It was impossible not to imagine this happening to one of his daughters and the lengths to which he would have gone to locate her and bring her home. No judgment on Virginia, but he wouldn't have been able to sleep until his daughters were tucked into their own beds again.

"When she didn't come back, did he have an excuse?" Darren asked.

"He'd already tried to track her cell phone," she said. "Couldn't find anything out of the ordinary on the call logs that ended the day before she left."

The lawman had mishandled the case from day one. He'd read somewhere that the first twenty-four hours were the most critical in an investigation. After twenty-four hours, trails went cold. Probably less than that when it came to children and stranger abductions.

"The person who abducted her could have made sure there would have been no way to track them," he countered, realizing he was preaching to the choir when Virginia nodded.

There was something to be said for a mother's intuition. He made a mental note of the two names Virginia had supplied. The first one would be difficult to track and he had no idea what Aiden was up to now. Darren didn't keep up with folks in his own grade, let alone kids who were two years older.

Virginia bit back a yawn. Her red-rimmed eyes looked like they were trying to close on her. Dredging up the past had to be awful for her. His heart went out to Camree's mother.

"Is there anything else you remember about that time?" he asked, figuring they'd learned enough for one evening. Besides, he wanted to get Reese home and to bed. She'd been through more than anyone should have to endure and needed sleep.

"Just those two names stick out in my mind," she said on a shrug. "As far as the other one goes, Aiden Archer, I didn't like the way he was always watching her when he was around. I asked if he ever tried to speak to her and she said he gave her the creeps. She brushed him off." She stopped and took in a deep breath. "What I wouldn't give to go back and do things differently with Camree Lynn. Hug her more. Tell her how much I love her." More tears streamed down Virginia's cheeks. She apologized as she wiped them away. "I certainly would have gone back and talked to those men once I suspected she didn't run away."

"No need to be sorry," he said to her as he stood up.

"I was drinking a lot back then to cope with the end of my marriage," Virginia admitted with an embarrassed look.

Reese closed the journal and scooted it across the table toward Virginia, who took it and then held it against her chest.

"Thank you for talking to us tonight," Reese finally said but it sounded like there was a frog in her throat. "It's really good to see you again."

"Stop by anytime," Virginia said, meeting them around the table. With her free arm, she embraced Reese in a quick hug. "She would be proud of you. You know that, right? You're doing everything the two of you said you would. You're successful in Dallas, organizing runway shows for designers. She was into art. You're successful and Camree Lynn is bursting with pride somewhere."

"It means a lot to hear you say that," Reese said. The hitch in her throat said she was holding back. It probably shouldn't surprise him that Reese had secrets. She'd kept a big one from him right up until she took off.

"I mean every word," Virginia said as she walked them to the door. She put her hand on Darren's shoulder. "If you ever want to talk…give me a call or come on by. I'd love to meet your girls someday."

"Will do, ma'am," he said.

Reese was quiet on the way to the SUV. He walked her to the passenger side with his hand on her elbow. Getting close to her was probably a bad idea on his part, but he could tell being in Camree Lynn's house again, seeing her journal, had nearly knocked Reese on her backside.

After opening the door and offering a hand, he helped her with the big step up to the passenger seat. One look at her said the adrenaline rush she'd been running on had expired. He rounded the front of the SUV, and then reclaimed the driver's seat.

It only took a few seconds to buckle up. He glanced over and noticed Reese wasn't wearing hers.

"You might want to put your seat belt on or this thing will start griping at you," he said, motioning toward the screen in his dash. Everything had technology in it now.

Reese stared ahead with a blank look on her face. "I recognized one of those names."

Chapter Eleven

"Phillip Rhodes." Reese involuntarily shivered after saying the name out loud. She buckled up so Darren could get on the road.

"The camp counselor?" Darren asked.

She nodded.

"He gave me the creeps. I even warned Camree Lynn about him. She seemed on the same page about avoiding the guy after he showed up in the barn and came on to me," she explained.

"Why was he there in the first place?" he asked.

"Duncan hired him for seasonal work after the camp closed for the summer," she said. "I'd forgotten all about him and the incident until Virginia brought him up again just now. I just wanted to block it out after it happened."

"Did you tell the sheriff about him before?" Darren asked.

Reese shook her head. "There didn't seem to be a reason to at the time. I mean, Camree Lynn didn't want to be around him to my knowledge. I feel like she would have told me if that changed at some point."

"Teenagers can be secretive," he said.

She nodded. No one in the community knew what a jerk her grandfather was to his family. All of the Hayes kids had been trained to keep the secret even though Reese didn't recall a particular conversation. It was ingrained in them not to discuss family matters outside of Hayes Ranch. Ranch hands were required to sign NDAs, so they legally couldn't discuss anything that went on.

"What exactly did Phillip Rhodes do to you?" Darren asked as he white-knuckled the steering wheel.

The memory was so traumatic, she'd blocked it out. The details were coming back now, though, and they made her hands fist. "He cornered me in a stall, pushed me up against the wall and tried to force me to kiss him."

"But you fought back," he said.

"Hell, yes, I did," she said. "He had grabby hands that were ridiculously strong. He pinned mine above my head easily." She needed a second to breathe through the tightening in her chest at the horrific memory that she'd suppressed for so long. "I wasn't going down willingly, so he dropped a hand and forced my face to be still." Bile burned the back of her throat as she thought about it now. "I was young, so I panicked. I was somehow afraid the whole incident would be twisted around to become my fault. Duncan was so hard on us, especially the girls."

"That son of a bitch," Darren said under his breath. It was so low, she almost didn't hear him. She had no idea if he was talking about Phillip or Duncan, but the label fit both, in her opinion. Phillip for being a jerk and Duncan for making her afraid to speak up.

More of the memory surfaced. "He licked my neck, which was disgusting, and then dropped his hand from my jaw and grabbed..." She didn't need to go into detail. The thought of what he did alone made her cringe. "Thankfully, my brother Tiernan came walking into the barn. Phillip threatened me if I told on him, and I clamped my mouth shut while he pretended to be helping me clean out the stall."

"Tiernan didn't catch on to what was going on?" Darren asked.

"I'm a very good actress," she explained. "So, no. But I suspect he had questions since I was shaken up. Before he could ask, I brushed the whole incident off."

Darren's silence hurt her feelings because he gave a small nod of agreement about her being a good actress. She didn't have a right to be mad at him. She'd kept a secret from him years ago when his uncle had first offered her an internship. She'd had to conceal the information or risk being shut down by her grandfather. And, honestly, talking to Darren face-to-face might have made her change her mind and stay. Dating Darren's uncle had been her worst regret. Matias Ossian had been the opposite of everything she'd known in Cider Creek. He wore hand-tailored suits and shiny shoes. He drove a sports car when she was used to pickup trucks and SUVs. On top of that, he had connections to a world in which she desperately wanted to belong.

The Hayes family had money, so his show of money wasn't what had impressed her—it was the way he carried himself. He was older, mysterious. In the beginning, though, she had no idea they would end up dating. Being alone in Dallas without family or friends turned out to be harder than she realized it would be. Matias had offered to bring over dinner a few times, so she wouldn't have to eat alone. Slowly but surely, he'd broken down her defenses and preyed on her loneliness. In fact, he'd played her like a fine instrument, all the while betraying her behind her back. She'd done it to herself, too, and was far too proud to admit she'd made a mistake. Tucking her tail between her legs and going home hadn't been an option. Not to someone with a stubborn streak a mile long.

Mistakes were always hard to admit, even harder to face.

He started the engine and put the gearshift into Drive, then pulled onto the farm road leading toward his home. He mumbled something about wishing he could spend five minutes alone in a locked room with the bastard. She assumed he was referring to Phillip, since he couldn't exactly read her thoughts. There'd been a time when she would have sworn he could. But that was a long time ago, he'd been proven wrong and a lot had changed since then.

Missed opportunities were the worst. But then, looking back, if she had stayed and—on the off chance—had actually married Darren, then he wouldn't have his beautiful twins. His life would look very different, and as much as he complained about being tired, his eyes lit up at every mention of those babies. So much so that Reese wanted to meet them to see what the fuss was all about. She'd never been much of a baby person. There were no longings about being pregnant or fantasizing about a wedding. Her brothers seemed to have found true love and she was happy for each and every one of them. Those things were great for other people.

And yet, being around Darren now did have her wondering what life might have been like if she'd made a different choice. But she couldn't have him and Dallas. Leaving Cider Creek had been a necessity and she was proud of herself for the career she'd built so far. She'd needed to know she could not just survive on her own, but make something of her life outside of Hayes Cattle. Surely, Darren could understand.

"Once we get back to my place, I'll do a little digging into Phillip Rhodes's current situation," he finally said. "He's a bastard but that doesn't mean he abducted Camree Lynn or Tandra. To be honest, I think I blanked out most of that time period of life."

"Same for me," she admitted. At least he was talking again. The silence had given her mind too much time to spiral. "A lot of the details are fuzzy." The thought of digging into her friend's disappearance made her stomach tie in knots, but she would face anything at this point for answers.

He nodded as he stared out the front windshield at the stretch of road in front of them.

"For what it's worth, I never had to 'act' when it came to how I felt for you," she said.

"Okay," he responded. The one word combined with his serious expression gave her the impression he would never be able to put the past behind them. She didn't expect him to run toward her with open arms, but a small hope had been building inside her that they could be friends. The wishful thinking was off base. She needed to remind herself of that fact every hour if necessary until it sunk in.

"WHAT ARE YOUR thoughts on Aiden Archer?"

The question from Reese yanked Darren out of his heavy thoughts. Those thoughts had gone on a path of their own the minute she mentioned being a convincing actress. He could personally attest to her abilities, considering he'd been the last to know she was planning to shred his heart and leave town. The breakup text from her had come when she was already halfway to her new city.

"I have no idea what he's up to these days. I never really liked the family, but that doesn't make one of them a criminal," he said.

"True," she responded. "As far as Phillip goes, I'd be interested to see if it's common for someone like him to escalate to something as extreme as kidnapping. I mean, I read somewhere that Peeping Toms actually do progress to break-ins and raping victims."

He nodded and mulled over the information on the rest of the ride home. It was getting late and Reese had had one helluva long day, so she needed rest.

As he pulled up in front of his home, he said, "I'm good without sleep for a few hours. Why don't you grab a nap and then I'll have an update for you."

"What about the girls?" she asked.

It was probably wrong to allow his heart to be warmed by the fact that her first thought was his children. "They'll be fine. I'll swing by at some point in the morning to check on them." He didn't like going more than a day without seeing them for himself, which had been a challenge during calving season without Hazel.

Reese didn't wait for him to come around to the passenger side before she exited the SUV.

She waited at the door for him to unlock it. The move surprised him at first, because he couldn't remember the last time he'd locked a door. With everything going on, he felt the need to now. He thought about increasing security with cameras and possibly an alarm, and hated the thought that his daughters might grow up in a world where they didn't feel free to come and go as they pleased.

Once inside, exhaustion started to hit him, too. He bit back a yawn, figuring he had another hour in him before he'd need to grab a few minutes of shut-eye.

"Mind if I curl up on the couch?" Reese asked as she twisted her fingers together. "The thought of being alone in a room right now..." She shuddered.

"Go ahead and make yourself comfortable while I grab a pillow and a blanket," he said, then exited the room. He returned a minute later to find her standing at the kitchen sink, drinking a glass of water. "Are you hungry?"

"A little bit, but I should probably get some rest," she said. "I'm so tired my legs ache."

He nodded, then made up the couch. It looked comfortable enough, although he couldn't imagine fitting on it with his six-feet-three-inch frame.

"I'll just change back into sleeping clothes," she said. It was her turn to disappear for a few minutes. He shouldn't like seeing her wearing his AC/DC T-shirt as much as he did, but Reese was a beautiful woman and they had a lot of good history before the one big bad event. It had been a heartbreaker, to be sure, but the old saying "don't throw the baby out with the bathwater" was beginning to seem relevant here. This was good. It meant he was starting to get closure. He'd mentioned to Stacie that he might be ready to move on and dip his toe in the dating waters. Shedding the past might allow him to open up to something all the way this time, instead of holding a piece of his heart in reserve for someone who was never coming back.

Reese positioned herself on the couch as he walked into the kitchen to make coffee.

He had no idea what her sleep habits were since they'd practically been kids when they'd dated and a lot could change. "Will noises bother you?"

"Not today they won't," she said. Her sleepy voice tugged at his heartstrings.

"You used to be a heavy sleeper, but I wasn't sure if that stuck," he admitted.

"I've slept through a tornado alarm that was right outside my bedroom window," she said. "So, yeah, some things will never change."

He didn't need to pay too close attention to what did or didn't change when it came to Reese.

She curled up on her side. From this vantage point, he couldn't see if she'd closed her eyes, but suspected so. After grabbing his laptop, he hit the power button, bringing his screen to life. Time to do a little digging into the cases and see if he could find any similarities.

The first name he typed in was Camree Lynn's. There were a couple of social media accounts with the name but no news stories of her disappearance. Then again, she'd been classified as a runaway. That fact was going to make this harder than he wanted it to be.

They would have to gain information by talking to folks. He could start with Stacie. She'd grown up not far from here. Her parents might know something. But the people who would remember the most were related to Reese. Her mother would have taken a keen interest in the case, considering it was her daughter's best friend. Then there was Granny. She was a firecracker with a great memory. She might have paid special attention to what was going on.

Between him and Reese, maybe they could piece together what happened or get enough to find a similarity with the Tandra disappearance. At least her parents were on the same page.

Based on the photo of Tandra, she and Camree Lynn were similar-looking with dirty blond hair and cobalt-blue eyes. Both were fifteen and Tandra's parents admitted to talking about divorce, which was hard on any kid, but especially a teenager going through an independent streak.

The crimes occurred in neighboring counties. Darren

suspected they could be related. He wondered how many other missing teens around the state had the same physical attributes. It was impossible to tell whether or not Tandra was the same height as Camree Lynn, but they had similar builds.

Scanning the search results of "missing or runaway teenage girls" in the news section, he located three other females in between Camree Lynn and Tandra who looked similar to them. All from Texas and spread around the state. He opened a document and made a note of their names and any family information he could find. If the same person was responsible for Camree Lynn and Tandra's disappearances, he'd chosen girls who had tumultuous family lives.

It was tempting to wake up Reese with this find, but he didn't want to disrupt her soft, even breathing.

A possible pattern was emerging, though. And Sheriff Courtright needed to be asked some hard questions.

Chapter Twelve

Reese opened her eyes, stretched and yawned. Light filtered through the slats of the miniblinds, so it must be morning. A figure was slumped over in a chair in the living room. A shirtless figure. The figure was Darren. Had he slept in that uncomfortable position all night long so she wouldn't be alone?

The least she could do was make coffee and cook breakfast. She freshened up in the bathroom before folding up her blanket and then stacking it on top of the pillow. With care, she sidestepped a squeaky toy and made it into the next room quietly.

The supplies for coffee were easy to find. His kitchen was orderly, so mugs were in the cabinet above the machine.

The living area might be messy with all the kid stuff lying around, but the kitchen had a place for everything. There were no dishes in the sink. He'd come a long way considering his mother used to be on him almost constantly to put his dishes in the dishwasher.

Darren Pierce was a grown-up now. She smiled. Sleep put her in a better mood. It helped that her head didn't feel like it was split in two this morning. Caffeine would clear the cobwebs. Food would keep her from getting queasy.

Once the coffee was working, she checked the fridge. There was a carton of eggs. There were green onions and bell peppers. She snagged shredded cheese and milk. With these ingredients, she could fix a mean omelet.

"What is that smell?" Darren asked. His deep voice raised goose bumps on her arms and caused warmth to spread through her. "Heaven?"

"My version," she said, turning her head enough to see him push to standing. The six-pack in his stomach was more like a twelve-pack. She forced her gaze back on the frying pan. "Almost done."

"What can I do to help?" he asked.

Being independent and taking care of twins wasn't something she could imagine pulling off on her own. It was high time someone took care of him for a change. "Take a seat at the table."

"You sure?"

The fact that there was a twinge of guilt in his voice, like he believed he should be helping, indicated that this man rarely got a break.

"Positive," she reassured him as she plated the food. She poured a cup of coffee for him and brought both to the table while he rubbed his eyes and yawned. "Eat. Drink. Once you get some caffeine inside you, I'd like to hear about what you found last night in your search."

Reese set down breakfast in front of Darren, who looked impressed by her cooking skills. A sense of accomplishment brought a smile to her lips. She had no doubt this day was going to be heavy once it got going, so it was nice to have a few quiet minutes this morning to share a meal.

After making her own breakfast, she joined him.

"When did you learn to cook?" he asked with a grin.

"Cooking shows." She returned the smile. "I know. Go figure. But you can learn just about anything you want to on the internet when you can't sleep at three o'clock in the morning."

"I'm surprised you have any time after hearing about your dedication to your job last night," he said.

"A girl has to eat," she said explained. "My mom was a good cook and takeout gets old." She shrugged. "I found a couple of shows that I liked and, more importantly, could pause as I followed along. Turns out, cooking isn't as awful or hard as I thought it would be. And I have a lot of satisfaction in knowing I can take care of myself."

"So-o-o-o-o." He drew out the word. "Just the omelets then."

"How did you know?" she asked.

"You overexplained your answer. It's always a sign someone is lying," he teased.

"Good to know," she replied. "I'll make sure to give short answers the next time I lie." Reese laughed and so did Darren. It felt good to laugh again. There hadn't been much laughter in her life since she left Cider Creek, and him. He'd always had a way of pulling a smile out of her. Good to know some things didn't change.

The plates were empty too soon, as were the cups. They needed to talk.

"Did you find anything last night in your research?" she asked.

He brought her up to speed.

"That makes five victims that we know about if they're all linked," she said.

"And gives us a trail to work with," he said. "We have two

names to start with and we can track them down to figure out if they have jobs that travel, for instance."

It sounded like a good place to start. "If we can figure out where they work, we might be able to get a hold of their vacation schedule." Hearing the words made her think differently. "Actually, I think this guy knows his targets. He would have to have a job that put him in those places long enough to find his target. The fact all the parents were in the middle of fighting and facing divorce means he had some kind of inside knowledge into their personal lives."

"Which could mean he contacted them on their computers, or via an app," he deduced as he tapped his finger on the table.

"Wouldn't that leave a cyber trial?" she asked.

"Yes, but these kids are classified as runaways, so no one is investigating too deeply. There are probably programs that can hide online activity," he informed her. "The crimes are occurring around Texas, so no link has been made up until now and we're just guessing here."

She nodded. "True enough. We are just going on flimsy information. We don't have evidence and, based on what you read, no bodies have ever been recovered."

"I imagine it's difficult to prove a murder case without a dead body."

Reese sighed. "This guy moves around to different locations. It's possibly Phillip Rhodes or Aiden Archer. Could be someone else, though."

"I take an accusation like this one very seriously," he said. "No one deserves to have their privacy invaded without clear evidence against them and we can't even prove any of these disappearances are linked."

She didn't want to be pessimistic about their amateur

investigation, but they needed to be honest and face facts. "The cases are cold, too." And they might be grasping at straws.

Darren studied the rim of his coffee cup for a long moment before lifting his gaze to meet hers. "All we're doing is asking questions."

She nodded.

"I thought we might want to start with my in-laws and then move to your family," he explained. "We have the best chance of someone remembering or having suspicions if we talk to the people who were closest to Camree Lynn's disappearance. Your family would have followed the story. Your mother, knowing how she is, probably brought meals to Camree Lynn's mother. At the very least, she would have dropped something off at her doorstep."

Why was it so easy to forget the good qualities in family members and focus on the bad stuff that happened? Reese was beginning to realize how shortsighted she'd been with her mother. In fact, she was starting to feel like a brat for punishing the woman for the behavior of Duncan Hayes. Rather than ask about the circumstances, Reese had made judgments about her mother being too weak to take on Duncan.

It might even be true. But her weak spot had been needing to provide for her children. Food and a roof over their heads cost money—money Duncan had but used to keep his daughter-in-law under his thumb after her husband, who was his son, had died. So, no, she wouldn't mourn a man who could be such a bastard to everyone around him.

But she didn't get off scot-free, either. The day she became independent was the moment she became responsible for her actions. She owed her mother an apology and a conversation.

Calling her couldn't be put off any longer.

DARREN MOVED INTO the bedroom to make the call he needed.

"How are my girls?" he asked the minute his former mother-in-law picked up.

"Amazing," she said, but she sounded more tired than she probably wanted to let on. "They've eaten breakfast and both are in their jumpy things." He could hear giggles in the background and the sound made the world right itself. "Have you had a chance to finish filling out the medical history on your side of the family? The nurse called and said your part has been left blank and they just caught it after the eighteen-month checkup."

"No. I haven't," he said, hating that he kept skirting this issue. The truth was that he wasn't one-hundred-percent certain the twins were his biological daughters. Hazel had moved out after picking a huge fight and didn't come home for a month. She'd said she needed time and space to clear her head and decide if being married was the right thing for her. What she meant was being married to *him*. Since she didn't go home to her parents' house or stay with her sister, he'd suspected and she'd confirmed she'd gone back to the musician boyfriend with whom she'd been in a relationship before the two of them met.

The timing of the pregnancy caused him to doubt he was their father, which didn't make him love the twins any less. He'd been ready to talk to Hazel about his concern once they got through the pregnancy and those early months. It had taken him a minute to do the math. Twins came early, Hazel had said. It wasn't unusual.

Darren had committed to his marriage. When Hazel came home, they'd talked and agreed to go the distance with each other, just like in their vows. He'd never wavered from his promise despite the fact that he loved his wife, but wasn't wildly in love with her like he'd been with...

He wouldn't go there.

After the girls were born, they were knee-deep in dirty diapers. A paternity test needed to happen, but he kept putting it off, trying to figure out the best time to spring the news on Hazel. Things between them had been going good and he hadn't wanted to stir the pot. Except the niggling voice in the back of his mind kept reminding him it wouldn't be fair to the girls or their biological father if they weren't his to stay in the dark.

Before he could bring up the subject to Hazel, she was gone. And then he was a single father with only a suspicion she'd cheated while they lived apart.

A year had passed by in a flash with the girls after their mother's death. Suddenly, they were eighteen months and he still hadn't taken the damn test.

Once Hazel died, her parents had come close to threatening to take the girls. They'd tap-danced on a line that shouldn't be crossed.

They seemed to realize cooperation was in the girls' best interest all the way around. Stacie had stepped in to defend him and help bring reason to an overcharged emotional mess.

They'd been a mess. But then, they'd lost their baby girl, so he couldn't fault them too much even if he'd been the one to take the brunt of their anger.

Apologies had been made and he'd forgiven them for the sake of the girls. They needed grandparents, and his folks were gone. They needed an aunt, and he had no siblings. And they needed their father, which had been him every step of the way.

Like they say, "if it ain't broke, don't fix it." But he didn't feel good about not knowing the truth. Plus, his math could have been off, the girls could have been that early and he could be stressing for literally no reason. Confirmation would be a good thing.

He couldn't ask Stacie for advice, considering she had no idea he was even questioning paternity. Could he ask Reese? She was objective. She could keep a secret. And yet, risking telling anyone else gave him chest pains.

He'd think about it.

"Darren?" his mother-in-law, Alice, said, sounding a little perturbed.

"Yes," he said, realizing he'd zoned out on their conversation.

"Do you want me to put the girls on the phone?" she asked but one of the babies picked that moment to belt out a good cry. "Oh, no. I better go."

"I'll call back later," he promised. Stopping by with Reese might not be his best play, especially after the way Stacie had reacted to her being in his home yesterday. Was Reese right? Did Stacie want more than to be the girls' aunt?

The situation was a potential powder keg. Just like paternity.

Alice ended the call before he could say goodbye or ask about the past.

He walked in and then handed his cell over to Reese, who traded rooms.

"How'd it go?" he asked, hoping she got more than he did when she returned after a couple of minutes.

"It was so long ago that she doesn't remember much," Reese said. "She set up a group chat, though, and is putting the question out to my siblings and Granny. I explained what happened to me, briefly, and reassured her that I'm fine."

"Good," he said.

"I didn't want word to get out and them to hear the news from someone else," she explained. "I also asked if they'd been expecting me and she said they were at some point soon but I didn't give an exact day."

He nodded.

"Wait a second," he said. "Granny is on the group chat? I thought she hated technology."

"Me, too," she agreed. "But then, a lot has probably changed in a decade."

He nodded. Hell, his life looked nothing like it had two and a half years ago, when he'd been newly married. The marriage happened after a whirlwind courtship and, to be honest, he'd had doubts about what they'd done, too. So he couldn't blame Hazel. She'd had doubts. His had to have been written all over his face, if not his actions.

"Anyway, maybe we'll get a few responses," she continued. "So much time has passed. I can see why cold cases become harder and harder to solve."

"Hell, I forget what I ate for breakfast yesterday, let alone try to recall anything but generalizations from a traumatic event that happened more than a decade ago," he said.

"True."

Darren fixed another cup of coffee, turned around and leaned his hip against the counter. The paternity test was on his mind, and he could use another opinion. Someone

who didn't have anything to lose or gain from the outcome
would be ideal. Could he trust Reese?

He studied her for a long moment, then decided to throw
it out there, for better or worse after shooting a warning
look. "Can I ask you a question?"

Chapter Thirteen

The seriousness in Darren's tone had Reese grabbing hold of the back of a chair to steady herself. "Absolutely. Ask anything." She had no idea where this was going but prepared herself for something deeply personal.

He stared at her for a long moment. After a deep sigh, he said, "First of all, this stays between you and me. I need your word."

After everything they'd been through, she was honored that he would trust her again. "You have it. Whatever you tell me never leaves this room."

He nodded as his lips pressed into a frown. Whatever was coming was going to be big based on how long it was taking him to get to the point. "There is a question as to whether or not I'm the biological father of the twins."

This was a bombshell she never would have expected in a million years. She needed to take her time to formulate a response, because he didn't need to be judged for whatever had happened in his marriage. She could also see why he couldn't talk to anyone else about this. His own parents were gone and he had no siblings. Stacie would most likely freak out and her parents might hire a fancy lawyer and file for custody.

"Have you thought about taking a test?" she asked, then realized he would have thought of that first. She held up a hand. "Forget I asked that. Of course, you have."

"Over and over again." He explained the situation with Hazel, and why he suspected the girls might not belong to him. "I'm at the point with them now that we've gotten through the first year without their mother, which, believe me, there were moments when I didn't think any of us would survive from lack of sleep."

"There wasn't a choice because you would never let them down," she pointed out. "It's easy to see that you would do anything for those girls. Period."

He nodded with a look of appreciation. "There was no way I was going to let those girls suffer in any way."

"It's also a big part of the reason that you put up with their aunt," she said. "You try to see the best in her because you need to keep her close for their sake."

"I won't argue that point even though I never really think about it," he admitted.

"When do you have time?" she asked. "You've been in survival mode for the past year. I can see it in your eyes."

Her comment might have gone too far and been too personal because he dropped his gaze to study the rim of his coffee mug. "That's a fair assessment."

She was relieved that he wasn't upset by the comment. Before she'd disappeared, they had been able to have honest conversations. Not only was he a boyfriend, but he had also been her other best friend.

"You're doing a great job with them, by the way," she added.

His gaze came up to meet hers as he cocked an eyebrow. "How do you know?"

"Kids need unconditional love," she pointed out. "Food, yes. Shelter, yes. Those basics are important, but love trumps all."

"They have that," he said and then dropped his gaze again. "But what if they're not mine, Reese?"

"You'll deal with it when it comes," she said. "Surely Stacie and her parents would agree that you are the best person for the job in bringing up those babies."

"I'm not so sure about that," he admitted with a frown. "They almost fought me for custody after Hazel's death. The only reason they decided to back off was because they had no real grounds and I think they realized their actions would put an unnecessary strain on our relationship and damage it beyond repair."

"Well, they would have been making a huge mistake," she said. "You're great for those children."

"I hope so," he said. "It's what Hazel would have wanted if she'd been able to speak up. Whether they were mine or not, she chose me as their father. She had to have done the math. She lied to me about how far along she was."

"You didn't go to any doctor appointments?" she asked.

He shook his head. "You know what work is like on a cattle ranch, even a small operation like mine. I have one ranch hand who does what I can't. He comes and takes care of my horse out back on his way to and from work so I can focus on the girls. Bradley is my lifeline."

"I'm guessing Hazel encouraged you to work so she could cover up the lie," she said.

"There was only a few weeks difference, so she probably figured she could keep me in the dark as long as I didn't show up and ask questions," he said. "She said everything was going fine and that she wanted me to save days off for when the babies made their appearance." He shook his head. "I should have been there for her and then she wouldn't have felt the need to lie."

"It might have been denial on her part or wishful thinking," she advised. It wasn't unusual for someone to hide from a scary truth until they couldn't any longer. "Did you have a conversation with her before she—"

"No," he interjected before she could finish her sentence—a sentence she didn't want to finish. "Because her death was unexpected. I'd like to believe she would have handled things differently if she'd known that day would have been her last."

"I'm sure," she observed. "You two were on a good footing and building a life together. She might not have wanted to believe the twins could be anyone else's."

"Part of the reason she and the musician broke up before we met was because he wasn't the settling-down type," he explained. "He was honest about it with her. Said he would be devoted to her but no marriage or children."

The way he said the last part stung because it hit a little too close to home.

"I have to believe Hazel chose the person she wanted to be with for the long haul, Darren. She chose you to be the one to bring up the twins with, and I know you—once you made a commitment to someone, you wouldn't go back on it."

"I took my vows seriously," he said before taking a sip of coffee.

"Bringing up those girls is no different," she said. "Even if they aren't yours biologically, Hazel chose you and her parents will respect her wish."

Darren took a lap around the kitchen. "I keep thinking

this jerk deserves to know he has children if they don't turn out to be mine and they are his."

"You know who he is?" she asked.

"I have a name, and I searched online to see who he was," he admitted. "Never wanted to know anything more about him than was absolutely necessary. Besides, she said she went to see the musician when she was gone for the month. I assumed it was him, especially after the way she talked about him when we first got together and discussed our pasts."

"I agree on some level that he deserves to know if he turns out to be the father, but maybe focus on one step at a time," she said. "Take the test for yourself and then decide what to do from there based on the result. Not doing anything is always an option. Hazel made a choice. She hid the truth for what I'm sure were good reasons. Even if they weren't, they were *her* reasons and we'll never know what they were."

"Respecting her wishes is important to me," he admitted. "But maybe you're right. Maybe I'm worried over nothing."

"I'll stay right here while you take the test if you'd like," she offered. "And I won't tell a soul about this conversation. I swear on my father's grave."

Darren took in a deep breath and then exhaled. "Okay. I'll take the test."

"Can I use your laptop?" she asked.

He nodded, so she walked over and searched for a nearby lab. There was one half an hour drive from here that could use a hair sample.

"All we need is eight strands of hair and we can drop off the samples at the lab. It's only thirty minutes out of our way," she said.

"How long before the results come back?" he asked.

"You're looking at a maximum of three days." She lifted her gaze from the screen to his face. "All I need is a zip-lock bag and the samples to make it happen. Are you in?"

Darren took another lap around the kitchen. He raked fingers through his hair. And then he stopped. "Okay."

Reese helped gather the supplies. The girls' hairbrush was easy enough to get samples from. The lab needed at least eight strands. Since the girls had been born with heads full of hair based on their pictures, getting enough wasn't an issue. He grabbed his own hairbrush and did the same, placing the contents in a separate baggie.

"We need to head out," she said. "Might as well drop this off on our way to see Tandra's parents."

"Let's do it," he said, then drained his cup. He'd been stressed about taking this test for so long now, it felt strangely calming to be taking action. "And thank you for helping me get my head on straight about this."

Reese walked over to him and placed a palm on the center of his chest. "You're a good man, Darren. You deserve peace of mind."

THIS CLOSE, he could see her pulse pound at the base of her throat. It matched tempo with his, which was climbing. He could also smell the citrus shampoo he kept in the guest bath, and it had never smelled sexier on someone.

He lifted his gaze to her full pink lips—lips that looked a little too tempting when her tongue slicked across the bottom one. It would be so easy to kiss her. Would she welcome his lips on hers?

His question was answered when he locked gazes and

saw an equal amount of desire in those beautiful eyes of hers. "Can I kiss you right now?"

"I'd be disappointed if you didn't," she said, pushing up to her tiptoes, making access that much easier.

With her lips this close, it didn't take much to kiss. Her hands came up to his chest and grabbed fistfuls of his shirt, then she tugged him closer. He parted her lips with his tongue, and she released a sexy little moan against his mouth that caused blood to flow south.

Kissing Reese was up there on his list of his favorite things. In fact, the sparks flying between them were something he hadn't experienced since—since… Since *her.*

By the time they separated, they were both gasping for air. He smiled as he brought up the backs of his fingers to brush against her cheek.

Beautiful Reese. Dangerous Reese. Foolish him. Because this would only lead to more heartache for him when she bolted back to her life. Normally, casual sex with her would top his list of favorite things. With their history, there wouldn't be anything casual about sex.

Darren took a step back and dropped his hands to his sides. "We should get going." He could hear the gravelly quality to his own voice, so he coughed to cover. It was an unoriginal move, but his head wasn't exactly on straight right now, or he never would stoked his desire with that kiss. Because it had him wanting more and Reese had limits—limits that would have her running for the hills if they got too close.

And he needed that heartache like he needed a hole in the head.

Besides, all his attention had to go to his girls right now. He could date casually, dip his toe in the water, but he

couldn't afford to get attached to anyone again. Especially
now that he was committed to taking the paternity test. The
results could add ammunition to a court case, but he vowed
right then and there to fight for custody with everything he
had if his former parents-in-law decided to challenge paren-
tal rights. His bank account was no match for their money.
They could afford to hire the best attorney—an attorney
who could run circles around him in court.

A noise sounded outside, in back. Normally, that wouldn't
register as alarming.

Darren locked gazes with Reese. "Stay away from windows and doors while I check this out, okay?"

Eyes wide, she nodded. And then immediately crossed
the room to grab a knife. Darren kept a shotgun in the hall
closet with a box of shells on the top shelf, far out of reach
of little hands. He grabbed both and loaded a pair of slugs.

Armed and ready with his finger hovering over the trigger mechanism, he slipped out the front door. Reese had
the presence of mind to lock it behind him. Good. He realized a few seconds too late that he should have told her to,
but she was on it.

Back against the house, he raised the shotgun barrel toward the sky before rounding the first corner. Adrenaline
pumped so hard that blood rushed in his ears, making it
difficult for him to hear.

Taking the first corner, he moved fast and lowered the
barrel. He scanned the area. No sign of anyone. Without
hesitating, he kept going until he could see the backyard.
Out of the corner of his eye, he saw movement.

Darren bolted toward the male figure who was running
fast and hard. Pumping his legs until his thighs burned,
Darren did his best to catch up to the bastard who'd been

in his backyard. Iris's tricycle had been pushed up against the house, near the kitchen window. He heard the back door open and assumed Reese followed.

Anger ripped through him. The runner was fast. He disappeared into nearby trees and then the sound of a motorcycle engine firing up filled the air. Darren released a string of swear words. Whoever was after Reese could be checking his home to see if she was there or coming for him. Finding answers and talking to Tandra's family just jumped up the priority list. So did carrying a weapon at all times.

As he headed back toward the house, an explosion rocked the ground. A ringing noise filled his ears as he bolted toward the sound. Fire ravaged his small home. His cell phone was inside so he couldn't call 911.

Where was Reese?

As he neared the blaze, he called out for her.

Just as panic coiled in his chest, he saw her. She was on flat on her back with her hand over her heart, lying in the grass.

"Reese," he said as he ran toward her full speed.

She didn't move.

Chapter Fourteen

Darren's panicked voice broke through the ringing sound in Reese's ears. She rolled onto her side, winced and coughed as he dropped down to his knees beside her.

"Hey," he said as she blinked up at him. "Where does it hurt?"

She could barely hear him. Her throat and lungs burned from smoke inhalation. Talking was next to impossible. She reached for him and grabbed on to his forearms.

"Help is on the way," he said to her. Reading lips helped her understand what he was saying. "Hang in there. Okay?"

Reese nodded. Movement hurt. Whoever the bastard was trying to erase her had another think coming. Trying to sit up was a bad idea. Moving was a bad idea. Looking into Darren's eyes and seeing his concern for her was a bad idea. That last one made her wish she'd done things differently. Since regret was nothing more than a waste of time, she pushed aside the sentiment.

"You're going to be all right," Darren soothed. His voice brought comfort even though the dark cloud feeling overhead made it feel like it would be short-lived.

"Your home," she said, managing to get the words out through a cracked, dry throat.

"I know," he said. "It's not important, though. Those are only things and things can be replaced. You're alive. You're safe. That's all that matters right now."

Because of her, his children had lost everything. The sobering thought kicked her in the teeth. She shook her head, determined to leave him out of this nightmare from now on. Plus, his former parents-in-law had threatened to fight him for custody of the girls once. How would this play out once they found out what happened here? He'd brought someone into his family's home who threatened their safety. Even though she would never do anything to put the girls in harm's way on purpose, reality seemed to have a mind of its own.

"Me being here puts your girls at risk," she said as sirens pierced through the fog in her brain.

In the next half hour, the fire was out and Reese was in the back of an ambulance on her way to the hospital. A deputy was supposed to meet them there to get statements. Darren's SUV hadn't sustained any damage and a neighbor volunteered to call in his construction crew to at least seal off the premises best as they could. Reese had an oxygen mask strapped to her face but was breathing fine. Her body was starting to ache, but nothing was broken based on the field exam. There would be bruising, no doubt. That wasn't anything she couldn't get over in a couple of days or a week depending on how bad it got. There would most definitely be a huge bruise on her right hip.

Thinking about leaving Darren caused her chest to squeeze, but it would have to be done for the sake of his family. She needed to lure whoever was trying to kill her away from the Pierce family. A thought struck. Darren would follow her if she tried to leave.

She would bang her head against the wall if it didn't hurt so much already. As it was, her brain felt like it might split in two from pain. Her hands fisted as she thought about the bastard who was after her. Had she opened a can of worms with digging into Camree Lynn's disappearance? That was the only explanation that made any sense. Why else would someone try to kill her? And then what? Make it look random? Or like she'd come across poachers yesterday?

Her thoughts shifted to Darren and the kiss that would now be the benchmark for all future kisses. He'd held the record since high school and had somehow bested himself. The grown-man version of Darren caused all kinds of sensations in her body—sensations she didn't need to focus on, considering there was no outlet for them no matter how much they sparked.

By the time the ambulance arrived at the hospital, Reese felt much better. She would argue about checking in but figured it might not hurt to have a doctor give her the all-clear just in case.

Darren's cell had been inside the house, which was now roped off as a crime scene. Or at least what was left of it. The thought of him losing everything gutted her. There had to be so many memories locked inside those walls. Memories of the girls in the form of pictures and toys. Memories of their mother. Memories of the short time they'd spent there as a family.

She was being sentimental, but those things mattered when people were building a life together. They took on a new importance when one of those people was gone. Thinking about all those little keepsakes going up in flames or being damaged by water when the firemen put out the fire, made her sick to her stomach.

The bastard responsible needed to pay.

Reese took in a deep breath as the doors opened. A few seconds later, she was being wheeled out of the ambulance and into the automatic glass doors of the ER. She went straight into a room, where Darren found her almost immediately. The look on his face was a mix of desperation, frustration and concern.

"I'm okay," she said after lifting the oxygen mask enough to speak. "I feel better already."

In the next second, he was by her side, reaching for her hand. The minute they made physical contact, she breathed a little easier. He was a lifeline in this chaos.

"I've been thinking that I must have been investigating Camree Lynn's disappearance on my way down," she said. "It's the only thing that makes sense to me as to why someone would target me."

"Just rest, okay?" He brought his free hand up to touch her face. The way he looked at her with such admiration hit her in the center of her chest.

"I almost got you killed," she said. "Why aren't you mad at me?"

"Because it wasn't your fault," he said. "Even if you were digging into Camree Lynn's disappearance. There's no way you could have known any of this would happen. You're not the bad guy here. And I know without a shadow of a doubt that there's no way you would have brought this to my doorstep." He stopped for a second and bit down on his lower lips. Then, he seemed to say "what the hell" because he opened his mouth to speak. "I think it's safe to say that I'm the last person you wanted to see when you headed back toward Cider Creek."

"That's not exactly true," she responded. "I've wanted to

reach out to you for years to apologize. But I didn't think you'd give me the time of day. And I didn't deserve it after the way I handled things, so I did you a favor and stayed away."

He stood there for a long moment, as though deciding for himself if he could believe her. Then, he gave a small nod of agreement.

"You're here now," he said after a long pause. "We've grown up. You have an important job. I have my girls and the family ranch to take care of."

"Speaking of which, will you be able to stay there now that your home is unlivable?" she asked, redirecting the conversation before he could give her a free pass.

"That's the plan," he said.

"Why don't you live there now?" she asked. "If you don't mind my asking."

"It was always my folks' place," he said. "This might not make any sense, but their memory is preserved there. I check in on the house every day while I'm on site. There's always food stocked in the kitchen, at least enough for lunches and the occasional dinner when I'm working late."

"It makes sense to me," she reassured him. "Maybe it's time to fill it again and still preserve their memory."

"A fresh start," he said.

"I think they would have enjoyed you and the girls living there and filling the halls with laughter again," she pointed out.

Could the two of them start over, too?

DARREN LIKED THE idea of his girls growing up around his mother's things. He could add a few touches of his own to make the place feel like home to them. His own home would take time to fix, even if insurance acted fast. He could fix it up and sell it, which would give him some breathing room with his finances. "It's time."

"Good," Reese said with a self-satisfied smile. She sat up a little straighter and took the oxygen mask completely off.

A loud beeping noise had her thinking she'd made a wrong move. A nurse came rushing in.

"Don't take that off unless you've been cleared," the short nurse with a name tag that read *Angela* ordered. She couldn't be more than five-two and her tone said she was not one to be messed with. Darren didn't dare cross her, and based on the look on Reese's face, she got the message, too.

"Yes, ma'am," Reese said, replacing the mask. "I do think I've improved."

"The doctor will be in soon. He'll decide that. In the meantime, don't mess with it again," Angela scolded, wagging a finger at Reese.

Angela checked the machine and then rushed out of the room, almost running into a deputy. She fussed at him, too, until he backed up into the hallway.

"I'll go see what he wants since you already gave a statement back at my house," Darren said.

She nodded.

He smiled as he left the room.

He almost made a crack that Texas could replace its former slogan from Don't Mess with Texas to Don't Mess with Nurses.

"I can try to answer any questions you might have, Deputy Lyle," Darren said as he read the deputy's name tag. The man looked to be in his midforties. He was roughly six feet tall and could be described as sturdy.

Darren offered his hand and introduced himself. After a firm handshake, he continued, "What can I do for you?"

"I dropped by to say we're opening up an investigation into Camree Lynn's disappearance despite this being a cold case," Deputy Lyle said. "I wanted to deliver the news myself."

"I appreciate you coming all the way here," Darren said.

"My place isn't far and I'm on my way home," he explained. Then he said, "I have a fifteen-year-old daughter. She's a handful sometimes. My wife says it's hormones and that it'll calm down eventually but there are days when I doubt that's possible." His smile faded when he said, "We're in the middle of a divorce and my wife noticed the Tandra St. Clair case on the news. She went digging around and found several cases around the state that had girls missing in the midst of a divorce who'd been classified as runaways."

"I found three," Darren admitted. He noticed the deputy used the word *wife* instead of *soon to be ex-wife*. It made Darren think the divorce might not be his idea.

"She did, too," Deputy Lyle said. "Anyway, it got her pretty worked up since we've been going through a rough patch like these other families. Our daughter is in a rebellious phase and my wife started overthinking, worrying. I guess she got me riled up, too. So I talked to my boss and he said I could reopen the case."

"Reese will be relieved to hear the sheriff is actually taking this seriously," Darren said. "The trail is cold, so it won't be easy."

"No," Deputy Lyle said. "But these other cases aren't as old, and we have something new to work with to bring to a joint task force. If they're related and we have a serial killer on our hands, we have to do everything in our power to stop him."

"I appreciate you stopping by to deliver the news," Darren said.

"Local law enforcement has a lot to make up for after Sheriff Tanner's arrest," Deputy Lyle said.

The statement didn't put Darren at ease with the current situation. "I better get back in."

Deputy Lyle nodded, then shook hands and headed toward the elevator bank. Darren didn't like being away from Reese for too long. He had a bad feeling that was probably nothing.

Chapter Fifteen

The door opened. The lights suddenly turned off, plunging the room into darkness. Reese opened her mouth to scream and then realized the oxygen mask would muffle the sound. She reached for the panic button and then remembered all she had to do was take off the mask.

As she jerked the thing off her face, she slammed her free hand into the machine next to her as she tried to scramble out of bed. Where was nurse Angela?

A hand gripped her arm as she opened her mouth to scream. An alarm sounded. The strong hand jerked her off the bed as she screamed.

Reese fisted her hands and threw punches, swinging at air. She kicked and finally connected. The male attacker grunted, and she thought it served him right. When she threw a second kick, he was smart enough to get out of the way.

He hauled her to her feet and then off the ground, so she unleashed a rampage of kicks. This time, he cursed under his breath and dropped her. Her feet hit the tile flooring too fast, too suddenly. She grasped for something to hold on to before she face-planted. Her elbow jabbed into something hard. Bone?

And then she heard whoever it was coming toward her. She readied herself for a fight, feeling around for anything she could use as a weapon.

The door opened.

"I thought I told you—"

Angela's voice was unmistakable.

"Excuse me," a deep male voice said as the light flipped on a second before he brushed past Angela and ran into the hallway.

"Stop him," Reese yelled as she scrambled to her feet.

Angela let the man brush right past her. She took one look at Reese and then turned back toward the hallway. "Stop that man!"

"Someone came into my room. I need my clothes. I'm leaving," Reese said.

Angela grabbed her cell phone out of her pocket and made a call to security as she put her free hand up to stop Reese. After making the request, she said, "Your friend is out there. What happened in here?"

"I already told you," Reese said, opening cabinets to locate the bag with her clothes inside. She distinctly remembered being given a plastic one but had no idea where it had gone.

"Did you know him?" Angela asked.

"I'm afraid I have no idea who that man was and he's the reason I'm in here in the first place," she said as Darren came barreling into the room. She made eye contact immediately. "He was here." She lifted her arm so he could see the grip marks.

"How?" Darren muttered a few choice words. "Did you get a good look at him?"

"Afraid not," Reese said as she opened the cabinet with

her personal effects. "There we go. Right here. Now if you'll excuse me." She made a beeline for the attached bathroom.

Angela seemed to know better than to argue. "Security is on its way."

Reese ripped off the hospital gown and put her clothes on, then slipped into her shoes. She couldn't wait to get out of there.

Darren waited at the door, reminding her, "The nurse called Security."

"Too late," she said, staring at him. "I'm not staying here a minute longer."

"I'm sorry I left you alone," he said, then reached for her hand and linked their fingers. "This is my fault."

"You had no idea this would happen," she said.

"This bastard slipped past me when I was right down the hall." He shook his head. "I never would have forgiven myself if something had happened to you."

"You have been sticking your neck out and putting your life on the line for me since I showed up on your property," she insisted. "You've done nothing wrong except try to help. If anyone is sorry, it's me. It's my fault your house is burned down. All your memories are gone."

Tucking her chin to her chest, she stifled a sniffle.

"Let's get out of here and then we can clear the air," he said, lifting her chin up until her gaze met his again. "Deal?"

She nodded. "I'm ready."

As they turned toward the door, it burst open. The deputy stopped in the door jamb, panting. "He got away. Any chance you got a good look at his face?"

"No," Reese admitted. "And I have no plans to stay here for him to finish the job, security or not."

She gave a quick rundown of what happened.

"How can I reach you?" the deputy asked.

"My cell burned beyond usage," Darren said.

Deputy Lyle produced a business card. "Once you get a working cell, program this number in."

Darren took the offering. "Will do."

"I'm taking her home," Darren said. "To Pierce Ranch."

"I believe I know where that is," Deputy Lyle said.

"If you are inclined to drive past it every now and then, it wouldn't hurt either of our feelings," Darren stated.

"It definitely wouldn't hurt mine," Reese added.

"Will do," Deputy Lyle said before escorting them to Darren's SUV. They arrived safely despite the bad feeling Reese had while walking through the parking lot. The hairs on the back of her neck pricked, which was never a good sign. Of course, at this point, she might be spooked and freaking out. But still. She had no plans to take chances.

Darren helped her into the passenger side of his SUV. The second the door was closed, she got a whiff of smoke. As soon as he claimed the driver's seat and turned on the engine, she cracked the window.

"You might want to crack the other windows, too," she said. "I didn't realize how badly these clothes smelled of smoke."

He nodded, then pulled forward out of the parking spot. Before he got too far, he hit the buttons to lower all the windows a little. "How's your head?"

"I have a monster headache but that doesn't seem to be anything new," she said.

"The guy back there," he continued after a moment of silence. "Did you get anything from him? A general build?"

"He wasn't big like you," she said. "I only saw him for a flash, but he looked slightly average height and build."

Average for Texans in this area was six feet tall. "He was strong. His grip strength caught me off guard. He had grabby hands."

"Did he say anything?" Darren asked after the muscle in his jaw clenched. "Did you hear his voice at all?"

"Not really," she said. "When the nurse walked back in, he mumbled but I couldn't get a clear take on his voice."

"The person responsible for the fire at my house must have stuck around to watch the rest unfold," Darren said.

"I didn't think about that before, but you're right," she said.

"He might know my property if he knows the equipment building," he continued. "Which means he might be local or someone who grew up around here."

"Phillip Rhodes spent summers here for years, even after the camp closed," she said.

"I'm almost thinking this person had to have grown up around here at this point despite the fact taking someone so close to home would draw attention," Darren said. "Camree Lynn's case was a long time ago. She might have been where he started."

"So you're leaning toward Aiden Archer?" she asked.

He nodded. "That seems to be the best name so far."

It had been a long time since she'd been to Darren's family home. A whole lot of good memories were stored there. Memories of going to his place after school to do homework, and stealing a few kisses when his mother wasn't looking. They'd held hands under the stars while sitting on the tire swing in his backyard. Her thoughts were flooded with good memories as he pulled onto ranch property.

Reminiscing about the past was a good distraction from what had just happened to her. Another attack and they were further from answers than this morning. How could this person act alone? How would a single person have pulled off what happened at the equipment building? She could have sworn she'd heard more than one voice.

Then again, she'd been pretty out of it. The blow to her head might have caused her to mix up details.

At least her head had been spared the floor at the hospital. And yet, nausea was still settling in as a monster headache formed. Thinking hurt.

DARREN PARKED IN the detached garage and then came around to the passenger side. He needed to do something about the lack of a cell phone. Being disconnected from his girls for the day caused a coil to tighten in his chest. Ever since their mother died, he'd worried something would happen to them. Like, maybe, he was cursed.

But the girls were thriving and, so far, hadn't met any accidents that didn't involve potty training.

"I need a phone," he said to Reese.

"We should have stopped along the way and gotten one of those throw-away phones. They come with service," she said. "I don't think they cost much."

"Can you make it to the store?" he asked.

"I don't want to stay here by myself," she said.

"Okay," he confirmed. "To the store we go." And then he stopped. "When we get back, we'll fill Buster in. He'll be sleeping in the bunkhouse."

"Buster still works for your family ranch?" she asked.

"That's right," he confirmed. He was also thinking it would be good to have another set of eyes around. Someone who could keep an eye out for danger. There were no security alarms in his parents' home, so all they had to work with would be door locks. He was seeing how easily the bastard targeting Reese was able to move through the hospital. It wasn't exactly reassuring how stealthy this guy could be.

"I'd love to see him and say hello," she said. And then she seemed to think better of it. "Unless he doesn't want to see me again."

"He'll be happy you turned up," he said. He held back the part about how many times Buster had asked when Reese was coming around again, or if Darren had called her to let her know how he felt before she got mixed up with his uncle.

Darren had been stubborn back then, digging his heels in. Some might say little had changed, but he would argue differently. Now that the girls were here, he'd learned to relax and cut back on his stubborn side. Especially as they started having ideas of their own, like when they wanted to be held and when they wanted to walk. It seemed the minute they learned they could move across the room without his help, they'd decided to do things on their own. Was it a sign of what was to come in the future? Probably. As much as he wanted to bring up strong young ladies, a piece of his heart would always want them to need their daddy.

By the time Darren drove them to the store and back, another hour had passed. Reese napped on the way. When he pulled up next to the farmhouse where he'd grown up, he parked the SUV and then touched her arm.

"Hey, we're here," he said quietly.

"Home?" Reese asked in a sleepy voice that tugged at his heart. Letting that voice penetrate the walls he'd built around his heart to survive would be just plain foolish of him. Determined not to make the same mistake twice, he shelved his emotions.

"We're at the farmhouse," he said, thinking how weird

it was going to be to call this place home. Then again, he was warming up to the idea of his children growing up here. Being around their grandmother and grandfather's things was the next best thing to being around them.

"Okay," she said, wiping her eyes. "Right. Are you going to see Buster?"

"I'll have him swing by," he said. "Looks like you need your rest."

"I'm good," she promised.

"You've been through a lot, Reese," he reasoned. "You're tired and need sleep. I'll be right here."

"But Tandra was the most recent and she might be out there in danger," she argued. "What if we can save her?"

Darren looked at Reese. "I'll make calls. It will be faster to do it that way, anyway. We won't lose time driving around."

Reese looked like she was about to put up an argument.

"I have this throwaway and I'll find numbers from the internet," he said. There was a desktop computer in the office that he could use.

She nodded.

He exited the driver's side and moved around the front of the SUV, then opened the door for her and helped her out.

"This place brings back a lot of memories," she said with a small smile.

"Sure does," he agreed. This was also the place where his heart had been shattered to bits, but he was certain she wasn't talking about that particular memory.

Bringing her here might be a mistake but he was short on options. Making those calls might bring answers.

Chapter Sixteen

Reese walked inside the house on her own, but her legs felt like they were made of rubber bands instead of bone. "I can't wait to get out of these clothes. Is there anything else I can wear?"

Darren nodded. He'd become quiet and she couldn't help but wonder what was going through his mind. Being back in this house with him brought back a flood of memories. They were good. They reminded her of why she'd fallen for Darren. Maybe that was the reason he looked so grim. Maybe he didn't want any of those memories.

Darren excused himself and returned holding out what looked like a complete outfit. "You left these here once when we fell into the pond."

"I wondered where these warm-ups went," she said. "These were my favorites." Thank the stars for the small miracle of a sports bra and underwear with the offering.

"You always kept them in your backpack on Fridays for when you came over and then we fell into that stagnant water out on the property, so we threw them into the washer and forgot about them," he said.

"Cool." The memory tapped into feelings she'd tried to

suppress a long time ago. She nodded and smiled. "Mind if I grab a shower?"

"Not at all," Darren said, but he was already programming a number into his cell phone. "I'll check on the girls and be in my dad's old... *My* office."

"Sounds good," she said, starting for the stairs.

"You might want to use the master," he said, motioning toward the hallway where he was headed. "I don't keep the upstairs stocked since no one lives here. I only keep towels and supplies downstairs for the occasional shower that needs to happen here before I head home."

Reese did an about-face and walked to the hallway where he was standing. He waited for her to go first. Him being in a room two doors down was a comforting thought after being attacked in the hospital. She made a mental note to call the sheriff to see what he found out on her phone records. She'd given him permission to check into her communication. Maybe he'd found something.

After the shower, Reese was beginning to feel human again. It was beyond good to get those smoky clothes off her skin. She couldn't help but think someone was desperate. Maybe their desperation would cause them to make a mistake and reveal their identity. She still had no idea who it was or why. That wasn't completely true. They had two names to start with. By the time she finished dressing and headed into the office, Darren might have an idea of which name to follow through on.

Darren was on a phone call while she stopped at the door. His body language was tense as he glanced up at her. The look on his face said he was being chewed out, or worse. The fire must have had his in-laws riled up.

"I know how to keep my own children safe," he said into

the phone in a quietly controlled voice that signaled he was on the verge of losing it. He couldn't afford to lose his temper right now. It would only make matters worse given the situation.

Reese walked in, squatted beside him and took his free hand. She gave a squeeze for reassurance that he appeared to appreciate, as he gave a small nod of acknowledgement. More importantly, he didn't let go.

"I'm moving into the farmhouse," he said. "I appreciate your offer but we have a home here. It's something I've been meaning to do, anyway. This pushes up my time line."

Darren paused.

Then he said, "I appreciate your concern. I know how much you love the girls." Another few beats of silence passed before he said, "They're all I have left of her, too."

Reese could scarcely imagine what Darren had been going through since figuring out those girls might not be biologically his. Their samples went up in flames, so they would have to regroup. Giving him a definitive answer was as important to her as being there for him when he found out the news. It was the least she could do to make up for at least some of the pain she'd caused him in the past. Maybe make a dent? Her guilt would last forever.

"I can swing by and pick them up anytime," he said into the phone. "Are you sure?" He paused a couple of beats. "Tomorrow at lunch. That'll give me time to get settled here. Sounds good."

He released her hand to push the end-call button. And then he set the phone on top of the desk and raked his fingers through his thick hair.

"What can I do to help prepare for the girls?" Reese asked, getting a second wind after her shower. "Diapers? Wipes?"

"I'll have to grab the portable cribs from the hall closet," he said. "There should be enough supplies here to last a couple of days."

"Then, we'll have time for a delivery," she said. "All we have to do is one-click our way into all the supplies you could possibly need."

"One-click is a little slower out here, but you're right about having enough to tide us over," he said. She liked the way he used the word *us*. She hoped he would let her roll her sleeves up and help. Then, it dawned on her that the fire might not be the only objection they had about him taking the girls back. "They know about me, don't they?"

He nodded.

"They're not happy about another woman being in your life," she said.

"No. They are not."

"Do they know that I'm only here temporarily?" she asked.

"They don't need to know every detail of my life," he countered. "I already tell them everything I can think of about the girls on an almost daily basis."

That couldn't be going over very well. "You always had an independent streak a mile long."

"Not when you have babies that have to come first," he said.

"They're lucky to have such a devoted father," she reminded him. He seemed to need the reminder. She would tell him that every day until he no longer needed to hear it.

"Thank you," he said. "It means a lot to hear those words."

He might not want to hear this, but, "If you feel stuck between a rock and a hard place about taking your girls or helping me, you know I understand you have to choose them."

"I do," he said, but the hint of gratitude in his voice said he appreciated her for saying it. He was taking care of twins, managing his former in-laws, and emotionally supporting his former sister-in-law while running his family's cattle ranch. Who took care of him?

"I might not be much in the kitchen, but I can dig around in there for food while you make an online order and set up the cribs," she said. "Did you call Buster?"

"I did," Darren acknowledged. "He's wrapping something up and will be on his way shortly."

Buster had always been like a big brother or uncle to her. "I'm glad he's still here helping the ranch run smoothly."

"I don't know if I'd call it running smoothly with me at the helm, but I'm doing my best," Darren said before making eyes that finally broke some of the tension.

"The place is still going," she said. "Sounds like success to me."

"The insurance money from the house will help. I've been running two places and it has been a drain. This is a small operation and can use a cash infusion."

Reese had a little money saved. She would offer her savings if it would help, but doubted he would take her up on it. "The ranch is solvent, right?"

"That it is," he answered.

"Like I said…success."

He smiled and nodded as she left the room and headed toward the kitchen. She wasn't kidding about her cooking skills. However, she'd managed to keep herself fed and she had a few tricks up her sleeve.

In the pantry, there were cans of pinto beans and boxes of boil-in-a-bag rice. This was right up her alley. In the fridge, she located a white onion and a nice spicy sausage. She pulled out a couple of pans and got busy. First, she chopped the onion and sliced the sausage. She threw those into a saucepan with a can of pinto beans. Next, she boiled water for the rice. Fixing a meal took less than twenty minutes. Pride filled her chest at what she'd accomplished because it actually smelled good. She located two serving bowls, using one for the rice and the other for the sausage and beans.

After grabbing a couple of glasses, she filled them with water and then put on a pot of coffee like she'd down countless times after school when they'd come here to do homework, because she didn't want to risk running into Duncan. Disappearing was the best way to fly underneath his radar, and she'd been good at it.

Had she become too good at disappearing?

DARREN MADE A couple of phone calls. Tandra's family didn't answer, so he left a message. If it wasn't necessary, he wouldn't bother them at all. But he might just be able to help find their missing daughter and connect a criminal to a couple other cases, so it was worth the intrusion.

Aiden Archer was more difficult to pin down. If he was around town at all, Buster would probably know something. He'd lived here for years and knew most of the families, if not personally than by association or reputation.

Phillip Rhodes, as it turned out, worked for a major distribution chain as a delivery driver, according to his mother. He went from house to house delivering packages and had moved three times in the past five years. There were five missing teens altogether, including the additional three cases that seemed connected to Camree Lynn and Tandra. He was on shift in Barrel City, which was a two-hour drive from the farmhouse, and he clocked out at midnight this evening. They could confront him and see what he had to say. His voice might be familiar to Reese, and could possibly jar a memory.

Or he could take one look at her, panic, and assume he was busted. He could run and that would tell them everything they needed to know about his innocence. But then what? Because it would also tip their hands. There would be no sheriff with them. Was it possible to get a current picture of Rhodes to show to Reese? Maybe on social media? Would that have the same effect? It was worth a try. He might have changed a lot over the years.

Darren performed a quick social media scan. He found several listings for Phillip Rhodes on the most popular platform. A few had actual faces attached. The others had pictures or memes. He scanned a couple to see if they gave away any details of where the person might work and didn't find anything related to delivery drivers. Of course, it stood to reason a man guilty of stalking, luring, kidnapping, and possibly killing teenaged girls with trouble at home wouldn't use his real photo.

And, a creep who preyed on teenage girls might be good at hiding. It dawned on Darren how easy it would be to find out intimate information about these targets online. So many shared too many details of their private lives, making it easier for someone to lurk. The bastard could become so familiar with the target, he believed they were in a relationship.

It also occurred to him someone like Rhodes could deliver gifts if the girls were home. Of course, it would be easy to trace if the interactions occurred on the computer. Law enforcement would certainly look there first.

The common thread of troubled teens bothered Darren. The parents fighting and talking about divorce could throw off the most grounded teen. Camree Lynn had withdrawn from everyone but Reese, and Reese's guilt must have crushed her at times that she couldn't save her friend. Young people had a habit of blaming themselves for everything that happened. He should know. He'd been just as bad.

Whatever was happening in the kitchen smelled good. Hunger pulled him out of the office, and he walked toward the scent. "I thought you said you couldn't cook."

"I said that I can survive in the kitchen," Reese said with a laugh. "I wouldn't call it cooking."

Seeing her standing there in what had been her favorite warm-ups wasn't helping him with the whole keep-her-at-arm's-length plan. Fresh from the shower, her hair still wet, he could already smell her clean, citrusy scent as he walked toward the table. The eat-in round table was set for two. There were serving bowls and plates. She'd even located a candle. He shouldn't be surprised. She'd spent plenty of time here when they were young, and nothing had changed. He hadn't touched any of his mother's stuff or rearranged any of the cabinets. When he ate here, it was usually off of a paper plate or fast-food carton. His mother would have had a fit. She despised fast food, but then she kept a garden of fresh vegetables and herbs. It was easy enough for her to walk outside and grab what she needed. Everything she'd touched grew. Having a green thumb was only part of the equation. There were people who made everyone and everything else thrive around them. She'd been one of those people. They used to joke she could touch a dying tree and it would come back to life. He imagined she had a huge garden and spent her days where she was happiest.

"I put on coffee but thought you should probably drink water with your meal," Reese said.

He walked over to her before taking a seat. He'd almost lost her today to whoever had attacked her at the hospital, right under his nose. So, yeah, he knew about guilt. As it turned out, some things from childhood don't change all that much.

"I should have stayed in the room with you," he said to her.

"There was a deputy with you," she said. "This guy is brazen."

"Or desperate," he responded.

"Point taken." She bit her bottom lip. "Either way, he won't catch us off guard again."

Darren leaned forward, close enough to rest his forehead against hers. "What if I'd lost you again?"

"You won't," she said. Those words shouldn't have warmed him as much as they did.

"I can't," he said, unsure how wise the statement was under the circumstances. It covered more than the bastard who was after her. And yet, he had no idea if he could, or should, try to open his heart, even a little.

Chapter Seventeen

With Darren standing so close, it would be easy to reach out and touch him. So Reese did. She grabbed a fistful of his shirt and held her hand against his chest. The feel of his rapid heartbeat against her fingers reminded her they were both very alive.

"I can't even think about anything happening to you, especially on my watch," Darren said against her lips.

Taking what she wanted, Reese pressed her mouth to his. A knock sounded at the back door, startling her. She took a step back.

"That must be Buster," Darren said as someone put a key in the lock mechanism. "He still knocks first even though he has a key."

"Should I set another plate?" She immediately turned toward the cabinet so Buster wouldn't see the flush to her cheeks.

"We can ask but he usually turns me down," he said.

Buster entered the room, then closed and locked the door behind him. Clearly, he was in the loop on what had been going on. His gaze moved from Darren to Reese. Buster was in his mid-to-late sixties. His skin was sun worn, his hair as black as night. Wise, pale blue eyes studied her with compassion. "It's good to see you here, Reese."

With that, he walked straight over to her and brought her into a hug. He smelled like leather and hay, with a dash of spice.

"It's really good to see you again, Buster." A tear escaped and rolled down her cheek before she could suppress it. She tucked her chin to her chest when more broke free, and sniffled. "Are you hungry?" Reese immediately turned away from him.

"Nah," Buster said.

"Thank you for taking care of the house," Darren said to Buster after a bear hug.

"I'm relieved the girls weren't there," Buster said. He had a gun tucked into a holster in the back of his jeans. Was that new? She didn't remember him carrying before. Then again, Darren's mother wasn't the type to allow a loaded gun inside her home. "Where are they now?"

"With their grandparents," Darren answered.

"Is this the longest you've gone without seeing them?" Buster asked.

Darren nodded. "They're coming home at noon tomorrow. And by home, I mean we're moving back here. It's time."

"Yes, it is," Buster agreed with a broad smile. "Your folks would be pleased, if you don't mind my saying so."

"It means a lot coming from you," Darren said. His comment pleased Buster, based on the smile on his face.

"Are you sure you're not hungry?" Reese asked.

"I just ate before I came," he said. "But, please, sit down and eat your meal before it gets cold."

"There's fresh coffee," Reese added. That got Buster's attention and approval. He walked over to the cabinet, grabbed a mug and then poured himself a cup before turning around and leaning against the bullnose edge of the counter.

Reese and Darren took a seat at the table and passed around the bowls. The food was good if she did say so herself. Simple but tasty. It reminded her of home, because this happened to be something her mother would throw in the Crock-Pot and let simmer on low for hours, filling the house with good smells.

Funny, she'd forgotten all about the food. Why was it so easy to remember every harsh word spoken and so easy to forget all the really good stuff, like Christmases around the tree in the living room? Baking cookies for half the afternoon on Christmas Eve while her mother's favorite holiday movie played in the background. *It's a Wonderful Life* was a staple during the holidays. As were *Elf* and *The Grinch Who Stole Christmas*.

It was probably the fact that it was December that had her feeling nostalgic. But she was happy to find so many good memories tucked in the back of her mind. Maybe it was time they came to the forefront, rather than replaying all those fights she'd overheard with Duncan and her siblings. Reese knew better than to go head-to-head with the man, especially after he'd methodically run off every last one of her siblings. Now that she knew the truth, she might never forgive him for breaking up the family and causing her mother so much pain.

"What do you know about Aiden Archer?" Darren finally asked Buster.

"Not too much," he said, pressing his lips together while he seemed to be reaching deep into his thoughts. "The

Archers were a tight-knit bunch—none of them were to my liking."

"Are they jerks or criminals?" Darren asked.

"Can't say that I would put anything past them," Buster concluded. "I don't know of anything in particular, but I steer clear of the family."

It was quite a statement if Buster didn't like them. He had a keen eye for judging folks. Said it came from years of sizing up young men for hiring purposes. She remembered him always talking about the eyes. All Buster had to do was look someone in the eyes and he could tell if they were bad.

The fact that he didn't care for the Archer family spoke volumes in her book. Aiden Archer topped her list at the moment.

"I didn't get a chance to update you on Phillip Rhodes yet," Darren said to her. Her stomach twisted in a knot at hearing the name. "He works for a delivery service and has moved around. He delivers packages to residential areas."

How easy would it be for him to stalk someone on his route? Especially if it changed every day. "That's convenient and fits the profile of the person responsible. Is that how you think he finds his victims?"

"He could work from the names on packages and then find the teens on their social media accounts," he mused.

"That's true," she agreed. Reese took a moment to let the news sink in. Rhodes could be exactly who they were looking for. She shivered thinking about it. Camree Lynn would have known him despite not caring for him. At least, that's what she'd said when Reese warned her friend to stay away from the man. Did Camree Lynn have secrets?

The short answer was probably yes. Even best friends kept a few things to themselves. Like the time Camree Lynn got busted trying to sneak a beer from her parents in middle school grade. Reese had overheard her friend's ninth grade boyfriend, Jaden, complaining about her getting grounded. When Reese asked her friend about it, Camree Lynn had said she was grounded for getting a D on a math test.

So, yes, even friends lied to each other at times.

Phillip Rhodes was definitely on the list of two names.

"Do you know anyone who might have the inside track on Aiden Archer or his family?" Darren asked Buster.

"I can ask around," he said.

Darren nodded. "That might be a better approach than us showing up to ask questions."

"I'd like to see his face when he sees me, though," Reese interjected.

"Part of me agrees and the other part doesn't think it's such a good idea," Darren stated. "He might see us coming and do something…"

Reese heard what he was saying and she didn't disagree. "I still want to see his reaction."

DARREN COULDN'T ARGUE Reese's point. It was logical. However, his heart strongly disagreed. His protective instincts kicked in with every word she was saying, and he couldn't apologize for it. Explaining it didn't seem like it would do a whole lot of good, either. When Reese Hayes dug in her heels, not much could change her mind.

Worse yet, if it was him in the position instead of her, it was exactly what he would want to do. So, coming up with an argument that could persuade her to change her mind without basing it on pure emotion was difficult.

"I hear you," he began, searching for the right words, "but it could be putting you in the line of fire and I'm having a hard time thinking about doing that to someone I care about."

"We could all three go," Buster interjected. "Reese could wear something to cover her face. We still have a cowgirl hat or two around here that might work. Or a baseball cap. Something to hide her until the last minute. If I'm there, you'll have backup."

"It takes a lot to run this place," Darren pointed out. "If we're both out, the animals suffer."

"Not if we're there and back this evening," Buster said. "In the meantime, I'll do some digging around to see if I can get a location on him."

"I'd appreciate it," Darren said. "Keep in mind the person we're looking for is dangerous and willing to destroy property. If he knows you're involved, who knows what he'll do to you."

The statement got a rise out of Buster. His eyes widened and his lips compressed into a thin line. "Let the bastard come at me."

Buster wouldn't be the kind to back down from a fight, but he needed to go in with his eyes wide open if he intended to help. Darren wanted his foreman to know the risks involved.

"Okay, then," Darren said. "As long as we're all aware of what can happen and willing to accept the risks, we can drop in on Aiden."

Reese nodded in agreement. She was about as stubborn as they came, but as beautiful, too, and his feelings toward her were clouding his viewpoint. He could admit it. Being with her again brought out feelings he didn't think existed any longer. He'd loved Hazel in his own way, but he could also admit to having closed off a large part of his heart after Reese that no one else seemed to have the key to unlock.

Which didn't mean he was saying they should go down that path with each other again. Hell, he didn't know where he stood when it came to Reese and didn't want to find out. Not now, in the middle of moving to his folks' house, fending off a would-be killer and trying to get settled for his girls so he didn't lose them to his former in-laws.

His cell buzzed, so he excused himself from the table after thanking Reese for the meal. The look of pride in her eyes wasn't helping with the attraction bit. He'd programmed in Stacie's number earlier and sent her a text.

She didn't wait for him to speak after he answered. "What happened?"

"There was a fire and—"

"Arson, you mean." Stacie wasted no time correcting him. "And I know this is because of your house guest."

"Right on both counts," he said.

The line went dead silent.

Then she said, "You have to choose between her and the girls."

He didn't like the demanding tone she used or the not-so-subtle threat. "Says who?"

"My parents, for one," Stacie returned. "And me."

"You?"

"Yes," she said with a little more fire in her tone this time.

"What do you have to do with it?" he asked.

"Darren, I don't think I've been secretive in telling you that I'm the best replacement for my sister." She'd said it like it was a job and she was the best candidate.

For this, he left the room and headed into the office. "We're not talking about a nanny job here."

"No," she replied. "We aren't. But you and I dated once. We had a spark and I think we can build something real on it."

There'd been no real attraction on his side. She was nice. They'd dated once to test the waters. "I appreciate how much you want to do what's best for the girls."

"And for us," Stacie interjected. "Hazel was always the fun one between the two of us, but I'm stable and won't aban—"

"Hazel's death was an accident," he warned. "So, I'm going to stop you right there before you say something you'll regret."

"She was reckless riding those ATVs and pushing the speed, Darren. We both know it."

"I'm about to end this call," he said. "Call back when you get your head on straight again. Okay?" He couldn't afford to anger the whole family, but this was out of line. "I'm about to hang up now if you don't say something."

"Are you sure you won't reconsider?" she asked. "Am I so horrific you can't see yourself with me. Ever?"

Again, he wasn't touching that statement.

"It's not about that," he said. "I was married to your sister, and we had these two lovely girls. It doesn't sit right with me to move on to my dead wife's sister."

"Well, putting it like that makes it sound different than I intended," she whined. "We would be two people committing to a life together. Two people who love those girls more than anything else."

"They're beyond lucky to have an aunt who is willing to sacrifice real love to make sure they're okay," he said, hoping it was enough to deflect this conversation for good. He had a sneaky suspicion it might come up again and he was already dreading the day. "And I appreciate the sacrifices you are willing to make for them."

Again, the line went quiet. Stacie didn't like what she was hearing but she wasn't rushing to respond.

"Keep me in mind," she finally said with an unusual calm. "It might be the best way for you to keep custody of the girls."

"Are you threatening me?" Darren didn't bother to hide the indignation in his tone.

"It's just my parents are, well…let's just say that I could tip the scale in your favor if we were together," she said.

Hell's bells. What was he supposed to say to that?

Rather than get worked up, he thanked her for the heads-up, and then ended the call. Were his former in-laws ready to fight? If it came down to a contest of who had more money, they would win.

The thought of losing his girls shook him to the core.

Chapter Eighteen

Reese was finished washing the last dish when Darren joined her in the kitchen. "Buster took off to make a few phone calls and get ready to leave tonight," she said with her back still turned to him.

Darren surprised her by walking behind her and wrapping his arms around her. His breath warmed her neck as his clean spicy scent washed over her and through her. Her knees went weak, but this time for a different reason. With her back flush with his muscled chest, all kinds of tingly sensations lit up her sensitized skin.

"Who was on the phone?" she asked, wondering if the call had anything to do with the sudden display of affection. Actually, *affection* might not be the right word for it. This seemed more like he was holding on to her to gain strength.

"Stacie," he said with a tone that said the call was anything but enjoyable.

"She heard about the fire," she said.

"Yep," he admitted, but there was a whole lot more to the story based on the dread in his tone.

"Your former in-laws must be awfully riled up if Stacie was calling to check on you and maybe smooth things over," she said.

"I wouldn't say that was the exact reason for the call, but yes."

"What then?" Reese asked, her curiosity spiked.

"Let's just say, you were right about her," he admitted.

"She asked you out?"

"A little more than that," he continued.

"What's more than…oh. She asked you to marry her?" Reese asked, mortified.

"Threatened me if I didn't is more like it," he said and then laughed. It wasn't funny, but Reese laughed, too.

"What in the actual hell?" she asked when she finally stopped laughing. "Did she think you would go along with a threat?"

"I guess she believed I could be swayed with the right words," he said. Then he continued, "We did go out on a date once. But to the restaurant where her sister worked. Hazel and I met, and ended up talking. I took Stacie home and that was it."

"Stacie is out of touch if she thinks what she just asked is reasonable," Reese said with a little more emotion than intended.

"She says it's for the girls," he explained.

"Because, yes, you being forced to marry someone you don't love would be in the best interest of those babies," Reese said, incredulous. Some people had a whole lot of nerve. "Please tell me that you would never be that desperate."

Reese turned around in his arms until they were face-to-face.

"I don't feel like this when I'm around her," he said, feathering a kiss on her chin. "Or doing this." He moved lower and pressed his lips to the spot on her neck where her pulse was racing. Darren was thunder and lightning, an electrical storm of impulse.

"Good," she said. "Because I haven't felt like this with anyone in a long time."

Those words stopped him. He took in a deep breath, like he was breathing her in for the last time. And then he took a step back.

"Need any help cleaning up?" he asked, changing lanes faster than an Indy driver on a hot track.

"I'm finished now," she said, wondering what she'd said that was wrong. Then, it dawned on her that he must think she was referring to his uncle. Rather than backtrack and end up making the situation worse, she bit down on her bottom lip to keep from talking.

"You lied to me earlier," he said with a serious voice that made her dread what might come next.

"How is that?"

"You said you couldn't cook," he said, but his voice was robotic. He was forcing himself to be polite. At least she was able to read him a little bit better now. When they'd first come in contact, she'd had no idea what he could be thinking. They were easing into a rhythm and she was very clear on the moments he shut down on her. Walls came up and walls came down, just not all the way.

"I have a few tricks up my sleeve," she said. "Besides, you had the right ingredients."

"Thank Buster's wife for that," he said.

Reese wasn't sure why she should be so surprised. "Buster is married?"

"Oh, right. You wouldn't know if you hadn't kept in touch with anyone in town," Darren said, then excused himself and headed back into the office.

Reese followed.

"No, I wouldn't," she said. "And, no, I didn't." The right words didn't come to her so she just went for it. "Remember how you said young people always blame themselves for everything, even things that aren't their fault?"

He nodded as he took a seat behind the desk. She perched on the edge, making escape impossible without asking her to move. He crossed his arms over his broad chest and leaned back in the swivel chair. "Yes."

"It's because young people make foolish mistakes," she admitted. "I was one of those young people who made a terrible judgment call, but I stand behind my reasons for leaving Cider Creek and the house I grew up in. Losing you was the only mistake I made and it was huge."

He held up two fingers. "No, you made two when you started dating my uncle."

"Not that it matters now, but he was much older and manipulated me," she said. "The only dating experience I had was with you, and it spoiled me into thinking all men were honest. I never believed I deserved that again after the way I treated you. I was young and naive. And, got what I deserved when I found out he was cheating with multiple women in the office." The admission was hard. Confessions usually felt good afterward, which was the reason people finally owned up to something. Admitting she'd been played for a fool was embarrassing. "I thought I was mature enough to handle anything when I left Cider Creek. But I was dead wrong. I sank into a hole because I missed you so much I could barely breathe. And then your uncle started showing up at my house, bringing food. He said I didn't look like I was eating, and he wanted to make sure his star intern was doing okay with the big move."

Darren sat there, stone-faced. She had no idea if she was getting through or just making a bigger fool of herself, but she had no plans to stop now that she'd gotten the ball rolling.

"Do I regret leaving home?" she asked. "The answer is no. Do I regret the way I left you? One hundred percent, yes. Would I change everything if I could go back and do it all over again?" She nodded even though he stared down at the wood flooring. "I'm sorry for the way I treated you and I have no right to ask anything of you, but—"

He looked up, catching her gaze and stopping her in midsentence. "We're already friends, Reese. You don't have to ask."

A tear escaped, streaking down her cheek.

"With the twins and running the ranch, I can't say that leaves a whole lot of time left over for anything else," he said. "But we started out as friends and I'd like it very much if we could get back to that."

"Same for me," she said. *Grateful* didn't begin to describe the way she felt at the possibility he wouldn't hate her for the rest of her life. The notion they might actually be friends, even if it was distant, made her feel like anything was possible.

She was also realizing how quickly she'd adjusted to being away from her cell. Normally, it was like an additional appendage and she got heart palpitations when she couldn't find it for even a couple of minutes. Then, there were those times she searched for it while it was still in her hand. Those were doozies. But, mostly, she was glued to the small screen.

Being around Darren almost had her wishing she could

lose her phone more often. This was probably the most she'd spoken to one person without constant pings from her phone. She babysat a lot of her clients and the term *babysat* was appropriate. They could be demanding and throw temper tantrums when they didn't get their way.

Despite someone being intent on erasing her permanently, she was surprisingly calm when she was close to Darren. It was a foreign feeling now.

DARREN DIDN'T HAVE the heart to kick Reese in the teeth when she was baring her soul. He was being honest, too. He didn't have a whole lot of time for friends, but this ordeal had brought them back together and he still cared whether or not she lived or died. He would like to hear from her every once in a while, even if it was from afar. The girls wouldn't be little forever and he needed to remember that fact, because he should also think about having a small life for himself. Something separate that wouldn't make them miss him like they already would their mother. Like he'd told Stacie, maybe it was time to think about dating again. The thought of having someone to talk to at the end of the day, even if it was just a phone call to check in with each other, was becoming more and more appealing.

Of course, that all had to be put on hold now that Stacie had lost her mind and his former in-laws might be suing him for custody.

"So as your friend, I'd like you to talk to me about what's going on right now," Reese said, interrupting his heavy thoughts.

"I was just thinking about custody and doing what's best for the girls," he said. "A long court battle where I'm in a fight with their grandparents will only push us further apart. We'd been working together okay. Or at least I thought we had. It's hard to believe they're bringing up the possibility of fighting me for custody again. I thought I'd proved myself more than capable of bringing these girls up alone in the last year."

"They are probably still grieving, which doesn't excuse their behavior," she said.

"I gave them plenty of latitude on that one," he said. "But at some point, I have to remind them that I was married to their daughter."

"You must have missed her something awful," Reese said with the kind of compassion that could heal an open sore in two seconds flat.

"I still do," he admitted. "When the girls do something new, like the first time Ivy walked. She's the youngest but is never to be outdone by her older by two minutes sister. Ivy got this big grin on her face and then just threw herself toward me. My heart nearly exploded at seeing my girl take her first steps, but then the sadness hit because her mother should be here to witness it, too."

"Kids shouldn't have to grow up without a parent," Reese agreed as a mix of emotions passed behind her eyes that she immediately tried to cover.

"I'm a jerk," he said. "I'm sorry. You grew up without your father because—"

"You don't have to apologize," she interrupted. "Besides, we were talking about your family, not mine."

He shook his head. Seeing the pain in her eyes made him wonder if he would see that same look in his own daughters one day.

"It's okay," she said. "Really, it is."

"Talk to me, Reese."

"No. It's just that my dad obviously missed a lot of my childhood...*most* of my childhood. I was so little when he died that I have no memories of him," she said. "We never talked about him when I was growing up, but I'm starting to realize that might have been Duncan's fault, too. All I want to say is that you should keep pictures of their mother up and tell them stories about her when they're older. They'll want to hear them but might be afraid to ask. Kids have a way of picking up on emotions, and talking about her makes you sad, so..."

"That's good advice, Reese." He locked gazes for a second longer than was good for his heart. "I'll keep that in mind."

"Good," she said. "That will keep her memory alive and they need that because it's the only way they'll know how much she loved them and what kind of person she was."

He nodded. "I bet your mother would love to talk to you about your dad."

"We don't ask because we think it'll be painful for her to talk about," she said.

"It's not," he said. "In fact, widowers want their children to know about your other parent. But I can see how life happens and the subject just doesn't come up after a while. Years pass and we move on with our lives, and it's easy not to go back and talk about it."

"Makes sense," she admitted. "But I can also see that I've been way too hard on my own mother. She deserves a break. And a hug, as far as I'm concerned. After talking to you, I'm starting to see how hard the job is."

"Marla is a good person," he said. "She definitely deserves a hug."

"She always liked you," Reese said. "I was half afraid she would never want to hear from me again after the way I treated you. It's probably the reason I took so long to get into contact with her along with many others. Plus, I believed she would try to talk me into coming back home, which she did."

"You've done good for yourself, Reese." He meant that. "You should be proud of the work you've accomplished."

She shook her head.

"I'm in an endless loop of taking care of people who are only bothered right now because they can't reach me," she corrected. "It's not like ranching communities, where people take care of each other."

"Careful there," he teased, trying to lighten the mood. "I'll start thinking you miss Hayes Cattle."

She looked him straight in the eye. "You know, I never thought I'd hear those words come out of my own mouth. I'm busy in Dallas and I do okay. But, at the end of the day, no one there is looking out for me or after me right now. The only people calling me want me to do something for them. And I convinced myself that was a real life, a better life."

"And now?"

"Being here at your parents' place—*your* place now—I feel like I'm at home for the first time in a long time," she said. "But then, that might just be because you're here. I felt it at your house before, too."

"Do you mean that?" he asked.

"I sure do," she said. "I'm not saying that I want to give up my business." She shook her head like she could shake off the thought. "I don't know what it means for my future but being away from it for the first time in…ever…has me thinking that maybe I want to make some changes in my life."

Did those changes involve him? Better yet, did he want them to?

Chapter Nineteen

The revelations hit Reese square in the chest, but she couldn't do anything about them until the person trying to kill her was caught. She'd showered and eaten. They had a big night ahead of them. If she stayed inside this office any longer with Darren looking at her like he was, she might just say something she would regret later.

"I should probably get some rest before we head out this evening," she said to him, needing an excuse to step away.

"Yeah," he said, and his voice was heavy with emotion. "That's probably a good idea."

"Mind if I rest next door and keep these open?" She motioned toward the door as she stood up.

"Be my guest," he said, then went back to studying the screen in his hand.

Reese walked to the master bedroom, then curled up on top of the covers. Darren had moved on to the computer keyboard and there was something reassuring about the *click-click-click* of the keyboard. There was a rhythm to his movements. Knowing he was right next door helped her doze in and out of sleep over the next few hours, then it was time to get up. She freshened up in the bathroom and headed down the hall toward the office.

She stopped at the door, took one look at Darren while he was deep in thought and a picture was imprinted on her thoughts. It was her, Darren and the girls living together in this home as a family. The tree was up, the girls were a couple of years older and Reese was resting a hand on her baby bump.

Did she want those things? Or was she having a career crisis? Was she burned out from working for a decade without a real vacation? She'd taken her phone with her on every trip, every weekend.

Reese flexed and released her fingers, realizing for maybe the first time how good it felt not to have them wrapped around a phone.

She was taking deeper breaths now, too, realizing life was short and she wanted to breathe fresh air again. If she moved home, she could probably run her business from here and only need to make trips to Dallas a few days every month to handle things in person. She could also hire a manager to help run her small service company.

"Hey."

Darren's voice pulled her from her deep thoughts. She looked up at him only to realize he was studying her.

"What are you thinking about?" he asked.

He probably didn't want to know all of it, especially the fantasy about him and the girls, so she said, "Changes that need to happen in my life if we're able to—"

"Not if," he interrupted. "When."

She stared at him, loving that he believed everything would work out great. Her reality didn't always go the way she'd planned. Still, his heart was in the right place, and she didn't have it in her to disagree. "Okay, *when* we're able to lock this bastard or bastards away."

Darren clicked off the computer he'd been working on and led the way into the kitchen. "Coffee?"

"I'd love some," she said, "but only if you let me help."

The two worked together to put on a fresh pot. She rinsed out their mugs from earlier.

"It'll be dark soon," she said. "When did Buster say he was coming back?"

Darren glanced at the clock on the wall. "We have about half an hour."

She nodded.

"I have bad news about Phillip Rhodes," he said.

"Oh yeah? What's that?"

"He just finished chemo recently," Darren said. "I was able to track down one of his family members. The guy is a jerk for what he did to you. Apparently, he found religion five years ago and has been working the same job ever since. His mother said that he had to move in with her six months ago so she could care for him during treatment."

"I hope he did get his life together," she said. It didn't change what he'd done to her, but she didn't have it in her heart to wish cancer on anyone. "But it doesn't sound like he would be strong enough to force someone to go with him."

Darren took a sip of coffee. "No. He's off the list. Which leaves Aiden Archer. He's more of a mystery."

"Which doesn't mean he's guilty," she pointed out, frustrated they didn't have a few more names to go on. It would be fine if Aiden was the one, but what if he wasn't? Narrowing down the suspect list to one name was hard.

"I know," he said. "We'll find this guy. I promise."

It wasn't a guarantee that anyone could make right now, but she appreciated him for trying to offer some reassurance.

"I heard you typing," she said, changing the subject.

"Ranch work is a whole lot of paperwork," he said with a look that said he saw what she was doing.

"Do you still love it?" she asked.

"I love being here on the land," he said. "You know how much I love the animals. The paperwork? That's not my favorite part."

"You never were one for doing homework," she quipped. "Despite the fact you tested better than me."

"It was busywork for people who couldn't understand the material," he insisted with a small quirk of a smile.

"Not everyone is a genius, like you," she said.

"Some genius," he countered. "I let the one person I truly loved get away without even trying to find you. How smart was I?"

The look on his face said his comment surprised him as much as it did her. An awkward moment passed before Reese took another sip of coffee and then walked over to the kitchen sink.

"This land always was beautiful," she said. "I loved coming here."

"Sometimes, I get so busy with life that I forget to stop and appreciate everything I do have," he said. "Having this place makes me feel connected to something bigger than myself."

"I can see that," she said. "My business might be successful and I like what I do most of the time, but there's no legacy. It doesn't tie into anything bigger in the way Hayes Cattle does."

"It's understandable how you might think that way, but you've built something from scratch," he said. "There is a whole lot to be proud of in that."

"Thank you, Darren." Those words, coming from him, meant more than she could say.

FORTY-FIVE MINUTES TICKED BY. Waiting was the absolute worst. If Darren paced anymore, he'd wear a hole in the carpet, metaphorically speaking, since the floors were wood.

Buster came through the back door at 6:30 p.m. "The Archer family sticks to themselves. No one knows all that much about them other than the fact they run the bee farm on the outskirts of Cider Creek."

"I don't remember much about Aiden from school, but I believe he would have been two grades ahead of us," Darren said as Reese listened intently.

"You probably don't know him because he dropped out of school in the ninth grade," Buster said. "I asked around and Mrs. Carmen said she was one of his teachers. Said he was a quiet boy who was unapproachable. He used to get bullied because he didn't talk much, and she remembered feeling sorry for him because of it. It's the reason he stuck out in her mind. His parents pulled him to homeschool him, saying they needed the extra help around the farm."

"The guy sounds like he could fit the description of a would-be serial killer," Reese finally said.

"It definitely doesn't rule him out," Buster admitted.

"I hate to say this, but living on a remote bee farm would give him a lot of places to bury bodies," Darren pointed out. "Aiden would know the land like the back of his hand and could have cameras set up, hidden."

"Which would also make it hard for us to confront him," Reese said. "We have no idea if he's home."

Buster lifted his index finger. "The place takes deliveries. Aiden is rarely, if ever, seen, according to several of the folks I spoke to but that doesn't mean he doesn't slip out at night and disappear for a couple of days to go somewhere. He's never seen in town, though."

"How would he know the girls if he doesn't leave the property?" Reese asked.

"Good question," Darren said. "Since the cases are stretched far apart, he might study each one and take his time with them."

Could it mean Tandra was still alive? Could they get to her in time?

"I'm ready when you are," Buster said.

Darren nodded before retrieving a baseball cap for Reese. Even with the disguise, Darren would know it was her from a mile away. If Aiden was targeting her, he would, too. So, basically, Darren had the drive over to convince her to stay inside the vehicle.

"Whoever is responsible for this also lit my home on fire," Darren said. "If we come driving up in my SUV, it'll alert Aiden and/or whoever else might be involved."

"Then, we'll take my pickup," Buster said. "It has a bench seat in front, plenty big enough to fit all three of us."

Reese put on the cap, lowering the rim to hide as much of her face as possible. Then, Darren waited for her to lead the way outside. It dawned on him that he might need a weapon of his own. His mother would never allow loaded guns inside the house and he respected her wishes to this day even though she wasn't there. It was one of many small ways that he kept her memory alive at the farmhouse.

It was already dark outside when Darren went to the locked shed at the back of the house. Clouds rolled across a blue velvet sky. He unlocked it and then retrieved the Colt .45 he kept there for shooting coyotes. It was the quickest way to get rid of the menace. There were wild boars on the property, too, and they were nasty creatures. Mean, too.

The drive over was quiet. The gate to the bee farm was closed. Was it locked?

Buster exited the vehicle and opened the metal gate.

The porch light was on at the ranch-style home. They were expected, so someone must have heard them driving up. And the prickly hair feeling on the back of Darren's neck was on high alert. He felt like they were being watched.

"You feel that?" he asked Reese and Buster. It didn't need explaining, not with how quiet they were. The cab was eerily silent.

"Yep," Buster finally said.

"I do, too," Reese agreed.

He pulled up beside the house and cut the engine. "Since they appear to know we're here, I say we all three go inside. It'll be safer if we all stick together."

"I was just about to suggest the same thing," Darren stated as he opened the passenger door and exited the truck. He helped Reese out next as Buster came around from the driver's side.

There was safety in numbers. He and Buster flanked Reese, ignoring the ominous feeling. This place gave him the creeps.

As they stepped onto the porch, the front door cracked open.

"Mrs. Archer, I'm Buster Wren." He stretched out a hand as a gray pit bull let out a low, throaty growl from her side.

"He's not friendly," Mrs. Archer said, referring to the dog.

Out in these parts with the house tucked behind a metal gate, Darren wondered what the need for an angry pit bull might be. He understood needing protection for cattle, but these were beekeepers not ranchers.

"I'm Darren Pierce," he said when her gaze shifted to him.

"And my name is Ree—"

"You're a Hayes," Mrs. Archer said in a disgusted tone. "I know who you are."

That tone sent a cold chill racing up Darren's back.

"We'd like to talk to you and your husband, if possible," Darren said. There was no way to get a peek inside the place with how little the door was cracked. All the brothers could be back there standing behind the door for all Darren knew.

Another thing occurred to him. The family had no storefront. They sold to businesses. And businesses needed deliveries. Darren would bet money Aiden and his brothers did the driving. There was a bigger question looming. Was this a family affair?

Chapter Twenty

Reese took a step back and to her right. Darren seemed to understand what she was doing when he brought his shoulder forward and tucked her behind him.

"What can I help you with?" Mrs. Archer said. The older woman looked hard. A couple of her teeth were missing, and her sun-worn skin was wrinkled, especially around the eyes. Hers were an intense shade of green, piercing and distrustful. Her mouth was bracketed by deep grooves. This was not a kind face. This was not the face of a good person. This was the face of someone hardened by life.

Mrs. Archer's strawberry-blond hair was in a messy pile on top of her head. Her clothing was a flannel dress, which oddly suited her. She kept her right arm hidden behind the door. Reese would bet money the woman was gripping a shotgun.

"Is your husband home?" Buster continued. Being the eldest of the group, he would command the most respect. His voice was calm but stern.

"I never said he wasn't," Mrs. Archer replied. Yeah, her responses were firing off warning shots left and right. A part of Reese wanted to head back into the truck, get inside and keep driving until she could no longer be tracked.

One thought kept her from turning around. Was Tandra still alive?

The feeling of pure evil was thick despite the cool breeze that said winter was gaining ground.

"Could we speak to him?" Buster continued, unfazed, but he had to be feeling the same thing as Reese. She could tell by Darren's tense muscles that he did.

"I'll see if I can find him," she said after a long pause. "Stay right here or Tyson will get nervous."

The door closed. While they waited, she figured it might be a good time to check out the place a little.

The porch was lit up. Seeing much past a small area was next to impossible since there were no other lights on the property. At least, no others that were on. Insects chirped, giving Reese a bad case of the willies. She might have been born in ranching country, but she never liked the thought of insects crawling on or around her. Field mice used to get inside the house occasionally and those really freaked her out. So, yes, she was on high alert.

Not to mention the possibility of coming face-to-face with a man who wanted to kill her.

Reese involuntarily shivered.

The door swung open wide. A tall man in suspenders she assumed to be Mr. Archer filled the space.

"What the hell do you want?" he grunted. "You have about ten seconds to tell me what you're doing on my property before I tell you to leave."

The door opened wide enough to give a glimpse of a shotgun. Reese had no doubts the man was prepared to use it.

Buster's hands came up in the surrender position. "Hold on there, Mr. Archer. We didn't come to get into a confrontation."

Reese started to back away slowly from the door.

"Then, why have you come?" Mr. Archer continued. "Because I don't take kindly to strangers meddling in my business or folks intent on trespassing on my land."

The reaction to their visit was over-the-top. Fear raced through Reese as she cleared the porch. She wouldn't put it past the family to make up a story about the three of them after shooting them. Then again, if Tandra was here, would they want to risk being found out?

The adrenaline jolt Reese was experiencing was the equivalent of a double shot of espresso. Her heart thundered inside her rib cage as her gaze scanned every place the light touched.

"We'll just be leaving now," Buster said as he hopped down from the porch.

The dog could be unleashed on them. They were on Archer land. Texas would back the land owners if they were mauled, especially if the Archers claimed the trio were trespassing.

Reese was torn between getting the heck out of Dodge and probing to find out if Tandra was here.

"Get inside the pickup as fast as you can," Darren said out of the side of his mouth. He spoke barely loud enough for her to hear.

She didn't wait for a second invitation. Reese turned and made a beeline for the truck, not stopping to look up until she was safely inside.

"Oops," Mr. Archer said before making a weak attempt to call his dog back.

Reese turned in time to see the dog clearing the porch in

one jump. Darren hurried inside the truck and Buster followed a few seconds later.

"Did that bastard just sic his dog on us?" she asked, incredulous.

"Are those the actions of an innocent man?" Buster growled. He started the engine and backed down the lane.

On the side of the gravel lane, the headlights showed two men with weapons hiding in the shadows. They looked like the Archer boys.

"Do you see those bastards?" Reese asked, motioning toward the left. They were about twenty feet apart on the same side of the road.

"Sure do," Darren stated, pulling out a weapon and keeping it behind the dashboard, out of view. He wasn't taking any chances but didn't want to instigate trouble, either. She appreciated his caution because this place seemed like a teapot on a burning hot stove ready to boil over any second. The tension in the air was thick.

"We can't leave," Reese said without a whole lot of conviction. They *had* to leave but they couldn't abandon Tandra if she was here.

"I know," Darren said quietly. "We just need a better plan to figure out if she's here."

Darren issued a sharp sigh. "If Tandra is alive, she might not be for long now that we showed up, poking around."

"Did we just issue a death sentence to a fifteen-year-old girl if she's not already dead?" Reese asked, horrified.

Darren let out a sharp sigh. He knew she was right. Buster didn't offer a differing opinion, either.

"It's impossible to know for certain," Darren finally said as they left property. "Staying here will get us killed and we are of no help to Tandra if we're silenced."

He made a good point, and it was along the lines of what she was thinking, too. They were stuck between a rock and a hard place.

"How about you guys drop me, and I'll circle back?" Buster said.

"With Tyson running around?" Reese asked. "You can't do that."

"Plus, the others might be walking the property for a while to make sure we didn't get any bright ideas," Darren said.

The sheriff believing them would make this a whole lot easier. Going back on the property without permission was trespassing, and it was legal to shoot them on sight.

"What can we do?" she asked in frustration.

"We'll think of something," Darren reassured her. He was picking up his girls tomorrow at noon. All investigating needed to stop for him at that point.

"We go back," Buster said. "Let's give it a couple of hours and then circle back."

As far as ideas went, it sounded like suicide. What else did they have?

DARREN WAS ABOUT to suggest the same thing as Buster, except that he was trying to figure out a way to keep Reese out of it. She would protest, and he didn't have a good argument as to why she couldn't go with them other than the same keeping-her-safe excuse that she'd rejected before. He knew her, and him asking her not to go while he risked his own life wasn't an option, either. She could be stubborn that way.

Buster drove a couple miles down the farm road before cutting the lights and pulling off the road. "Those folks are guilty as sin of something."

"Yep, they are," Darren agreed.

"Murder is a serious accusation," Buster continued.

"Kidnapping and murder," Reese added. "If this is true, they're preying on teenagers."

"Deliveries across the state sure make a good excuse to be in various places," Darren added.

"Not to mention, they use trucks, which would make it easy to hide someone," Reese added.

"It's all circumstantial," Buster said. "We don't have any proof. Just a theory."

"A good one at that," Reese stated.

"Not enough for the law to step in," Buster said. "Like we already said, the best they could do would be to drop by and ask questions. The Archers don't have to allow them inside even if they have a kid strapped to the couch. The law wouldn't be any wiser. Without a search warrant, they can't walk through the door or make demands."

"So we go back," Darren said. "This could be like searching for a needle in a haystack."

"Not to mention these people are beekeepers," Buster added. "They'll have storage buildings for their honey and others for equipment. There's no telling where they would stash a fifteen-year-old."

"Assuming we're right in the first place and she is actually here," Reese added.

"And still alive," Darren pointed out. The odds weren't great they would be able to make a hill-of-beans difference. And yet, if this was one of his girls, he would hope folks would move heaven and earth to find out before walking away.

"What if we're off base?" Buster asked. "Just playing devil's advocate here."

"Then, we know for sure the Archers are innocent," Darren said. "We keep looking for Tandra while trying to figure out who is trying to kill Reese." Those last words tasted bitter in his mouth. "Because whoever is behind this is intent on making sure she doesn't see her next birthday."

"And they don't mind taking down anyone who is helping me," Reese added. "Now that the two of you have shown your faces, neither one is safe."

Darren nodded. He was well aware of the danger, considering his house had been torched. Those smug bastards weren't getting away with it, either. "With the whole family involved, they could easily cover each other's tracks."

"Seems like everyone has a computer, laptop or smartphone these days," Reese said. "Any one of them could be responsible for finding the next target and grooming them."

"If that's true, the family isn't just criminal, they're…" Darren stopped himself right there. His emotions were running high, and he didn't need to finish his sentence. The thought this could happen to one of his girls at some point in their lives was enough to make him crack a tooth from clenching his teeth so hard.

"We'll figure something out," Reese insisted. "I wish we had a reason to be on property. That would make this so much easier."

"Or an invitation," Buster quipped.

"I wonder if there are any other dogs like Tyson on property?" Reese asked.

"I'm guessing just the one since we haven't heard barking, and it seems like they keep him at the house," Buster mused. "We would have heard others mouthing off once Tyson got riled up."

There was a small miracle. Still, if they made the pit bull

angry and got anywhere near his mouth, the bite from his jaw would apply something like three hundred pounds of pressure. The jaw would lock, too, so there was no opening it again or wriggling out. Plus, this one looked trained to defend. Not good.

"So, with the Archers, we're dealing with at least two young men, a mother, a father and an aggressive dog," Reese recapped.

"I wouldn't underestimate any one of those," Darren added. "To complicate matters, we're going on gut instinct these folks have done something illegal. They might just be nasty folks who keep to themselves. Jerks but not criminals."

"This family strikes me as pure evil," Reese said.

"We can all agree there," Buster interjected.

"We know that we want to circle back and explore the property," Darren said. "But doing it safely is the issue."

"Hell, I forgot all about that drone thing I got for Christmas last year," Buster said. "My wife thought it would be a good way to check on the cattle near Dangling Creek. You know how one ends up there stuck in the mud every spring."

"I do," Darren said, liking the sound of this idea. "I'm guessing it has some kind of light for a night feature."

Buster nodded. "We can go back and study the property using those internet maps."

"That would help us figure out where we could best enter," Darren agreed, starting to gain a little more momentum with the idea.

"It could also save one of us from getting shot," Reese added.

"And give us a bird's-eye view of who might be patrolling around," Darren said.

"I would bet money the family will be setting up patrol at least over the next couple of hours," Buster said.

"A couple of hours gives us enough time to go home, collect the drone and figure out the landscape," Darren said. "The actual ranch land will be blurred online, but we'll get a sense of the periphery."

A plan was taking shape. It was still risky, but doable with minimal collateral damage, he hoped. The thought of something bad happening to Buster or Reese sat hard on his chest. He was a single father. His girls needed him. He needed to come home in one piece.

Would voluntarily stepping into a life-threatening situation be enough for him to lose custody if his in-laws had a good lawyer?

He couldn't ignore the possibility. Or the developing feelings he had for Reese. They went beyond ensuring her well-being. He could be honest with himself about it. The thought she might not make it off the Archer property alive nearly gutted him. As much as he was ready to make sure justice was served, the idea of going back to his old routine—a routine that didn't involve Reese—sat heavy, too.

But could he open his heart to her a second time?

Chapter Twenty-One

The drive back to the farmhouse was spent in quiet contemplation. Reese leaned her head on Darren's shoulder and closed her eyes for most of the ride.

Buster pulled up beside the farmhouse.

"I'll grab the drone and meet you at the house," he said, then headed toward the barn and bunkhouse, where he and his wife lived.

Reese followed Darren inside and straight to the laptop on the counter. She claimed one of the bar stools and Darren took the open one next to her. He turned on the computer and then pulled up the map. As expected, the actual property was a blur. However, since it butted up against roads, they could move that way to get a sense of the periphery.

"It would be nice if we could bring this with us," she said.

"I could create a hot spot with my cell..."

He shook his head.

"Not sure about this throwaway," he said. Then he got up and retrieved a pad of paper and pen from the office. "Then again, nothing like going about this the old-fashioned way."

Darren drew a rough map of the Archer Bee Farm.

"We should probably be ready to call the law at any moment while we're there," Reese pointed out.

"Do you want to be in charge of that?" he asked.

She nodded.

"Good," he said. "When we get there, I'll hand over the phone."

"I imagine Buster will man the drone," she said.

"I have some night-vision goggles that we can bring," Darren added. "They'll come in handy if we need to go on property."

"How long does a drone battery last?" she asked.

Darren's fingers danced across the keyboard after he pulled up a search engine. "Let's see. Not long. Maybe half an hour."

"Which is why we need a solid lay of the land before we send it in," she said.

"Says here they can fly anywhere from forty to sixty miles per hour," he stated.

"That should help cover a lot of ground."

Darren leaned back. "It's the safest way to get on the property and the most efficient. But I'm thinking that any evidence we gather won't be able to be used in a court of law."

"Which could mean those bastards might walk away," she said.

"If we find Tandra and she can testify." He paused for a few seconds, stopping before saying *if* she can testify, because he hoped she wasn't dead. "Then we're okay."

"We had a question for the family and stopped by to ask," she proposed.

"But if we don't find anything, or something truly bad happens, all three of us can be arrested, sued or both," Darren said. Which meant he was risking more than his livelihood.

Darren stood to lose everything. They needed to find something or leave without getting caught.

Before she could tell him that he didn't have to do this, he said, "I'm all in, Reese."

"I wouldn't be able to live with myself if anything happened to you and those girls were orphans or, heaven forbid both scenarios, you were sued and couldn't provide for them any longer," she said as a tear escaped.

"I love that you are always putting my girls first, but I am, too," he said. "How could I call myself a father or live with myself if Tandra is alive in there and we could save her? I understand the risk I'm taking, and I didn't commit to this lightly. As much as I'm doing this to keep you safe, my girls are always at the forefront of my thoughts, and I wouldn't be able to look them in the eyes if I let someone else's daughter die when I could have saved her. Plus, this might help resolve the other cases, as well."

"You're an amazing father, Darren. And an even better human being," Reese said. She'd known it back in high school, and she'd been an idiot for letting him go. At least he'd agreed to be friends, moving forward. She wanted very much to be in his life.

Buster knocked, then unlocked the back door and walked into the kitchen. "The drone is in the pickup. We can head out whenever you two are ready." He took a step inside and waited by the door.

Darren stood up. He picked up the notepad and showed the rudimentary map to Buster, who gave a nod of appreciation.

"I think we should come from the opposite side to confuse them," Darren said, pointing to the east side of the property.

"Good idea," Buster said. "I was just thinking along those

same lines. We definitely don't want to go in the way we came earlier. They'll be expecting that."

"My thinking exactly," Darren said. "Plus, there's a cluster of small buildings tucked over here, away from the main house."

They headed out the back door, making sure the place was secure before making their way to the pickup parked beside the farmhouse.

Reese looked at the house as Buster backed up and was overcome with a strange sensation. Was this the last time she would see the place that had been a second home to her? She cleared her throat, unable and unwilling to allow herself to believe all three of them wouldn't make it back alive. Besides, she was working herself up for the worst-case scenario. The whole thing might end up a bust. The drone could reveal no wrongdoing and they could end up turning around to come back home.

Home? Interesting word choice.

Ready or not, it was go time.

DARREN STUDIED HIS homemade map like his life depended on it, and was using the flashlight app on his throwaway cell phone on dim. He'd mapped out the house, the tree line on the west side of the driveway. He'd made two dots where the pair of boys had been standing. They'd been protecting their home while taking cover. Had they believed things might go south during the visit? Were they meant to be a warning?

The fact they'd decided to stand where they could be seen meant they were sending a message. They meant business. Darren made no mistake about it. If what they believed was true, members of this family would be locked away for a very long time, if not the rest of their lives. Even if their mother wasn't involved, she would go down as an accomplice. He didn't need to be in law enforcement to know these folks had nothing to lose, which made them even more dangerous.

Of course, if they were innocent...

Darren stopped himself right there. The place had the security of a meth lab, and he seriously doubted the Archer family was running drugs out of there. Although, he couldn't be one-hundred-percent certain about that, either. Uncertainty was the worst.

Archer Bee Farm was a family operation, so were there cousins, uncles or nieces who were involved with the business?

More questions looped through his thoughts as Buster passed by the entrance to the farm. He circled around to the west side of the property, driving along a dirt road. A few miles into the turn, he pulled to the side and parked.

The area was surrounded by trees and scrub brush. The pathway was well-worn, which meant vehicles used this stretch a fair amount since it wasn't gravel or pavement. That might be a good sign they weren't totally off base with the theory.

"Since this thing has a light on it, I'll have to maneuver it through the trees instead of over them," Busted began as he exited the driver's side. He retrieved the drone from the back as Darren slipped out the passenger side before helping Reese out.

That was the hope.

Darren took in a deep breath before releasing it slowly.

"Before we move ahead, I just want to thank both of you for everything you're doing," Reese whispered. "I do realize this isn't just for me, but that doesn't take anything away from my gratitude."

"You'd do the same," Buster said, waving her off.

Darren reached for her hand, and then squeezed for re-assurance.

Buster motioned toward the fence line. "I'll head down this way with the drone. Do you want to follow or stay by the pickup?"

"We should keep watch here until you find something," Darren said. "In fact, you might want to hand over the keys in case we need to get away fast."

Buster reached into his front pocket and then tossed them over. This pickup was old enough to need an actual key. "I'll give you a shout if I find anything."

"Got it," Darren said. "Good luck."

If Tandra was being held here, he hoped they were in time. It was late at this point, long past midnight. They'd visited hours ago and might have caused the Archers to panic. Would they lie low? Would they ramp up? Would they kill her and dispose of the body? Once again, the property was large. But there were only a few areas that might be good for dumping a body. They wouldn't do it near water, so as not to contaminate it as the body decomposed.

Darren stopped himself from going down too morbid a road. Waiting for Buster to return was the pits.

Thankfully, they didn't have to wait too much longer. Darren came running, waving his arms in the air.

Darren immediately jumped into the pickup, as did Reese, and then cranked the engine. Buster hopped into the back and rolled, keeping a low profile.

"Stay low," Darren said to Reese as he backed down the drive without headlights. He didn't plan to stick around long enough to find out what had spooked Buster. They could regroup when it was safe.

Reese ducked down in the seat and he made himself as small as possible. Not an easy feat for someone his size and stature. In fact, he was the biggest target in the vehicle.

Half-expecting gunfire to break out and half-expecting someone to jump out from behind a tree, he was surprised when nothing happened for a couple of miles until he made it onto the farm road.

Buster knocked on the glass, so Darren took that as a sign to stop. He joined them inside the cab.

"What did you get?" Darren asked.

"They were patrolling on that side," Buster said. "I had to get out of there."

"On foot?" Darren asked.

"They must have anticipated us, or this is their normal routine," Buster said. "One of them heard the drone but didn't know what it was."

"No one would be out walking around this time of night unless they were concerned we would come back and find something," Reese interjected.

Darren nodded. "We can go back to the other side to the entrance area and watch."

"It's the best we can do for now," Buster said. "I didn't see any buildings on this side of the property, anyway."

"Do you know how many of them were out there?" Darren asked.

"I'm pretty sure it was the pair from earlier," Buster said.

"Seems like they would send someone else to cover this side if they had them," Reese pointed out. She wasn't wrong. Darren made the same assumption.

"At least we can reasonably assume we aren't dealing with a small army here," Buster said.

It was a small miracle. One he'd take. The family consisted of three boys, who would now be grown men. Two had been on patrol. Where was the third one?

"At this point, we know there are four people in the house, possibly involved," Buster said. "I have enough battery left on the drone to investigate the area around the house."

"You don't think they would keep her in the main house, do you?" Reese asked, sounding mortified.

Buster shrugged his shoulders as Darren turned on the fog lights and kept driving. No one was out on the road this time of night. This area could be described as one that rolled the streets up by 8:00 p.m. Not much happened past sunset. Of course, folks would be up in a few hours. Rising at four o'clock in the morning was normal rancher hours.

Darren drove around to the entrance of Archer Bee Farm, and then continued twenty yards past it. He pulled over and turned off the engine. He retrieved the notepad, then handed it over to Buster. "Mark the spot where you saw the guys on patrol."

Buster did.

"I wish we had our bearings," Darren said. "My map could be off."

"We aren't getting anywhere," Reese said.

Giving up when they were this close to figuring out the truth wasn't something Darren wanted to consider. And yet, Reese had a point. They weren't getting any closer to finding Tandra and it was too risky to barge onto the farm at this hour.

But what choice did they have?

Chapter Twenty-Two

Reese twisted her fingers together, tying them in a knot. "We have to go in."

"I know," Darren said and then Buster agreed.

"Good," she said.

"It's not ideal," Darren continued. "But we can get a cursory look through the drone and possibly get enough intel to know how to target our search."

"Otherwise, this is an almost impossible find," Reese agreed.

"Let's do this again," Buster said. "It's getting late. Or early, depending on your point of view."

All three exited the pickup. This time, Reese took the keys and they decided to stick together. After backtracking toward the entrance, they found a hole in the fence and slipped through.

"The closer we get to possibilities, the longer life we get out of the battery," Buster pointed out as they moved through scrub brush and trees. They stayed close to the gravel drive as they moved, making as little noise as possible.

The occasional rustling of leaves nearly stopped Reese's heart. She reminded herself to breathe.

On foot, they made it close to the family residence, sticking to the tree line. The house was pitch-black now and there was no sign of movement inside or around it. She'd been praying they hadn't tripped a silent alarm, but the men patrolling and the dog seemed to be the two main sources of security.

Once safely past the house, Buster sent the drone out. He kept it low to the ground until he found a clearing. He located the hives about a quarter of a mile from the house.

"Looks like the hives are spaced around five hundred feet apart," Buster informed them after studying the screen on the control panel. "There has to be a building where they keep supplies and jar the honey. Right?"

"I would think so," Darren concluded.

"Might be a good place to hold someone against their will," Buster said.

"Is it the obvious choice, though?" Reese asked. "The Archer family doesn't strike me as the most brilliant people in the world based on the parents, but that doesn't mean they aren't criminally smart."

"What's your idea?" Darren asked in a voice barely above a whisper.

"I don't know," she admitted. "I'm just thinking out loud."

Her eyes had adjusted to the dark enough to see Darren nod. It was getting cold outside. She shoved her hands inside her pockets to keep them warm. What were they missing?

And then it dawned on her.

"What about the trucks?" she asked.

"It would make for an easy escape if she was already loaded up," Darren said.

"I got a building," Buster whispered. "What do you think about splitting up again?"

"It's risky, but we'll cover more ground that way," Darren said.

Reese agreed, so she didn't speak up. There was no denying the risks or the fact they would be more productive this way. Time was of the essence and their window of opportunity was quickly closing. So, yeah, they needed to do whatever it took.

Buster gave each one a quick hug before heading toward the building. She and Darren circled back to the trucks that were lined up near the main house. There were three trucks parked off to the side of the home. The house was a side yard away from the small gravel lot, so roughly half a football field if she had to guess.

They couldn't afford to make noise and awaken the scary dog in the house. Darren tucked her behind him as they neared the first truck. It was a small commercial delivery vehicle with one of those rolling metal doors in the back. A twist of a handle revealed it wasn't locked.

Slowly, methodically, Darren raised the door. He palmed his cell and tapped the flashlight feature. There were bucket shelves lining the sides, easy for tucking in jars of honey for transport. The vehicle was empty. They moved to truck number two. It was empty as well. Truck number three was no different.

So much for the truck idea.

Darren turned around and sat down on the bumper of truck number three. "Something is off." He shook his head. "I can't quite put my finger on it."

"Any word from Buster yet?" she asked in a whisper, but she knew full well it was too early for him to make it to the building closer to the bees, even at a dead run.

Darren shook his head.

"I was so sure we would find something in a truck," Reese whispered. "In the end, I'm just grasping at straws here, convincing myself we're going to find her."

Guilt reached all the way back to tenth grade, when she'd lost Camree Lynn.

"Something is off…what it is?" Darren asked. "Let's check the trucks one more time."

Considering they had no Plan B and it was too early to hear from Buster, they had nothing to lose by checking. This time, they worked in reverse. Truck number three revealed nothing different, but they got inside and walked through it, feeling around for something even though they had no idea what to look for.

Walking truck two, Reese got the same uneasy sense as Darren. "It's this one. Something is off."

She walked through it again.

"It's shorter than the other one," she said as Darren nodded. They walked to the back of the truck and felt around.

"I got something," Darren said as he bent down and reached for a handle. He cranked it as they heard a gasp.

Reese held her breath as he opened the panel. A teenager was curled in a space that was about two feet deep. There was a bottle of water and another bottle that looked like it was for urine. The smell was the first thing that struck Reese.

And then, two wide eyes blinked up at her as Darren turned the flashlight beam away from the girl's face.

"Tandra?" Reese asked, scanning the girl's body, looking for bindings. It stood to reason it would be her since years passed in between abductions and she was the most recent.

Tandra sat up, and scooted away from them. She had bindings on her wrists and feet. Wide-eyed, her face bleached-sheet white, she shook her head as though urging them to forget they'd ever seen her.

"It's okay," Reese soothed. "You're safe now. We're going to get you out of here and take you home."

Darren took a step back while Tandra's gaze stayed locked on to him. Fear radiated from the poor girl.

"He's not going to hurt you, Tandra," Reese said. "And neither am I."

Tandra's gaze finally shifted from Darren to Reese. The teen's chin quivered before the tears started to fall. She released a sob that cracked Reese's heart in half.

"I need you to be as quiet as you can, okay?" Reese said, looking around for something to use to cut the bindings.

Darren produced a pocketknife but maintained a distance. In fact, he turned his back so he could face the opening of the truck, then palmed the gun he'd brought along with him. If anyone showed up in the opening, he would be ready for them.

Reese worked quickly, cutting the ropes off Tandra's wrists and ankles. The teen immediately lunged for Reese, wrapping her arms around Reese's neck in a death grip. "I've got you. You're going to be okay now. You're going home."

Tandra nodded but she didn't speak. The teen was crying softly and buried her face in Reese's shoulder. All they needed to do now was notify Buster, the law and then get the hell out of there.

DARREN HAD ENOUGH life experience—or maybe just plain old bad luck—not to take this find for granted. Locating her was only half the battle. The rest was getting off the property with Buster, with all four of them in one piece.

If anyone made too loud a noise, the dog would come unglued and wake up the house. The men on the east side of the property would be here in a heartbeat. They, no doubt, had some mode of transportation to get them from one section to the next while they hunted for trespassers.

Darren exited the truck first after shooting a text to Buster, and then waved Reese to follow suit. With the teen hanging on one side, Reese managed to get them both out of the vehicle without making much noise.

He scanned the area. It looked clear.

Moving to the tree line, the trio made their way toward the pickup. There'd been no return text or acknowledgment from Buster, and that had Darren worried. He wouldn't exactly call this extraction easy, but they seemed to be flying under the Archer family's radar for the time being.

With every step toward freedom, Tandra's sobs grew louder. Reese did her best to keep the teen quiet, but only so much could be done without her cooperation. At this point, the teen was most likely in shock. She was just a kid, doing her best after what had have been the most traumatic event in her life.

Darren's heart went out to her and her parents. Losing a child had to be a parent's worst nightmare, but having a kid abducted would be a close second.

But this wasn't the time to celebrate. He had a bad feeling deep in his gut. That Buster wasn't answering the text wasn't a good sign. The hairs on the back of his neck pricked again as the dark-cloud feeling returned, threatening to smother him.

He took the lead, keeping Reese and Tandra tucked right behind him as he moved through scrub brush toward the pickup.

Once they were safely out of earshot of the house, Reese asked, "Has Buster checked in?"

"I'm afraid not," Darren said. He could put these two inside the pickup, hand her his cell phone and go back for Buster.

Reese would protest the move, but they were short on options and even she would have to agree getting Tandra to safety had to be their first priority. She would also understand that he couldn't leave Buster on the property.

Breaking through the tree line onto the road, they cut right toward the pickup. Now that they were off property, Darren allowed himself a burst of hope that he could get this child through this ordeal. Could they call 911? If they did, was Buster as good as dead? Was he already?

Air squeezed out of Darren's lungs. Breathing hurt.

He gave himself a mental shake and kept moving.

Finally, the truck was in sight. All hope Buster might have dropped his cell phone or the battery died disappeared.

When the truck was twenty feet ahead, two large male figures stood up from squatting in front of the vehicle. Darren muttered a string of curses, palmed his cell and sent a 911 text. He could only hope it went through.

"If you're smart, you'll put your hands where I can see them," one of the men said. Darren recognized the voice as Alexander Archer's.

Tandra's cries became louder. That poor girl.

As much as Darren wished he could bum-rush these bastards, he couldn't. Two against one, especially when both of them were carrying guns, wasn't the kind of odds Darren could handle. If he was killed, where would that leave Reese and Tandra? He would be making his babies orphans.

"The law is already on its way," Darren said, hoping they

wouldn't call his bluff. "Your only choice is to let us go. We'll say that we found her walking down the street and she won't say a word about where she's been or who had her. Just leave her alone and she won't talk."

"Nice try," the other one said. Darren recognized the voice as Aiden's. There was one more brother, but who knew where he was? He might not even live at home. "All three of you are coming with us."

"You won't get away with killing three people," Darren argued. "Think this through."

"We've gotten away with a whole lot more than that," Aiden said before being shushed by his older brother.

"Your mouth was always going to get us busted," Alexander admonished. "It's the reason Mama and Daddy keep you on the property while me and Andrew do all the work."

"Our brother isn't even here right now," Aiden complained. There was something simple yet threatening about the tone of his voice.

"He'll be back in a few days, and you need to be quiet," Alexander said, his tone more of a threat.

So, it was two against one at this point, since Reese had her hands full with Tandra. Speaking of Reese, he had an idea. He reached behind and placed the pistol, along with his cell, in the flat of Reese's palm. She got the idea and immediately gripped it. He pointed toward the tree line. They were close enough to zigzag through the trees to avoid being shot.

"You might as well stop hiding," Alexander said. "Come out, come out, wherever you are."

Darren stopped himself from pointing out they were standing in plain sight. With Andrew out of the picture, there was at least a little hope they could survive these twisted bastards. He took a small step back. The farther he could get them away from these jerks, the better chance all three of them had at getting out of this alive.

What he needed right now was a miracle. If he could get them close enough to the trees and distract them, Reese could run with Tandra.

"I told you to get your hands up," Alexander said, his voice filled with rage.

Darren complied. There wasn't anything to hide, anyway, now that Reese had the gun and cell phone. She also had the keys. Could Darren draw the men away from the ladies?

"Don't do it," Reese said so quietly that he almost didn't hear her. "Don't risk it. We'll figure something out."

"Now, send us the bitches and no one will get hurt," Alexander demanded. "It's just like Mama said. The only woman we can trust is her. The rest are evil just like Me-ma. Me-ma used to torture Mama. Now, all Mama was trying to do was find ones for us and teach them how to be good girls. She said we have to start young before they become too worldly."

One on one, Darren had no doubt he could take these men down despite their hefty size if they didn't have weapons. But as it was, one wrong move and one of the ladies behind him could end up paying the price.

"Hold on," Darren hedged, trying to stall for time.

"Time's up," Alexander said, weapon aimed at the center of Darren's chest while the man walked right toward him.

"Go," Darren said out of the corner of his mouth.

A second before Reese and Tandra could react, the buzz of a small airplane or helicopter came roaring up. The drone. It was the drone. That must mean Buster was alive. His condition was unknown, but he must still be breathing, conscious, and reasonably coherent.

The drone attacked Alexander, who waved his right arm around to stop it from smacking him in the face. Aiden's gaze was fixed on his brother, his mouth agape.

Darren didn't waste the chance to bolt into the tree line with Reese and Tandra. He stopped as soon as they reached cover, took the gun from Reese, aimed and fired. A look of shock stamped Aiden's features. It took a second for him to realize he'd been hit in the calf. He squatted down to one knee and used his hand to stop the blood squirting from his wound, dropping his weapon in the process.

If only Darren was closer, he would take the bastard's gun.

The drone was bouncing around, just out of reach for Alexander. Darren took aim and shot, hitting Alexander in the shoulder. He dropped his gun as he shrieked in pain.

"Freeze and I'll let you live," Darren shouted from the trees.

Aiden put up his hands in the surrender position. Alexander came gunning toward the trees. Darren had no choice but to shoot. This time, he hit his thigh, bringing him down.

A sound coming from behind said Darren's luck might have just run out.

Chapter Twenty-Three

A deep growl came from behind Reese. She spun around and tucked Tandra behind her. Whatever came out of those trees would have to get through her first.

Darren handed her the gun one more time. "Shoot if you need to but know what or who you're shooting before you fire."

He was gone before she could tell him she had no idea how to handle a gun. *Point and shoot.* She'd played video games with her brothers when she was a kid. This must be close to the same thing. Right?

Not thirty seconds later, a figure emerged. Her finger hovered over the trigger mechanism. But then she froze.

"Buster," Reese said as he stumbled out from behind a tree. And then he collapsed. "Darren, it's him. He's alive."

With Tandra clinging to her, she ran toward him. A siren sounded in the distance, the welcome shrieks filling the air. This would also alert Mr. and Mrs. Archer, but Reese couldn't care about that right now. She needed to get Buster off the Archer property.

Reese dropped to her knees, not caring that she was stabbed by scrub brush in the process. Tandra stayed right beside Reese but let go of her neck, which was helpful. "Buster."

He didn't look as though he was breathing, so she unbuttoned the top couple of buttons on his shirt. His eyes were closed and his breathing shallow. She checked for a pulse and got one, but it was faint.

"What do I do?" Reese asked, searching her brain for something that could wake him up.

"Move over..." It was Tandra's tiny voice. "We learned CPR in school. Let me try something."

She pinched his nose, opened his mouth and blew measured breaths into it. Then, she switched gears, placed her fisted hands together on his chest and pumped as she counted.

And then she repeated time and time again, until paramedics arrived on the scene. The pair of young men, who looked to be in their early twenties, took over, and placed an oxygen mask over Buster's nose and mouth.

"You might have just saved a life," the EMT named Jerry said to Tandra. "I didn't catch your name."

"Tandra," she said.

Recognition dawned as Sheriff Courtright came jogging over.

"Tandra St. Claire?" the sheriff asked.

"Yes, sir," she responded as Buster was lifted onto a gurney. The teen was shaking by this point.

Jerry turned to Reese and said, "His vitals are good. It's looking good for him."

"Thank you," she said a moment before he was taken away. She scanned the area for Darren, and found him giving a statement to a deputy near where the Archer brothers had been cuffed and placed into the back of a service vehicle.

"The parents were inside the house," Reese said to the sheriff. "They're involved."

"I have a deputy heading that way now," Sheriff Courtright stated.

"There better be someone from animal control with him," she quipped.

The crack of a bullet split the air.

Tandra shrank.

"It's okay," Reese soothed. "You're going to be okay now."

"I want my momma," Tandra said, reverting back to what she probably called her mother as a child.

Reese looked to the sheriff.

"She needs to be checked over by a doctor," Reese pointed out, still in full-on protective mode.

"Yes, ma'am," the sheriff said. "We're heading to the ER where her parents will meet us after they've been informed."

Tandra seemed satisfied with the answer as she clung to Reese.

"What the hell was that?" Reese asked the sheriff as he listened to his radio. She clamped her eyes shut, afraid the dog had just been shot. Her chest squeezed.

The sheriff spoke quietly into the radio strapped to his shoulder. He turned to Reese and said, "A warning shot was fired by the Archers, but once they were informed their sons were going to jail, they surrendered."

"And their dog?" she asked.

"It's fine, but it'll need a new home once this family goes to jail," he said. "We plan to lock them up."

"Andrew Archer is out there somewhere but the others were clear about him being in on it," Reese informed the sheriff.

"We're tracking him down right now," the sheriff said. "So far, we believe he is unaware of the circumstances here."

"Someone needs to throw the book at him, too," she said, disgusted these murderers had gotten away with their crimes for so long.

"They said I was going to die," Tandra finally said. "Just like the others before me."

The teen released a sob as Reese did her best to soothe the young girl. Teenagers were caught in the space between being a child and an adult—it was a difficult time where they needed independence, but also needed to be watched more than ever.

"You're going to be just fine," Reese said, walking her over to the sheriff's SUV. She looked at the sheriff. "She's shivering." The teen had on jeans and a sweater that was filthy and had been ripped.

Reese also acknowledged what the teen had just said. *Just like the others before me* meant they were all gone. Tears overwhelmed Reese.

"I have a blanket in the back of my vehicle," he said, then went to retrieve it. As he walked away from them, he also communicated on the radio. Reese walked Tandra to the opened passenger door of his SUV.

"Sit inside here," Reese said, only able to focus on the teen right then. "This will keep you warm."

The heater was on, and this kiddo desperately needed to warm up.

"Don't leave," Tandra said as the sheriff returned.

"I won't," Reese promised. "I'm right here until your parents arrive."

Tandra nodded, then sniffled and wiped tearstained cheeks. "I never should have talked to him at the store."

"Who?" the sheriff asked.

Tandra gave her statement. By the time she finished, Reese was ready to throw a punch at one of those bastards presently in the back seat of the deputy's SUV wearing handcuffs. It was probably good that Courtright climbed inside the driver's seat and then pulled away. Justice would be served when the book was thrown at those jerks.

Darren walked over and stood behind Reese. She leaned back into his chest as he looped his arms around her. His body was all the warmth she needed. And yet, she also realized this was the end of it.

"You came asking questions on your way to the ranch," he said in her ear. "I overheard Alexander telling the deputy they had to stop you."

It explained why she'd been abducted and nearly murdered.

"But first, they intended to torture you by showing you where your best friend was buried. They planned to dig a grave next to her," he said quietly, reverently. "Nothing will ever happen to you on my watch."

Tears streamed down her cheeks. Tears for Camree Lynn. Tears for Tandra. Tears for the fact it was time to go home to the family ranch and face the music, leaving Darren behind. She would be leaving her heart behind with him.

That was life, though. It was messy and unpredictable, coming so close to giving her everything she could have ever wanted before ripping it all away again.

Walking away from Darren a second time was going to be the second hardest thing she'd ever done.

DARREN WATCHED AS Tandra's parents were reunited with their daughter in the ER. He listened as the fifteen-year-old detailed the Archers' plan to kill her by Christmas. The horror of what she'd gone through would last a lifetime, but she would sleep in her own bed tonight and that was something to be grateful for.

His cell buzzed, so he immediately answered. "Hello?"

"This is Jeanie," the familiar voice said. "I just thought you would want to know that Buster is going to be just fine."

"That's great news, Jeanie," he said to Buster's wife. "Really great news."

"If not for someone knowing how to administer CPR, then…"

Her voice cracked on the last word.

"I'll pass along the message," he said to her. "I'm sorry that I let him come with us."

"He wouldn't have taken no for an answer, but his heart isn't what it used to be," she explained.

"Then, we'll figure out a way to force him to rest," Darren said, realizing that by selling his personal home and moving into the ranch, he could afford to hire another hand to lighten the load. Ever since the twins, he'd been busy with his children and wasn't pulling his weight on the ranch. "Things are going to change for the better."

It was a promise he intended to keep.

"Thank you, Darren," she said. "I know how much you care about him, and he's such a mule. I've been asking him to talk to you for a while now."

"No need," he said. "I'm clear with what needs to happen. Plus, he can use a little more desk time. I hate managing the books. I'd much rather be outside more."

"I don't know what to say except thank you," she said.

"Loyalty means everything," he said to her. "Your husband was loyal to my parents and now to me. I won't let him down. You two are the only family I have left at the ranch."

They exchanged goodbyes before Darren ended the call. Change was in the air. And he had a few things to say to Reese before she walked out of his life forever.

The sheriff took a phone call. He said a few *uh-huhs* and an *I see* before thanking the caller and ending the call. "Looks like Andrew was pulled over on a minor traffic infraction and arrested. He went peacefully and said he would testify against his brothers. He's willing to cooperate for a lighter sentence."

"I don't know who he is," Tandra said honestly as her parents hugged her tight. She was waiting for the doctor to confirm she could go home.

Her father stepped up to Darren and Reese. He was a big man. Someone who looked proud. Tears ran down his face, and droplets stained his overalls.

"I don't know how to thank you for bringing me my little girl," he began with a shaky voice. "There's no way in the world I can ever repay something like this."

He didn't finish his sentence before Reese and Darren started shaking their heads.

"You don't owe us a thing," Darren said. "We are happy enough that your daughter is alive and well." Darren paused as emotion clotted in his throat. He looked Mr. St. Claire straight in the eyes and said, "I'm a father. Twin girls."

Mr. St. Claire nodded. He gave a look of understanding.

"I hope your girls stay safe," Mr. St Claire finally said. "And if they ever need an uncle or guardian angel…they can count on me."

Now, Darren was the one trying to hold back tears.

"It takes a village, right?" he asked but it was more statement than question.

"It sure does," Mr. St. Claire agreed before his daughter wrapped her arms around him. They weren't long enough to clasp her hands together, so she grabbed fistfuls of his overalls.

"I won't ever talk to strangers online or otherwise and I'll never leave the house again without you and mom knowing where I'll be at all times," she promised.

"You did nothing wrong," her mother said. "But your father and I plan to be home every night, together, to take care of you."

Tandra beamed through big teary eyes.

The family of three huddled together.

"Are you ready to get out of here?" Darren asked, turning toward Reese.

"Yes," she said, then added, "But I'm not ready to leave you."

"Then don't," he said. "Let's go home and clean up. I'd like you to meet my girls before you go to back to your family's ranch."

"I'd like that very much," Reese said, warming his heart.

After saying their goodbyes, they walked outside and to his vehicle. She scooted over to the middle seat for the ride back to the farmhouse. They sat in companionable silence with her curled up against his arm.

Back home, they showered, ate and set up the place for his girls. He should probably be tired, but going to sleep meant losing his few precious hours with Reese before she walked out of his life again. They'd promised to be friends, but he knew as much as she that their schedules would make it a challenge to stay in touch.

Still, it was better than nothing.

By the time the house was set up, his former in-laws called. They were on the way, saying they wanted to check out the new space for the girls. Darren heard something in their voices that alarmed him, but he'd been running on adrenaline all night and tried not to read too much into it.

"Is it strange that I'm worried I'll make a bad impression on eighteen-month-olds?" Reese finally said after pacing around the room a couple of times.

"They don't always take to new people right away," he warned. "But don't let that put you off."

She nodded as a knock sounded. And then she followed him to the door before he opened it.

His former in-laws were normally put together to a T. His mother-in-law's hair was pinned in back and his father-in-law had bags underneath his eyes.

"Who are these angels?" Reese said as the girls were carried inside and then set down on the soft rug in the living room.

"Our granddaughters," his former mother-in-law Alice quipped.

Reese walked right over to her, extended a hand and introduced herself. Alice's eyes widened at the last name Hayes.

"It's a pleasure to meet you, Ms. Hayes," Alice said, taking the offering. "Darren didn't tell us it was you."

"Would it have made a difference?" he asked. It clearly did, considering Alice didn't answer. "Reese is going to be part of my life and I'd like her to know my girls."

Alice nodded but she was hiding something. He prepared himself for them to say they planned to fight him for custody.

"Let's clear the air, shall we?" he asked. "Before you fight me for custody you should know how much I love those girls and—"

"Oh, we do," Clifford Brown said. "And they are lucky to have you." Cliff shook his head. "We've had them for two nights and realized the amount of work they are."

"It's twenty-four-seven," Alice added. "Believe me when I say we are happy as larks being grandparents. We don't want to go back to being full-time parents. It's hard work."

Well, that news really made Darren laugh. But when he turned around to see Ivy reaching for Reese to hold her, his heart would never be the same.

"In fact, we don't want to be rude, but we'd like to go home and take a nap," Cliff said.

Then they all laughed, including the girls, who were clueless. He hoped to maintain their innocence for as long as humanly possible. But they were also going to be signed up for self-defense classes before their fifth birthday.

"Thank you for keeping them," he said, waving to Alice and Cliff as they couldn't get out of the house fast enough. He turned to Reese. "I guess that's settled."

Her smile lit a dozen campfires inside him.

"If you ever need a babysitter," she said as Iris cooed at her, "I'm your girl."

Darren wasn't sure if this was the right time, but he decided to throw caution and logic to the wind. Because those last three words spoken out of Reese's mouth made him want to make it a permanent arrangement.

"I know it's been a long time since we've known each other," he began, running with the first words that came to mind, "but I know you, Reese."

She practically beamed at him.

"And I know me, too," he said. "Being friends isn't going to be enough. Not when I haven't been able to find anyone else who holds a candle to you. I fell in love with you in high school and I've been in love with you ever since." His heart pounded the inside of his ribs with the next words. "I guess what I'm saying is that I don't ever want you to leave again."

Reese walked over to him.

"You would forgive me?" she asked, blinking those beautiful eyes up at him.

"Already done," he said. And it was the truth. "I can't push away the woman I love."

"Because I don't think I ever stopped loving you, either," she admitted. "And now, these girls, it just feels like the family I'm supposed to have."

Darren dropped down on one knee. "Then, I have one question for you."

Tears welled in her eyes before rolling down her cheeks.

"Will you marry me?" he asked.

"Yes," she said, pulling him up to standing. "I love you and I would be proud to be your wife."

Coming home was exactly what Darren and his girls needed. With Reese, his family was complete.

Epilogue

Darren wasn't sure he wanted to wait any longer for the lab results. In fact, getting the pediatrician involved might have been a mistake. "I'm not sure any of this is necessary. These are my girls and no test can say—"

"I know," Reese reassured him. "*We* know. But there could be medical history questions that come up later, and they need to know. It's just biology, Darren. *You* are their father, and they love you."

He nodded, tapping his fingers on the chair of the waiting room of the pediatrician's office.

The door leading to the exam rooms opened and a nurse appeared.

"Darren," she said, smiling warmly at him. Was that a good sign?

He stood up, linked fingers with Reese and followed her into the green exam room.

"The doctor will be with you shortly," the nurse said. He should know her name by now. It felt like he'd been in here every other week during these first eighteen and a half months.

"Can you check the chart?" he asked her.

"I'm afraid not," she said before closing the door behind her.

The door barely closed when it opened again.

"Hey, Dr. Michaels," Darren said. "This is my fiancée, Reese."

"Pleased to meet you," Dr. Michaels said to her. The two exchanged pleasantries. He had an envelope tucked underneath his arm. He grabbed it and held it up after closing the door and washing his hands.

Darren took in a deep breath. No matter what that envelope said, he was the one who'd changed their diapers. He was the one who'd sat up with them when they couldn't sleep. And he was the one who'd promised their mother that he would never walk away from those girls.

Dr. Michaels opened the envelope and scanned the contents. He handed over the top piece of paper. "I'm sorry to say the probability that you're the biological father of Iris and Ivy is almost none."

"Which doesn't change a thing," Darren quickly said. "I'm still their father in every way that matters."

"No, it doesn't," Reese added. "And, yes, you are."

"Hazel mentioned to me during one of her solo visits that it might come to this test someday," Dr. Michaels said. "She asked me to keep the information confidential, so I honored her request."

"She talked to you about him?" Darren asked.

"I have an address," he said. "If you're interested."

Darren nodded.

The doctor handed over a slip of paper. "You'll let me know if this changes anything about their care, right?"

"Absolutely," Darren said. "I will always want what is best for them."

"It's your name on the birth certificate," Dr. Michaels pointed out.

"They deserve to know the truth," Darren stated. He folded up the piece of paper and thanked the doctor, then they left.

"Where are we headed?" Reese asked.

"Nowhere," he said. "There's a phone number."

He stopped at the SUV and stood on the sidewalk before opening the slip. He fished out his cell phone and made the call.

"Speak," a hard, gruff voice said. He coughed like he'd just smoked a pack of cigarettes.

"Do you know Hazel Montgomery?" Darren asked.

"I knew her," he said and then seemed to catch on. "But those kids aren't mine. And even if they were, I'd want nothing to do with them."

"Are you sure about that?" Darren asked.

The man belched.

"I'm a rocker and a drunk," he finally said before the sound of a bottle crashing against the wall interrupted him. "Oh, hell. That's going to cost me. But, no, I told Hazel when she first said she was pregnant to go the hell away."

"Hazel died a year ago," Darren informed him.

The guy released a string of swear words.

"But not before having twin girls," he continued. "I'm the man she was married to when she had an affair with you."

Those words should be bitter, but he realized he'd never fully given Hazel his heart even though he'd wanted to.

"Like I said, I want nothing to do with them," the jerk said.

"Then I'll send over paperwork to make it official," Darren stated.

"Fine by me," the guy said. "That everything?"

"As a matter of fact, yes, it is." Darren ended the call before looking toward his future. "He doesn't care about them."

"His loss," she said, "because they are two little miracles."

"Our miracle babies," he said, then kissed his fiancée. "I like the sound of that."

Reese pulled back. "Are you ready to go home to our family, and then to mine to see why I've been called back to Cider Creek?"

"I thought you'd never ask."

* * * * *

COMING SOON!

We really hope you enjoyed reading this book. If you're looking for more romance be sure to head to the shops when new books are available on

Thursday 9th November

To see which titles are coming soon, please visit

millsandboon.co.uk/nextmonth

MILLS & BOON

LET'S TALK

Romance

For exclusive extracts, competitions and special offers, find us online:

- **f** MillsandBoon
- **𝕏** @MillsandBoon
- **◉** @MillsandBoonUK
- **♪** @MillsandBoonUK

Get in touch on 01413 063 232

For all the latest titles coming soon, visit
millsandboon.co.uk/nextmonth